For Rachel
Who tended me
& Cheered me up

Enjoy

Three Masons Exposed

Three Masons Exposed

A Far from Fraternal Fable

John C. Hackett P.A.G.D.C.*

* The Mnemonic indicates Past Assistant Grand Director of Ceremonies. Any Masonic rank which includes the word 'grand' with no qualification (such as Provincial Grand) indicates the brother so entitled has been honoured by United Grand Lodge and is known as a Grand Lodge Officer.

Masonic Ranks are either acting or past. Only about 2 per cent of Brethren become Grand Lodge Officers—the majority with 'past' rank. Grand Ranks are usually written in bold and capitals in Masonic publications.

Three Masons Exposed: A Far from Fraternal Fable
John C. Hackett

Published by Aspect Design 2016
Malvern, Worcestershire, United Kingdom.

Designed and Printed by Aspect Design
89 Newtown Road, Malvern, Worcs. WR14 1PD
United Kingdom
Tel: 01684 561567
E-mail: books@aspect-design.net
www.aspect-design.net

ISBN 978-1-908832-91-7

Dedicated to my patient wife, Diana, and my talented daughter, Fiona, who never believed I would write a whole book; my late mother, Linda, who always believed I would; and my many friends in Freemasonry—they may be fewer after this.

'Injuries are revenged; crimes are avenged.'

(Joseph Joubert)

My object all sublime
I shall achieve in time –
To let the punishment fit the crime,
The punishment fit the crime.

And make each prisoner pent
Unwillingly represent
A source of innocent merriment –
Of innocent merriment.

(*The Mikado*, lyrics by W. S. Gilbert,
a Freemason, set to music by Sir
Arthur Sullivan, also a Freemason)

ACKNOWLEDGEMENTS

Grateful thanks to:

My wife, Diana
My late mother, Linda
My clever daughter, Fiona
Detective Inspector/W.Bro. Paul Hughes
W.Bro. Terry Wilcox
W.Bro. Fred Lee
W.Bro. Roger Hall-Jones
Mac MacBeth
Graham S. Orr. M.A.
All the other helpful people who have encouraged me.

Plus, ruefully and ironically, the brother whose un-Masonic conduct, (immodest and incorrect behaviour in a lodge room) provoked this book. (I try to forget him but . . .)

FOREWORD

It is reliably reported and unreliably refuted that the principal, and preferably *only*, motive for becoming a Freemason is entirely altruistic. Thus the United Grand Lodge of England and Wales proudly pronounce, and throughout their entire global jurisdiction (there are overseas districts affiliated) lodge orators and provincial information officers faithfully, and often in complete sincerity, repeat the official fiction.

For a few—a very few it has to be said—the motivation *is* altruistic. But curiosity; hopes of 'better' (more influential) friends; greed; and family tradition (often forced) were notable, albeit ill-concealed persuasions for many to become Freemasons. Another inducement, albeit altruistic, neither hinted at or admitted, is the natural 'herd instinct' of the human male (and female—there are Lady Freemasons).

It is the 'gang' of one's youth, now authorised and grown-up; something to be part of, proud of, and protected from those less worthy. A superior body of persons in which one can, simply by 'time serving', become a nominal leader. Self-aggrandisement or self-confidence depending on the individual.

Once 'in' then everyone is the embodiment of kindness and consideration for everyone else; one's brothers whom one loves, relieves (assists in times of need), and with whom one is truthful. Such is the basic premise—the prevailing ethos—fervently preached by the diehards of the fraternity. Such is often the practice. But theory and practice do not always go together . . .

CHAPTER ONE
AVONBRIDGE MASONIC HALL
MONDAY 25 JANUARY 1988, 8.30 A.M. TO 9.30 A.M.

Mrs Scarlett Jones had never had hysterics—until the morning of Monday, 25 January 1988, when she discovered three naked Freemasons in their lodge room. Her husband dropped her off outside the Masonic Buildings in Avon Street, Avonbridge, at her usual time of 8.30 a.m. She had been employed there as a part-time cleaner for the last two years—a nice little job she had been glad to be awarded by that nice Mr Fawner. She let herself in with her key, hung her coat on one of the many pegs beyond the glass display cases and, as had become her habit, placed the vacuum cleaner at the foot of the stairs (it made it appear that she had begun work). She then tried to make her way into the big downstairs room where 'they' dined. It was locked. Grumbling to herself about not making up their minds, she retrieved from her handbag the big bunch of keys with which the kind Mr Fawner had entrusted her, unlocked the dining room door and made her way to the kitchen where, as usual, she made herself a cup of tea and enjoyed her second cigarette of the day. That done, she heaved the Hoover upstairs, past the changing rooms to the smaller of the two rooms of what Mr Fawner called 'the temple complex'. Mrs Jones was not one for complexity and she had long since ceased to be curious as to what went on in there: her husband, Bert, was convinced it was devil worship—but she habitually ignored his ramblings.

Born Scarlett Smith in 1940, Mrs Jones owed her forename to her mother, Mrs Hilda Smith's admiration for Vivienne Leigh's petulant Oscar-winning performance in *Gone With The Wind*. So taken with the film was Mrs Hilda Smith that, despite the beginnings of labour pains and the threat of breaking water, she resolutely refused to leave until the bitter end of the film—frankly not giving what Clark Gable said but she shouldn't. She stoically stood for the national anthem—at that time always played at the conclusion of cinema performances—before hastening to the hospital where, three hours later, she was delivered of the daughter to whom she had promised, and had bestowed by the local vicar, the lifetime embarrassment of her unusual forename.

That morning, Mrs Jones was surprised to see the door to the big upstairs room (they called it the temple) very slightly ajar and the lights still on inside. This was unusual, as was the warmth seeping from the room. Thinking someone must be in the room she called out a nervous "Ello?' No answer. She tried again—"Ello in there.' For answer there came a muffled sound—as though someone was calling from a long way off. She pushed open the door. The sight that met her eyes caused her to stagger back, scream, and flee.

If she had been asked to define hysteria, Mrs Jones would have looked shocked and evaded the question—believing, as she did, that it was an operation for ladies one did not speak of in polite company. On Monday 25th January 1988, she was, albeit briefly, in company—if the almost inert forms of three, bound, gagged and naked old men unable to conceal their shrivelled or shrivelling private parts could be classed as company. Mrs Scarlett Jones, gripped—although she did not know it—by hysteria, ran from the dire and awful sight. That she did not fall down the stairs was amazing, and possibly due to fear lending wings to her non-Mercurial calloused feet. She did stumble on the steps outside the entrance before recovering to run, screaming, across the car park and into Avon Street where, as luck would have it, she was discovered and calmed down by an off-duty male nurse. Nurse Greg, for such was his name, listened to, and tried to still, the ungrammatical ramblings of the distressed woman.

"Orrible bodies . . . 'orrid men, all . . . all . . . all . . . in there. Bodies all . . . there's blood, there is, orl over . . . . It ortn't ter be allowed, it ortn't—it's 'orrible, it is. Blood . . . . 'Orrible . . . . 'Orrible . . . . They're in there, they are . . . all . . . . Aargh! In there they am. Orl exposed . . . the bodies . . . in there . . . Someone ort ter be arrested, they 'ad . . . .' *Ad infinitum.* Accusatory gesticulation towards the Masonic building accompanied each stressed utterance of *there.*

Amongst those squeezing past the onlookers gazing in fascination at something unusual, Greg spotted Phil—a nursing colleague—and, sensing that all was not as it should be in *there,* summoned his assistance. Phil agreed to find a telephone and call the police. Having done that, driven in equal measure by professional training and human curiosity, Phil returned to report that the police would send someone when they could and to offer his help to Greg should he need it. Greg welcomed some practical assistance.

No one noticed David Horseman eavesdropping before he slipped away from the onlookers. He hastened to his office as fast as his nicotined lungs and developing beer belly would allow and signed out a small camera.

None of the curious onlookers in Avon Street recognised David Stanley Horseman as 'that ambitious and unscrupulous young journalist from the *Avonbridge Gazette*'—a label already attached to him by several local bodies and organisations. Horseman's ambition had not, as yet, ensured sufficient success for him to own a car, so he counted it fortunate that the most recent recruit to the local newspaper, Derek Carl Peters, was in the outer office trying to look busy and efficient—and succeeding in neither. Peters came of a wealthy family who had indulged the young man's fancy with a car as his eighteenth birthday present—making him an invaluable asset to the paper as free transport.

'Come with me, Derek,' ordered Horseman. 'We could have a scoop here. I need you and your pad.'

The rookie appeared to think this an assignment on foot and was already on the pavement looking around before Horseman ran back from the car park shouting, 'We need your car, as well, Derek. This is urgent!'

Young Peters was fresh to the world of journalism and such an invitation so early in his career both excited and frightened him. More than that, it imbued him with a false sense of importance.

Calmed by the attentions of Greg and Phil and their promises to accompany her, Mrs Jones agreed to be taken back into the Masonic Buildings.

'But only to get me 'andbag and coat, understand. I'll not go up them stairs, agen.'

The two nurses sat her down on one of the several chairs in the hallway and whilst Phil, under Mrs Jones's direction, retrieved her coat from the pegs and her handbag from the kitchen, Greg, seeing a telephone in the Masonic hall—somewhere he had never expected to enter, though he could not have said why—asked Mrs Jones if there was anyone she wanted him to ring on her behalf. Calmer now and restored to as logical thought as she was able, the distressed 'daily' reasoned that Bert would baulk at coming into the building even (or especially . . .) to help her. Mrs Jones was, by now, determined that the 'nice little job' was over and Mr Fawner, having got her into association with a place which now seemed to have confirmed her husband's opinion of it, ought, by rights, to get her out of it. Thus resolved she answered Greg, 'Mr Fawner,' she said. ''E ort ter sort it out. I want to speak to 'im.'

Alongside the telephone was a typed list headed 'useful numbers'. Atop the list, and therefore to be assumed *most useful*, was inscribed: 'W.Bro. D. Fawner—Secretary and Manager'. Greg dialled the given number.

Douglas Fawner was a committed and ambitious Freemason who

revelled in the conviction that he was indispensable to local Freemasonry. His appointment as secretary of the Masonic buildings, Avonbridge, closely followed the management committee's relief that someone should volunteer for the dogsbody position of secretary, the designation *manager* was self-styled. He had stopped short of describing himself as *director*, despite having been known as one such before his early retirement. Douglas Fawner was one of those who, had there been such a publication, would have been an earnest subscriber to the *Sycophant's Monthly*. His wheedling and toadying had eased his promotion to positions for which his self-confidence enabled him to give assurance he was well-suited: assurances swiftly contradicted by his complete lack of ability. To avoid embarrassment, his ill-advised employers continued to move Fawner in an upward direction in the management structure, if only to avoid other able staff, whom Fawner had an amazing ability to upset, leaving the firm. Eventually, at the early age of forty-nine, he became an administrative director with no greater responsibility than to shuffle paper across his large desk and attend directors' meetings at which such utterances as he made were promptly acknowledged and as promptly ignored. The board were relieved of his pompous presence by the advent of an amicable takeover— opposed only by Fawner—the first act of which was to offer a generous and, thankfully, gratefully accepted redundancy package to Fawner. The lump sum and pension enabled him to inveigle himself into several more Masonic lodges and orders in addition to his original lodge. Despite applying himself diligently to learning his various Rituals he failed to shine in whatever Ruler's Seat he arrived in by determined progression. As is often so, his wife was inordinately proud of his several statures—having heard only her husband's account of his relative importance and ability.

After receiving his routine appointment to Provincial Rank at a level below that to which he felt himself entitled, Fawner had welcomed the vacant post as secretary of Avonbridge Masonic Buildings as something he perceived to be an opportunity to alert the Provincial Rulers to his abilities and willingness to serve. He was due, by time-served rotation, to be promoted next year and entertained high hopes for himself. Little did he realise further disappointment would await him.

Fawner disliked being telephoned or disturbed in any way before he had finished his morning ritual of breakfast, coffee and the crossword— easy version. His wife, Marion, summoning him to the telephone before nine o'clock, 'To speak to someone about your cleaner, Mrs Jones— sounds urgent,' was not a good start to what would prove to be a very bad day. Greg introduced himself and briefly outlined all he knew. Fawner agreed to speak to Mrs Jones and, after some mumblings, his eardrums were assaulted by her loud wailing. Mrs Jones was one who considered communication at a distance should be conducted at great volume.

'Oooh, Mr Fawner it's 'orrible. 'Orrible. The lights is still on and I saw 'em, I did. 'Orrible it is. In yer big room, Mr Fawner, they am. Disgustin'. I never thought that sort o' thing went on, Mr Fawner. I'd not have taken the job, I'd not, if I'd knowed that . . . . Disgustin' it is. 'Orrible . . . I ain't never goin' up there again, I ain't. Never! But I'm owed me wages, I am. And me cards, Mr Fawner—and me cards.'

The phone was, it seemed, dropped. Fawner could still, distantly, hear Mrs Jones uttering inarticulate sounds. There were other, indistinct voices—presumably seeking to calm the cleaner. The telephone was recovered and Fawner heard Greg telling him Mrs Jones was 'getting all upset, again' and asking if he could 'come down to sort out whatever the problem might be.' Reluctantly, Fawner abandoned his coffee and crossword, the last clue he solved was 'terrible fate or judgement. Four letters' Fawner had just written 'doom' into his crossword as the phone rang.

An irritated Douglas Fawner made his way upstairs where he cleaned his teeth and carefully brushed his still thick hair before donning his tie and jacket and returning downstairs to explain to his long-suffering wife that he must go to the hall for some problem no one else seemed to want to deal with. Marion was her usual, unsympathetic self, 'Down there again—and at this time of the morning.' Fawner left her in mid-complaint and, clad now in his smart new car-coat, activated the automatic garage door—an improvement of which he was inordinately proud. He reversed his shining car out onto his well-swept drive. After closing the garage door he allowed the engine to warm up for the usual three minutes (good habits should never be changed). Fawner then drove carefully, as he always did, towards town. He stopped at the newsagents to buy a magazine and, chatting with the shopkeeper, accepted that it was sufficiently close to the month's end to settle his paper bill—which he duly did. Had he made more haste he might have arrived in the Masonic Buildings before David Stanley Horseman and Derek Carl Peters of the *Avonbridge Gazette*.

CHAPTER TWO
JONATHAN JUSTIN WHITEHOUSE-MARTIN
1974 AND BEFORE . . .

One of Jonathan Justin Whitehouse-Martin's reasons for completing the application form (Form P!) to become a Masonic initiate was to still his father-in-law's irritating insistence that he would enjoy it. He knew his male trustees were Freemasons in another county (he would later come to know Masonic areas were designated provinces), but circumstances made it in many ways easier and, due to demand, more expeditious, to remain local. His father-in-law, Freddie Wells, was worshipful master of Chandlery Lodge Number 5590 for the year 1974. Freddie reasoned that proposing and initiating his son-in-law could cull kudos both within the lodge and with the rulers of the province. It also afforded the said Freddie personal gratification and pleasure—although he would never admit to either. Worshipful Brother Wells had ventured into Masonic realms eleven years previously at the age of thirty-nine in the hope of bettering his social contacts. His venture had succeeded. The many contacts he made through his involvement, allied to the unconditional trust membership implied, ensured his further success as the pre-eminent local builder. As time and success rolled on, the local designation covered an increasingly large area. The slogan prominently displayed on each of his building sites, 'WELLS BUILDS WELL' arose from an exchange of banter with a visiting brother working in advertising who had been so seduced by the joviality of the festive board (the meal after a lodge ceremony) that he overlooked making any charge for what proved to be an invaluable publicity aid. In fact, Freddie Wells was a very good builder.

The love affair between Jenny, the daughter of Freddie and Doreen Wells, and her handsome husband was one of genuine love. Until Jonathan Justin Whitehouse-Martin courteously asked her to dance, no one in Avonbridge had ventured to partner 'Fat Jenny'—apart from easily detected fortune-hunters aware of her prospects as the only child of the wealthy Wells. For Jonathan Justin—known to most as JJ—her fully fleshed figure contrasted so markedly with every other female conquest he had recorded on his mythical bedpost that true love blossomed for the first time in his life. The passion was mutual. Never in her wildest dreams, or fantasies culled from reading romantic fiction, could fleshy Jennifer Doreen Wells, with her thick, mousy, hard-to-control hair, have imagined being paired with a tall, handsome, flaxen-haired Adonis who not only delighted her, but quickly gained the respect of her doting parents. Freddie's business affairs were, although profitable, not as well arranged as they might have been and JJ's expertise as a qualified chartered accountant expert in company law and taxation, made significant improvements to the Wellses' fortunes. The 'gift-in-anticipation-of-marriage' (free of any gift tax) comprising shares in Wells Building (Holdings) Limited awarded to JJ and his buxom bride did, unbeknownst to Freddie and Doreen, effect little significant increase in the accumulated wealth of JJ. Despite, as some thought, having been plucked from the poverty of Vicar Martin's gloomy manse, Jonathan Justin Whitehouse-Martin had an inherited fortune far in excess of the bombastic Wellses' wealth.

Jonathan Justin Whitehouse had been conceived out of wedlock ten days after the subdued celebrations for the first anniversary of V.E. Day. The conception had little to do with the victory in Europe and far more to do with twenty-one-year-old Sylvia Armitage's naively eager libido being mistaken for sexual awareness by her flaxen-haired serial seducer Roger Whitehouse—ostensibly a salesman of ladies' foundation garments. The resultant pregnancy shocked all concerned—from the thin-lipped respectability in the Armitage family to the knowing acceptance on the Whitehouse side. The latter tended to feel he should be forgiven—their perceptive pre-judgement now vindicated by Roger's just deserts for his past conduct. The strangely matched pair of persons principally involved were content to combine.

CHAPTER THREE
ROGER WHITEHOUSE
1901 TO 1946

Roger Whitehouse was born in 1901—the eldest son of Baron (an old Black Country forename—certainly no indication of ennoblement) Whitehouse and his wife, Cecilia. The family fortunes originated in eighteenth-century chain making. Whitehouse and Barker was the first firm to gather together some of the previously scattered outworkers of the Black Country into one large forge: an initiative from which all prospered—particularly Messrs Whitehouse and Barker. Blake Barker died early, unmarried and without acknowledged issue or close family, leaving the Whitehouse family with sole control and augmented affluence. As was often so with the magnates of the area, their apparent simplicity concealed shrewd, calculating and, where necessary, ruthless abilities. The firm prospered and the family future was secured by prudent investment. Roger and his younger brother, Charles, wanted for nothing their parents could conceive of in education and luxury. They were both boarded out as pupils at the small private grammar school correctly titled William Sebright's Endowed School for Boys at Wolverley, but generally known by the simple soubriquet Sebright. In 1931 the school did change its name to Sebright School. Wolverley is a village five miles to the north of Kidderminster—unremarkable for much save the school, which was founded from the bequest of the village's only famous son who became a sixteenth and seventeenth century town clerk to the City of London —a contradictory title in terms acceptable to history. By prudent investment in property—principally in Bethnal Green—William Sebright became a rich man and felt it incumbent upon him to endow a seat of learning in his place of birth—an obligation established by his last will and testament of 1620. A small village grammar school suffers from the inbuilt restriction of the size of village dictating the number of pupils. Thus, in time and without betraying the terms of the original bequest, Sebright became a small boarding school. Faithful to the endowment, it continued to offer 'a classical education fitted to qualify for university entrance'. This appealed greatly to Baron Whitehouse's ambitions for his sons who were duly enrolled and left home to be 'classically educated'.

They slept at Bury Hall—the principal and original boarding house of the school—and studied in a fine Gothic building at the centre of the village.

Opinion as to whether Roger would have qualified for university entrance was divided amongst his tutors, and remained conjectural since, succumbing to the postered clarion call beneath the accusatory finger of Kitchener, Roger, in common with other keen contemporaries, falsified his age and, in 1917, enrolled to serve his country's needs in the Royal Flying Corps. Charles was neither as patriotic nor as likely to deceive the military as to his maturity; his aptitude for both Latin and Greek allied to a fine brain easily gained him acceptance to New College within the dreaming spires of England's oldest university. His first class Oxford law degree brought him to the attention of many prominent firms of solicitors from whom, influenced by family associations, he chose to pursue his career with the respected Birmingham practice of Rixon-Reed. At the early age of thirty, Charles was installed as a partner of the firm—an appointment not entirely dissociated from his having wooed and wed the delectable Miss Charlotte Reed. Charles's legal acumen was to be of inestimable assistance to his elder brother.

Roger was intended for the family firm. A good education—Classical or not—terminated early by volunteering to 'do one's bit' in the Great War ill befits a young man for the life of a chain maker in the fire and grime of the area rightly titled the Black Country. Roger's apprenticeship to the ancient art of making chain was, for him, a time of misery and resentment. He bore it as best he could until the sudden demise of 'The Baron' following a second, ill-advised double brandy to wash down the game pie. His death left Roger and Charles, at twenty-six and twenty-two respectively, to arrange a chain maker's funeral and either secure the succession of or sell the family firm. Roger and Charles found the canny foresight of their predecessors had garnered an unsuspected spread of investment in land, property and 'blue-chip' stock exchange holdings which, they were advised, it would be best to retain until improvements in the market added further worth; as, in time, they did. Whilst the national prosperity following the General Strike was not conducive to securing the best bargains, the decision to sell Whitehouse Chain to their traditional rivals in the trade was easy. The Baron having died intestate, a deed of family arrangement was drawn up. It ensured that old Mrs Whitehouse retained the family home—including the snooker room into which she had always resolutely refused to venture—for her lifetime with sufficient income to support herself and the staff required for the management and maintenance of the old house. Roger and Charles divided the shareholdings and other investments between them, together with the valuable land, property and blocks of luxury flats to the west of Birmingham. The brothers moved themselves into apartments in their respective and prestigious Hagley Road properties.

When clearing their father's study they had discovered, in a bottom drawer of his desk, a brown leather case approximately nine inches by six with their late father's name etched into the leather. The case contained a Masonic apron and an impressive certificate. The certificate was headed with the Royal Coat of Arms beneath which was inscribed, in a fancy form of script: 'United Grand Lodge of Ancient, Free and Accepted Masons of England.' There followed, in a further fancy form of lettering, the name 'His Royal Highness the Prince of Wales, K.G. Grand Master.' Beneath this, in both English and Latin, was witnessed that Brother Baron Whitehouse had been initiated into Freemasonry in 1898. There were two signatures on the Certificate: one of someone described as 'G. Sec.' and the other the well known scrawl of their late father. There was a lodge name and number that, when Charles later researched it, proved to be in Staffordshire. As Roger was little interested, his brother took charge of the case and its contents. Subsequently, Charles was initiated into a Warwickshire Lodge, and was far more Masonically active than his father—easily accomplished since the Baron had not been master of his lodge. Charles proceeded a great deal further in the fraternity than the Baron had ever envisaged.

Mrs Cecilia Whitehouse never recovered from her husband's sudden demise and almost a year to the day from his passing was discovered dead at the door of the neglected snooker room by one of the soon to be redundant staff. The family home was sold to an ambitious local entrepreneur, the staff dismissed with generous severance packages— unusual for the time—and Roger and Charles became even richer young men. To the credit of both they never flaunted their wealth and were always generous to good causes and their friends.

Roger had been one of the talented flyers of the Royal Flying Corps which morphed into the Royal Air Force. He was one of the few who survived the Great War in which, during the battle of Arras, two thirds of British airmen were lost due to the superiority of the German Albatross aeroplane over the British DeHavilland BE2F. Roger's daring exploits culminated in crazily crashing his sick plane, one of the new rear engined SE5s, between the lines in no man's land from which he miraculously escaped with a few bullet wounds and was given a decoration for gallantry. His injuries healed, but he never returned to combat or reconnaissance—

thereby missing the chance to fly the new Sopwith Camel, a plane with two forward mounted machine guns that several historians credit as a significant factor in winning the war.

His filial devotion to Chain at an end his share of the inheritance and the guarantee of a secure rental income allowed Roger to acquire and maintain a private aeroplane, initially a Sopwith Camel—though without machine guns. It was hangared at a small airfield near Bridgenorth. But flying could only be a part-time occupation and a life of ease did not suit his active nature. The offer, by way of another former flyer, to travel the country purveying 'sensual undergarments for ladies of taste' offered not only variety but easy access to many ladies of (varying) taste throughout the land. He bought a motor car and his increased mobility boosted not only his sales and attenuated commission, but also his amatory conquests. Word of this dashing and decorated flying ace soon spread and invitations to stay in more amenable circumstances than the commercial travellers' hotels found around England and Wales were willingly accepted. The word was usually supplemented by the whispered confidence that the prodigious size and versatility of his male appendage—an inherited trait—warranted more than close inspection. The offers of free accommodation became almost embarrassingly frequent. Roger enjoyed his life as a travelling salesman—as did his accommodating hostesses.

The Second World War saw Roger Whitehouse, despite his age, re-enlisting in the Royal Air Force where, although denied active flying duty, he served with distinction as an increasingly senior officer and the darling of not only Whitehall, but most of the Women's' Royal Air Force. In 1945 he was demobbed with an officer's pension and a small retainer against future consultation service. Eschewing boredom he discovered that demand for ladies' foundation garments, and his own attentions to ladies both in and out of the flimsy vestments, was even greater than pre-war. His travels resumed—although petrol rationing meant he became a frequent traveller by train. The car—the best he could buy—was utilised only for weekend leisure or business trips within the Midlands. And it was on one such Friday business trip prior to the weekend that he met, bedded, impregnated, and then, as he thought, consigned to pleasant memory young Sylvia Armitage. The memory was to return to both haunt and delight him.

CHAPTER FOUR

SYLVIA ARMITAGE

1925 TO 1946

Sylvia Armitage was the adopted child of Julian and Ethel Armitage, proprietors of Armitages, 'Family grocers of quality in Stourminster'. The 1925 adoption was a closely guarded family secret—although the less discreet of their customers and congregation at the Modern Methodist Chapel were firmly of the opinion that Julian and Ethel would not have known how to start a family had they so wished and adoption was their only course of attaining such social cachet. Discerning acquaintances— the Armitages were not fans of friendship—detected that young Sylvia's luxuriant yellow locks, bright blue eyes and fresh complexion almost certainly denied her having being born of the sallow skinned, dark haired Ethel and her short, fat husband whose greasy black locks carefully combed across his large cranium failed to conceal his early baldness. Julian Armitage would have preferred to adopt a boy, but Ethel was adamant that they had nasty habits and she would rather have no child than have a boy about the house. Thus the succession to the old established firm of family grocers—of quality—would, seemingly, pass to a woman. Julian sometimes wondered how his late father, Julian Senior, would have viewed such a democratic disaster, but put aside such thoughts to concentrate on being a good grocer and, his latest unprecedented success, a town councillor.

Life for the child Sylvia was divided between home, school and chapel. Despite a fiercely independent spirit she generally conformed to the narrow confines dictated by her home and the chapel elders. At the age of sixteen, despite being of above average intelligence and scholastic ability, she was withdrawn from Stourminster High School for Girls— against the advice of the headmistress—in order to work in the shop. Wartime restrictions and rationing limited the scope of family grocers— of whatever quality—and the Armitage fortunes, although of greater size than most, were not as healthy as Ethel or Julian would have hoped. He remained on the town council, of course, and the chapel was a great comfort. The frustrated ambition of their seventeen-year-old adopted daughter—it could only be in the genes, they felt—was of no comfort. Sylvia patiently and persistently explained that she did not want to be a grocer—of any quality—but wished to become a schoolteacher. Somehow she had obtained details of a teachers' training college in Dudley which was prepared, on the recommendation of her former, highly respected headmistress, Miss Polly Meadows, to accept her as a trainee. After weeks of being bullied by their adopted child, the Armitages relented and Ethel, being now convinced that educating the young was at least as worthwhile as supplying victuals for their sustenance, allowed that Sylvia might be trained as a teacher. The journey from their Stourminster home to Dudley posed a problem: the time necessary to effect a daily commute would mean Sylvia leaving home at such an early hour and returning so late that her necessary home study would not be accomplished. Julian felt this ended the matter. Sylvia did not and, with a reluctant and apprehensive Ethel in support, the availability of a small apartment was discovered above the premises of Weatheralls, 'Olde established drapers of Dudley'. Situated in a respectable area close to the college, to Julian's dismay and expense, it was secured. The cost of this independent accommodation being less than that of commuting daily by public transport proved small comfort to Julian who was, reluctantly and unexpectedly, financing this advance in his daughter's life. Not that he saw it quite that way but . . . .

In September 1943 the Allied Forces landed at Salerno and Sylvia Armitage left the family shackles of quality grocery to train as a teacher. She loved it. Evenings were free to talk with new friends without the boring chore of inflicted Bible readings. After two tiring weekends travelling back to Stourminster for little save two or three chapel services and lengthy lectures on 'being good' she announced that she would only return home for holidays. Having informed the entire congregation of the Modern Methodist Chapel and most of the town council that Sylvia was training to be a teacher, neither Julian or Ethel could envisage admitting they had deprived her of the opportunity, so she remained in Dudley during term time where she prospered both socially and educationally. She enjoyed tennis—particularly the attentions of the college coach—and her doubles partner, Jane Aspinall, became a close friend with whose nearby family she enjoyed weekly relaxed evenings of happy conversation and playing card games—another new experience. Sylvia joined the college choir as a second soprano standing next to the bright, bubbly Thelma Denness—a fellow student from Sutton Coldfield—with whom she formed a firm and fond friendship. They became almost inseparable and in their final year as student teachers Thelma insisted Sylvia spend the second week of the half-term break at her parents' home. This required persistent persuasion of Ethel and Julian—but the lure of possible acquaintance with someone of quality (other than a grocer) finally persuaded the Armitages. The arrival of a large motor car with liveried chauffeur and smart young lady passenger to transport Sylvia to the north of Birmingham was a talking point in Acacia Avenue—the Armitage's home street—for many months.

Sylvia had never ridden in a posh car—her motoring trips having been hard-sprung rides in Julian Armitage's delivery van and, on pre-war weekends, the occasional outing in the Austin Seven. As the luxurious car purred its way northeast she and Thelma excitedly planned their week together—it would be a significant few days for Sylvia. Having been told that Thelma's family dressed for dinner in the evening—Jane and Mr and Mrs Aspinall had explained to Sylvia the implications of this, to her, unusual formality—two suitable evening dresses had been conveniently purchased from Weatheralls. Despite discount for a good tenant, Julian ineffectively complained, and effectively paid with a resented but sound cheque.

CHAPTER FIVE

SYLVIA AND THELMA
MONDAY 6 TO MONDAY 13 MAY 1946

Archie Denness was an apparently successful and wealthy dealer, industrialist and engineer whose fortunes had begun before the war and had been greatly enhanced during hostilities by profitable war work in his several factories. The Dennesses' home was Holt Hall—a ten-bedroomed mansion with extensive grounds. Sylvia could not contain her admiration as the car swept up the drive between the rhododendrons and the immaculate lawns. The evenly spaced wooden posts lining the drive seemed curious; Thelma explained that the ornamental chains between them had been 'taken away by the munitions people'. As, indeed, had the elaborate iron gates that once stood between the now stark gate posts. They alighted from the car at the foot of a flight of stone steps leading to a double front door from which Mrs Denness, a jolly, buxom lady, emerged to embrace both Thelma and, to her surprise and embarrassment, Sylvia. Such familiarities were unknown at the Modern Methodists or in Acacia Avenue.

'Hello, dears. Welcome Sylvia—make yourself at home. You'll need to freshen up after the journey—I hope it wasn't too bad? Sylvia's in with you, dear, and tea's in the drawing room in half an hour or so.' Mrs Denness spoke without any apparent pause for breath whilst ushering the young ladies indoors.

Sylvia entered a vast hall with a polished, parquet floor from which an impressively wide, red-carpeted staircase swept upward to balustraded landings. Enormous life-sized portraits in oil paint and gilded frames hung on every wall in the hall and beside the stairs. Entertaining in the tiny Armitage household was an unknown and frowned upon indulgence, so being received into such a magnificent mansion was daunting to Sylvia. Acceptance of familiarities hitherto unsuspected made her nervous and confused.

'Come on, slowcoach' urged Thelma, already several steps up the stairs. Sylvia forced a smile, gripped her small suitcase more tightly and followed her friend. Corridors branched away from the landing. Thelma led her along the second on the right to an impressively panelled door she pushed open with proprietory familiarity.

'This is us,' said Thelma, dropping her case beside the only bed in the large room.

Sylvia had never shared a bedroom before. To now be facing the apparently inevitable sharing of a bed—albeit a double one—was daunting. In vain she looked for a second bed whilst fighting rising panic. Thelma was her friend. What was there to be concerned about? She stood rooted to the spot clutching her case.

'Which side would you like?' asked Thelma, effectively bringing the matter to a *bed*.

'I don't mind, really,' replied Sylvia.

'Well, we'll start this way round and see how we go, shall we?'

'Yes . . . yes, of course,' said Sylvia, placing her case on the opposite side of the bed.

'That's the spare wardrobe. Hang your stuff in there, Sylvia.'

'Thanks.'

'I'll wash first, if you don't mind,' said Thelma.

To Sylvia's surprise, and almost before Sylvia could look away, Thelma stripped herself down to her underwear and walked past her through a door beyond which the amazed Sylvia saw an adjoining bathroom and toilet. She had never seen such luxury. Deciding that she must accept things as they were, Sylvia unpacked her suitcase and hung her few clothes, including the two new evening dresses, in her wardrobe. Thelma was still in the adjoining bathroom. The injunction to freshen up before tea not having been lost on her, Sylvia removed her dress and, feeling rather embarrassed in only her underwear, sat on the side of the bed. A tear worked its way from her eye. Irritably she dashed it away, but another swiftly followed and, before she could contain herself, she was weeping and sobbing uncontrollably.

'Your turn . . . ,' began Thelma, emerging from the bathroom. Then, 'Whatever is it, Sylvia?'

'Oh, I'm sorry, Thelma. This is all so . . . strange to me. I shouldn't have come. I don't know what to do or say, and I'll let you down and embarrass you with your parents.'

'Stop that at once,' said Thelma. 'If I'd thought you'd embarrass me I wouldn't have asked you.' She seized a linen handkerchief from a drawer beside the bed and began wiping away Sylvia's tears. She then put her arms around her friend and gathered her to herself in a warm, friendly embrace. Never having been so held by another human to her recollection, Sylvia had now been twice taken into the arms of kind, caring persons. Despite her distress, she realised that she liked being hugged. She gripped Thelma tightly. The warmth of a fellow human was comforting and addictive, Sylvia wanted to stay held by Thelma for a long time . . .

'Better now?' enquired Thelma, holding Sylvia at arm's length. 'Wash your face and we'll see what there is for tea, shall we?'

As they dressed, Thelma assured her frightened friend that no one would be trying to find fault with her—she was a guest and, as such, entitled to respect and consideration. It made sense and Sylvia resolved to enjoy her visit. A resolution well fulfilled.

After dinner—a quite delicious meal since the shortages of wartime seemed not to apply to this household—Mr and Mrs Denness, Thelma, her sister Rita, their neighbours Mr and Mrs Masters, and Sylvia repaired to the large, comfortable lounge adjoining the dining room where Mrs Masters sat down at the grand piano and began to play. It was a wonderful evening. Sylvia appreciated that this was probably normal behaviour for everyone else but, for her, the communion of happy people sharing the joy of singing together and to each other seemed so natural and joyous that she wished it would go on forever. It appeared to be almost traditional that the last song of the night was a catchy tune about a funicular railway, rendered with practised verve by Mrs Denness, in which everyone joined the final chorus. For the first time in her life, Sylvia had drunk good wine with her meal and afterwards, around the piano, enjoyed a glass of sherry. She could never recall feeling so happy. As she and Thelma made their way upstairs she tried to explain to her friend how remarkable it all was for her.

'Glad you're enjoying yourself, my dear,' said Thelma. And, again, she put her arm around Sylvia. Sylvia liked it. She put a tentative arm around her friend and, clasped together, they walked to their bedroom.

Apprehension began to eat at Sylvia again as Thelma slipped out of her evening dress and then began to remove the remainder of her clothes. Sylvia had only taken off and hung up her new evening dress preparatory to finding her nightdress in her case when she turned to see her friend wearing only brief knickers and a smile.

'Oh . . . sorry,' said Sylvia.

'What, dear?' asked Thelma.

'Well . . . you've got nothing on . . . hardly . . . I mean . . .'

She wasn't entirely sure what she did mean. Naked flesh was not proper—or so she had always been taught. She stood—rooted to the spot in her petticoat, underwear and embarrassment, trying not to look at Thelma—yet strangely drawn to do so.

'Sorry, Sylv, didn't mean to upset you. It's what I usually do. I didn't think you'd mind. I was just going for a wash.'

Thelma paused before adding, 'Would you like me to cover myself up?'

'Yes . . . . No. I mean . . . . No. Of course not. It's your home and . . .'

'And it's my bedroom and my body, Sylvia. And, apart from being a bit pudgy around the bust and middle, there's not a lot wrong with it.'

Thelma stood, near naked, almost challenging Sylvia. They regarded each other for a long moment. Slowly, Sylvia allowed her gaze to move from Thelma's face to her body. Thelma stood totally unashamed, still smiling. Then, slowly, she removed her knickers and walked towards Sylvia.

'There's nothing wrong with being bare, dear,' she said.

'No . . . no. It's just that I've never . . .'

She left the sentence incomplete as Thelma passed her and entered the bathroom.

'You should try it, Sylvia,' said Thelma from the bathroom. 'I'm going to wash and turn in before I catch cold.'

Sylvia had always washed before going to bed. She had never been naked in the company of another—only stripping for a solitary bath on Friday nights.

She could hear Thelma in the bathroom washing. As she stood irresolute she recalled Mrs Aspinall saying, 'When in Rome, do as the Romans do,' meaning that she would need to adjust to the ways of her hosts when she visited the Dennesses home. Nudity had certainly not been anything she could have envisaged, but Thelma had been so kind to her— and so natural in her nakedness—that, on impulse, Sylvia determined to see how it felt. It felt strange—yet, somehow, liberating. She stood naked and alone in the midst of her scattered underclothes before gathering up her discarded clothing, storing it in the wardrobe drawer and following Thelma in to the bathroom. And, for the first time in her life, reflected in the bathroom mirror, Sylvia saw herself as nature intended. She blushed.

'Gosh, you've got a lovely body, Sylvia Armitage,' said Thelma.

'Have I?' she said—not entirely sure how to conduct unclothed conversation.

'Gosh, yes,' replied her friend. 'Hurry up into bed before you catch a chill.'

And, giving Sylvia a friendly pat on her buttocks, Thelma was gone.

Sylvia washed herself and, still feeling self-conscious in the extreme— and nude—returned to the bedroom. She automatically took her nightdress from her case, but as she held it up preparatory to putting it over her head, Thelma cried out, 'What on earth is that for?'

'It's my nightie, of course,' replied Sylvia. She looked at Thelma who now sat up in bed. It was obvious that Thelma was not wearing a nightdress.

'Oh. You don't wear one,' said Sylvia—stating the obvious. 'Don't you feel cold?'

'Good Lord, no. Once you cuddle down it's fine. Try it if you like— it's up to you, dear.'

Sylvia stood holding her nightdress in front of her. Should she? 'When in Rome . . .'

Boldly she put the nightdress back into her case and, not without apprehension, climbed into bed with Thelma.

'Ooh, Sylv, you're quite cold. Come here and get warm.'

And once again in this eventful day, Sylvia Armitage was gathered into a warm, loving embrace—this time by her naked friend. And, after a brief initial hesitation, she returned the cuddle. It was lovely. She felt wanted; she felt Thelma's warm body against her own; she felt naughty, but she had stopped feeling guilty. She was liberated and she felt the better for it. Eventually she slept—at ease in the arms of her bosom friend.

Sylvia awoke as light streamed through the curtains of Thelma's bedroom and, after an initial pang of unease, a great wave of happiness engulfed her. She was happily and confidently aware of herself and her own body—Thelma had told her how lovely she was. And, indeed, she felt lovely. She reached out and touched Thelma's warm breast. Thelma returned the gentle caressing squeeze. They lay comfortably together—far closer friends than ever.

'Good Morning.'

'Good Morning.'

'Sleep well?'

'Better than I ever remember.'

A knock on the door announced Mrs Denness in a shiny, floral dressing gown bearing a tray with two steaming cups of tea.

'Nice morning cup of tea, dears,' she said, placing one cup on Thelma's bedside table.

'Sleep well, Sylvia?' she asked—placing tea on her bedside table. As Mrs Denness bent, Sylvia was very aware that under her silky floral dressing gown there was only Mrs Denness. Truly she was in a different world. But she liked it. She liked it very much.

'Shall I start you both a bath?' asked Thelma's mother.

'Please, mummy,' replied Thelma. 'Let it run in slowly.'

'As usual,' answered Mrs Denness, moving into the bathroom from where the sound of running water began.

Thelma sat on the side of the bed sipping her tea. Sylvia followed her example, almost forgetting that she was naked. Mrs Denness returned from the bathroom.

'Don't let it run over,' she said. Then, looking appreciatively at Sylvia, she added, 'You're a very lovely young woman, Sylvia.'

'Thank you, Mrs Denness,' was the only reply Sylvia could think of. But she was, she knew, flattered. After years of prudery and narrow attitudes, she was not only aware of herself, but actually feeling proud of her own form. It was a new and wondrous experience. As was sharing the bath with Thelma and washing each other.

The week in Sutton Coldfield broadened Sylvia's outlook and awakened in her a hitherto unawakened sexual awareness. Thelma's sister was even more uninhibited than Thelma, and through the talks they had, the facts of life—which Sylvia had formerly only vaguely comprehended—became clearer than they ever had through Mrs Lloyd, the district nurse whom Ethel had imported at the appropriate time to explain to Sylvia the basics. Mrs Lloyd had certainly never mentioned anything about erogenous areas—only referring to private parts in a lowered tone accompanied by furtive looks and gestures. Rita Denness had, she boasted 'had' a man. Far from seeming ashamed, she appeared proud of having lost her virginity. She promoted it as exciting and life affirming—which to a chapel girl was, initially, a foreign and utterly confusing attitude; yet, by the end of the week, Sylvia almost craved the attentions of a male partner to supplement her erotic enjoyment of her bosom friend Thelma. She returned to her Dudley lodgings on a sunny Monday morning a different young woman.

Within a week she had met, known in the Biblical sense and been impregnated by Roger Whitehouse. Despite his vast knowledge of women he would later admit that the eager surrender of Miss Armitage had deceived him into thinking she was not only experienced but at a safe time. He did realise that he had de-flowered her, but was content that his usual brand of protection was adequate. For once it was not . . .

CHAPTER SIX
ROGER AND SYLVIA
FRIDAY 17 MAY 1946

Roger Whitehouse usually visited Weatherall's of Dudley on the second
and fourth Thursday of each month. The London re-union of former
RAF Officers in early May 1946 delayed his call to the 'Olde Established
Drapers of Dudley' until late Friday afternoon. It made him easy prey for
Florrie Graves.

Miss Graves was an institution at Weatheralls. A committed spinster
of notably unattractive visage and comfortable body, she easily outsold
every other Weatherall employee in both volume and revenue. She was
also a devotee of the local theatre, the Hippodrome, newly opened after
the war. Many citizens of Dudley, and, indeed, the surrounding areas, had
made their first theatre visit as a direct result of dear Florrie's unending
persuasion to buy tickets. Roger had always avoided committing himself
to the Hippodrome as Thursdays required him to move on to other
calls further north, or south, or wherever. On the fateful Friday, Roger
sealed another good order from Mr Leonard Weatherall with the usual
handshake. Leaving Mr Leonard's office they passed an attractive, yellow-
blonde young lady using the telephone in the outer office.

'Please excuse us, Miss Armitage,' said Mr Weatherall, as they passed.

'Miss Armitage, our upstairs tenant. No telephone upstairs, of course,'
explained Mr Weatherall once they were out of earshot.

Roger again shook hands and bade farewell to Mr Leonard who returned
to his office. Fatefully, Roger paused to exchange pleasantries with Miss
Graves. Florrie just happened to have the last pair of tickets for tonight's
performance of *The Desert Song*—being performed by the local Amateur
Operatic Group. Florrie Graves was a committed and enthusiastic—if not
particularly talented—member of Dudley and District Light Operatic
Society—prized for her ticket selling abilities despite her penetrating
and often out of tune mezzo-soprano voice. Having ascertained that Mr
Whitehouse, being in Dudley on a different day, intended to stay at the
Castle Hotel—almost opposite the Hippodrome, Florrie determined it
was high time he enjoyed a night at the theatre.

'And what should I do with the other seat, Miss Graves?' said Roger, mischievously. 'Put my hat on it?'

'Surely you could find someone to accompany you?' replied the indefatigable Florrie.

And, as fate decreed it, at that moment Sylvia Armitage, having finished her dutiful weekly telephone call to her mother, walked toward them.

'I'm sure Miss Armitage would love to go with you, Mr Whitehouse,' cooed Florrie, indicating the approaching Sylvia with an inclination of her tightly permed head.

Sylvia should have walked on by. Roger should have resented the scheming procuress and pleaded another engagement. Neither thing happened.

'What would I love to do, Miss Graves?' enquired the ever polite Sylvia.

'Accompany me to a performance of *The Desert Song*, tonight,' Roger quickly interjected—feeling he should seize the initiative and introduce himself, 'I'm Roger Whitehouse,' he extended his hand, 'and I would be delighted to have your company, Miss Armitage.'

'Why, thank you, kind sir,' answered Sylvia, taking his hand and shaking it.

Feeling that an evening in the bar of the Castle Hotel would be poor comparison to the company of this lovely young woman, Roger dutifully paid Miss Graves for the tickets. Together the ill-matched pair walked toward the door of Weatheralls with Florrie Graves's command to, 'Enjoy your evening,' and their simultaneous thank yous echoing behind them. They laughed together for the first of many times.

'I gather you live above here?' asked Roger as they emerged from the shop.

'Indeed I do,' answered Sylvia.

'In which case it makes offering to walk you home rather pointless.'

Sylvia laughed. 'Shall I join you at the theatre?' she enquired of her handsome—if rather older than herself—new acquaintance.

'Good Lord, no' he said, consulting his watch. 'Why don't I wait here whilst you change and then we can have dinner together at the Castle? I'm staying there. And I really would be glad of the company—especially of such a lovely young lady, if I may say so?'

'You may say so, sir,' answered a flattered Sylvia. 'But, forgive me, what should I wear for dinner at the Castle and afterwards at the theatre.'

Roger admired her honesty.

'Let's be informal, please,' he replied. 'I wasn't expecting to wine and dine anyone and I only have this suit with me. So a nice dress such as that you are wearing, would be ideal.'

'In which case all I shall need is a moment to powder my nose and gather a handbag—if you really don't mind waiting?'

'I shall contain my impatient soul upon this pavement,' replied Roger.

Sylvia had never been to the Castle Hotel, let alone dined there. She silently blessed the experience of social life gained with the Dennesses and was only slightly nervous. Roger Whitehouse was an expert at calming female nerves. It was early for dinner so they enjoyed a sherry in the lounge whilst getting to know a little of each other; they liked what they learned. Dinner was unremarkable and paled in comparison to the fare at Holt Hall, but Roger kept the mood light and Sylvia enjoyed herself. They walked across the road to the Hippodrome and took their dress circle seats. Whilst neither Sylvia or Roger could claim to be experienced judges of light opera it was readily apparent to each of them that the performance was staged as much for the benefit and enjoyment of the performers as that of the paying patrons.

Whilst the two leading performers possessed good voices—very good in the case of the young lady—the disparity in their age and height lent a farcical element to the attraction it seemed should develop between them. The moment when the dashing Red Shadow, a thin man of forty summers and five feet seven inches in height, had to lift and 'carry off' the heroine who, despite being only half his age, was a buxom lass standing only an inch under six feet in her bare feet, evoked mirth where Rudolf Friml and his librettist had intended a quite different reaction. The strain of the hero's effort was clearly visible in his bent knees and the panic-stricken eyes of the heroine. Want of breath curtailed the vocal climax to The Shadow's supposedly triumphant song. The staggering exit drew sympathetic applause, fortuitously drowning out the ill-suppressed giggles of Sylvia, Roger and several others.

On leaving the Hippodrome into a balmy night—they conveniently 'forgot' Miss Graves's invitation to join her after the show—they were able to give full vent to their hilarity at the well-intentioned, yet sadly comical, presentation of the *Song of the Desert* they had endured. That they both had a well-honed sense of the ridiculous was evident. That Sylvia had as good a singing voice as he had heard all evening became obvious to Roger when she parodied the 'Love Lament' in response to his off-key rendition of the Riff's Song. As they arrived at her door beside Weatheralls she thanked Roger for what had been a most enjoyable evening and for his delightful company.

'We may never meet again,' she said, with genuine regret.

Before he could stop himself, Roger was inquiring what this delightful young woman might be engaged in the following day that might prejudice her from accepting his invitation to go for a drive into the country.

'You've got a car?' queried Sylvia incredulously.

'Yes. I wasn't proposing to bring a pony and trap to your door.' They both laughed. 'Suppose I pick you up here after breakfast at, shall we say, ten o'clock?'

'Oh, yes please,' replied Sylvia, relishing a break from her intended studying.

'It's a date,' replied Roger, turning to go.

'But, Roger,' Sylvia timorously asked, 'what should I wear? Sorry—I always seem to ask that,' she added.

'Something warm—we might have the top down,' was the reply. Sylvia was not entirely sure what 'having the top down' entailed but, before she could frame a query that didn't make her seem too ignorant, Roger added the almost taunting *coup de grâce*, 'And if the weather and you are good, we might fly a little.'

There was a pause. Sylvia could believe that this mature man possessed a motor car, but flying, even 'a little', had to be a joke.

'I'll wrap up against the breezes,' she said. 'Goodnight, Roger—and thank you again.'

CHAPTER SEVEN
ROGER AND SYLVIA
SATURDAY 18 MAY 1946, DAYTIME

At ten o'clock the following morning Sylvia emerged from her flat clad in her thickest clothes with an outer coat and a headscarf covering her hair to find a sleek, red sports car and a be-capped Roger Whitehouse awaiting her. It was a fine morning and, as he had threatened, Roger had folded back the top—he called it the hood—of the car.

'It's an MG,' Roger proudly explained. 'That stands for Morris Group.'

'And where are you and your MG car taking me this fine morning?' asked Sylvia.

'Well if you would like to go for a short flight, not far,' answered Roger, as he held open the car door. Sylvia stopped in her tracks and looked him full in the eyes, 'Oh . . . I thought you were joking about that,' she said.

'Not a bit,' replied Roger, adding, 'If you're game for it?'

They sat in the car for a while whilst Roger assured her that he did, certainly, possess an aeroplane and a pilot's licence and she would be quite safe. If, however, Sylvia felt too scared to fly he would not be offended. But he did have to make a short flight and she would have to wait on the ground should she not wish to go with him. Sylvia was having the most exciting fortnight of her life and, she assured Roger, would love to be taken for a flight. That settled, they set off Westwards.

They left Dudley and, after passing through Himley, Sylvia noted a sign indicating the quaintly named Halfpenny Green Airfield.

'Is that where we're going?' she asked above the roar of the engine.

'That is precisely where we're going,' replied Roger, 'but not until we have the proper things to wear. We'll just pop in to my little place in Bobbington for flying gear. I prefer to keep it under my own roof rather than in the lockers at the airfield.'

And very soon they were in the Hamlet of Bobbington. Roger drew up beside a small, black and white cottage with a tiny porch and a front door so low that both of them had to stoop as they entered. Small it may have been, but the quaint nature of the cottage delighted Sylvia who eagerly expressed her admiration of the little house.

'I keep it for when I'm flying to save going to and fro,' explained Roger to an increasingly amazed Sylvia, before apologising that he had no smaller flying jackets but she could 'snuggle into one of his spares.' She did. And was then 'fitted' with a flying helmet and unflattering goggles before they made another short journey in the MG to Halfpenny Green.

The sheer exhilaration of being airborne and seeing Middle England laid out below her as a patchwork of fields and houses was something Sylvia had never expected to experience. She loved every short minute—there were only fifteen—and after landing with only a few bumps, she jumped into Roger's helping arms, was lowered to the ground and, excitedly asked when she could do it again. Roger regarded her affectionately, she really was different to the ladies with whom he usually spent his weekends, and he was enjoying her company.

'I do have to go on a long flight tomorrow,' he said, thoughtfully, 'but I could make a telephone call if you would really like to go with me. It would mean a very early start—just after daybreak, in fact.'

'So we'd have to drive here in the dark?' answered Sylvia

'Yes, we would,' answered Roger.

'Is that what you usually do?'

'No . . . I usually sleep at the cottage,' answered Roger, looking keenly at his young companion.

'Well, isn't there room for one more?' asked Sylvia.

With all his experience of the fair sex, Roger was surprised at her eager forwardness.

'Wait until I've telephoned, please,' he asked. 'Do you mind waiting here for a short while?'

Sylvia shook her head—glad to have her hair released from the strictures of the flying helmet. She was curious as to why she had been able to fly today but, it seemed, had to have permission granted to fly tomorrow. It was a glorious spring day, birds sang and everything in her world seemed wonderful. It was a far cry from measuring out flour and sugar in a Stourminster grocer's shop . . . quality notwithstanding. After several minutes she saw Roger emerge from the small control room, turning to thank the resident controller. She clearly heard him instructing a 6.00 a.m. take off, 'fully fuelled and everything, as usual, please.'

'Well, young lady, the powers that be are in a kind mood and, if you still want to come with me, all will be well.'

'It's still yes, please,' interrupted Sylvia.

Roger held up his hands in front of himself, 'Whoa, there. I need to explain a little before you finally commit yourself. There are conditions to be complied with . . . . Let's sit in the car.'

And before Sylvia could answer, Roger was half way to the MG. Consumed with curiosity, she followed and, as he held the car door open, lowered herself into the passenger seat. Roger walked around the front of the car and settled himself into the driving seat, but he made no attempt to start the car. He turned to face Sylvia, a far more serious expression on his face than she had hitherto seen.

'Now, please, listen carefully, Sylvia, dear,' he said. Sylvia liked the use of her name with added endearment. But she dutifully listened as bidden.

'Firstly, I must ask you to keep tomorrow's trip strictly between us. By all means tell a friend or two that you've been up in a plane but, for my sake—and, indeed, your own—don't mention where we are going or even how long we are up. Okay?

'Yes, of course—if you say so,' replied Sylvia. 'But am I allowed to ask questions?'

'You're allowed to ask me questions, but I have to reserve the right not to give you answers. Anyone else you meet, and there will be others, please refrain from any curiosity. You must agree to and be content with that, or there's no trip, I'm afraid.'

There was a long pause. It was obvious to Sylvia, despite her excitement, that unless she complied with the secrecy stipulated, she would be studying in her flat tomorrow.

'Right,' she said. 'It seems I have no choice in this, so I agree. Is that all there is?'

Roger smiled, 'You're very perceptive, aren't you?' he replied. 'So here's the rest; when we get to where we're going try not to recognise anything about the location. I shall be away for some time, maybe several hours, but you will be indoors most of the time and, I can assure you, you will be looked after and as well fed as you could wish for.'

'Sounds super—and mysterious too—if I can say that?'

'Yes, dear, you can say that to me—but try to be more circumspect in the company in which I shall be leaving you at the other end. Act as though you were used to being left waiting for me and are well aware of the need for avoiding what we called 'careless talk' during the war.'

'Sounds okay,' answered Sylvia. 'I'll have to keep my wits about me, it seems, as well as not asking questions.'

'Good,' said Roger. 'Now there's only one thing to be settled.'

Again he looked seriously at Sylvia.

'I can either drive you back to Dudley and call for you at an ungodly hour tomorrow morning, or you can stay in the cottage. But, you should know, there is only the one bed—albeit a double. Your pilot is prepared to sleep on the settee.'

'Gosh, I can't ask you to do that,' laughed Sylvia. 'I've shared a bed, before, Roger.'

Which of them was more surprised at Sylvia's last utterance would be debatable. Sylvia felt the opportunity to 'beat Thelma' to sleeping with a man justified her forwardness. Roger looked with ill-concealed delight at the tall, well-proportioned young woman beside him who was so freely offering herself and, feeling there was nothing further to be said, started the car and drove back to the cottage. On the way he suggested a 'wash and brush up' before an early dinner at a nearby restaurant.

'Need to get some sleep before the early start, of course,' he said.

'Sounds lovely,' said Sylvia.

Although she had enjoyed a few dates with fellow male students from college, she had never been treated so lavishly. She decided she liked it. She liked it very much.

CHAPTER EIGHT
ROGER AND SYLVIA
SATURDAY 18 MAY 1946—EVENING AND NIGHT

At the cottage, Sylvia shrugged off the heavy flying jacket and hung it with Roger's similarly discarded jacket in the small hallway. She was looking forward to a good wash after the drive and flight.

'Where's the bathroom, Roger?' she enquired.

'Upstairs, Sylvia. This is what is known as a 'two up, two down' residence. Lounge and kitchen down here and bedroom and bathroom up above. Follow me, please, ma'am,' he said and opened a small door at the side of the hall to reveal a steep winding, staircase. The few uneven steps—Sylvia counted ten—brought them to a tiny landing from which two open doors led, as forecast, to a bedroom and a bathroom. The latter, however, was not what Sylvia had expected—if she had formed any preconceptions. There was no bath. A modern washbasin and toilet stood at one side of the small room and where, she supposed, a bath had once been, there was a shower. A large shower. She had seen showers before at school and college but, in her shy days, had always managed to avoid using them and 'displaying herself', as she had then thought of it—something Thelma had dispelled in one exciting week at Holt Hall.

'Can I have a shower, please?' she asked timidly. 'If there's time, of course.'

'There is time and you may,' answered Roger. 'In fact, I ought to do the same, myself . . . . But, after you. I'll make a cup of tea downstairs for when you've finished, if that's alright?'

'I would love a cup of tea—but I would also like to be sure I know how the shower works, please.'

Roger had started towards the stairs but now turned, wondering how he might explain the shower without demonstrating and getting his clothes wet. To his surprise—and delight—Sylvia was already in her underwear—and about to discard that, too. His expectations of her unadorned beauty, kindled only since her forward statement in the car, were not disappointed. She was, indeed, a remarkably lovely young woman with everything in the right proportion and size. He realised he was staring—as did Sylvia. As she discarded her last vestments she could not resist echoing Thelma's naked maxim of last week, 'Nothing wrong with being bare, Roger,' she said and smiled coyly.

'No, indeed, Sylvia,' he answered, moving into the bedroom and swiftly transforming himself to the state where no wrong had been decreed. Sylvia was impressed. He might be more mature than she had anticipated her first conqueror to be, but he was in fine physical form, with a taut belly and slim waist above . . . she had definitely not anticipated *that*. To say she had never seen anything like it would be not only true but, had she been so inclined, expostulatory.

'It would be far easier if we showered together and I handled the controls,' said Roger.

'You handle . . . controls very well,' answered Sylvia, coquettishly.

'I can handle most things I want to . . . handle,' said Roger, taking her hand and leading her toward the large shower.

'Hop in,' he said, standing aside and, as Thelma had done less than a week ago, patting her gently on her buttock.

'You stand at that end until the warm water comes through and I'll brave the cold,' he joked.

They soaped each other at Roger's suggestion, willingly acted upon by Sylvia. After a quick, vigorous, although not entirely thorough towelling, he led her to the bedroom and, for the first time, they made love. There was an awkward moment when it became apparent that this was Sylvia's first surrender, but with her eagerness and willingness, and Roger's gentleness and skill from long experience (experiences to be precise) this passed and the dinner at a nearby restaurant was not quite as early as might have been originally envisaged. Nor was the night devoted entirely to sleep.

CHAPTER NINE
ROGER AND SYLVIA
SUNDAY 19 MAY 1946

Without the benefit of an alarm clock, Roger arose at 5.00 a.m. He looked affectionately at the soundly sleeping Sylvia, then washed and dressed himself before gently rousing her.

'Oh, hello,' she said, adding with a coquettish, anticipatory smile, 'Again?'

'Not now, darling. We have a flight to make . . . remember?'

Leaving her to fully waken, wash and dress, Roger descended to the small kitchen where he made coffee for two. He considerately added a little more sugar to Sylvia's cup for energy—explaining that their first food of the day would be at the 'other end' of the flight. They were glad of the heavy flying jackets in the car in the chill, early morning air.

Whilst cognisant of the caution impressed upon her by Roger, Sylvia could not suppress her curiosity as to their destination. She recognised from above a few of Dudley's landmarks away to their left and, to her surprise and her right, Kidderminster with the tower of St Mary's Church and the spire of St George's Church. Far away to their left was a vast conurbation she assumed to be Birmingham, after which there was nothing she recognised. Later there was nothing she could recognise in the increasingly flat land far below. Eventually she spied, away to her left, the sea. Below them, as they began to descend, she saw slashed across a huge field, like some monstrous sign of plague, a concrete X surrounded by low, wooden huts, aircraft hangars and other buildings above which towered a strange, circular edifice with glazed observation panels all around its upper storey. And, atop what she was later told was the control tower, she was amazed to see the flag of the United States of America. Her geography had not been top of the class, but neither had it been so abject as to let her believe they had crossed, unobserved, the Atlantic Ocean. As Roger helped her from the plane she laid her head alongside his and said quietly, 'I know you said no questions but . . . is that the American flag up there?'

Roger held her close and said that indeed it was and they were on a United States airbase in East Anglia, that being all she needed to know.

She nodded and tried not to look too amazed or to gaze around too obviously.

A large black man in immaculate uniform with sergeant's stripes on each arm saluted Roger before contradicting the gesture of respect by adding, 'Hi, Roger.' He then ushered Roger and Sylvia into the rear seats of a peculiar, open motorised vehicle.

'Breakfast coming up soon,' said the sergeant over his shoulder and the whine of the engine as they sped across the black tarmac towards the serried ranks of buildings. Sylvia noted, but did not comment upon, several soldiers in light khaki uniforms and brown boots.

'We thought the annexe to the officers' mess for the young lady and yourself,' they were informed. Roger thanked the sergeant saying it would do nicely—a phrase Sylvia would hear several times that morning.

The buffet breakfast laid out for them to select from was beyond anything Sylvia could have imagined. There seemed to be even less shortage here than at Holt Hall. Unused to such quantities, but not wishing to offend her hosts, Sylvia served herself with two fried eggs, a very large slice of greasy bacon, the smallest sausage she could see and one of what Roger quietly told her was a hash brown. Having managed to eat it all she felt as though she would not need to eat for the rest of the day, but when she told Roger this he laughed and told her she had better find room for lunch before they left. Before Sylvia could reply they were joined by, and Sylvia was introduced to, Gloria—a dark-skinned female sergeant of quite enormous proportions—in whose care she was to be left. Roger excused himself and, with an apparent knowledge of the base, departed elsewhere.

Sylvia spent the next two hours endeavouring to keep up with Gloria who moved with startling alacrity for one of such bulk. The tour over they returned to the annexe to the officers' mess for enormous mugs of coffee and, declined by Sylvia but enthusiastically consumed by Gloria, large sugar-coated brown rings —referred to as 'do nuts' by Gloria who, either to save Sylvia embarrassment or simply to satisfy her own appetite, ate Sylvia's doughnut after her own. As she finished the second doughnut a young attendant yelled, 'Phone, Sarg.'

Gloria excused herself to take a call on the telephone in the corner. Leaving the phone hanging from the receiver she came back to Sylvia, 'Sorry, honey, there ain't time for the fillum show we'd got all lined up for you.

'Seems they were quicker than usual with their jawin', today. Mr Roger wonders if you'd mind skippin' lunch and gettin' on your way.'

Silently grateful for the 'quicker than usual jawin',' and Roger's consideration of her stomach's capacity, Sylvia said she wouldn't mind at all providing no one was inconvenienced. Opining that, 'You talks funny, honey,' Gloria transmitted this intelligence to the telephone and returned to the table where, shortly, they were joined by Roger. Gloria was thanked and they were returned to the strange vehicle, which seemed to be called a Jeep, and their plane. Despite the lovely day and the thrill of what was only her third flight, Sylvia slept for part of the return journey—waking as they descended to another slightly bumpy landing at Halfpenny Green. As they walked to the MG Sylvia risked another question.

'So you go there quite often, Roger?'

He smiled. 'As often as I am needed,' was the enigmatic reply. 'And that is all you need to know, young lady,' he added.

After a short pause, Roger stated that the early return meant he could return her to Dudley in the light and get home to prepare for the week ahead. Realising that this was a firm statement of intent and that dissent would only sour a memorable weekend, Sylvia hid her disappointment and climbed into the MG. After briefly visiting the cottage to leave the flying wear in the small hall, they motored to Dudley in an uncomfortable silence. Sylvia rallied sufficiently to effusively thank Roger before she left the car, and as he helped her out, she gave him a grateful kiss—surprised that he only allowed it to be applied to his cheek and made no attempt to return the affectionate gesture.

'I expect you'll be back in Dudley soon?' she ventured in what she felt to be a tactful overture to a future meeting invitation.

'I expect so, Sylvia,' he replied and leaving her standing on the pavement outside her flat he drove away.

CHAPTER TEN
AROUND AVONBRIDGE AND DISTRICT
FRIDAY 22 JANUARY 1988

George Jeffries was a careful, fastidious and conceited man. He had been, as was his employer's wont, retired from Lloyds Bank at the age of sixty after forty-two years' diligent service. Despite his diligence, he had only attained the rank of manager in his last five years—taking over a small branch in an industrial town. The branch had lost the few prestigious customers it had held during the stewardship of Jeffries's predecessor, who had spent too much time perfecting his hobby of ballroom dancing. Whilst this had elevated him to sufficient status in the dance world to represent his country, it had done nothing for the bank who were only too pleased when he reached sixty and could be pensioned off. Jeffries disliked the town to which his employers had promoted him on sight. The citizens of the town developed similar feelings towards George Jeffries, and his five years' tenure did no more for the bank locally than had that of his predecessor. Relieved to be rid of the under par pair, but concerned that two poorly performing managers in succession at the same branch represented an unfair view of the bank's reputation, the area management of Lloyds appointed a young up-and-coming, ambitious man on the basis of third time lucky. They were, indeed, fortunate since, in a remarkably short time, the new man regained former customers and added others, thus vastly increasing the reputation of both himself and his employers in the town. George Jeffries neither knew nor cared.

The thin, socially conscious Judith—the third Mrs Jeffries—and George selected a bijou villa on the outskirts of Avonbridge as their ideal retirement home and moved in during June 1980. Over six years they transformed the extensive garden into a veritable show piece—not that they showed it to any but carefully selected acquaintances. Within their villa, imitation of the better glossy magazine features continued in an almost sterile manner, everything was exactly and carefully placed to give maximum impression of the Jeffrieses' gracious lifestyle. In George's study everything was precisely where he felt it should be. The filing cabinet's drawers were each clearly labelled to indicate their exact contents—all maintained in immaculate files. The second drawer down contained, as the labelling indicated, files for Chandlery Lodge No. 5591 of which George had been secretary for three years following his arrival in Avonbridge and successful application to become a joining member. The brethren of the lodge were grateful for George's precise efficiency— although several resented his affected snobbery. Yet since they could find no other brother able and willing to undertake the demanding office of secretary they tolerated his prissy ways.

The ordered manner of the Jeffrieses' lives dictated that they left their home at 9.15 a.m. every Friday, holidays excepted, to effect their carefully planned weekly shopping. Their invariable intention was to return at 11.30 a.m. for a late coffee. Their habits had been covertly observed over several weeks—both before and after the Christmas period. On Friday 22nd January 1988 at 9.16 a.m., the same unremarkable man who had observed the Jeffrieses' comings and goings, now clad in an old duffle coat and jeans and carrying a large bag of nondescript towels, cleaning materials and other cheap items, began knocking at the doors of houses further down the short road. At each house he mumbled incoherently whilst presenting a dirty, printed card stating him to be impoverished and selling goods to ease his life style—it was couched in precisely those terms. It took him eight minutes to be repulsed or rejected at four homes before he reached the front door of the Jeffrieses' now empty home. To the casual observer, and there was only one, he remained at the door no longer then it took to ring the bell twice and assume there would be no answer.

At 9.20 a.m., as planned, a nondescript van with registration plates rendered indecipherable by mud and grime parked in the lay-by opposite the Jeffrieses' home. Its overalled, be-capped and mufflered driver took his time dismounting from the driving seat before limping to the rear of the van where he slowly opened the doors and leaned inside. From this vantage point he was easily able to observe, through the gap between the door and the van side, the progress of the unsuccessful door-to-door salesman. As the salesman turned from the Jeffrieses' door he gave a pre-arranged signal towards the van before trudging on his way to the next house. The man-with-the-van then straightened up, removed from the rear of the van a small tool-bag, and closed and locked the van before, slowly, limping across the road and entering the Jeffrieses' front hall. The door was unlocked thanks to the salesman, and all he had to do was disarm the burglar alarm. He confidently entered the Chandlery Lodge number into the control panel and the system bleeped its acknowledgement of being correctly disarmed; Mr Jeffries should be more careful to whom he confided his security details, he thought.

Exhibiting a knowledge of the house one might not have expected of a visiting workman, he quickly made his way to George's study where his tightly-gloved hands extracted from the desk-top stationery container several sheets of notepaper headed 'Chandlery Lodge No. 5591'. Removing the cover from George's Underwood typewriter, he inserted a sheet of the selected paper and, with great care, typed out his planned message. This he repeated on second and third sheets before selecting three envelopes from George's neat store, typing a different address on each before inserting the letters. The envelopes were attached together with one of George's paper clips and carefully placed in the side pocket of the tool-bag before the typewriter was re-covered. Checking that he was leaving the study exactly as he had found it, he re-armed the burglar alarm, left the house, closed the self-locking front door behind him and, assuming the limp (intended to confuse any subsequent identification) made his way to the van. The van drove away. The only person who observed the workman's departure was Miss Jenkins at the adjacent bungalow, but since she was never questioned on the subject she divulged her observation to no one.

The van drove into the next street where it stopped to pick up the salesman before being returned to its accustomed place of rest over the last few weeks. The salesman hastened to the toilets to change before emerging in his more normal daytime apparel to transport the van driver/workman to his temporary resting place where he, too, transformed himself to his usual appearance and relaxed with a book for the rest of the day.

The letters so diligently typed on George Jeffries's typewriter that morning were signed in ink with a well-practised simulation of the present worshipful master's signature. The three envelopes were addressed respectively, but without respect, to the homes of Worshipful Brother Maurice Fisher, past master (a nervy, ex-teacher); Worshipful Brother Raymond Hughes, director of ceremonies (opinionated, bombastic furniture retailer); and the unwitting owner of the typewriter, Worshipful Brother George Jeffries, secretary. The workman/clandestine typist placed them in the case he needed for Sunday. Part one of the master plan was complete.

CHAPTER ELEVEN
SYLVIA
MAY TO JULY 1946

Late Sunday afternoon did not feel right to Sylvia as a time to resume her studies. Especially after the weekend she had experienced. She wanted to share her excitement with someone. So, after washing her face and hands, she set out to visit Thelma before it got dark. The ten-minute walk eased her stiffness from being cooped up in an aeroplane and small car. But Thelma was not at her flat. Almost everyone else, she decided, would either be preparing for, or already at, evensong. She did not feel it would be entirely proper to join them and, as it might be, give thanks for the last two days.

Finding no-one with whom to share her tales of adventure Sylvia returned to her flat and a reluctant spell of study. The following day was no better. Thelma was not in class and, when she enquired at the bursar's office she was told that Miss Denness had returned home due to a family crisis. Nothing further known. Sylvia's request for more details only earned her a reproving frown for being inquisitive. Jane Aspinall was absent from class with a severe cold and Mrs Aspinall said Sylvia, 'Ought not to come in for fear of catching anything, dear.' Descent from excitement is always difficult—particularly so when one's closest friends are missing and there is no one with whom to share one's thrills and enjoyment. Anticlimax dispelled adrenaline and Sylvia's week was not her happiest.

The next month her misery deepened. She began to feel sick in the morning.

Thelma had not returned and enquiries at the bursar's office were greeted with ever-deepening frowns; a telephone call from Weatheralls to Holt Hall was unsuccessful—the unusual sound signifying, so Mr Leonard informed her, that the number was unobtainable. A fact he kindly had confirmed for her through directory enquiries. She wrote to Thelma at Holt Hall but received no reply. Jane returned to classes looking pale and weak: invitations to her home were not forthcoming as had previously been the case since, it seemed, Mrs Aspinall was now 'laid low'. Sylvia did not feel up to tennis and the choir seemed, somehow, less fun than it had been. Roger had not called at Weatheralls in the two weeks following their weekend and when she casually enquired of Miss

Graves during the third week Sylvia was told that he had made his usual call the previous afternoon and, as usual, had moved on to the north.

She missed a period—something that had not happened before and she felt miserable. When she missed for a second month and was actually being sick in the morning she suspected the truth and, reluctantly, made an appointment with the college doctor. He confirmed what she had suspected. He obviously disapproved.

As the college paid his bills Doctor Moresby seemed morbidly pleased to inform Sylvia it was his duty to inform the college authorities. He added that, in his opinion, Miss Armitage would not be completing her course with the college. His opinion was endorsed and his disapproval exceeded by the bursar and on 19 July, only a week before she would have qualified, Sylvia was expelled from college. Worse, and in accordance with regulations, her parents were to be informed in writing of the expulsion and the reasons therefore.

Sylvia returned, thankfully unobserved, to her little flat. Continually wiping away her tears she packed as many of her clothes as the suitcase she had originally brought would hold. The formal dresses bought for Holt Hall she had to leave hanging in the small wardrobe: she consoled herself with the mournful thought that they would not be required at Acacia Avenue. She wrote out formal notice of leaving the flat, inserted the flat keys in the envelope and, not daring to face any questions, dropped the envelope through Weatherall's letter box very early in the morning.

It required two bus journeys to reach Stourminster. Although the travel seemed interminable Sylvia almost hoped it would never end—dreading, as she did, the attitude of her parents. Her reception was more torrid than even she could have imagined. Her mother simply looked at her with distaste and cried. The grocer of quality stormed and raged, alternately condemning her to eternal damnation and demanding to know the identity of the 'bounder who did this to you'. She was constantly in tears herself and all she could bring herself to tell the raging Armitage was that the 'bounder' was named Roger Whitehouse, a sales representative who called at Weatheralls and had taken her to the theatre.

'Taken you to more than a theatre, you shameless hussy,' was the response. 'Where can I find him?'

Sylvia's ignorance of Roger's whereabouts further enraged the little grocer. She was glad to retire to her former little bedroom—despite having to make up her bed. She cried herself to sleep with the sounds of her father's raging promises to 'find the filthy fornicator' and 'give him his just deserts' still ringing in her ears.

CHAPTER TWELVE
Dudley Bell
Monday 22 to Friday 26 July 1946

Julian Armitage's enquiries proving fruitless, but with the distressed compliance of the weeping Ethel, he remained determined to 'discover the scoundrel' and 'have him accept his responsibilities'. It would, of course, also serve to have an unmarried and pregnant daughter removed from the prying eyes of the Strict Methodist Congregation. Julian engaged the services of a private detective courting respectability by advertising himself as an 'enquiry agent': a status enhanced by the halting recommendation of Armitage's slightly shocked solicitor, Mr Ivor Morton.

Dudley Bell, enquiry agent, happily accepted the Monday mid-morning instruction of the recently promoted deputy mayor. It would make a welcome change from arranging trysts where he burst upon supposedly surprised persons and photographed bare-chested, guilty husbands in bed with hired for the occasion scantily clad ladies: the easy way of obtaining divorce amongst unfaithful and dissatisfied spouses of the 1940s. Early Tuesday morning, additional increment for swift results having been promised by his new client, Bell embarked on the reverse of the two bus journeys that had returned Sylvia to her unwelcoming home. Researches in his own interest had made Bell aware of the greater cost of rail fares to Dudley: costs that he would, in time, include in the plus expenses agreed to be paid by the quality grocer.

In the absence of Mr Leonard Weatherall his secretary innocently supplied the details of Mr Whitehouse—offering Roger's business card to save the nice gentleman writing it all down. He wrote it down anyway. Sustenance being necessary for his concentration, a calorific lunch at a convenient café/restaurant was taken and, for a small gratuity, an inflated receipt supplied. Having ascertained the cost of a rail ticket to Birmingham, Bell then boarded a bus for the city.

'Roger Whitehouse, Freelance Representative' ran the legend on the business card conveniently supplied at Weatheralls. The address was stated as 7, Stirling Road (off A456), Birmingham 16—the additional direction being useful since Bell's map of Birmingham included three roads designated Stirling. The bus conductor helpfully took his fare only as far as necessary and agreed to advise him of the nearest stop where he could alight in order to walk to the said Stirling Road. He was even more helpful in advising the bus fare from Birmingham's Snow Hill railway station to Monument Road—the stop nearest Bell's destination—thus unwittingly supplementing the enquiry agent's 'plus expenses'. Bell did not have far to walk on the A456, usually referred to as the Hagley Road, before branching off onto the narrower Stirling Road. After a similarly short walk he discovered number seven to be a small, semi-detached house in 1920s architectural style. A well-polished brass plate proclaimed it to be where Roger Whitehouse—Freelance Representative was to be found and, whilst he examined the gleaming brass that so easily confirmed his destination, the gleamer of the plate in the person of a cleaning lady emerged from the front door enquiring what help she could be. Bell was grateful for any good fortune that came his way and, after subjecting the cleaning lady to some well-practised flattery, he was invited in to have a cup of tea in view of his exhaustion from walking all the way from Snow Hill station.

Over strong tea with sterilised milk which Bell pretended to relish, he elicited the information that, 'Mr Roger is away on 'is travels like 'e uzualy is. Mr Roger's weekly ritual is to return on Friday night to sort 'iz mail and so on. Mr Roger is most often away all week.'

Had Bell been a better enquiry agent, he would have discovered that, despite the stairs, the upper storey of the small semi-detached building housed no more than office space and storage for samples: there were no beds or provisions for sleeping. That he contented himself with the basic information given whilst he forced down the sterilised tea resulted in a depletion of Julian Armitage's assets to the benefit, as if he needed further financial increase, of Roger Whitehouse.

Roger Whitehouse, being wealthy by inheritance and his own improving application to his affairs, did not reside in Stirling Road. Both he and his brother, Charles, lived in the owners' flats of their respective Hagley Road luxury apartment blocks. Charles with his lovely wife, Charlotte. Tenants of their apartments were constrained by legal covenants from use for business purposes and the brothers Whitehouse were too wise to abuse their position as owners by flouting restrictions. Charles, of course, worked from the city centre offices of Rixon Reed. Roger, as part of his inheritance, owned through one of the brothers' limited companies several 1920s built houses in Stirling Road—making compliance with the restraint on conducting business from his apartment a simple matter of utilising the nearest Stirling Road house to his apartment as office and recipient of his business mail. It was not intended as any form of subterfuge: it serving as such was entirely due to Bell's lack of diligence.

After thanking the cleaning lady for the tea and assistance, Bell repaired to a nearby tea room where he cleansed his palate of the taste of sterilised milk with several glasses of orange squash supplemented by slices of cake—receipted as dinner at double his expenditure. He then returned to Stourminster where he busied himself with telephone calls to various drapers and ladies' clothing shops both in and beyond the Midlands. Having traced four or five who were happy to acknowledge their business relationship with Mr Roger Whitehouse, Bell then noted rail fares to these distant sources of information into his plus expenses of the Armitage enquiry before busying himself on the few other investigations in which he was currently instructed.

On the following Friday, well before the forecast arrival of Mr Roger in Stirling Road, Bell was in position opposite number seven with the latest in photographic equipment—a necessary asset of his occupation—ready for use. And after only thirty minutes of patient waiting a tall, fair-haired man alighted from a taxi cab—a luxury Bell detected as necessary due to the large sample case carried by the passenger. With his long lens Bell was easily able to obtain several good shots of Whitehouse before he disappeared into the house. Pausing only to take pictures of the house that would enable his client to readily identify the building, Bell walked briskly to the Hagley Road and joined the late afternoon queue at the bus stop opposite Monument Road. He was fortunate enough to be the last allowed to board the next Stourminster bus and, after standing as far as Halesowen, he completed his journey in seated comfort. By nine o'clock that night he had not only developed the roll of film with satisfactory images of Whitehouse and his little house, but had also laboriously typed both his report and invoice to Mr Armitage. Both were dated on the Sunday evening (double time!) and included time and costs for seven full working days: an undetectable discrepancy/falsehood of which only he and his conscience—had he had one—were aware.

CHAPTER THIRTEEN
JULIAN ARMITAGE, IVOR MORTON AND ROGER WHITEHOUSE
MONDAY 12 AUGUST 1946

Julian Armitage, despite his impatience to trace the vile seducer of his adopted daughter—her guilt had been impressed upon Sylvia as the fault of her natal genes overcoming her proper upbringing—and place her future care into the bounder's keeping, gave Bell's report a guarded welcome. The presence of the local enquiry agent in his grocer of quality shop did not present the sort of image he felt befitted him and that presence should, Julian felt, be removed as soon as possible. He was even less pleased with the invoice, but business was business and a cheque was written and placed into Bell's greedy grasp before Bell was none too politely ushered from the premises.

Within two hours of Armitage taking delivery of the report, at an emergency appointment, solicitor Mr Ivor Morton had read it, discussed it—so far as any discussion was warranted—and noted his councillor client's intentions for safeguarding his mayoral year from scandal.

'It will be a heavy cost, Julian,' stated Morton—quietly relishing his own fees and unaware of the extortionate sum already disbursed to Bell.

'Not nearly as heavy as the social and business cost to me should this disgrace be made public,' responded Armitage. 'How soon can you draft a suitable deed, Ivor? I want to confront the bounder and get him to sign it. Then we can remove the strumpet from this locality as soon as possible. Ethel and I find her presence under our roof intolerable.'

Morton made no answer to this. Secretly he felt more than a pang of sympathy for Sylvia—but, of course, he was not a strict modern Methodist.

At 11.13 a.m. on Monday 12 August 1946, Julian Armitage, quality grocer and deputy mayor/mayor elect of Stourminster accompanied by Ivor Morton, solicitor of said town, arrived hot, footsore and twenty-three minutes late for their appointment with Mr Roger Whitehouse at 7 Stirling Road, Birmingham 16. The train from Stourminster had been late; there had been no available taxis and the bus from Colmore Row had seemed to stop at every lamp-post. Armitage's temper had not improved during the interminable 'necessary professional time' which had elapsed since Bell's report. Taking time away from the quality emporium was something he disliked—unless it was for council business, of course. He had had to suffer Morton's attempts to calm him throughout the train journey and having Morton begin this meeting with an obsequious apology for their lateness only served to sharpen his irritation.

The deputy mayor's original intention had been to 'confront the evil seducer' as soon as possible. Morton's narrow professionalism and golf commitments allied to Whitehouse's apparently being 'otherwise engaged' had frustrated his wishes and, after far too many telephone calls, he had been forced to agree to this time and place. Morton had prepared a deed in accordance with his client's wishes and had constantly impressed upon the irate Armitage that he, Morton, should do the talking and that such imprecations as scum of the land and womanising Whitehouse would be of little assistance to their negotiations. Privately, Armitage saw no need for negotiation believing, in his narrow, conceited way, that Whitehouse had no alternative but to accept his more than generous ultimatum.

Bell's photographs had shown a well-dressed, tall, fair-haired fellow. They had given no indication of his age or education. Morton's telephone exchanges with Roger had indicated a more mature and refined intelligence than he had expected, but Armitage remained convinced they were about to meet a young shifty seducer of limited intelligence and similar means. The first sight of Roger Whitehouse, civilly greeting Ivor Morton, excusing their lateness and inviting them to enter, elicited the sort of ire against which Morton had so insistently counselled, 'Good grief, he's old enough to be her father,' exploded Armitage—pointedly ignoring Roger's outstretched hand and level gaze.

'Please, Julian, restrain yourself. We agreed . . .'

Armitage managed to restrain himself, despite wanting to correct Morton. He had not agreed, of that he was sure—it had been Morton who had continued to insist that, as his legal representative, it was he who should do the talking. Roger led them to a small, carpeted sitting room with one easy chair and a small settee and with practised ease made it clear they should sit together on the two-seater. It was not only the seating arrangements that had occupied Roger Whitehouse's time since the telephone calls from Ivor Morton. Whilst the intention and motive for the visit had been kept unclear, the identity of Morton's client had, inadvertently been disclosed, 'Councillor Armitage is a very busy man,' and Roger had instantly recalled spending a most pleasant weekend with a Miss Armitage who had originally hailed from Stourminster. Whilst certain that he had taken the usual precautions during their relations, he was aware that there had been instances of what courser colleagues termed equipment failure and the general tone of Morton's conversation had led him to suspect the true purpose of this possibly bad start to the week. Consequently, he had consulted with his brother Charles. Charles had listened to all Roger had to say, reproved his elder sibling—not for the first time—concerning his penchant for 'bedding anything in a skirt,' and wisely advised that it would arouse suspicion were he, Charles, to be present at this initial meeting. He was insistent, and Roger agreed, that under no circumstances should Roger agree to anything until they had further discussed the matter. Whatever it might be. He agreed that, as the other party seemed to be aware of no other address for Roger than 7 Stirling Road, Roger should maintain the image of that being his only address.

Once Morton and Armitage had seated themselves, Roger made the naïve query, 'I shall be interested to learn why you wish to see me so urgently, gentlemen.'

'You know damn well why we're here, you lecherous cur,' burst out Armitage before Morton could reply or restrain his client.

'Please, Councillor, abusing Mr Whitehouse will serve no purpose.'

'All he deserves, in my opinion,' was the grumpy reply before the red-faced grocer—exhibiting little quality this Monday morning—slumped back onto the settee.

'Get on with it, then, Ivor,' he sulkily instructed before Morton could resume.

Morton managed to extract a file and pad from his briefcase and, resting the case on the floor beside him, opened the file.

'Let me get straight to the point, Mr Whitehouse.'

'About time.'

'Please, Julian.'

'Hmph . . . alright, alright.'

'As I was saying,' resumed Morton, 'we are, initially, concerned with events of the weekend of May 24th to 26th last. During that weekend it is believed you were, . . . how shall I put this . . . in the company of a Miss Sylvia Armitage?'

'He was in her bed, the swine,' interjected Armitage before being silenced by the admonitory hand of Morton.

'I believe you are correct, Mr Morton,' replied Roger calmly. 'But let me check with my diary, to be certain.'

Morton placed his hand firmly on Armitage's knee and, for once, succeeded in restraining his impatient client. Roger, as slowly as he dared, went through the motions of checking his diary before looking back at Morton and saying, 'It is correct that I was with Miss Armitage—a delightful young lady—that weekend.'

Morton's grip on Armitage's knee tightened.

'We had dinner together and, afterwards, attended the theatre in Dudley.'

'And, if I may be direct, Mr Whitehouse, did you, during that weekend, have . . . er . . . have . . . well—sexual congress with Miss Armitage?'

'Of course 'e did, the swine,' exploded Armitage—forgetting both his imposed silence and an aspirate. Morton's patience, already stretched by having to speak of what he felt to be unpalatable matters, was wearing thin. He turned on his client, 'Julian, if you want me to handle this on your behalf, then please allow me to do so. Otherwise I'll leave you to abuse Mr Whitehouse in his own house and see where that gets you.'

Councillor Julian Armitage, grocer of quality, pillar of the chapel and mayor elect was not used to being publicly reprimanded. So taken aback was he that, uncharacteristically, he mumbled an apology and sank meekly back into the corner of the settee. Morton composed himself whilst mentally resolving to increase the fee levelled for this unpleasant assignment.

Roger had observed this interchange with concealed humour whilst also forming a strong revulsion for the bigoted father of the lovely young lady he recalled from May. Observing his brother's advice, he decided to let matters take their course only so far as Morton's stilted questions and his client's obnoxious interventions indicated. Morton cleared his throat and again looked directly at Roger.

'Apologies for that, Mr Whitehouse. You will appreciate that Mr Armitage is under some strain concerning this matter. Could you now answer my question, please, as it is, in terms of legal niceties, the crux of the matter.'

'Yes, Mr Morton, I can confirm that Miss Armitage and I were sexually intimate—although I prefer to term it that we made love together. But——'

Roger's intention, contrary to Charles's advice, had been to state that the liaison was with the consent and, indeed, urging of Sylvia but, again, Armitage's offended and offensive manner and manners prevailed against his own interests.

'There you are, Morton. He admits it. He's flaunting it and taunting us. You deserve to be flogged, you filthy bounder you. Getting an innocent young girl pregnant is evil and deserves far worse than you are going to get, you foul sinner. And you're old enough to know better, too. You've brought disgrace on us. My wife and I regret the day we adopted the slut and we can't wait to be rid of 'er. You've no idea how this could affect us. If this sort of thing gets out my reputation will be ruined. I'm due to be made mayor later this year, but that'll not happen if the council get to know of the disgrace you've brought on us. I could be thrown out of my Masonic lodge and our customers would take their business elsewhere. But what do you care, huh?'

Armitage's rage had brought him to his feet and he had stepped toward Roger with his fists clenched. Morton struggled to his feet, spilling his file onto the floor as he tried to seize his trembling client from behind. He was not as swift, however, as Roger who had risen and stood, towering a good six inches over the suddenly uncertain grocer. Armitage allowed Morton to guide him backwards to the settee where he sat, gazing impotently at the now reclining Roger Whitehouse. If Roger had been at all uncertain of how he might re-act to a situation he and Charles had discussed hypothetically, he was now sure that anything agreed would, if he could influence it, be to the detriment of this obnoxious little man. The evident self-interest and, even more despicable, lack of care for Sylvia evinced in his selfish rant had entirely prejudiced Roger against Armitage. He sat calmly regarding his visitors. Almost inconsistently he found himself unsurprised that Sylvia was not the natural child of this sad little man. He looked at the uncertain Morton who was gathering his file together and decided he should wait to see what might be the next move.

'Mr Morton?' he said, not unkindly.

'Yes, Mr Whitehouse. Again I apologise.'

'Shall we take it as agreed that Mr Armitage is, understandably, upset? And, as I think you have tried to make clear, outbursts of uncontrolled anger will serve no useful purpose?'

'Yes. . . . Thank you for that, Mr Whitehouse. . . . May I take it that you were unaware until . . . today of Miss Armitage's . . . er . . . condition?'

'That is correct, Mr Morton.'

Both Morton and Whitehouse looked at Armitage but, his last utterances having had so little effect, he merely sat, head down, in the corner of the small settee.

'Then, that being the case,' replied Morton, 'my client and I have the advantage of what I think I might call prior knowledge. Having given careful thought to the situation we have a proposal which, I feel, you would do well to consider.'

'I shall be interested to hear your proposal and to give it consideration, Mr Morton.'

'Thank you, Mr Whitehouse.'

Again Morton cleared his throat and, opening his file, extracted papers to which he referred whilst talking. Roger listened with growing but well-concealed amusement and incredulity as Morton continued, 'My client appreciates that the income of a commercial traveller may scarcely be sufficient to support his daughter and her future child and that it is unlikely that you will have the means to finance the costs of birthing and removal from this address, which is considered unsuitable for family life. He hopes and expects that you will do the honourable thing and, as soon as possible, quietly marry Miss Armitage. Having ascertained that this house is leased from Baron Estates Limited, Mr Armitage is also prepared to purchase for his daughter and yourself a small house adjacent to the Martha Spence Maternity Home in Avonbridge where he will make arrangements for her to be delivered of the child. Neither Mr Armitage or his wife wish to visit or to have any future contact with their daughter, her husband or their child. Mr Armitage will make a one-off payment to yourself of three hundred pounds to cover the cost of surrendering the lease on 7 Stirling Road and removing yourself, plus any other incidental costs which might arise. Future support of your wife and child will be your own responsibility and any attempt at recourse to Mr Armitage will be refused and may lead to deferred action against yourself. Apart from in that contingency, no action is to be instituted against you providing you are willing to accept and agree to these proposals in writing. This is all detailed in this draft agreement. Here is a copy for you to study and consider. I suggest you have it examined and approved by a legal representative, Mr Whitehouse.'

'If he's got one,' was Armitage's sulky observation.

Morton rose and handed the draft deed to Roger, who had also risen.

'Thank you, Mr Morton. I shall certainly consider your proposals with my solicitor.' He looked at Armitage as he said the last three words, but the grocer was struggling to rise whilst still controlling his temper. Roger continued, 'I have your telephone number and I shall be in touch very soon. Thank you, Mr Morton.'

Roger and Morton shook hands. Armitage, as before, ignored Roger and swept from the room with his nose in the air. Unfortunately for him, he had to not only wait for Morton, but for Roger to open the door.

CHAPTER FOURTEEN
Sylvia, Roger and Jonathan Justin
February, 1947

At 11.34 p.m. on Tuesday 27 February 1947, Mrs Sylvia Whitehouse gave birth to a healthy baby weighing nine pounds and two ounces. Her husband Roger was not present at the birth—such presence not being permitted in those days. He was, with other fathers-in-waiting, in an adjacent room where he was so delighted to be informed he was the father to a healthy boy that he gave the matron a big, grateful kiss—something never before known at the Martha Spence Maternity Home. Nor had anyone previously seen Matron Jameson blush.

Having admired his son and dutifully kissed his exhausted wife, Roger made the short journey home through the deep snow—their home being, thankfully, but a few houses distant—where he enjoyed a celebratory glass of whisky before retiring to bed. At 9.00 a.m. on Wednesday the twenty-eighth, he was, despite the weather, the first customer at the post office from where he sent his wife's parents the following telegram:

'To Sylvia a son stop Weight nine pounds and two ounces stop Mother and child well stop Roger.'

He neither expected nor received a reply.

CHAPTER FIFTEEN
Sylvia and Roger
1946 to 1947

Pregnancy for Sylvia Whitehouse had not been easy. Not due to any physical reasons—she was fit and healthy and her new doctors in Avonbridge constantly encouraged her in her diligent exercise and diet. The emotional stress of being unexpectedly with child; expelled from both college and her childhood home; hastily married in a mid-week ceremony at Birmingham Registry Office with no bridesmaids, family or personal friends; and learning to be a housewife whilst expectant, had all taken their toll. Her unexpected husband had been kind and solicitous and, materially, she had wanted for nothing. His kindness had begun as soon as he had nocturnally smuggled her from Acacia Avenue to his former bachelor flat where Roger had sat her down and, at his readily agreed to suggestion, they had a frank exchange of views. It had cleared the air, but had not entirely allayed Sylvia's apprehension of an uncertain future. She mourned the loss of, as she viewed it, her hard-won independence; she rued the apparent loss of her dear friends from college; but her bitterest regrets were for the loss of the career on which she had set her heart.

A forced marriage is a personal stigma. A completely new environment inhibited Sylvia's need to make fresh social contacts. The disparity of age allied to their inordinately short acquaintance prior to being wed made life difficult and, when Roger was at home, conversation became stilted—however hard they both tried. Despite the 'daily' being a chatty, helpful little soul, she and Sylvia had nothing in common save the cleanliness of the house—and Mrs Marriott attended to most of that. During the coffee and tea breaks, Sylvia listened as attentively as she could to the seemingly incessant tales of the family Marriott—none of whom Sylvia was inspired to meet. Had it not been for the regular visits to the doctor and midwife—and she went as often as she dared in order to break the monotony—she envisaged little before her but a dreadful passivity. She recalled from her chapel days a phrase from the King James Bible, 'an awful looking-for of judgement.'

For Roger the transition was less of a problem, although there had to be adjustments to his previous pattern of life. Commission on sale of ladies undergarments was not a wholly necessary income and he reduced his commercial travelling to three days in most weeks. The costs of accommodation away from home remained negligible as his collected coterie of more-than-accommodating hostesses continued to eagerly await his free samples and nocturnal attentions. Occasional excursions by air remained as a condition of his RAF retainer but, whether she would have been welcomed or no, Sylvia's condition made it initially inadvisable and latterly, due to her size, untenable. After the birth her company in-flight was not even contemplated since having their infant son in an open plane was a nightmare scenario neither parent was willing to contemplate.

Roger's office remained at 7 Stirling Road, Birmingham 16. For the sake of satisfying his strange, estranged father-in-law's lawyer, the lease from Baron Estates Limited had been surrendered (copy to Morton, Kaye & Co.) and ownership and a new lease arranged with another of the Whitehouse Brothers property companies (no copy to Morton Kaye). Later all the Birmingham properties on lease were transferred into Roger's personal ownership at his request as part of the re-drafting of what proved to be his last will and testament. Leasing his owner's flat in Hagley Road produced rental income considerably in excess of his lost commission and, on the rare occasions he needed to stay-over in Birmingham, brother Charles and his wife Charlotte were pleased to have his company.

Charles and Charlotte had been the chosen witnesses at the register office wedding, the only other person behind Sylvia and Roger having been a constantly embarrassed young clerk from Morton, Kaye & Co. who, as soon as he had taken possession of a copy of the marriage certificate for the Armitage file, muttered a truculent good luck before hastening to the nearest bus stop and returning to his native Stourminster. The four Whitehouses posed with forced smiles for photographs before taking the hired limousine to the select Plough and Harrow Inn on the Hagley Road where they dined and, as a nod to convention and for the sake of appearances (though to whom they would have been hard-put to explain), Roger and Sylvia occupied the bridal suite for their wedding night. They had then spent two weeks in a similarly named, but less luxurious, suite in The Bull at Meriden as a token honeymoon. During this time together they found, despite their enforced nuptials, they still shared a sense of the ridiculous and Sylvia was even able to laugh at Roger's account of Julian Armitage's conduct and misunderstandings. She was a little ashamed to find she relished his discomfiture and subsequent financial 'sacrifice'. Roger had explained that he was sufficiently secure to support her without any contribution from Stourminster—not that any would have been forthcoming—but had stopped short of disclosing the extent of his wealth. Sylvia had also been amused at the subterfuge employed as Roger had been accompanied by one of Charles's clerks when signing the slightly amended—for the sake of legal ego as understood by both professional parties—deed; such subterfuge having continued to conceal his relationship to Charles.

After their far from unpleasant sojourn in rural Warwickshire, Roger and Sylvia had moved to the acceptable comfort of Charles and Charlotte's guest room until the conveyance of Morston, Park Road, Avonbridge into the name of Mr and Mrs Roger Whitehouse was complete. Finally, on the last day of September in 1946, the said Mr and Mrs Whitehouse duly arrived at their new home. Inquisitive neighbours had already noted delivery of several furniture consignments from the best suppliers of the time: Sylvia and Charlotte had busily combed the Birmingham stores to select the finest Roger's money could buy. Whenever Sylvia had expressed concern over cost, Charlotte had assured her that Roger could easily afford it. The curiosity of the neighbours was further aroused by the arrival of young local builder Freddie Wells's small army of workmen to install a double garage alongside the house and pave and widen the sloping drive from the road to one of the few local brick-built car accommodations.

On moving day, a sleek, red MG made its first ascent of the new drive before disappearing behind the smartly painted double doors. The Whitehouses had arrived—and in some style.

CHAPTER SIXTEEN
SYLVIA
FEBRUARY 1947 TO NOVEMBER, 1950

Whatever difficulties they have, two intelligent people with determination and a common cause—in this case the welfare and future of their child—can find agreement on most matters. Roger and Sylvia had no difficulty deciding their son's names: Julian and Baron were swiftly discarded and, despite an alliterative similarity to the never-to-visit maternal grandfather, they settled on the names Jonathan Justin. Ease of address swiftly abbreviated this to JJ as the boy became known for the rest of his life. Choice of godparents was more of a problem: Charles and Charlotte needed no persuasion to stand in that capacity, but a second godfather was not easily found. Their short residence in Avonbridge had afforded little opportunity to acquire friends considered suitable and it was not until a few weeks before the actual christening that the second godfather problem was solved.

The tiny Mrs Marriott—known as Weeny—cleaned and polished the house; the large, lugubrious and aptly named Mr Greening carefully cultivated the garden; the local grocers (quality evidenced though not advertised) delivered twice weekly. Adding to this the weekly visit of the nearby laundry, made a life of ease for Sylvia a certain passage to complete boredom had she accepted Roger's proposal to hire a nanny for little JJ. She very firmly insisted on being a hands on mother, despite the early lack of sleep.

Sylvia's generous and considerate husband, knowing her interest in music, had bought her a piano and arranged lessons at home for her. She enjoyed her Wednesday classes with Mrs Harriet Morris, a good music teacher, and she began to prepare for the grade examinations of proficiency in music recommended by Mrs Morris; the published successes in which assisted in maintaining Mrs Morris's local reputation and supply of pupils. Through Mrs Morris she was able, after a year, to join the local Choral Society at their Thursday rehearsals as they were so well organised as to provide a crèche service for young musical mothers whilst rehearsals took place.

Young JJ's early years were spent in a happy, loving environment. His big, loving father spoilt him as much as Sylvia would allow and JJ retained memories of joyful times playing and being driven very fast through the Midlands with his father. If he noticed that his father was considerably older than the other male parents wherever they went, he gave no sign of it and in later years had no clear recollection of it being something that had bothered him.

Due to Sylvia's diligent application of her near-complete training, JJ was literate at an early, pre-school age. Not all of his pre-school tuition had been for him alone or only at home. Park Road ran past St Bartholomew's Church and, feeling that their son should not be deprived of having his name conferred in a more dignified and socially-acceptable manner than their austere nuptials had allowed, Mr and Mrs Whitehouse arranged the christening of Jonathan Justin on Sunday 18 May. They forbore to inform the vicar that it coincided, as near as could be managed, with the lad's conception. Sylvia, with JJ in her arms, began regular attendance at the family services and, when he could, Roger joined them. They made the acquaintance of a few neighbours and, of course, the vicar—but it was whilst booking the christening with the parish secretary, Mrs Linda Brown, that Sylvia found not only a new friend, but an employer.

Mrs Brown, in the course of conversation, informed Sylvia that she ran pre-school and infants classes at her home, adding, 'I don't suppose you know of any teachers who could help out—we're in desperate need?'

Sylvia could not believe her luck—but she felt she must proceed with caution. It was, therefore, with more hope than expectation that she told Mrs Brown that she had trained as a teacher but had not been able to complete the course.

'Well, I don't wish to pry, Mrs Whitehouse, but were you very far into the course when you found yourself unable to continue?'

'There were only two weeks of the course left when I . . . had to finish,' Sylvia said—feeling rather silly and hoping that Mrs Brown was sincere in her wish not to pry. It seemed she was as she immediately invited Sylvia to come and have a chat the following evening.

'Perhaps we could manage something to help both of us,' she said. Then adding, 'Bring the baby—we're used to them.'

The 'we' in this instance referred to herself and her delightful, caring husband. The three adults struck up an instant rapport and friendship—Sylvia was pleasantly surprised at their non-judgemental acceptance of herself and her history of which she, to her own surprise, had recounted a shortened version. Surprise was then transferred to James Brown who, despite the short notice and acquaintance, consented to be the required second godfather.

Thus it was that Sylvia Whitehouse became a practising teacher—despite never having qualified as such—and JJ was found a 'full set' of godparents. Sylvia joined Linda and James's small staff at the Brown's rambling house—only four minutes walk from her own house—as a part-time assistant and very quickly became indispensable. She had a natural facility to communicate with young children and many children of the late 1940s brought up in Avonbridge owed their early literacy to her skill. There was no problem with JJ—he, along with one or two other babes in arms, were attendees and, as they grew older, pupils. The small salary was of little importance to Sylvia as Roger's munificence provided more than she could wish for, but she accepted the weekly envelope gracefully rather than create mutual embarrassment. She was happy and more fulfilled than she could have hoped for during the miserable months of her pregnancy. She even, with the baby-sitting agreement and co-operation of the Browns—who accepted the story of Roger needing to fly his plane for a full day occasionally—accompanied Roger to East Anglia on two occasions. On each visit she was looked after by Gloria with whom she found a sympathetic friendship during their time together.

Sylvia still had to return to an empty house on three days of the week as Roger continued to travel, but for three years life was far better than either of them could have envisaged. When he was at home, Roger was kind and attentive and normal marital relations were certainly as frequent as Sylvia desired. No further pregnancy resulted, however, Roger exercising more caution than he had done during their first physical encounter. He also took time and great patience to teach Sylvia to drive—JJ again being cared for by Auntie Linda during the early staccato lessons in Roger's car. She proved an apt pupil and, as Roger confided to his brother, a natural driver. It was, therefore, no surprise that she passed her driving test at the first attempt, giving her further freedom whenever Roger travelled away by train. For her twenty-fourth birthday Roger bought Sylvia a small, second-hand convertible Morris 8—at the same time taking the opportunity to change his two-seater MG for the latest must-have car: an Armstrong-Siddeley Sapphire. Family outings were comfortable and much envied by neighbours. Sylvia's life became more enjoyable and fulfilled. It was not destined to last . . .

CHAPTER SEVENTEEN
Sylvia, Linda, and Claude (and a Stuffed Horse)
November 1950

On Wednesday 15 November 1950 Roger Whitehouse suffered a massive heart attack and died in bed. It was not Sylvia's bed. Nor was he alone when his heart failed—probably consequent upon yet another bout of encored copulation. His shocked Wellington hostess had no idea that her regular supplier of free frillies and sexual satisfaction was a married man—indeed she had nurtured faint hopes of luring him to an altar. Nor was she very concerned to advise whoever might be dear Roger's nearest relative—such things being, in her estimation, better left to the authorities. An ambulance took Roger's remains to the Shrewsbury mortuary. The obliging hospital staff asked the police to inform his nearest and dearest at the home address found on the first page of his diary. Had their research continued further into the diary, Roger's brother Charles would have been the first to be told.

The Avonbridge police were more caring and conscientious than their Shropshire colleagues. A female police constable accompanied her sergeant to Sylvia's door on the morning of 16 November. Sylvia was about to leave for school—a short walk she did not make that morning. In accordance with Sylvia's tearful request the sergeant left her with the tea-making and handkerchief-supplying W.P.C. and walked up the road to inform Mrs Brown. Whatever the demands of the school and nursery, an emergency such as bereavement of one who had become a trusted colleague and friend took precedence in Linda Brown's Christian conscience. Leaving her staff to manage she hastened to Sylvia's side. Feeling the need for more Christian solace than she could effect whilst also tending to the young JJ, she unwittingly gave a helping hand to fate by telephoning the recently arrived local vicar, Claude Martin.

Claude Eustace Martin was a dedicated churchman and cleric. He was born on Christmas Eve 1918 of a strong mother and a father too disabled to serve his country in the Great War, yet able to serve his demanding wife. Claude's devout parents, feeling his birth date a divine sign, intended their third son for holy orders—his elder brothers having followed parental direction into the army and teaching respectively.

Claude's academic attainments far exceeding those of his siblings, he had duly gained admission to Durham University where he achieved a first class degree in theology. His intention to attain a doctorate in divinity was delayed by the call to arms in 1939—prior to which he was swiftly ordained into the Church of England. This allowed him to serve as an army chaplain—an experience that broadened his outlook and unuttered vocabulary and persuaded him to abandon any intentions of further study for the doctorate his parents would have prized far more than he and serve any community to which he might be appointed. His early enthusiasm withered over the five immediate post-war years he spent in a remote Leicestershire parish. Claude could have remained there as a faithful, though slightly disillusioned, curate had not the career-minded vicar of Avonbridge persuaded his cousin Bishop Berowne that the vacancy of dean at Worcester Cathedral would be best filled by his own immediate appointment. This left Avonbridge parish without a vicar and a swifter search for a replacement than proper prudence might have dictated resulted in Claude Eustace's unexpected promotion and removal to a large, tied vicarage—more a manse many felt—adjacent to St Bartholomew's Church, Avonbridge, in October 1950.

Claude's eagerly anticipated debut sermon proved far too erudite for the majority of his new parishioners and even the more biblically learned were inclined to surreptitiously consult their watches before Claude Eustace arrived at his unfathomable conclusion. His sincerity was evident, but the caution that caused Claude to base his first address to the faithful of Avonbridge more on his diligent studies in the North East rather than his armed services experiences failed to initially endear him to his new flock. The parish council, by a small majority, decided that their new vicar needed to be educated in the ways of their world. Consequently, the early weeks of his life in Avonbridge were consumed in an orgy of dances, whist drives, parish socials and parties where the strength of the alcoholic refreshments loosened Claude's tongue and elasticated his legs. The size of the tied dwelling was far too great for his needs and the cost of a twice weekly cleaner ate into his stipend such that even his poor financial awareness became alarmed. Ministering to the spiritual and emotional needs of his parishioners had been his avowed intent upon taking the unexpected appointment. The whirl of social life had quickly acquainted him with many of his flock—although he was uncertain how many of the party set were safely gathered-in on Sundays—but he longed to be, as he felt, useful.

That charming Mrs Brown's call to his parish secretary on 16

November 1950 was the first real cry for help he had heard in Avonbridge. Consequently, he hastened as fast as his sturdy legs could carry him to the charming house named Morston. Little did he realise how the mysterious movings of fate and his maker led him on that day.

Due to other demands on Roger's weekend time whilst Claude had been their vicar, Sylvia and Claude had never met. Consequently, his words of sympathy for Sylvia needed, Claude felt, to be carefully chosen. He was certainly surprised and uncertain how to respond when Sylvia acquainted him with the disparity in age between herself and her newly late husband. He was pleasantly surprised into further uncertainty by how attracted he felt towards this newly aggrieved young lady; although he was careful to conceal his admiration given the circumstances. His attempts to ingratiate himself with the young boy, 'And what do they call you?' proved a marked failure and he swiftly returned him to the care of Mrs Brown. Time would show no better relationship for several years than an uneasy truce between JJ and Claude—a sadness for Sylvia. For the present, however, Claude, despite his lack of any romantic experience, trod a careful and correct line between sympathy and practicality.

Resultant upon Claude's practical queries, Charles Whitehouse was, at last, informed by telephone of his brother's demise. He promised to get things moving before he and Charlotte came over. From his own experiences in Leicestershire, Claude could impart the cautionary advice that a post mortem examination would need to be conducted due to the distance from home before Roger's body could be transported to Avonbridge. He promised to contact the local undertaker and, through him, to arrange whatever form of funeral service her late husband would have wished. Sylvia had no idea what Roger might have wanted said or sung at his funeral. Nevertheless, she promised to inform this kind, caring vicar as soon as she had reached some decision. Claude left her with the nice Mrs Brown, who promised to remain with Sylvia for as long as she wished.

Together the two friends debated the best manner of informing a not yet four-year-old that his daddy was not coming home—ever. In the way of young children, JJ absorbed the news with little apparent interest and continued playing with his favourite toy—a stuffed horse on wheels which Roger had given him for his third birthday. It had a handle at the back with which caring adults could push along the mounted child. JJ had soon discovered that not only could he push the horsey along himself but that, without resource to studying Isaac Newton's law, the sloping drive allowed him to ride unaided down to the gate against which poor horsey impaled himself before being dragged back to the top for another roller coaster ride. Despite this damaging for the horsey and potentially damaging for JJ exercise being expressly forbidden, whenever JJ thought he was unobserved another ride was essayed. The potential danger of horsey riding only became horrifically apparent when a careless postman left the gate open and a stuffed toy horse on wheels with a mounted child joyfully yelling giddy-up horsey drifted across the main road to the accompaniment of alarmed, horn-sounding motorists. Child and horse survived intact but horsey was, thenceforward, confined to the house.

CHAPTER EIGHTEEN
THE WILL
THURSDAY 16 NOVEMBER 1950

Charles and Charlotte Whitehouse arrived at Morston in the early afternoon of Thursday 16 November and, after introductions and thanks, Linda Brown was able to return to her school and pre-school business. Charles had not been idle since the distressing news of his elder brother's death had reached him. He had learned all he needed to know at this time from the Shrewsbury mortuary and the Wellington police; his awareness, from an early age, of his elder brother's sexual adventures and free lodgings whilst away had completed in his mind the rather sordid picture of which, he had little doubt, Sylvia would be either wholly or partly unaware.

He had retrieved Roger's will and quickly re-acquainted himself with the terms thereof, some of which he had advised against without avail. On the drive from Birmingham he had confided to Charlotte that informing Sylvia of the will's provisions and, probably worse, the circumstances of his brother's death would be, at best, difficult.

'Does she really need to know?' a shocked Charlotte asked.

'Not all of it, certainly, but these things have a nasty habit of revealing themselves. Better she knows the basic facts of dear old Roger's deviant ways. The will is only going to make things worse for her, I fear.'

After some discussion they stopped at a village shop on the journey and purchased a few edible offerings for sustenance, and a bottle of Bell's whisky for shock and mild anaesthesia. The edible offerings were little consumed—something that could not be said of the whisky. It seemed that Sylvia, whilst not wholly cognisant of her late husband's free accommodation whilst on his commercial travels, had drawn the correct conclusions from his reluctance to talk of hotels at which he had stayed— they had been few—and his insistence on making any telephone contact during his absences himself, 'No need for you to bother receptionists, dearest. I'll call you when I can.' The bottle of Bells had remained unbroached whilst that awkward obstacle was removed—Charlotte correctly suspected the removal was only temporary. Charles secretly shared her apprehension. He found himself moving to the testamentary problem rather earlier than he had anticipated. He was helped by Sylvia who, in the way of those who seek refuge from one unpleasant aspect of a situation in another problem, was worrying about Claude's queries.

'The vicar was asking what form of funeral Roger would have wished for, Charles. Did he make you aware of anything about that?'

Charles was well aware and relieved, for the time being, to divert from the manner of his brother's death to the manner of the disposal of his earthly remains.

'He wanted to be cremated, Sylvia. Before that he wished for a church service at St Bartholomew's—the church where JJ was christened. He liked that church . . . the hymns and the reading are all detailed in the introduction to his will.'

At this stage, not only for Sylvia's benefit, but his own fortification, Charles forcefully suggested drinking whisky. He met no opposition. There followed a short silence whilst the spirit was savoured.

'I'm glad Roger made a will,' said Sylvia, nervously breaking the awkward pause. 'He wouldn't talk about it, but I thought he would have.'

Charles took a large gulp of whisky before beginning to inform his young sister-in-law of the financial facts of her late husband's wealth and its disposal, 'I checked the provisions of Roger's will before I came over. He has had a will in force for some years, but he revised it from time to time to suit circumstances as he saw them.'

Charles took another gulp of whisky. Fortified he looked at a tearful and curious Sylvia before continuing, 'He last had it re-written in early June 1947, shortly after JJ's christening. I have to tell you, Sylvia, that I advised him against the extent of some provisions, but he insisted on his own wishes—as was his right.'

'That doesn't sound too promising, Charles,' interrupted Sylvia. She seemed about to say more but the quick-thinking and wise Charlotte, putting an arm gently around her shoulder, cautioned, 'Let Charles finish, please, dear.'

Sylvia nodded. What else was fate to throw at her this day? Charles resumed, 'I don't propose to read the whole thing. You are, of course, entitled to a copy if you wish: but the main provisions are these:

'There are bequests to the RAF Benevolent Fund and St Bartholmew's Church. His plane he leaves to George Seymour—an old flying friend. His medals and uniforms (they're at Stirling Road) he leaves to the RAF Museum.

'To yourself, his wife, he leaves this house and contents; the small house at 7 Stirling Road, Birmingham 16, and its contents other than the uniform and medals of course; his car; whatever sum stands to the credit of the household account and the sum of £10,000 to be invested for your future.'

Charles paused and looked at Sylvia. 'I'm sorry, Sylvia. I did urge him to make better provision for you.'

'It seems a lot to me,' said Sylvia. 'But, I suppose, I never really knew how much Roger was worth . . .'

'Well,' said Charles, bracing himself to confront what he had feared Roger might have concealed from his young, and initially unexpected wife, 'in all fairness I should answer that question first, Roger was, as am I, worth in excess of one million pounds. This, I have to say, is largely due to our parents and grandparents from whom we inherited far more than we ever expected to. That, however, is by the way—please let me finish before you ask any more.'

He paused to take another sip of whisky. Sylvia sat, dumbfounded, waiting on his words. At last Charles continued, 'The residue of Roger's estate, comprising several properties on and around Hagley Road, Birmingham, yielding rental income in excess of £25,000 yearly; a considerable portfolio of shares; cash deposits with Barclays and Lloyds Banks and sundry small accounts with provincial building societies which, I suspect, he used whilst travelling to avoid carrying an excess of cash is all left to JJ . . . . Of course, due to his age, it will all be held in trust for him. The details are rather complex but, basically, there are directions for two trusts. The first is for his education and maintenance and is be utilised until he attains the age of twenty-one when any monies remaining transfer into what is termed the capital fund. That capital fund is to accumulate until JJ reaches what are described as 'ages of discretion'—I have to say I disagree with the ages specified, but Roger was adamant. At eighteen, which—as I say—I feel is too young, JJ will be entitled to one quarter of the capital fund; at twenty-one he inherits a similar portion—which will almost certainly amount to more as the other fund will have swelled the balance; and at twenty-five the balance passes to him entirely and the trust is wound up. He's a very lucky young chap. The trustees to be appointed are yourself, myself and Mr William Burroughs of Harvey, Smith and Thomas—our Birmingham accountants.'

There was a long silence. Sylvia simply did not know what to say—a state in which both Charles and Charlotte found themselves similarly trapped. It seemed almost apposite that the silence should be broken by JJ bursting into the room to tell his mother something of great import to the young lad. He, too, became enmeshed in the aftermath of his father's legacies being disclosed since, whatever he intended to impart after the initial urgent shouts of 'Mummy, mummy,' were stifled by said mummy gathering him to herself with agonised cries of, 'Oh, JJ.'

Charlotte was the first to recover her composure, calming both mother and child and, tactfully, taking JJ to 'play in the garden'.

'I should advise you,' said Charles to the still stunned Sylvia, 'that you have the right to challenge the will, should you so desire.'

'What good would that do, Charles?' answered Sylvia. 'It was what Roger wanted. And I've never had much money. Ten thousand pounds seems an awful lot of money to me, you know.'

'I appreciate that Sylvia—but you have to consider that it has to last for the rest of your life. The income will be worth less and less as time goes on, you know.'

'I do know, Charles,' replied Sylvia, 'but what Roger seemed to overlook was that, despite not completing my diploma course, I can teach and earn a reasonable living.

'And Linda, my friend and employer—you met her when you arrived, of course—she says there is a chance I could return to complete the course and gain my diploma. That would mean I could earn more if I wanted to. I'll abide by what Roger wanted and see where it gets me, thank you, Charles.'

CHAPTER NINETEEN
AVON STREET, AVONBRIDGE
SATURDAY 23 JANUARY 1988

The bridge over the Avon from which the town derives its unoriginal name is not exemplary of bridge building—being neither by Telford nor by Brunel. Nor is it on one of the main arteries of the county, for which the highways agency has cause to be grateful since any increase in heavy traffic passing across it would make major repair necessary. The modern river crossing for vehicular conveyances being less than a mile outside the town boundary is, mercifully, more convenient for the majority of drivers. The road across and beyond the town bridge, as locals affectionately refer to it, is unimaginatively called Bridge Street. It leads directly uphill into High Street which houses the majority of the town's small shops and, reflecting town planners usual consideration, boasts complete prohibition of parking. Frequently ignored as is also usual. To the left of High Street, on the former site of the Tennant School, are two not very cheap car parks opposite but inappositely facing the nineteenth-century town hall, with crumbling facade and an interior last decorated shortly before V.E. Day for the muted celebrations. The town hall stands not very proudly beside several Regency style houses—now occupied by the professional offices and surgeries of Avonbridge. At the far end of the block is the office, complete with unimposing frontage, of the *Avonbridge Gazette*—established 1905.

To the right of High Street, on North Road, are various commercial enterprises, a petrol station and the town's only small supermarket—two larger stores more entitled to call their market 'super' are to be found 'out of town'. Off North Road are several smaller streets bordered by early twentieth century dwellings, many now converted to flats, and several failing and failed small shops. In Avon Road North are to be seen the imposing older houses that still provide home to the better of the town families. Avon Road South once boasted a small park named for a once prominent, but now long forgotten, citizen; the now neglected open space reduced to sparse grass, rusting swings and immovable roundabouts. Even dog walkers have long since ceased to walk here. Opposite the former park is a builders' merchant store that also caters for the DIY market, where Wells Builders began their expansion from mere builders to merchants and other associated (and sometimes dissociated) enterprises.

Avon Road South narrows and leads to Avon Street where an agglomeration of shops, estate agents, foreign restaurants and take-away food vendors keep commercial company with a well-run and enterprising charity shop. Towards the end of Avon Street an imposing brick wall shields the large car park of the Avonbridge Masonic buildings. The generosity of a former stockbroker and Freemason funded the practical masons who built the hall in the early twentieth century. Next door to the Masonic hall, frowning on its very existence and dark-suited members, stands the gospel church, beyond which the road turns ninety degrees into Versey Street, a very narrow lane of mostly bed and breakfast establishments whose guests, providing they can navigate the tight access, park in what were once rear gardens. Opposite the Masonic hall is a disused factory where once dedicated artisans produced artistic metal-wear for which demand has long since ceased—as did their occupations. Where Avon Street makes its turn into Versey Street and facing oncoming traffic are two imposing metal gates supported by equally impressive brick pillars. The gates once led to a boatyard and chandlery established in more leisurely times when Avonbridge was a popular sailing venue and the now closed canal disgorged narrow boats for the journey downstream on the Avon to the major waterway of the Severn. The ornamental crests that once adorned the gates were removed by a saddened and near-bankrupt proprietor before he finally departed the premises and allowed the receivers' representative to attach a large chain and padlock securing entry to the unprotected waters edge.

Those who were frequenting Avon Street on the afternoon of Saturday 23 January 1988 took little cognisance of the two unmarked vans drawing up before the gates to the old boatyard—from time to time minor maintenance took place. It was, therefore, unremarkable that the gates should then be opened and the vans, with very dirty number plates—intentionally illegible—should drive into the boatyard. One of the drivers closed the gates and wound the chain around them before the vans drove down past the old chandlery and out of sight on the old wharf. Even an observant onlooker, of whom there were none, would probably have failed to recognise the men, clad, as they were, in dark blue overalls and voluminous caps—which was as they intended. The observer, had there been one, would have needed to be extremely near to realise that the two workmen had had no key to the padlock securing the gate but had picked the lock. Nor would it have been observed that when they left, in only one van, they secured the chains holding the gates to with a different padlock—one to which they had a key—taking the old padlock with them in the van. The second van was locked and remained out of sight of the road behind the boatyard buildings.

During their short stay beyond the gates, the pair ensured that the unseen stay of three further vehicles would be unobstructed and easily accessed. They departed as unobtrusively as they had arrived. The van in which they left did not travel far before the passenger alighted and quickly walked out of sight. The van was then driven to a local used car lot where it was quickly cleaned and a 'for sale' sticker and asking price re-secured to the windscreen. The driver then retrieved his own car from a locked garage and, unobserved so far as he could be certain, drove to his home in the distant village of Cookley.

CHAPTER TWENTY
Sylvia, Charles and an Acquaintance Renewed
November 1950

Arranging a funeral with the body detained by officialdom some miles away can be a frustrating exercise. Charles had provided several copies of the relevant portion of Roger's will which was very specific. A meeting between Sylvia; the Reverend Claude Martin; and the local undertaker, Christian Harley, was very helpful and eased Sylvia's concerns: together they drafted the order of service, including who did what according to the wishes of the deceased and Chris Harley took the draft away to be proofed by a trusted printer. Only a date was needed to complete arrangements and printing.

Meanwhile, Charles was busy gathering together Roger's assets and discharging his few liabilities. He and Sylvia visited 7 Stirling Road and, with Charlotte's help, discovered everything that Charles needed in the form of deeds, pass books, and the log books of his car and aeroplane. The decision to sell the small house where her estranged father had dictated the terms of her future with Roger was an easy one and Charles undertook to instruct an estate agent on Sylvia's behalf. Mr George Seymour was contacted and set in train arrangements to take ownership of the plane and fly it to his local aerodrome. There remained the problem of Roger's car and such personal effects as were with him at the time of his death.

The car had been, Charles was informed, removed from the Wellington bed and breakfast to a car dealership near Shrewsbury. Although Sylvia had twice driven Roger's most recent car, she much preferred her own small runabout: she and Charles agreed that the Siddeley Sapphire should be sold—Shrewsbury seeming as good a place as anywhere else to find a good price for it. Tracing Roger's personal effects proved difficult for Charles and his staff. The hospital had little to offer since he was clad in little more than a deathly pallor when they received his body. The lady of the house in whose bed Roger had inconsiderately and suddenly expired was difficult to contact and, once contacted, aggressively reluctant to assist. The suggestion of some reward, subsequently unfulfilled, eventually extracted the information that she had been so eager to remove all trace of the episode that Roger's clothes, samples and brief case—in fact anything he owned that she had not felt she could retain without being prosecuted (sentimental remembrances, you will understand) had been packed into the car before it was removed. Subsequent investigation revealed that the sentimental remembrances consisted of Roger's silver-backed hairbrushes: it was agreed that no action for their recovery would be commenced, as in all likelihood, they had been disposed of for the best price offered.

Charles and Sylvia decided to transport the car's log book and themselves to Shrewsbury and, at the same time, retrieve Roger's belongings. Both had been aware, without the other's knowledge, that Roger kept what he had called 'reserve funds' beneath the false floor of the car boot—something that made the trip more necessary. Accordingly, on Tuesday 21 November, a cold but mercifully dry day, Charles collected Sylvia from Morston and drove them both north by way of Kidderminster and Bridgnorth on the A442 toward Wellington and Shrewsbury. Following instructions they arrived at the Upton Magna Car Showrooms—an establishment in evident need of external renovation. A selection of used motor cars for sale were on display both outside and within the rather ill-lit showroom.

'We're to contact a Mrs Bateman,' said Charles, to the obsequiously fawning individual who stood full square in their way as they entered the gloomy showroom. The fawning one, who appeared to assume that anyone entering the car showroom must be there for the sole purpose of purchasing a vehicle from he and he alone, swiftly changed from servile to surly as Charles explained that he had made an appointment with the said Mrs Bateman. With little grace he conducted Charles and Sylvia to the rear of the showroom where scuffed panelling and frosted glass partitioned off what was grandly designated the office by a faded board loosely attached to the door.

'She's in there,' informed the now surly one before leaving them.

Charles knocked on the door and, brusquely bidden to enter, walked into a tidy, efficiently arranged small room furnished with a desk, three chairs and several filing cabinets—all of which had seen better days. Before one cabinet they observed the back of a woman—presumably engaged in filing.

'What is it, now, Denis?' she said without turning around.

'Mrs Bateman?' queried Charles.

At the sound of an unfamiliar voice the woman turned smartly—an apology on her lips, 'I'm so sorry. I thought you were my husband worrying about . . .' She stopped, gaping open-mouthed beyond Charles.

'I'm Charles Whitehouse and this is my sister-in-law Mrs Roger Whitehouse,' began Charles before his voice trailed off in confusion. He followed Mrs Bateman's amazed gaze . . . only to observe the same expression on Sylvia's face.

'Sylvia?'

Thelma?'

To Charles's embarrassment the two women rushed into each other's arms and began sobbing and talking together. After a few moments of unintelligible talk between them Charles felt he should attempt to restore some semblance of sense into proceedings, 'I, er . . . assume you two know each other?' was his unthinking and, he realised, obsolescent enquiry. Nevertheless he hoped for enlightenment.

Sylvia and Mrs Bateman disentangled themselves from each other and turned toward Charles. He noted Sylvia's tear-stained face.

'Oh, Charles, I'm sorry,' began Sylvia.

'We're sorry, Mr Whitehouse,' added Mrs Bateman.

'We were at teaching college together, Charles,' said Sylvia, 'and Thelma was my best and dearest friend. But we . . . we . . .' Sylvia seized a handkerchief from her sleeve and mopped her eyes.

'We lost touch, Mr Whitehouse,' said Thelma, completing her friend's sentence.

There was a pause. Charles felt he should take charge—something he was used to.

'It seems to me you both have a great deal of catching up to do. Can I suggest that I search Roger's car, if I may, whilst you tell each other what you've been doing since you . . . lost touch?'

'Good idea,' replied Thelma. I'll get Denis, my husband, to show you to the car. It's on the back lot—but securely locked.'

Denis, the obsequious one, was summoned and on being introduced and instructed suggested that it might be easier to transfer the clothes and things to Mr Whitehouse's vehicle if he brought the deceased's car round to the front.

'If you stand by your car, sir, I can bring it alongside, for you,' he added.

'Thank you,' replied Charles.

'Thank you, Denis,' said Thelma by way of dismissal, adding, 'We'll be upstairs if you really need us—but only if you really need us.'

Charles and Denis, obviously Mr Bateman, departed in different directions.

'You come with me, Sylv,' said Thelma. 'We've a little lounge upstairs that's more private than here.'

After quickly closing the filing cabinet and shuffling some papers from the desk into a drawer which she then locked, Thelma escorted Sylvia through a door at the rear of the small office that had been almost hidden by the hat and clothes stand. A short flight of stairs led them to a small room overlooking the showroom. Motioning Sylvia to sit on the small, two-seater settee, Thelma switched on an overhead light and drew blinds across the windows.

'There we are. As private as it gets round here,' she said, sitting herself down beside Sylvia and giving her a lingering kiss.

'Now tell me what's been happening in your life,' said Thelma.

CHAPTER TWENTY ONE
Sylvia, Charles and the Batemans
'Could Auld Acquaintance Be Forgot'

Thelma's request sounded almost like an order, but Sylvia decided to ignore what she may have imagined.

'Well,' began Sylvia, 'after I left your home in Sutton Coldfield I met . . . this lovely man, Roger Whitehouse—later my husband—and . . . well . . . I found I was pregnant. At first I didn't know what to do. I couldn't find you. I wrote to you but you didn't answer and——'

Sylvia started crying again.

'Oh God, Sylvia. I'm so sorry. I never got any letter, I'm afraid.'

'But . . . but what happened?' sniffed Sylvia.

'I'd better tell you all. Obviously it didn't feature in any newspapers you read.'

'I wasn't reading newspapers at the time, Thelma,' retorted Sylvia. 'I was pregnant and alone and I . . .' she paused, suddenly uncertain as to how much to say.

'Yes?' said Thelma, encouragingly and undoubtedly curious.

'Well, I was . . . expelled from college before I could qualify.'

'That makes two of us who failed to qualify, I fear,' said Thelma. 'Sorry. Go on.'

'Then I married Roger and we moved to Avonbridge where I had our little boy . . . But what should I have read in the newspapers?'

Thelma drew herself a little apart from Sylvia and sat upright, looking straight ahead rather than at Sylvia. Sylvia began to dread what her friend was about to say.

'I had to go home because daddy was arrested—please don't interrupt, dear, it's hard enough to talk about.'

Thelma sniffed and dabbed her nose with a hanky. Sylvia didn't interrupt. After a few moments, Thelma continued, 'They said daddy and Mr Masters—you remember the Masterses from next door?'

Sylvia nodded, not intending, as instructed, to interrupt.

'They said they'd been misappropriating government funds and accused them of treason. I'm sure it was all Mr Masters's doing, but the court decided they were both guilty. The hall and everything was seized and sold off. To help repay the country, they said. Mummy and I were thrown out and homeless. We moved into a tiny flat with Mrs Masters. I hated it, but it was somewhere to live. All our mail was impounded by the court—that must be why I never got your letter . . .'

Thelma stopped and looked at Sylvia. Sylvia was lost for words even though it appeared she was now expected to say something. Suddenly she recalled Thelma's sister.

'What happened to Rita?' she asked tentatively.

'Ah . . . yes,' answered Thelma. 'She went off to live with the man she'd been sleeping with and—sorry, Sylv—she got pregnant as well. . . . Unlike you, she decided to get rid of it. They went to some back street woman who took their money—they didn't have a lot—and botched the job. Rita ended up in hospital where they had to operate to save her life. The baby didn't survive, of course, which was what they wanted; just not that way. Then her chap left her and she took herself off to Birmingham, we believe—but we never heard from her after that.'

There was an embarrassed pause. Sylvia regretted having asked about Rita and decided to change the subject back to Thelma. 'But you got married?' Sylvia asked.

'Oh . . . yes. Yes, I did. Denis turned up to buy the car they left with mummy—it was in her name but she couldn't afford to keep it so we'd advertised it for sale. This business is his—he inherited it. We went out a couple of times and, suddenly, he said he loved me—I think he does, in his way. If I'm honest, getting married was a way of escaping from that crowded little flat in the back streets of Sutton . . . But, enough of me, though. Who was this Roger Whitehouse you married? It was Denis's aunty's bed he died in, you know . . .'

Sylvia gasped, held her hand to her mouth and stared at Thelma. It was obvious she had not known the precise locale of her husband's demise.

'Oh, sorry, Sylv, I thought you'd have been told.'

'No, Thelma. I hadn't.' It was Sylvia's turn to dab at her face with a hanky. Making an effort, she pulled herself together and continued, 'I can't say I'm altogether surprised. Roger was . . . I think the word is promiscuous. I always had my suspicions but, to his credit, he never flaunted his affairs or, so far as I know, was unfaithful near to home. And he was very kind and attentive to JJ—that's our son—and me and . . . well, we never wanted for anything. And now he's . . . gone.'

Sylvia paused—again uncertain how much to disclose. Why she had become so cautious she could not have said. This was her dear friend . . . yet, somehow, Thelma seemed less sympathetic than Sylvia might have expected. Thelma's next query further enhanced her doubts.

'I assume, from what you've said, he's left you quite well off, though?' asked Thelma.

Whereas previously Sylvia might have stated some specifics she found herself resorting to a white lie. 'Comfortable might be nearer the mark, Thelma,' she said.

'Lucky you,' replied Thelma. 'My miserable man told me he owned this place and it was a roaring success.'

'Doesn't he own it?' asked Sylvia.

'In name only, love. The bank are very close to closing us down unless we manage a miracle in the near future.'

Sylvia sat dumbfounded, staring at her friend. Whilst she tried to keep it from showing in her face she sensed that Thelma was nowhere near to being as close and friendly as she once had been. Looking anew into Thelma's eyes, Sylvia seemed to discern a look of almost predatory greed. She decided she should excuse herself to see how Charles was getting on, but before she could say anything Thelma pursued the course Sylvia feared she might, 'I know it's an awful nerve to ask, Sylv, but we are old friends and . . . well, as you said, you're comfortably off . . . . If you could loan us, say, a couple of thousand pounds we—well I, really—could get over the immediate problems and be able to carry on without all the worry . . . . You see?'

Sylvia saw very clearly. Whilst Thelma had been stating her case, she had been wondering how to make a polite refusal before collecting Charles and returning to Avonbridge as quickly as possible. The answer, which occurred to her just in time, was not only simple but honest.

'Thelma. Roger's been dead less than a week. Whatever he may have left me won't be legally mine until the will's been properly processed—or whatever the phrase is that makes it possible for me to take control of anything. Until then I only have the housekeeping to keep our son and myself.'

She watched Thelma's face contort with disappointment and . . . was there something else? For some reason, she instantly regretted, she felt obliged to add a sorry.

Thelma was evidently not to be so easily deflected.

'That's alright, Sylv,' I understand. No offence. Of course, I see. But . . . look . . . the car comes to you, doesn't it?'

'Yes, it does,' answered Sylvia—uncertain where this was leading and feeling wary and increasingly uncomfortable.

'Well,' persisted Thelma, 'it's a nice car, a good recent model and should sell easily. Suppose we sell it but keep the proceeds as a sort of private loan. It would help us and, as you've said, you've got the housekeeping. The money would be of more use to us than you, if you see what I mean?'

Again Sylvia did *see* what she meant. But before she could offer the excuse of needing to consult with Charles as her solicitor, Charles himself knocked at the door and entered the room smiling; he failed to see the warning look Sylvia was desperately giving him.

'Denis suggests we all go out for lunch at a nice hotel down the road. His treat,' Charles said cheerfully, adding, 'if that's okay with you ladies?'

'What a nice idea,' answered Thelma before Sylvia could say anything. Equally swiftly, Thelma rose, decisively drew back the blinds and, edging herself between Charles and Sylvia, followed Charles down the stairway, through the office and into the showroom where a smiling (or leering as it seemed to Sylvia) Denis waited.

'What say we go in your car, Charles?' said Denis, quickly adding, 'It'll save moving some of the stock around.'

'Alright,' replied Charles. 'I've got *all*'—he stressed 'all' with a knowing look at Sylvia—'of Roger's things in my boot. And it's not far, you say?'

'Hop and a skip, really,' answered Denis. 'Hardly worth using the car—save for the ladies, of course.'

Charles politely held open the rear door for the ladies. To her great discomfort, Sylvia found herself sitting hip to hip with Thelma whilst Denis joined Charles in the front. She consoled herself that it was only to be a short journey—a consolation based upon Denis Bateman's smooth deceit. Charles was too polite to comment during the two-mile trip to the Manor Hotel.

Sylvia desperately wanted to talk to Charles alone, but the Bateman's astute manoeuvres prevented any opportunity. The Bateman's were also well-skilled in conversing on irrelevancies which, allied to Charles natural social graces, made an hour of eating, drinking and small talk pass with relative ease for all save Sylvia. Charles did wonder at Sylvia's silence, but was too considerate to enquire as to her reticence in front of the others. Sylvia followed Charles's lead in refusing a sweet or a brandy; looking meaningfully at Charles she suggested they should be thinking of the return journey before it became late.

'Quite right, Sylvia,' he replied.

A short, embarrassed pause ensued before Denis summoned the

waiter to request the bill. It was duly delivered and placed before Denis—the ostensible host. He glanced at it and then extracted from his inside pocket a very distinctive leather wallet. With what Sylvia and Charles afterwards agreed was a well-practised ploy, he opened the wallet and looked shocked and surprised.

'Oh, gosh. Oh dear, oh dear me,' he said. 'I seem to have run out of money. Look, this is embarrassing, but I wonder if you could settle the damage, Charles. Pay you back, of course, but . . . bit embarrassing, actually.'

'That's——' began Sylvia.

Her indignant objection was forestalled by Charles—whose recognition of the wallet had been as swift as her own. Charles's hand shot across the table trapping Denis's hand and the wallet.

'Run out of *whose* money?' demanded Charles; his voice as hard and cold as Sylvia had ever heard from him.

'What d'ye mean, old boy? And let go of my hand; that hurts.'

'I'm just wondering—as, I think, is my sister-in-law—where you obtained that wallet?'

'Gift from a grateful customer, old boy. Now do let me go. This is not on, you know.'

'What I do know is that that wallet belonged to my late brother.' With his free hand Charles seized the wallet. 'Now the property of his wife, I feel.'

'I think you ought to apologise, old boy. My wallet.'

Denis endeavoured to snatch it back, but Charles was too quick. He opened the wallet. Again he spoke quietly and coldly, 'If it's your wallet, how do you account for the initials "R. W." inscribed inside?'

The opened wallet clearly displayed Roger's initials. Denis made no reply. Charles continued in that cold, rather frightening voice, 'If you wish to dispute ownership, I have a precisely similar wallet, save that the initials are mine. They were given to my brother and I last Christmas by my wife.'

'You bloody fool, Denis,' spat Thelma, through clenched teeth.

'I think that settles it,' said Charles, emptying Denis's few papers and cards from the wallet onto the table, 'Sylvia, I'm sure you agree we should now leave?'

'But how're we going to pay?' whined Denis. 'And get back?'

'I'm sure your local will allow you credit,' replied Charles. 'And it's only "a hop and a skip" back, isn't it? After you, Sylvia.'

Sylvia and Charles left the restaurant. Out of sight of the Batemans

Charles quickly and quietly explained to the hotel receptionist they were leaving and left fifteen pounds—far more than the meal had cost—with instructions not to speak to Mr and Mrs Bateman for ten minutes and to keep the change. The flushed receptionist willingly agreed to participate in what she perceived as a joke between friends—one from which she profited considerably.

In the car, Charles handed Roger's empty wallet to Sylvia.

'Lord knows what else they pilfered but, so far as I can see, it's not worth pursuing,' he said. Sylvia heartily agreed—not wishing to ever again set eyes on her former friend and her equally dissolute husband. Tearfully, she outlined the gist of her conversation with Thelma and Thelma's proposition. Sylvia had already formed a firm resolve that the Bateman's should not, under any circumstances, retain Roger's car. Although she had only driven it for short journeys, she was grimly determined that she would drive it back to Avonbridge where it could be sold. Fortunately, Charles still retained the log book. He had also noted where Denis Bateman had hung the keys to the car—knowledge that enabled him to stride confidently into the showroom, retrieve the car keys. 'We came to collect it,' he assured the spotty young salesman left in charge, and informed him that Mr and Mrs Bateman would be along shortly.

Anger fuelling her grim determination, Sylvia doggedly drove the big, powerful car in the wake of Charles. Charles had never driven so far with his attention almost equally divided between the road ahead and the rear-view mirror. Alone in her deceased husband's car, Sylvia found it increasingly difficult to maintain her concentration. Her mind constantly returned to her past and regrets that she knew she should not entertain began to overwhelm her. How could she have been so blind to the mean, calculating nature of Thelma and her crooked family? And had she not accepted the invitation to spend that week in Sutton Coldfield and Thelma's bed . . . Anger turned to remorse. The tears started to flow. She seemed unable to wipe them away quickly enough to see where she was driving. Just as she felt she must either crash or stop the car in the middle of the road, a garage with a café sign loomed on the left. She leaned on the horn, extended the left hand indicator and frantically gave an exaggerated turning left hand signal in the hopes that Charles would realise in time to turn in. He did.

The forecourt of the café was sufficiently large for the two big cars not to cause a major obstruction. Charles leapt from his car and rushed to Sylvia who, by this time was weeping uncontrollably.

'I'm so sorry, Charles. I thought she was my best friend,' sobbed

Sylvia. 'It all just . . . '

'I know, love,' answered her considerate brother-in-law. 'Let's see if we can get a cup of tea here and I'll ask them to let me use the telephone.'

Sylvia could never have wished for a kinder, more caring brother-in-law. She sipped the strongest tea she had ever been served from the thick cup. When Charles was satisfied that she was sufficiently calm, he left her with her tea and began a series of telephone calls. With an efficiency that amazed Sylvia, arrangements were made that, in her distressed state, Sylvia could never have envisaged. Money, of course, had a strong persuasive influence, but without Charles's calm, decisive and positive attitude little could have been achieved.

Bridgenorth boasted but one hotel. It had a large car park and the two best rooms were vacant for the night. Most of the other rooms were also vacant, but the nice, generous Mr Whitehouse only required two. The café proprietor's brother would have driven the powerful 'posh' car simply for the pleasure it gave him: the tip the tall lawyer offered was more than he often earned in a day—let alone the half hour it took to drive to Bridgenorth and be taken back to the café by his friend with whom he shared the tip. The free drinks he derived whilst endlessly recounting this experience were his alone.

Sylvia's twin-bedded room seemed not only extravagant but lonely: until, after less than an hour of trying to calm herself, a gentle knock on the door preceded her sister-in-law Charlotte.

'Charles felt you ought not to be alone tonight,' said Charlotte—leaving her over-night case on the bed and gathering Sylvia into her arms. 'Cry it out, dear,' she added.

Dinner was late. It could not, by any stretch of imagination, be described as haute cuisine, but it satisfied what little appetite Sylvia had. Later she found herself, for the second time in her life, sharing a bedroom with a member of her own sex. This time, however, each was demurely clad in night attire—Charlotte having, considerately, brought a nightdress and spare toiletries for Sylvia. The embraces they exchanged before climbing into their respective beds were those of sympathy and comfort with no sexual connotations.

Charlotte learned a great deal more about her young sister-in-law—and indeed her late brother-in law—than she would ever have imagined likely. Very little of what she learned that night was ever shared with Charles—or anyone else; the daughter of a solicitor who then marries another solicitor knows all about discretion.

Roger's car was returned to its home garage the following afternoon and a tearful re-union of mother and child effected. Charles arranged the sale of Roger's car for a reasonable price through the dealer from whom Roger had originally purchased the vehicle. Sylvia never went near to Shrewsbury again in her whole life. Having read of it in mid-1951, Charles bided his time telling Sylvia of the Batemans's bankruptcy; neither of them were surprised or, being basically decent persons, delighted. Charles succinct judgement of just deserts sufficed for both of them.

CHAPTER TWENTY TWO
Sylvia
1950 TO 1953

On her return home from the Shrewsbury experience Sylvia collected JJ from Linda and put him to bed before she sat down and, again, surrendered herself to the tears and self pity she had been suppressing. She still felt betrayed. The more she reflected on the now exposed perfidious nature of the woman she had regarded as her bosom friend and leader to a liberated life, the worse she felt. The dictates of her young life in the confines of the modern Methodists, Acacia Avenue and the grocery of quality came back to her with all the force of forgotten condemnation to eternal damnation and she descended into a maelstrom of misery. That night she cried herself to sleep.

The morning brought little comfort or respite. Feeling she could not face a morning teaching, Sylvia prevailed on the generosity of Linda and, offering a rather lame excuse that yesterday had not resolved matters completely, she left JJ in Linda's care for a second day. Having done which she returned home and sat, sad and bewildered, in a house that she now began to feel was only hers due to having erred and strayed from the righteous path of life. It was in this state of piteous self-recrimination that she decided prayer might help. Suiting action to the thought she walked to St Bartholomew's Church where, in a back row pew, she sank to her knees and surrendered herself to such a surfeit of prayer as she had not entered since childhood. It gave her little comfort.

The Reverend Claude Eustace Martin, discovering a distressed parishioner in his church, and finding her to be the young widow he had so recently comforted and admired, offered coffee and comfort. So understanding did he seem that, to her own surprise, Sylvia unburdened herself of the self-imposed guilt the previous day had occasioned. Claude Eustace listened sympathetically to Sylvia's shamefaced confession. Concealing his surprise at her revelations and carefully avoiding the platitudes usual to many of his calling, Claude chose, rather, to offer practical suggestions for Sylvia that could, eventually, consign the past to a dreadful memory. To the surprise of both of them they relaxed into a tender cuddle of commiseration—only parting when the imminent entry of eager and earnest ladies to arrange flowers became audibly evident. Sylvia thanked the vicar for his kindness. Claude thanked Sylvia for her confidence—which he would respect. They agreed that regular sessions of prayer allied to 'keeping busy' would help Sylvia allay her grief.

Claude secretly hoped that more cuddles could ensue—nor did he feel any guilt for his desires.

Roger's funeral, when his remains were eventually released from Shrewsbury, was made a greater trial for Sylvia by the unexpected attendance of numerous landladies from all parts of the land. Their ladylike status was somewhat dubious but each, in a brazen but genuinely saddened way, insisted on clasping Sylvia to huge bosoms and leaving lipstick markings on her cheeks and blouse. As if this were not enough, most chose to confide in Sylvia's ear their carnal envy of her proprietary right to Roger's 'great . . . you know . . .' More specific descriptions of his Priapus were whispered which Sylvia would have blushed to repeat. The knowledge that the deceased's brother was present in the Church Hall wake occasioned so many lascivious landladies' to cast unladylike looks at his lower frontage that Charlotte, aware by experience and her husband's shared confidence of the family immensity, felt obliged to constantly stand in front of Charles.

Sylvia was pleased and surprised to find Gloria, the large American sergeant, amongst the mourners and was vastly relieved that during her embrace Gloria made no reference to Roger's physicality. Gloria was accompanied by a small body of uniformed personnel from the United States Air Base. The Royal Air Force sent a uniformed detachment of men to carry the coffin and act as a guard of honour. There were also a few very superior looking gentlemen in black jackets and striped trousers—identified by Charles as senior civil servants—who regarded the ladies of the land with distaste, whilst remaining unfailingly civil and sympathetic.

The most distinguished of these gentlemen shook Sylvia's hand and, after saying how much they would miss Roger, confided, 'There will be a small pension, of course, to yourself. Roger contributed, you know. I'll let Mr Charles Whitehouse have the details.'

With which intriguing confidence he was gone. In the confusion of the day, Sylvia almost forgot this small exchange. Charles did not and was able, later, to inform Sylvia that she would be in receipt of an 'inflation proofed' pension commencing at £240 per annum.

Sylvia's nearest and dearest—Charles, Charlotte, Linda and James—

were all very complimentary concerning Claude Eustace's conduct of the funeral and, particularly, his touching eulogy on Roger. Claude and the two couples accompanied Sylvia to Morston after the wake and, to the mild, unspoken surprise of the two couples, Claude remained when they departed. Sylvia was pleased that he had stayed behind and, not for the first or last time, they sat together in comfortable silence or talked of shared interests.

Time is a great healer, as is the presence of a kind confidant. The Reverend Claude Eustace proved to be both kind and sympathetic. As the weeks passed, Sylvia found herself spending more time at the church. As the months passed her calls at the vicarage became increasingly regular. She felt, rightly, that the old house definitely needed a woman's caring touch rather than the perfunctory cleaning effected by the daily—who, perversely, performed her duties on Mondays, Wednesdays and Fridays— bank holidays excepted. Sylvia gradually found herself leaving school and going directly to the vicarage rather than home. JJ seemed to like the vast rooms in which he was able to play to his heart's content—often getting filthy in the process and needing to be bathed in the vicarage's enormous bathtub with the gurgling taps which always made him laugh. On fine days he was allowed to play behind the house—where an area of rough grass apologised for the lawn it had once been—until the day he decided to explore, and became lost in the jungle which abutted the former lawn and stretched to unknown distances. Panic ensued until, scratched, happy and filthy almost beyond recognition, JJ, responding to his mother's distressed calls, emerged from the overgrown tangle of weeds, trees, shrubs and plants. He was instantly forbidden from ever again venturing beyond the confines of the patch of trampled grass and weeds.

The following day Sylvia discovered a distressed Claude whose blistered hands had been incurred during his unavailing attempt to make a better playground for JJ by the restoration of some semblance of lawn. Claude's gardening skills matched his other practical abilities: a blunt kitchen knife and bare hands proving not to be the ideal means of trimming grass. Sylvia was so touched by his attempts, however, as to give him a spontaneous kiss and cuddle. To her surprise and, she had to admit, pleasure, Claude returned the physical contact with considerable enthusiasm. Sylvia's confession and account of her mad week in May had aroused erotic feelings in the vicar that he had never imagined could trouble his mind or loins. His pent up love and lust surfaced with almost alarming fervour before his usual reticence and regard for Sylvia caused him to release his tight hold on her and, holding her at arm's length, he began to frame an apology, 'Oh, dear Sylvia, I'm so sorry to get so carried away, but I've loved you from the moment we met and you giving me a kiss just made me forget myself. Will you ever forgive me, dear Sylvia?'

'What's to forgive, Claude? You're a man and I'm a woman and we've shared a lot together in the last two years,' replied Sylvia. Then, gathering him to her she added, 'Dear Claude.'

'Oh, my darling,' gasped Claude. 'I want you so much I . . . Oh, I'm sorry.'

'Stop apologising, Claude. I can see and feel that you want me and . . . it's all right for you to feel that way, you know.'

'But . . . but, Sylvia it's only been two years since Roger——'

'I know, Claude, and the world at large might judge us severely,' said Sylvia. 'But what the world doesn't know it can't judge, can it? And as long as we have clear consciences we can live happily ever after, my dear. I'll be right back.'

Sylvia dashed to the car from which she removed JJ and, to his delight and despite the cool day, sent him to play in the back garden. She returned to a smiling, flustered Claude and, taking his hand, led him upstairs to his neat, tidy bedroom. The neatness and tidiness did not long remain. Sylvia felt no guilt over initiating Claude for, truth to tell, they truly loved one another—true love for the first time in each of their lives. Adding physical affection to Claude's spiritual comfort made Sylvia feel a complete woman again, the vicar's organ afforded her, she admitted to herself, though not to Claude, greater vaginal comfort and ease than had the inherited enormity of her over-endowed late husband. Claude's spirits soared and he, too, felt a more complete person.

Over the next six months they managed to conceal their intimacies from the congregation—indeed from everyone save Linda in whom Sylvia, correctly, felt she could confide. Sylvia's gardener, house cleaner and laundry service commenced regular attendance at the vicarage which was looked on kindly by all as improving the life for the dear vicar.

In May of 1953, to no one's surprise, they announced their engagement and, there being no real reason to delay, they were married on Saturday 18 July. After a short honeymoon in Cornwall, Sylvia moved herself and JJ into the vicarage and, with Charles's permission and cognisance, sold Morston. Stirling Road had long since been sold and, for the first time in her short but eventful life, Sylvia was happy, content and secure.

CHAPTER TWENTY THREE
JJ
1950 TO 1956

Life for the infant Jonathan Justin Whitehouse was as idyllic as he might have wished—had he had the luxury of his own pre-destination. Although daddy was not constantly living at home, he dearly loved his playful and, as he later appreciated, generous father. At the age of three years and almost nine months the memories of most children are small and selective: their capacity for emotional adjustment far simpler than in later life. Hence JJ had only happy, hazy memories of his father and was able to bear his loss with the equanimity of the young. He retained recollections of two early disruptions to his routine: although he would not have known the precise dates on which they occurred were the 16 and 27 November 1950. On the first day a policeman and a police lady had came to the house and talked to mummy: then Auntie Linda ran in and everyone seemed to be crying until Uncle Charles and Auntie Charlotte came. But mummy still seemed awfully upset. On the next day, and not long after (a child does not count eleven days) things were all upset again: mummy, dressed in unaccustomed black, gave him a very wet kiss (tears—not saliva) and left him with Weeny, the house help, for almost the whole day until Uncle Charles and some other people came into the house and drank tea, and mummy was very upset again.

Life, then, resumed some of its former normality although he did seem to be in the church far more than before. Mummy and his aunties (real and adopted) had told him that daddy was not going to be here any more and his demands to know why seemed not to be appreciated, so he stopped asking. He and mummy still went up the hill to Auntie Linda's where he had some little friends and enjoyed playing, reading, starting to write, and singing whilst mummy or, more often, Auntie Linda played the piano. The quiet man with his collar on backwards also seemed to call very often and he was encouraged to address him as Uncle Claude; he didn't like that very much. He did enjoy exploring the big house where Uncle Claude lived.

At the age of five JJ began the, then mandatory, three years at infant school.

After resenting change for the first day or so, he enjoyed school and made friends easily. He hated the smelly communal lavatory in the playground, but he enjoyed the music lessons—especially when he was allowed to play the tambourine or the drum and Mrs Gardner told mummy that he had a natural facility, whatever that was, for the trumpet. He never blew one from the age of seven. What Mrs Gardner, or any one else at that time, failed to appreciate was that JJ had an almost perfect sense of pitch—a gift given to few. This allowed him to demonstrate to mummy an innate ability to pick out a tune on mummy's piano after only one hearing. This being reported to Mrs Morris prompted that perceptive piano teacher to seek for and be granted tutelage of the young JJ. Harriett Morris's blinkered view of piano tuition took no account of those who could, as did JJ, play better by ear than from the music she supplied—at a pleasant profit. Consequently, JJ's musical ability became hampered by stricture. Lessons for both he and mummy acrimoniously ended after the lesson at which JJ deliberately played the set piece demonstrated by Mrs Morris with his eyes shut and more fluently than his teacher. His development as a pianist thereafter continued at his own will, all he owed Mrs Morris was a basic ability to read music when he needed.

Infant school lessons wherein JJ was forced to knit a sampler and embroider coloured circles on a brown (hessian) bag were periods of extreme distaste to he and his friend Christopher. They never finished either task themselves, but had them completed in indecent haste by Miss Pittaway so that they could take them home to mummy, to their credit neither boy attempted the deceit of claiming to have produced the unwanted articles. All the boys and girls walked to and from school. After a year at school, JJ was increasingly told to walk back to the vicarage instead of home; mummy seemed to make the tea there several days a week and Uncle Claude always tried to ingratiate himself with the boy—with little success. The vicarage was a big, rather dark house that had lots of rooms in which to play—he got quite dirty at first, but later Weeny could be sighted at both home and the vicarage and the dusty rooms became more habitable and less fun. The garden looked to be a great place to explore, but initially JJ was forbidden to go out there where he might be stung (or lost). JJ missed Auntie Linda and Uncle James. Uncle Charles and Auntie Charlotte came to see them less and less. JJ entered a period in which he became a solitary child.

During this time his reading ability advanced rapidly. His membership of the local library afforded access to the exciting adventures of Arthur

Ransome's *Swallows and Amazons* and other worthy literature for children. His mental advancement was most affected by Uncle Charles's and Auntie Charlotte's gift for his fifth birthday of a set of Arthur Mee's children's encyclopaedias. He kept them in the room at the top of the vicarage of which Uncle Claude allowed him exclusive use and could be found there on most wet days avidly studying.

In the July of 1953, JJ was summoned to the front room at home and a strange woman, who smelled very odd, made him put on a white, satin suit. He felt silly—but it seemed to make mummy happy so he walked around as asked and the smelly woman, who now had pins in her mouth, pulled and pinned the material before he was told to remove it 'until the big day.' JJ had no idea what the big day was, mummy had told him they were going to a church for a wedding and he would be a page boy. He had to walk behind mummy and hold up her long trailing skirt. There was a practice in the hall he found rather boring but, again, it seemed to please mummy so he did as he was asked, though with little enthusiasm. It was after that that he became upset. Mummy sat him down and told him that they were not going to live at home any more and that, after a holiday by the sea, they would live at the vicarage with Uncle Claude. And the vicarage would be home after Saturday. This wasn't right. *Morston was home*!

'Not any more, JJ,' said mummy.

'Why not? I like it here.'

'Don't you like the vicarage?'

'It's alright.'

'Of course it is, JJ. We're going to be very happy there. And after Saturday, I would like you to call Uncle Claude daddy.'

This was a step too far. Funny collar Uncle Claude wasn't his daddy and he never would be, and so on *ad infinitum* until a compromise was reached. The truculent JJ finally consented to call the former Uncle Claude 'papa' or 'pa' for short. The compromise remained exactly that until JJ's mid-teens.

The change to his surname puzzled him but, not understanding what it meant, he accepted it with the equanimity of a child. After all when people addressed him by his full name they said 'Whitehouse' before 'Martin'—and he always answered politely.

On the last day at infant school, JJ, Christopher and all of their form were walked in a long line into the middle of Avonbridge where they would spend the next three years as intermediate pupils of the then prestigious Tennant School. Their introduction was a reading aloud test in which he and Christopher—both sons of talented teachers—simply read as they usually did and were surprised to be told they were excellent young readers and would be in the top class. Mummy and Christopher's mummy seemed amused when they were told; nevertheless they complimented their sons. Their new headmaster was a tall, dignified gentleman whom everyone seemed to like and respect; when he met JJ's mother there were mutual exclamations of surprise and delight—it seemed they had trained together. Denis Dunkerley—known to generations of admiring pupils as Daddy Dunkley made it very clear to JJ that he should expect to be treated no differently to any other pupil, despite his mother's acquaintance with him. And so it was.

JJ liked this school better than the previous one and, with his natural intellect, progressed well. His days as a loner were behind him. The school boasted a bicycle shed and, in response to his repeated demands, Sylvia and Charles agreed to purchase JJ his first bike. He swiftly mastered the art of balance and rode alone for many miles around Avonbridge, thus becoming better acquainted with the local geography than Uncle Claude and enabling him to demonstrate a superiority whenever the confused vicar wondered aloud how he might travel to any part of his parish to which he had been summoned. JJ's concise directions sometimes led to problems for Claude since a solo cyclist can access areas where the vicar's new car—a gift from Sylvia—could not travel.

The vastness of the vicarage was not confined to the house with its six big bedrooms, three reception rooms, enormous kitchen and scullery. From Church Road the vicarage visitor passed between high, unkempt hedges to a wide, unweeded driveway that meandered—it had once justified the description *swept*—around before both house and stabling. The double fronted dwelling boasted a porticoed front door almost twice as wide as had, later, become fashionable—and practical. When opened it gave onto a wide, deep hall with red tiled floor that, when polished, gleamed impressively and been dangerous to the less than sure-footed. The days of polishing and gleaming were long gone and the front door had became a redundant entrance; all save the uninformed using the side door that afforded easier access to the vicar's study and the living areas of the rambling house. The side door was approached by way of a pathway between the house and the former stables—now converted into a double garage, bike shed and repository of rusting garden tools. To the rear, a long garden of former splendour was entirely enclosed by an eight-foot high wall. Years of neglect had allowed the long garden to become so overgrown as to be almost impenetrable to all—except for a determined four-year old boy.

The incident of JJ's excursion into the unknown depths, allied to Claude's inept attempt at lawn culture, prompted Sylvia to approach Mr Greening the gardener for his help in, initially, restoring the former lawn.

"Taint worth the bother of tryin', missus,' was his horticultural judgement. 'Gorn too far, it 'as. Better to dig it orl up und lay noo turf, I reckons.'

So it was that gardener Greening came to cultivate the vicarage gardens, and the remaining space in the former stables became occupied with garden machinery and shiny new implements of cultivation and maintenance. JJ had always liked gardener Greening, his slow, funny way of talking appealed to him and the fact that the old man always treated him as a person and not a child endeared the grubby Greening to JJ. The young lad's enthusiastic attempts to help in the laying of new turf hindered as much as helped the older man, but he patiently persuaded the lad to minor attenuated tasks that, though of little assistance to the lawning, satisfied the lad into believing he was being useful. After the lawn laying came a period when, to his frustration, JJ was not allowed to tread on the grass whilst it 'bedded in', Greening explained it carefully to the lad who, whilst comprehending, remained impatient for somewhere to play. The next step in the Greening of the vicarage was to reduce the front hedges to a reasonable height—during this exercise JJ was, advisedly, confined to the house. When the superfluous hedging had been *ditched*—the old man liked that little joke, in which oft repeated affectation he remained alone—and light once more bathed the frontage of the old house, it was obvious to Sylvia and anyone save Claude that the attentions of a painter and decorator were required. Claude pointed out that such expense should be borne by the church authorities, but their miserly prevarication would, in Sylvia's opinion, have allowed sufficient regrowth of the hedge as to conceal the house before it was re-painted. Her pecuniary legacy had been swelled by the sale of Stirling Road and Roger's car and the interest on her capital, allied to the unexpected pension and her teaching salary made Sylvia, for the time, if not a wealthy woman at least comfortably off. Sufficiently comfortable to engage and pay a local decorator to restore the outside of the old vicarage to a much-admired state.

Due to the trusts in Roger's will, Sylvia had no need to dispense money for JJ's education and maintenance; not that his education, until the age of eleven, incurred more than minor costs. The clauses by which JJ was to be afforded pocket money at an extortionate rate (a father's indulgence and earlier than expected demise was Charles's explanation) could have proved an embarrassment and spoiled the boy, but the wisely chosen Mr Burroughs of Birmingham chartered accountants Harvey, Smith and Thomas devised a means by which JJ received the money in such a way as to be both guarded against childish extravagance and allowed to commence early education in financial prudence. The pocket money was paid, as directed, from the trust to a savings account in a local bank from which account JJ, with Sylvia as counter signatory, was empowered to draw such sums as Sylvia thought fit for the boy to have as spending money. The income of the savings account was, for several years, far greater than the expenditure (cash drawings)—something that JJ increasingly understood and jealously guarded. He needed little in the way of money and, unbeknownst to Sylvia, he actually hoarded at least half of the cash dispensed to him in a padded bag hidden behind books in his bedroom.

It was from his secret hoard that JJ bought some packets of seed to supplement the flowers around the new lawn that gardener Greening had planted.

The lad's desire to please and surprise proved an embarrassment to poor old Greening when carrots and leeks began to appear amongst the daffodils and tulips he had so carefully arranged for madam's pleasure. The best mistakes are those from which lessons can be learned; once the source of the vegetables was detected, gardener Greening was deputed to instruct the young lad in the basics of gardening. Instructor and pupil were almost equally pleased with the position and sat for hours in the garden stall of the stables as JJ listened, rapt, to the old man's tales of gardens he had known. Once the borders beside the front hedge and around the rear lawn had been satisfactorily seeded and the rose bushes Sylvia so wanted had been bedded in, JJ was deputed to do the daily watering ('Not too much, now yung un—downt wanna drown 'em'). The younger partner of the gardening team, inspired by the older man's stories, urged expansion into the overgrown tangle beyond the lawn. Sylvia agreed with gardener Greening that it did look 'a orful messy site' and authorisation was granted for clearing to begin. It was at this stage that JJ confided in his horticultural mentor that not only had he trespassed on the first known occasion, but had also made several undetected excursions beyond the boundaries dictated to him.

From the lad's uninformed descriptions, the older man realised that hidden from view were a summer house, a pathway with pergola, a greenhouse, and a brick-built garden house. It took a year of back-breaking work and the assistance of gardener Greening's son and younger brother before the mass of weeds, foliage and self-seeded trees were cleared and burned or, in the case of less flammable detritus, removed. The wooden summer house had rotted beyond redemption, but Sylvia was so entranced by the new possibilities that she funded a new, glazed and upholstered version of the original in which she could sit and read and where Claude subsequently felt he composed some of his best sermons. 'Nearer to nature is nearer to God' was one of his new maxims.

Around the summer house a profusion of flowers, bushes and ornamental trees began to flourish: the restored pergola—truth to tell it was almost all new, but on the same ground and in the same pattern as before—gave a peaceful walk through the garden. Beyond the floral displays the demolition team, urged on at all times by JJ, had come to a 'cross wall' with a gateway (now just an opening) to what had once been part vegetable plot and part small orchard. Beyond this, against the end wall of the vast vicarage tract of land was, as originally discovered by JJ, a large greenhouse with the end wall of the gardens as its rear support. The roof frames had rotted in half-glazed despair and several shards of dirty glass hung ominously poised to fall upon the unwary. Tendrils of an unpruned vine perversely protruded into the chill air where they should not have survived. Two neglected, brick based cold frames nestled uncomfortably against the left hand wall beside the greenhouse. These were converted into composting bins on which smelly receptacles old Greening lavished almost as much loving care as he gave the rest of the garden. Opposite the compost bins, against the right hand wall and the last quarter of the end wall, a brick built potting shed adjoined a small gardener's cottage with running water, and an intact Belfast sink and a toilet. A water supply had, in an enlightened former time, been piped from the main house serving both the cottage and an outside tap, its lagging only part rotted, for watering the gardens. Sewage seemed to dispose of itself towards whatever lay behind the end wall. In the corner of the cottage stood a rusted stove set into a fireplace from which smoke had once issued into the brick chimney protruding above the wall.

With the enthusiasm of youth and the little knowledge that could be dangerous, JJ urged the development of this far plot. Sylvia and Claude, aware that a ready supply of fresh fruit and vegetables would be advantageous and (this was Claude) cheap, sanctioned Greening to clear, dig over, restore and begin planting. Clearing the soil by the planting of potatoes was urged and, reluctantly ('What can we do with all the potatoes?') agreed. What was to be done with all the potatoes was no problem for the guileful Greening; unfortunately for him he confided his estimate of the crop's value to JJ. Managing his own small savings and secret hoard had imbued the lad with an elementary commercial sense. A bicycle ride to the local greengrocery (no mention of quality) supplied JJ with a more precise retail valuation for a crop of King Edwards. The indulgence of an initially unsuspecting greengrocer who rapidly revised his opinion of this young upstart led to a deal being struck—to include the arduous burden of collection. Tentative future deals for apples, plums, soft fruits and grapes, tomatoes, lettuce and any other surplus vicarage produce were also agreed on handshakes. Before his ninth birthday, JJ was in business. He liked it.

Restoration of the greenhouse, potting shed and cottage proved more costly than Sylvia anticipated and, with the agreement of her fellow trustees, a sizeable contribution from JJ's education and maintenance fund was advanced; the boy's interests in gardening and horticulture being considered sufficient justification. Old Greening's time was fully occupied clearing and planting the vegetable patch and pruning the neglected small orchard; which was as well since— despite protestations to the contrary—his skills did not include glazing, plumbing and building work. The almost ubiquitous Wells Builders made swift and efficient work of restoring the greenhouse, and the potting shed and cottage were combined, at JJ's suggestion, by the simple expedient of removing one wall and erecting an archway from one to the other. As the last task, one warm Friday night, the old stove was removed and taken away.

'We'll be back next week to repair the fireplace, young man,' was Mr Wells's man's parting shot as he left for the local. JJ followed him up the garden for his tea.

CHAPTER TWENTY FOUR
JJ AND BILLY BAKER
1956 TO 1958

A boy of nine, albeit sometimes solitary, still has the usual ambitions. So JJ, in addition to and in part due to his potato and produce business, desired a den of his own. To be sure Uncle Claude—or 'Pa' as JJ called him when wanting to please him—allowed him almost exclusive use of the attics in the house, and he did enjoy playing an old piano that he found there beside an early electric organ that he had begun to master. But it was the *almost* applied to the *exclusivity* that rankled. Weeny and another cleaning lady came up there at least once a week. A lad, particularly one who has had a time as a loner, prizes his privacy. With this in mind, he had harboured proprietory thoughts toward the gardener's cottage. The first claim on it, even JJ had to acknowledge, should have been with gardener Greening but, to JJ's relief, the old man spurned its use in favour of the section of the old stables he had already organised for his vicarage gardening. Mummy was warily agreeable. Pa seemed as unconcerned as ever where any practical matters were concerned. JJ had his den.

Being a bright but thoughtful boy, JJ deliberated long and hard as to how he should arrange his den: these were not idle periods of thought, but practical considerations allied to near-scale drawings made on squared paper even whilst the builders restored the neglected buildings. The raised section of the potting part—originally for drying seeds, etc.— JJ decided could be a sitting area for which soft covering and cushions would be needed. The toilet, although not flushed for several years, was cleaned and restored to full working order; Sylvia was relieved that her son could function similarly without returning to the house or, worse, fouling the garden. The brick floor of the potting part was removed and close boarded to the same level as the cottage. Plaster only remained in a few areas of the walls and was swiftly removed and replaced. JJ was fascinated by the skill and speed of the plasterer who applied what he termed browning and when that had dried—an interminable wait—a skim. JJ was delighted with the finished interior. He was sternly told not to hang anything on the walls or knock in any nails or such for at least a month. He had, in his elementary planning, assumed that heating would be provided by the ancient stove. After the useless stove was removed, heating remained an unsolved problem.

New window frames were installed followed by a nice new door with, as proof that even a builder could understand a lad's right to privacy, a knocker and letter box. The glazing of the small windows was allied to the restoration of the greenhouse. Each of the tradesmen were so taken with the young lad's enthusiasm and polite gratitude that the painting of the woodwork was thrown in at no cost. After five weeks of hectic activity, heating apart, the greenhouse and JJ' s den were complete and almost ready for occupation by plants, pruned vine and small boy.

It was on the Friday evening of the stove removal that JJ, returning to his den after his tea, first saw Billy Baker—more accurately he saw Billy Baker's head since he appeared, rather like the Cheshire Cat in Alice's adventures, as a dark, disembodied head peering through bright blue eyes from the den's empty fireplace.

'Hello,' said JJ.

''Ello,' replied the head.

'What are you doing?'

'Just lookin' . . . nice place.'

An awkward pause followed in which each boy regarded the other. In the way in which opposites sometimes attract there seemed to each boy that there was more to be said—although what it might be neither was very sure. JJ spoke first, 'How did you get there?'

'Crawled through from our side—we gotta place like yourn ower side.'

'Oh. Right. . . . What's your name?'

'Billy—what's yourn?'

'I'm called JJ—it's the initials of my Christian names.'

' OK. . . . 'Ello JJ. Can I come in?'

And before JJ could consent—he would have anyway—a blackened Billy launched himself into JJ's den. He was shorter than JJ, but squat and seemingly strong. His blue eyes twinkled above a snub nose in his grimy face and his grin—an almost permanent fixture—showed even, white teeth. The soot only added a different shade of black to his tousled hair.

'Cor—this is bigger than wotz on ower side, is this. Wot yer goin' ter do wiv it?'

'It's going to be my den,' answered JJ. 'I'm getting some carpet and chairs and other things when the heating's been done.'

'Goin' ter be rite posh, en it?' said Billy.

'When I can get some heating', said JJ.

'Oh, I got 'eating—and lighting ower side,' replied Billy. 'D'ye wanna come and see?'

Boys will be boys and with no further bidding both crawled through the sooty fireplace opening to the other side. Standing upright and dusting off some of the black residue, JJ found himself in a smaller but very similar gardener's cottage to the one he had just left. Similar save that, despite dusk descending, it was far lighter and warmer than that which he had left. From the ceiling hung an unshaded, but illuminated electric bulb. Against the wall the three glowing bars of an electric fire shed a welcome warmth. JJ's enquiries elicited the information that Billy's 'bruvver' had 'run a cabul'.

'Cum out 'ere un I'll show yer,' JJ was bidden.

JJ emerged into a short, uncultivated garden, mainly occupied by unidentifiable mounds beneath grey covers. To his right, and only a short distance away, was the first in a row of almost identical three storey houses—their gardens separated by wire fences and some sparse hedges. The nearest house had white walls, the back door was painted a bright red and blue curtains hung at nearly all the windows. A washing line hung with assorted garments and sheets stretched from one corner of the house to a tall pole almost half way down what would have been a garden had it not been what JJ could only suppose was a storage area. Atop the pole a Union Jack flag hung limply awaiting a breeze in which to flutter. This was, obviously, the home of clean patriots.

'Is this where you live, Billy?' he asked.

'Yus—for now, aneeway,' was the enigmatic answer. JJ decided not to query that, but could not suppress his curiosity concerning the tarpaulined mounds. The answer left him, for the time being, little wiser, 'Me dad deelz, dunne?'

Billy indicated the route that the electric cable had taken and then, to JJ's surprise, offered to have his wiring extended into JJ's cottage. With the impulsiveness of youth, and untroubled that electricity might incur a cost, JJ accepted. His offer of payment was airily dismissed before a stentorian bellow issued from Billy's mouth in answer to which a larger version of Billy, named Bobby, stumped from the patriotically decorated house to join the young lads. He seemed only too willing to extend electricity into JJ's den—his only condition seeming to be that the fireplace opening be enlarged to permit of his easy access. JJ felt that he could persuade the builders to do this and, thanking Bobby he said his goodnights to the Baker brothers, returned to his den and, closing the door behind him, walked slowly up the garden pondering how he might explain his sudden acquisition of light and heat. He concluded that it would be best to wait until the installation was complete and he had acquired an electric fire—he had seen one on the high street at Mr Russell's shop—and then deal with any questions as to the *fait accompli*. It was a strategy he would utilise at appropriate times in his later life to good effect. The success of this first trial of this manoeuvre proved encouraging since both mummy and pa accepted with little demur the explanation of extended wiring. That they had, at the time, other problems relating to the church distracting their logical thought processes, failed to occur to the exultant JJ—although he was pleased that he had made no mention of the enlarged fireplace—access to his new friend's den or the rather large safe—from Mr Baker's surplus stock—that Bobby Baker had helped them move into position off the recess where the fireplace once stood. The safe, locked by both key and combination (JJ and Billy's months and year of birth: 02-05-47) was to prove invaluable to their future fortunes. JJ moved his pocket money surplus from his bedroom to the safe.

Thus the unlikely lifetime friendship of Jonathan Justin Whitehouse and William (Billy) Baker began. Young boys will either use their differences to distance themselves or adapt those varying characteristics of intellect, talent and circumstance to their advantage: JJ and Billy chose the latter path to what they would always consider their mutual benefit. Mr Wells's men agreed to enlarge and strengthen the fireplace opening, although the elder one tried, without offering good reason and consequently without success, to dissuade JJ from association with 'them next door'. From his hoarded monies, JJ purchased sufficient underlay and carpet to effect the covering of both his and Billy's dens, Bobby Baker, actually Billy's half-brother and ten years his senior, laid their floor-coverings. His practical talents seemed boundless. Listening to talk between the Bakers when he was supposed to be elsewhere awakened JJ to the fact that the electricity he and Billy were using was not actually diverted from the Baker's home but somehow connected to the street lighting in the road beyond their house; he decided to maintain silence on the subject. He was learning discretion.

Almost at once and without question or discussion, the two young friends shared everything that happened or was based in the dens. The removal for collection of garden produce was effected via Billy's address— thus removing any likelihood of discovery by Claude or, more probably

Sylvia. Naturally the supply of free vegetables and fruit extended from the vicarage's wants to the Baker home. From his paper round Billy was able to procure (a very polite description of his acquisitions) comics. The *Beano* and *Dandy* were supplemented by more brazen and daring imports from the USA that the wily newsagent kept under the counter. Later *The Wizard* and *The Hotspur* would be similarly smuggled into the boys' dens and eagerly read by both. The lowering of JJ's literary tastes was not total—indeed he regarded them as being broadened—and it was he who introduced Billy to the exploits of Captain W. E. Johns's hero Biggles and the wider ranging works of Percy F. Westerman.

Nor were their activities confined to trading and reading. As a result of continual conversation and some persuasion, Billy's speech, to the amusement and sometime mockery of his parents and half-brother, but the delight of his sister, became more refined. Tutored by JJ, Billy found the addition of basic manners and a little flattery increased his tips from those to whom he delivered daily papers; it also served him well in the regrets he expressed when, as occasionally occurred, the absence of a comic was queried. Billy's natural guile and contacts (via his father) allied to JJ's commercial sense combined to improve the marketing of the garden produce to not only their benefit, but to that of a greedily grateful Greening. Billy's initial repugnance for writing it down was gradually replaced by appreciation of JJ's meticulous records and the proven fair distribution of their gains: after a year he, too, was able to effect the proper and correct book-keeping entries—although neither boy realised what they were doing was book-keeping.

For the best part of two years the boys prospered and enjoyed themselves but, as he knew it would, this had to change when JJ, aged eleven, followed his father and Uncle Charles to Sebright School as a boarding pupil.

CHAPTER TWENTY FIVE
EDUCATION—IN MANY SENSES
1958 TO 1961

JJ had previously enjoyed school. At Sebright he positively revelled in the academic and sporting life. The uniform for the first year together with other specified items of clothing, both daily and sporting, had been purchased and, where necessary, fitted at the recommended establishment in nearby Stourton where two rather fey gentlemen, permanently wearing tape measures, had expressed the admiration and slight envy of former pupils toward the new pupil whilst efficiently assembling the various garments. Neither of the effeminate old gentlemen remembered Mr Whitehouse, the boy's uncle, who promptly paid all their bills—Charles had been a Wolverley pupil after they had left school for the narrow world of outfitting gentlemen and schoolboys. It had been no surprise to Sylvia, and even less so to Charlotte, that Charles had sentimentally insisted on delivering JJ to the school for his first term.

JJ was to be, as had been his father and uncle before him, in Bury Hall House—although it was by now, the junior house for first and second years. The house was almost as great a revelation to Charles as it was to JJ. What Charles recalled as a lawned area in front of the house had been tarmacked over and now served as the parade ground for the school cadet corps; an old schoolroom was now the indoor rifle range and armoury for the same cadet corps; and a former store shed on the hill above the house had been extended and now served as the school sanatorium for infectious, sick pupils.

JJ's first visit to Sebright had not been to Bury Hall, but to sit in the school's assembly hall in the main building at the top of the hill on the opposite side of the village to Bury Hall. The school hall was where he and others had sat the entrance exam, 'Ever so easy, Mum,' had been his verdict. He had been impressed by the bright, clean and airy hall with its stage, on the proscenium arch of which were the words 'wisdom, knowledge and understanding' inscribed in foot-high gold lettering. He was later to learn they were words spoken by Stanley Baldwin, MP for Bewdley and three times prime minister when he had officially opened the school hall.

Charles had not been able to take JJ to Wolverley for his entrance examination—Sylvia having done the honours—so now, leaving JJ in the care of Mr Buttermere, his house master, Charles took the opportunity to drive from Bury Hall through the village, up the hill between the sandstone cliffs—forever known as the Holloway—to the school where he requested a tour of his alma mater as it now was. The bursar was delighted to show him the new swimming pool and gymnasium. The centre for learning endowed by William Sebright had grown beyond recognition from the time when Charles and Roger had arrived to be classically educated. With the building of the main school atop the hill had come the acquisition of the former Woodfield House—a senior boarding house and living accommodation for the headmaster and his family, plus a resident house master within the main building, further boarding for pupils and a suite for the house master of School House. To avoid any suggestion of unearned superiority, School House soon became re-named Baldwin House. Each house had its own colours, delineated by braid quartering on black caps, 'Always wear it properly and not over your ear, boy.' Blue for Baldwins, red for Woodfield, green for day boys, and yellow braided caps identified pupils of the most recently acquired boarding house with its own master, Eric Knight House. The school had been admitted to the headmasters' conference—become a public school—in 1947. Despite still bearing his name, it was a far cry from what the former town clerk of the City of London may have envisaged.

JJ found the camaraderie of Bury Hall—plain green caps with no piping for the junior house—and sleeping with new friends in a dormitory novel and enjoyable. He had, ever since he began riding his bike, been fit: he enjoyed cross-country running, PT, cricket and, especially, rugby, to which he took as a duck to water. Being tall for his age he was initially a second-row forward with responsibilities for the line out, but as his pace, fitness and ball-handling skills became more obvious, he was tried as a back, but JJ preferred to be in the thick of things and was wisely switched to open-side wing or loose forward—a position he would occupy for the rest of his twenty-year playing time. He was considered a natural and, exceptionally, became a regular in the Colts' game and, in only his first year, played three games for the School Colts XV—the side for under fifteens. Bury Hall, being a junior house, could not compete for the house XV trophy, but had their own grudge match against an under thirteens team from day boys house. Day pupils did not have separate quarters for their junior boys as they came and went every day of the six-day school week. Day boys had no boarding facilities but, as did each other house, out of class they gathered in their own common room. They also had their own changing rooms with showers. To no-one's surprise, in his second year, JJ was made captain of the Bury Hall team and became the youngest regular in the under fifteens school team.

Academically, he found no difficulty with any subjects save physics and chemistry—in which he could summon no interest and the standard of tuition failed to stimulate in him any desire to cultivate concern. Despite his failings in science he was consistently placed in the top three of the fortnightly order for his class—often being top. He was popular with masters and his fellow pupils—the latter, as boys at an age of puberty will, admiring or envying him for his physical and mental prowess, but exhibiting an enduring and crude fascination with his immense pubic patrimony. Communal showers and the bedtime habits of lads ensured that all JJ's contemporaries were not only aware of his enormity, but most had viewed and marvelled at Whitehouse-Martin's 'thing'. Word, as it does, soon passed beyond JJ's contemporaries and masters and senior pupils found themselves inventing excuses to pass by the Bury Hall showers after games. JJ could not feel flattered by this attention to what he had always had. He tended to regard with a wry amusement the prurient attentions his laving attracted. He had, as was only to be expected, found the physical thrill of what the masters referred to as self abuse but felt, and always did feel, it to be a personal and private matter. He was well aware of the 'mutual masturbation' sessions apparently enjoyed by some sexually inclined boys but, despite several invitations to join in, he spurned the activities of the 'wankers'.

In JJ's third year—when he became a member of Baldwin House—there was the unusual occurrence of a senior boy, Malcolm Grenson from the fifth form, being expelled. No announcement was made and the cause was, initially, a mystery to almost all the boys until the unthinking use of the departed as a scapegoat by another senior who had been attempting the seduction of a junior (who had—unforgivably?—blabbed) revealed that the expulsion resulted from Grenson's attempts to involve juniors in mildly homosexual affairs. As rumours do, this flew through the school with alacrity and exaggeration before, almost as quickly, fading into distant memory in the face of some further talking point.

When JJ was summoned to the study of the deputy head boy, Gary Smithson, he was innocently curious as to the reason. He was quickly disabused of any fears he may have had that he had transgressed by the senior boy asking him to come in and shut the door and then, with no preliminaries, dropping his trousers to reveal his swollen organ which he waved at JJ.

'I'm told you've got a big one, too,' said the deputy head boy. 'How about this, Whitehouse-Martin?'

'You seem proud of what you've got, Smithson,' replied JJ. 'Can I go now?'

'No, you may not, you cheeky Arab. Get yours out and let's see how it feels.'

JJ was, despite himself, rather excited by the attention, however incorrect, of one of the most senior pupils. Reluctantly, he undid his trousers and lowered them to his ankles. Though not tumescent, he was tending that way whilst feeling both guilty and tremulous as to what might or might not follow. Smithson had no doubts as to the course events should take and after admiring JJ's mid-section he placed JJ's hand on his own eager organ and seized hold of the Whitehouse (no Martin involved in this) pride. JJ had no way of fighting off this insistent senior who stood several inches taller than he and was renowned for his strength. He let events take their course after which Smithson expressed satisfaction and donned his trousers. JJ did likewise. Smithson then sat down and invited JJ to take tea. The invitation was so ludicrously incongruous as to make JJ, despite himself, laugh.

'What's so funny, Whitehouse-Martin?'

After Smithson's vulgar assault, the unexpected request to partake of afternoon refreshment was so absurd that it not only made JJ laugh, but allowed him to gather his mind together.

'You are, Smithson,' he replied, now feeling himself on certain ground.

'Don't you laugh at me, boy. I can have you beaten you know,' said Smithson angrily.

'And I,' said JJ looking calmly at the senior boy, 'can have you expelled.'

'You . . . you bloody wouldn't,' gasped Smithson, glaring from his protruding eyes. It was obvious to JJ, even in his youthful innocence and abused state, that not only was this unjustifiably promoted senior used to having his own way, but that the recent event was almost certainly not the first such violation of the trust placed in him by the masters of the school.

'I might,' answered JJ—certain he had the initiative and determined to retain it.

'You wouldn't dare. You did it as well, JJ.' wheedled Smithson.

'Only under duress is, I think, the correct phrase,' said JJ looking the senior boy in the eyes. 'You being the senior by years are in the same position as Grenson found himself, I'm the injured party here, Smithson. I'm entitled to complain and demand justice, you know.'

JJ smiled and waited for the confused Smithson to gather his thoughts. At last it dawned upon the not terribly quick-thinking deputy head boy that there might be a way of avoiding the treatment meted out to Grenson and, what would be worse, the shame of facing his parents.

He looked, pleadingly at JJ, 'What sort of justice are you referring to, Whitehouse-Martin?'

'I understand from my uncle, a lawyer in a large Birmingham firm——'

The squirming Smithson interrupted, 'You're not going to sue me, are you?' pleaded the now desperate senior boy.

'If you would let me finish,' said JJ, relishing the superiority he had obtained by calm reason, 'I was about to say that it is sometimes the case that, for first offences——' he looked hard at Smithson who confirmed his previous suspicions by refusing to return his look '——it is sometimes adjudged that a substantial fine and guarantee of future good conduct suffices to correct the conduct of the offender.'

There was a long pause. Smithson looked goggle-eyed at JJ who continued to stare him down. Eventually, some semblance of reason seemed to enter Smithson's mind, 'Now see here, JJ—you don't mind if I call you that do you?

'Whitehouse-Martin will suffice, thank you,' replied JJ, determined to keep the senior boy subservient.

'Yes, OK . . . Whitehouse-Martin. I'm told you're sent more pocket money than anyone else. How much are we talking here—you don't need the money, do you?'

'My allowance,' replied JJ, determined to remain calm and in control, 'has nothing to do with this and you know it. If you insist on prevaricating and making me both judge and jury'—JJ recalled this phrase from a book he had recently read and felt it was rather good as well as apt—'then I suggest you pay me one pound a week until you leave. As you will probably be leaving in July that's not a large fine, 'specially as it's only payable in instalments.'

There was a long pause whilst JJ looked around Smithson's study— his choice of reading betrayed a carnal pre-occupation—whilst Smithson studied his stockinged feet and pondered how he could defeat this precocious boy he had so unwisely picked upon or, alternatively, how he might reduce or avoid the penalty his victim had demanded. At length he could think of nothing but to try a counter-threat, 'You know this is blackmail, Whitehouse-Martin?'

'Correct, Smithson. That, too, is against the law. If you want to accuse me then go ahead. But do consider this, I would then have no alternative but to disclose the shameful event that led me to ask for money in return for silence.'

After a further long silence agreement was reached as to where and when payment would be made and, after further emphasising the penalty for non-payment or any form of retaliation, JJ left the study and returned to the Baldwin common room. He was quite pleased with the outcome, if not the earlier actions that had precipitated it, but thinking it over he became more and more certain that Smithson would not leave him alone for long. Other boys had suffered mysterious cuts and bruises for which unsatisfactory and unconvincing explanations had been offered and JJ was not naïve enough to suppose that he would be spared unless, he reasoned, he took both precautions and, an even better thought, insurance. He gave these matters deep thought—little knowing that the answer to the second, and more difficult defence, was to become available at half-term—the weekend after next.

JJ had not been looking forward to this half-term. Mother (no longer mummy now he was older and a public schoolboy) had written explaining that pa—how he still despised that compromise even though he no longer despised Claude himself—had to go to an ecclesiastic conference and she, never having been to York, was going with him. She hoped JJ would be OK without a visit just this once. Smithson would not be aware that he was without parental company, so the absence of his quickly-formed bodyguard—being popular made recruitment easy—with their respective visitors might not be realised until too late for any action against JJ to be organised; he hoped. An unexpected summons to his housemaster's study set his nerves jangling. Had Smithson devised some diabolical plan? JJ's apprehension was quickly set at rest by Mr Philipson.

'Sorry to get you along, Whitehouse-Martin, but I've had a telephone call from your uncle asking if we can allow you to be released a day early for half-term. He said there was nothing for you to be alarmed about, but he was most insistent. As you had nothing urgent on the timetable I agreed and have made the necessary arrangements.'

JJ felt a mixture of relief and apprehension, but Philipson was not going to salve the latter concern. The house master continued in his dull voice, 'Your uncle is collecting you in his car at 1.30 this afternoon so, I suggest, you get a quick lunch then go and do some packing; it seems you're being taken somewhere for half-term and a day.

With a quick, 'Yes, sir. Thank you, sir,' JJ took leave of his housemaster. How like old Philipson to stress the allowance of the extra day, he thought. But where was Uncle Charles taking him—and why? Time would tell, he thought, as he packed the essentials for a long weekend. At half past one JJ was waiting at the end of the school drive. As promptly as traffic allowed, Uncle Charles' Rolls Royce drew up and the rear door opened. If only some of his fellow pupils could see him getting into a Roller . . .

The first surprise was the sight of Billy Baker sat in the back seat of the car smiling uncertainly at JJ; Uncle Charles was driving. No chauffeur. No Auntie Charlotte. What was going on, wondered JJ. Uncle Charles was not about to wholly enlighten him yet.

'Settle down, JJ, we're off to Birmingham for a meeting. You two have been found out, and it's time to face the music.'

'What do you mean, Uncle Charles?'

'You'll see, young man. Nothing to get too upset about and, hopefully, we can resolve everything this afternoon.'

The car was already speeding smoothly away from Wolverley across country towards Hagley and Birmingham. JJ turned, helplessly, toward Billy.

'Dunno, JJ. Mr Whitehouse won't tell me any more, either,' said Billy aloud. But he then leaned across to whisper in JJ's ear, 'He came down your garden while we were loading up the tomatoes and started asking questions. I 'ad to tell 'im—sorry *him*—what was happening. He didn't seem very pleased. He made me get all the books from the safe, then he put me in the car and went round and asked me mum if it was all right for me to come. Before we started he went into your house and, he said, made a phone call.'

JJ stared. He sat back—obviously Billy was waiting for him to solve this strange problem. And he had no idea what the problem was, even though he could hazard some guesses. Uncle Charles had always been so good—and kind to him. Surely he wasn't going to stop their profitable little scheme? He had to know, 'Uncle——'

'Oh no, JJ, I said not to get upset, so do just that. Young Billy has had to wonder for longer than you, so copy his example, sit back and enjoy the journey.'

And Uncle Charles reached forward and turned a switch so that classical music was all the boys could hear unless they, rudely, whispered into each other's ears.

They sat back and tried to enjoy the journey, if not the music.

There was another surprise for JJ as the Rolls continued past Uncle

Charles' apartment home and went on towards the city. Poor Billy, never having travelled in a Rolls Royce, or into Birmingham, remained completely bemused, silent and fearful. He also hoped they would stop somewhere so that he could relieve himself soon—a feeling JJ, too, began to experience due to the nervous tension. Uncle Charles steered the Rolls along Hagley Road, past Five Ways and into Broad Street from where they moved smoothly into Great Charles Street and then left into Newhall Street. The Rolls was obviously expected as a parking space was being indicated by a waiting man who opened the doors to allow them to alight before taking the wheel and driving the car away to a secure, private parking area behind the imposing buildings. As Uncle Charles ushered the bewildered boys through swing doors, JJ noted the brass nameplate beside the door identifying the offices of Harvey, Smith and Thomas, Chartered Accountants. He knew that was the firm where Mr Burroughs, who looked after his trust monies, worked. That might have been a comfort—but why had Billy been brought along? Uncle Charles had a big, leather briefcase in his hand so, presumably, the garden records were in there. JJ was confused. Billy was frightened and confused. At their joint request, a gents' toilet was indicated and they were able to relieve at least their bladders. Since Uncle Charles also visited the same convenience they felt unable to discuss any of their anxieties.

They took a silent ride in a lift to the first floor where Uncle Charles was greeted by a smiling lady in an area labelled reception, and all three were conducted to a large, airy office with an imposing desk and, obviously pre-arranged, three chairs set before it. The name on the door was W. Burroughs and it was that very person who rose and greeted Uncle Charles with a warm handshake. JJ had met Mr Burroughs on previous occasions, though never at his offices, and he too was afforded a firm handshake. Mr Burroughs looked at Billy, 'And you, I suppose, are JJ's friend Billy?' he said extending his hand to Billy.

By now poor Billy was almost totally overcome. He had never been to Birmingham, never been in a posh office and never, ever, met anyone like JJ's Uncle Charles and this white-haired, genial gentleman.

'I'm Mr Burroughs, one of young JJ's Trustees. Pleased to meet you.'

Billy nodded and, weakly, shook Mr Burroughs's hand. He didn't trust himself to say anything but, with the others, accepted the invitation to sit in front of the desk. Uncle Charles opened his case and, as JJ had suspected, produced the exercise books in which he and Billy—and latterly only Billy—had recorded the results of their garden business.

Meanwhile, Mr Burroughs was talking to the boys whom he regarded over half-moon spectacles. 'Well, now. It seems you two have been running a little business enterprise from the vicarage garden. Thank you, Charles. And these, I understand, are the records of your transactions?' He looked over his glasses at them.

Billy was frozen in his seat, his half-brother had been on probation twice and Billy was imagining himself in a similar predicament—through no fault of his own he felt—and he was beginning to wonder if, as Bobby had questioned, he had been wise to befriend a posh kid. JJ seemed better composed, Billy was pleased to see, and it was JJ who replied to the genial gentleman.

'I . . . sorry, we kept details of everything, Mr Burroughs, so that all of us could see that we were getting our proper share.'

JJ stopped as Uncle Charles intervened, 'JJ, Billy, please understand you are not in any serious trouble and Mr Burroughs and I are here to help you understand the things you should have done and to put it all right. But to do that we need to know what has been going on—and your records will, we hope, tell us that.'

Mr Burroughs had been looking at the exercise books.

'As far as I can see, Charles,' he addressed Uncle Charles, 'our hopes will be easily satisfied.' He turned his head to the two boys, 'You seem to have kept remarkably good records, young gentlemen. I congratulate you. What I'm going to do, whilst we have something to drink and Mr Whitehouse and I talk to you, is have one of my staff make what are known as accounts from these.'

He had picked up the telephone and dialled as he was speaking and now excused himself to address that instrument, 'Ah, Norman, Burroughs here. Who's the best and quickest from your department at sorting sense from incomplete records? OK, can you send him down, please. There's a little rush job—a *pro bono*—here I'd like him to sort for me p.d.q. . . . Thank you, Norman.'

He turned to the boys, 'Just a few questions before Greenhow gets here. Is the first date in these books the date you actually started . . . er, business?'

Everyone looked at JJ. This was rather like the team talk before rugby—something to which he was used. Except that now he was not, definitely not, in command. With as much confidence as he could muster JJ explained that he had not written down their first sale—the first potato crop. Burroughs was taking notes of the date and proceeds of the initial potato harvest on a large pad with columns ruled up and down it.

'And is there anyone else, besides you two, involved in this?'

At the mention of Greening, Mr Burroughs and Uncle Charles exchanged meaningful looks—the meaning of which eluded JJ. Before he could ask whether Greening was in trouble, there was a knock at the door and, being bidden to come, a man in a shiny suit with scruffy hair and bitten fingernails entered and announced himself as, 'Ian Greenhow, sir.'

'Yes, Greenhow. Thank you for doing this—it's a bit of a rush, please. Records here.'

Greenhow was beckoned to Mr Burroughs's side of the desk and shown the exercise books and Mr Burroughs's notes. They muttered together and JJ overheard them mention premises, rent, equipment and wages. He was posed more questions. Did either he or Billy have any gardening tools? Greening the gardener had all those. Had everything been paid and received in cash? It had. And what had each of them done with their share? JJ had banked his; Billy had spent his; they had no idea what Greening had done with his share. Greenhow, who had taken over the note-taking, then departed with the instruction to be back as soon as he had finished.

A tray of tea for four was ordered by Burroughs, delivered and drunk. As they consumed their tea the boys were told, gently but firmly, what the laws of the land stated about establishing a business and paying taxes. Billy was asked what he received for his paper round, 'Never mind the tips, young Billy, they aren't much are they?' Mr Burroughs shook his head as he said this and Billy, with the first return of his cheeky grin that afternoon, reported only his basic weekly wage. The grown-ups then turned their attention to JJ, explaining that his trust was intended to exempt him from any need to earn further monies and that, dependent upon the accounts that Ian Greenhow produced, 'There might be a few problems with the income tax.'

Both adults were surprised and impressed by JJ displaying remarkable understanding and mental agility by asking whether it would help if he paid his share into the trust.

'We'll see, JJ . . . but smart thinking. We could make a good accountant out of you, you know,' answered Mr Burroughs.

JJ had never thought about what occupation he might pursue in life, but it is certain that this was the moment when he began to perceive a career path. He wanted to ask Mr Burroughs how to become an accountant, but felt that this was not the most opportune time. His accountancy education and the bemusing of both he and Billy took a step forward with the return of Ian Greenhow who, almost proudly, announced to Mr Burroughs that he had managed to make them show a loss. Even more of an affront to the young entrepreneurs was Burroughs not only accepting what Greenhow said, but actually congratulating and thanking him. Both boys protested that they had made a profit.

'Not on paper, young gentlemen,' was the reply. There followed a long explanation, of which JJ understood only part and Billy even less, of something called 'overheads' and the 'rental of tools, equipment and premises.' They were, JJ particularly, cautioned to communicate and seek advice in the future. In answer to JJ's question—one Billy wanted to ask but didn't dare—they were told to continue as before with the sale of garden produce—but to be sure to issue something called an invoice for every sale. On another of those lined pads Mr Burroughs sketched a specimen invoice and instructed them—this they both understood—how to get them printed and how to fill in the numbered documents. They were also told that they had to make payments to Mrs Sylvia Martin for rent of the garden and shed. It would all be set out in a letter to them both.

JJ was still in business. He still liked it. Billy's enthusiasm was a little dented. Both liked the conclusion of the meeting when Uncle Charles offered high tea with Auntie Charlotte, a night at their flat and, on the morrow, a half-term excursion to the sea. Billy began to revive his enthusiasm for being in business.

And, later that night, before he joined Billy in Uncle Charles's and Auntie Charlotte's guest bedroom, JJ—with not too many blushes—recounted to Uncle Charles the episode with Smithson: his rather shameful solution; the bodyguard he had hastily but effectively recruited by sharing the blackmail proceeds; and his perceived need of some form of insurance. Uncle Charles was, as ever, patient and understanding. He even attempted a joke when he told JJ, 'As you know, I've got to tell your mother about the gardening business, but I think we'll keep this matter strictly between ourselves. As it happens, I know Smithson's father through one of my lodges; he's about as charming as his son from what you tell me—but we can't all be as good as we want to be. Leave this with me, JJ, and I'll see what I can do for you. See you in the morning, sleep well.'

For the first time since his encounter with the deputy head boy, JJ slept well. The following morning the boys were transported in the Rolls Royce to Borth in Cardiganshire where they occupied a small, but well appointed, attic room in the Grand Hotel for two nights. JJ felt happy. Billy decided that being in business was a good thing if these were the rewards to be expected.

CHAPTER TWENTY-SIX
Continuing and Further Education
1961 to 1965

On his return to school, JJ was relieved, 'though a little puzzled, to discover from announcements at assembly on the first day back that deputy head boy Smithson had left the school earlier than expected in order to help with his father's business. He was not the only puzzled pupil. Smithson's sold cars in East Birmingham and schoolboy opinion held that unless he became more pleasant, Gary Smithson would be as likely to sell ice to Eskimos as cars to Brummies.

Little more had been said between JJ and Uncle Charles on the subject of Smithson other than his uncle quietly advising him after breakfast in the Grand Hotel, Borth, that it 'might be best to disband your bodyguard— that sort of thing doesn't look good.' In answer to JJ's puzzled look of apprehension, Uncle Charles had assured him that he was sure everything would be alright. JJ had tried to accept his uncle's assurance, but it was not until he heard the school assembly announcement that he felt truly safe. He was also sure that his Uncle Charles was able to exert influence in more ways than JJ might have imagined. The reference to 'one of my lodges' made by Uncle Charles had also intrigued JJ, but clarity on that issue would not be forthcoming for some years.

The return from the west coast of Wales had culminated in a meeting of JJ's trustees to which he was summoned for most of the session. He duly, and unbidden, apologised to Sylvia for not keeping her informed of the extent of the garden business and a sum was agreed for settlement of unpaid rent for the garden and orchard. Sylvia expressed Claude's concern that he might be reprimanded by the church authorities for allowing commerce on church property; he felt he should inform them. Mr Burroughs told Sylvia to inform Claude that as the business had been carried on for over two years under Claude's nose, the commissioners—if they ever reached a decision—would be more likely to discipline him for not reporting the matter earlier.

'Tell Brother Claude that what they don't know won't hurt them, Sylvia.'

JJ was slightly puzzled by the appellation of 'brother' to pa, but felt it best not to enquire. He assumed his mother had passed on the advice since Claude never made mention of the matter and he, Billy and Greening continued on as before, save for the regular payment to Sylvia. JJ suspected she donated it to the church collection but, as with Claude and the church commissioners, what he didn't know failed to harm him.

Life at school was, as it had been before the Smithson incident, thoroughly enjoyable. Classes and homework (despite it not being taken home by boarders, work after class retained the traditional label) posed no problems—apart from physics and chemistry in which subjects the respective masters reached reluctant agreement on an impasse and no subsequent attempts to improve JJ's scientific knowledge were attempted—to the immense relief of the pupil. In both rugby and cricket JJ represented the school and was fast becoming the star player—indeed in his last year he was trialled for the England schoolboys rugby team. His failure to be selected seemed to disappoint Mr Taffy Evans, the games master even more than it did JJ. It may have been a subconscious wish to compensate Old Taffy that led JJ to postpone leaving in the July of 1964, despite his excellent grades in the examinations (he was exempted from the physics and chemistry papers), until the Easter of 1965 in order to captain the XV to a totally victorious season. The option of university, involving another full year in the sixth, more exams, and being approved, did not appeal. He discussed it at some length with his trustees and, in the end, the decision being agreed as his alone, JJ opted to take up articles of clerkship to Mr Burroughs, work for Harvey, Smith and Thomas and become a chartered accountant.

At home the decline in old Greening's health and his sudden death at seventy-three led JJ and Billy to re-consider their business as embryo market gardeners. The new opinionated gardener appointed by Sylvia and Claude made it very clear that he had no time for young boys meddling. This, allied to the apparent difficulties the exposure of the business had created for Greening's income tax had made the cessation of vicarage produce an easy decision. Sylvia was undismayed at the loss of the rent and Claude was vastly relieved. Being honest with themselves, both JJ and Billy had begun to lose enthusiasm for the garden. There was still the offshoot business that had evolved from the need to prepare invoices, statements and letterheads, Billy had initially, through his father, acquired for them a Roneo duplicating machine with inks, paper and all the necessary impedimenta for its operation.

Both boys quickly realised that the production of their own stationery utilised the machine for only a short time. With a little marketing amongst their friends and Claude's congregation, they established a flourishing trade, of which they kept records equally as meticulous as those of the garden sales. Having learned from their exposure as purveyors of garden produce, they regularly submitted the print business records to Mr Burroughs. As time passed and the demands for printing grew, they sold the Roneo machine and, again with Baker senior's assistance, acquired a flat-bed platen printer and the skills to operate it. The church magazine had never looked so good. Many of the advertisers asked for their business printing to be done and, at JJ's expense, but to be recouped from future income, a small premises was secured and an ambitious printer—later to be made a partner—employed. 'J & B Printers' established itself in the town. It continued to prosper.

As JJ and Billy grew towards puberty and greater awareness, other things became of more importance. The supply of under-the-counter literature had evolved from *The Wizard* and *Hotspur*, through amused and furtive examination of *Health and Efficiency*—naturists of all shapes and sizes cavorting with ill-disguised gooseflesh in the English outdoors— to more lurid and expensive glossies in which leering females flaunted amazingly large breasts for the camera and the subsequent satisfaction of the red-blooded men of the nation. The natural effect of such study on two teenage boys led to the regular relief of pressures mutually felt and, after discussion—including JJ's confession of the enforced and thus resented intimacy with Smithson—led to each of them losing any inhibition with each other, and enjoying mutual relief. Despite being less well-built than JJ, Billy was not ill-endowed; compared to JJ, of course, he lacked exceptional proportion in that department but, as JJ assured him from observations in his school showers and changing rooms, he had nothing to be ashamed of.

One evening, not long after their fifteenth birthdays (Billy was three months younger than JJ), when the friends had relieved their pent up passions, Billy broached a question that, bearing in mind JJ's greater experience of the world, Billy felt may have elicited either of the possible answers.

'You ever *done it* with a woman, JJ?'

'You mean . . . had sex?'

'Yeah. Have you?'

'No. . . . Have you?'

'No. But I'd like to.'

'That makes two of us,' said the curious JJ, adding the careful and cautious, 'But I wouldn't want to pay for it. You can get some nasty things from prostitutes, you know?'

'I know that,' expostulated Billy. 'We had some doctor chap talk to us this term about it. The older chaps call it the clap. It's nasty. . . . But, if you could, safely as it were, and for free, you would, wouldn't you, JJ?'

'Of course—but, so far, every girl I've kissed jumps as if she's been scalded if I as much as try to touch her tits—let alone go any further. . . . What are you getting at, Billy? I know you. You've got some scheme or other, haven't you?'

Billy explained how his big sister, Zoe, aged all of seventeen and not long begun work, had walked in to the unlocked bathroom as he was getting out of the bath and, to his embarrassment, admired his big dick. In a mixture of confusion and pride as he grabbed for the towel, Billy admitted to his friend that he had, without thinking, retorted that his friend JJ's was bigger. Zoe, undeterred, had expressed eagerness to not only see but 'have a bit of your friend.'

'I said it was unfair to me 'cos I couldn't have my own sister. And, you know what, JJ, she says she'll bring her friend Janice from work for me so we can both be . . . done.'

There was a short silence whilst the two friends looked at one another—a mixture of anticipation and apprehension etched in each face.

'When's this supposed to happen, Billy?' asked JJ conscious of the, remote though it might be, possibility of interruption or discovery. Billy, too, appreciated this. Together they discussed when there was least likelihood of either set of parents, or the new gardener, finding them at it. The curtains at the den windows were rarely drawn. The locks on the doors—supplied and fitted by Bobby Baker—were rarely used. Starting at once they determined to establish the principle of regularly preserving their privacy by closing the curtains and locking the doors.

Zoe and Janice, JJ learned, were both seventeen and had left school to be trained locally as hairdressers. In some manner the boys initially failed to understand the girls had access to a seemingly inexhaustible supply of contraceptives. Later enquiry elicited the fact that Janice's brother worked for the men's barber shop adjacent to the girls' place of employment and was able to avail himself of the barber's failure to control his stock. Janice, having discovered her brother's minor thefts were not only for his own use, but were sold to supplement his income, was easily able to secure supplies *gratis* in exchange for her silence.

Every Saturday afternoon, Mrs Baker joined her friends at the local bingo hall whilst Mr Baker and Bobby indulged themselves in the frustrations of supporting the local football team. As this coincided with Sylvia and Claude's regular trips to outlying parts of his parish, it meant the girls comings and goings (and activities in between) could remain unobserved. JJ and Billy were initiated at fifteen. The lads', particularly JJ's, initial regret that neither girl was greatly-fleshed in the chest department was more than compensated for by the discovery and exploration of the ladies' lower charms.

Zoe and Janice's regular Saturday afternoon visits during JJ's school vacations were eagerly anticipated and mutually enjoyed. What arrangements Billy chose to make with Janice during term time, though subject to similar subterfuge, were not queried by JJ, nor were Zoe's bus trips to Wolverley on the Wednesday evenings (when senior pupils were allowed out for recreational walks) of interest to Billy and Janice. JJ's equally impelled relations with the village postmaster's sixteen-year-old, skinny, but very willing daughter remained as unknown and undiscovered in Wolverley as it was in Avonbridge. Before familiarity could breed any contempt, time, the disparities of age and cultivation of further interests—both sexual and otherwise—combined to ensure that copulation in the dens became less regular and finally ceased. There were no recriminations. All four retained pleasant memories and gratitude.

JJ and Billy left their respective schools and Zoe and Janice completed their training. Had any of them been told that they would become further involved later in their lives, they would have dismissed it as fiction. Yet such were the dictates of fate—assisted by JJ's generous nature and business mind.

CHAPTER TWENTY SEVEN
Avonbridge Masonic hall
Sunday 24 January 1988, morning

Many, although by no means all Freemasons attend Sunday morning service at their local church or chapel. It was, therefore, unusual to observe, were anyone sufficiently interested to make such observation, a member of the fraternity or anyone else admitting himself and a quantity of strange luggage into the Avonbridge Masonic hall at 10.45 a.m. on Sunday 24 January 1988. The entrant carefully closed the front door behind him and, with great care, activated the safety lock—ensuring that, without knocking or ringing, no other would be joining him among the fraternal furnishings on this quiet morning. With similar care and caution he then locked the downstairs doors from the hallway so that the only accessible exit from the hall other than the toilets was the stairs that led to the robing rooms and temple.

Up the stairs he carried his two bulging bags and, initially, put them down in the robing room, but within easy reach of the temple. From his first bag he took several rolls of clear plastic sheeting with which he carefully and completely covered the temple's black and white chequered carpet with its elaborately woven border and the boarded area beyond. Next, he made a radical re-arrangement of the lodge furnishings by placing the three large chairs—those of the wardens and the secretary—halfway up the room in line abreast facing the door. With several lengths of plastic-coated washing line he securely tied together the three chairs. He closed and folded up the now empty first bag and carried both bags to the desk usually occupied by lodge secretaries and treasurers. From his second bag he first removed and then carefully positioned receptacles never before introduced into a Masonic meeting room. Next he unpacked and set out on the desk several rolls of Sellotape; two lemons; three lengths of towelling; a pack of five incontinence cushions; and some items purchased some months previously from a London supplier of theatrical make-up and other aids to dramatic effect. He added the temple's two daggers and the tyler's sword to the table's collection after first honing each to razor-like sharpness with a whetstone brought for the purpose.

He surveyed and approved his handiwork. Now he positioned a further large chair —that used by the officer of the lodge designated inner guard—further inside the temple and to the left of the entrance. From the store cupboard reserved for the members of the Knights Templar Order he fetched a 'spare' black tunic and cloak—as worn by those of the order designated Knights of Malta. He folded and placed the tunic and cloak on the inner guard's chair and added a cheap, black balaclava and a spontaneous and, he felt, inspired purchase from the London theatre shop. He took one last look around and, satisfied that everything was as he intended, he placed the two empty luggage bags tidily beside the inner guard chair and exited the temple, leaving the lights on.

In the robing room he stood on a chair and systematically removed all the light bulbs from the robing room, the outer room of the temple, and the toilets. Despite having on a previous occasion surreptitiously tested, as far as was then possible, the effect, he was pleased to confirm that the light 'shedding' from the temple was quite sufficient for anyone approaching from the stairs to avoid bumping into any furniture whilst finding their way into the temple. Content that he had overlooked nothing, he took from his pocket a small torch before switching off the temple lighting and returning downstairs. Restoring the outer door lock to its normal function he left for what he considered the riskiest part of his morning's task.

'Fortune favours the brave', and 'the best hiding place is under the light' are adages from adventure fiction that can prove equally as successful in the real world. So it proved to be on this cold, wet, Sunday morning. No one was so foolhardy as to be cleaning their car or tending their garden; the few who ventured forth into the miserable morn bowed their heads against the driving rain and took little or no note of others— particularly of the black-clad man hastening from an anonymous old van to three doorways in different parts of the town where he delivered to each address a confidential summons to an 'Urgent and confidential meeting with the licensee/caterer to consider an important matter of concern' at the Masonic rooms that very evening. The summons were identical, indefinite and mysterious—the only variation being the times cited for this suddenly necessary gathering. The first delivery requested attendance at 7.00 p.m.; the second summoned the recipient to be present at 7.20 p.m. and the final delivery gave 7.40 p.m. as the time to gather. Each missive cautioned the recipient to maintain a strict secrecy concerning this meeting 'in case of problems that discussion with other Brethren might engender'. They purported to be signed by the present master of Chandlery Lodge No. 5591 in which each recipient held membership—yet the delivery man was well aware that the present master was neither privy to the notes nor due to return from a trip abroad until the morrow. That worshipful brother had left two days earlier for an emergency business meeting in Madrid where he would find, to his embarrassment and in quick succession that there was no meeting; no one could be found who had telephoned the misleading urgent information to his secretary; and the earliest return flight was on Monday morning. The Monday when he was due to install his successor as master of the lodge. Fortunately, he had taken his ritual book with him and the period of his enforced Spanish sojourn was not wasted, he could, and did, study the ceremony uninterrupted.

Relieved that he appeared to have made each delivery unseen, the carrier returned to his temporary lodging in a disused flat at the rear of a shop where he had a short sleep before the exertions he had set himself for the evening.

CHAPTER TWENTY-EIGHT
JJ—THE AGE OF MATURITY AND THE FIRST INHERITANCE
FEBRUARY 27TH, 1965

Although JJ did not, by his own choice, leave school until the end of the Easter term on 9 April 1965, he attained what had, unwittingly presaged by his father's will, now become the new age of maturity on 27 February of that year. His trustees, with the permission of the headmaster, had arranged a celebratory meal for him with friends—Billy included—at a well-known country restaurant. Before eating he had been closeted with his trustees for over two hours and had been informed of the value and composition of one fourth of the capital fund that now became his by right. A sensible sum for investment was agreed and advanced; JJ was rich—and likely to become richer. Sylvia kissed her mildly embarrassed son and hoped he would have a lovely night before she and Claude departed with Auntie Charlotte. Mr Burroughs shook his hand, reminded him that he started work on Monday 3 May, and told him to expect no 'special favours or treatment' before he, too, left for 'the grown-ups' party'. JJ was left with Uncle Charles—a situation so obviously contrived that Charles felt no apology necessary.

'JJ, dear nephew,' he began, 'you are the nearest thing I have to a son. Claude is only too happy to cede to me the 'grown-up lecture' tradition says you should get.

'We would both be naïve if I tried to teach you about what used to be called 'the birds and the bees'—you can probably teach me a thing or two about some aspects of sex.

'Mature relationships come later in life, I hope, before which it's only natural that you 'sow a few wild oats'—you probably have already— but I don't want to know about that and you shouldn't want to tell me. What I have to say to you, and this *is* the serious part, JJ, is that I'm aware you've inherited the . . . er, distinguishing feature, if I can so call it, of male Whitehouses in the size of your penis: accept it as a fact. Don't flaunt it and, whatever you do, don't be too eager to succumb to temptation. You are probably not aware that your father, my brother, was more than usually active in many ladies' beds— something you may not want to know, but it's better you hear it from me than from someone more biased later on. What Roger was, however, was both calculating and discriminating in his choices of sexual partners: he was careful not to risk infection and his assignations bought him free lodging in his travels as a salesman. It was his choice of occupation, financially unnecessary, but it kept him busy while waiting for the RAF and the government to make their infrequent demands on him.

'You should, overall, be proud of your father—he was a fine man and served his country, your mother and yourself as well as anyone could wish. I'm telling you this not only as a precaution against future gossip, but as a form of warning. Times are different to in your father's and my time and talk and mud-slinging are more prevalent now.

'So far you've been a credit to all of us—try to continue as that. If you ever need us, any of us, don't hesitate to ask, if you don't ask you usually don't get what you need. You will make mistakes—we all do. Make sure they are both minor and as well-hidden as possible. One last thing before I stop boring you, the only advice my father gave me—and he couldn't say it to Roger as he'd already enlisted and gone to war—is this: if you must make a mess—don't do it on your own doorstep.'

Uncle Charles stood up and extended his right hand. JJ took it, gratefully, and they solemnly shook hands.

'End of lecture, young man. Good luck with everything.'

Before JJ could respond, his uncle was gone from the room leaving him a little tearful, very grateful and, after a moment to gather himself together, ready for his eighteenth birthday party. The 'float' from his capital trust and the genuinely warm friendship of the assembled company ensured it was a memorable party.

CHAPTER TWENTY-NINE

JJ—Articled Clerkship and Professional Education
1965 to 1970

At 8.50 a.m. on Monday 3 May 1965, slightly self-conscious in a new suit, Jonathan Justin Whitehouse-Martin presented himself at the reception desk of Harvey, Smith and Thomas, Chartered Accountants. It was, in point of fact, his third visit to the Newhall Street offices following first being 'hauled in' with Billy by Uncle Charles, and then a week ago—and again with Uncle Charles—to sign and have witnessed his articles of clerkship. This time, as both his male trustees had warned him, he was on his own.

A buxom, laughing lady welcomed him and introduced herself as Thelma. If everyone is like this, thought JJ, I shall enjoy working here. Not everyone was like Thelma but, overall, JJ would enjoy his time with the firm. Thelma, as he later learned, was everyone's friend and confidante to most; she, herself, appeared to have no close friends and, seemingly, confided in no one. On JJ's first day she not only knew who he was but with whom he was scheduled to spend his first few weeks.

'You'll be with Mr Arnold,' she informed JJ whilst dialling the telephone into which she announced, 'Young Mr Whitehouse-Martin's here, Johnnie.' She turned to JJ, 'He'll be with you in a moment, JJ, wait over there, please.'

And sure enough, in only a few moments, a tall, gangly man in a dark, shiny-with-wear suit approached from the hallway, extending his bony hand in greeting.

Despite Johnnie Arnold's friendly grin, JJ was fascinated by the fact that Arnold had one brown eye and one blue eye: for many years he was the only person JJ encountered with such a peculiarity. He became used to it and, as it was never spoken of in his hearing, it was apparent others were similarly accustomed.

JJ was led to the end of the corridor and into the stairwell. Until that morning, JJ had not consciously appreciated that his employers' offices extended over several floors of the impressive building. As they ascended the stairs—'We don't use the lift unless we have to'— and without seeming to hurry, Johnnie Arnold swiftly explained a few basic rules of engagement within Harvey, Smith and Thomas. Only partners and the senior manager had offices on the reception floor; on the floor above were the tax, estates, company law and small business departments and above them, inverse importance applying, were the audit staff, managers, assistant managers, seniors and juniors spread over two further floors. Audit managers were allotted a small office each; assistant audit managers, when they were in, occupied desks at the approach to their respective manager's office; audit seniors, of whom Johnnie Arnold was one of many, took precedence in the claim for desk space in the large outer offices leaving juniors, amongst whom JJ was now numbered, to find any working space available should they so need. JJ's lack of a brief case was noted and a temporary plastic envelope was substituted. Into the small envelope went various 'necessities' in the form of different coloured Biro pens; one pad of plain paper; and one columnar ruled pad. All the pads had the firm's name and logo printed at the head of each sheet of paper. Finally, and too bulky for the temporary substitute case, came a staff manual. JJ was advised to study the latter in his own time and to ask any questions the next day. The absence of a brief case was more generously dealt with; Johnnie Arnold introduced JJ to Arthur Hill, a short, squat audit manager whose lack of inches was amply compensated for by his larger-than-life personality—he had been one of the few Battle of Britain pilots to survive the war—and Arthur Hill offered to obtain JJ a smart, new leather briefcase from one of his clients in Walsall, the Midlands centre of leather manufacture.

'It'll cost you, even at trade prices (which it will be), but it should last you a lifetime, JJ,' stated the cheery Mr Hill, waving away the offer of payment in advance. He was due to visit Walsall on the morrow and, if JJ were to call into his office before 9.00 a.m. on Wednesday with his cheque book, he would become the proud possessor of his very own briefcase. The Wednesday morning surprise, as JJ duly took delivery of, and paid for, said briefcase was that, without being bidden, Arthur Hill had arranged for 'J. J. W.-M.' to be inscribed on the flap. The cost was far less than JJ could have imagined and, indeed, it did last him almost his entire life.

Before 9.30 a.m. on his first Monday, JJ found himself leaving the Newhall Street offices and hastening in the wake of the long-striding Johnnie Arnold uphill to Great Charles Street where they turned right and, by way of underpasses and roads JJ had never known—but would come to know well—to a well-known motor trader's showroom and offices. He had begun the unexciting, but demanding and strangely educational task of auditing.

His 'induction' continued with verbal information from Johnnie Arnold and, subsequently, other seniors. Allied, of course, to the practical staff manual that he duly studied that evening and night, being conscious of the instruction to ask any questions concerning it on the morrow. It was not the most exciting read of JJ's life, but he conscientiously noted his queries and posed them to Johnnie Arnold the following morning.

'You didn't really read all through that last night did you?' was Johnnie's incredulous reply. 'We've got work to do—you'll pick things up as you go along. Probably be best if you ask Mr Hill your posse of questions tomorrow morning,' added Johnnie Arnold—looking warily at JJ's three pages of notes and 'passing the buck'.

Arthur Hill's reaction was similar to Johnnie Arnold's, 'I've got better things to do than lecture on the staff manual, young man. All I would say to you is don't take everything you're told too seriously and learn as you go along. Now go along, JJ.'

First lesson learned. JJ quickly learned that partners were always addressed as 'sir' and referred to by their initials; managers were addressed and referred to as mister; and clients were to be treated with respect—whether it was felt they so deserved or not. The firm, as Uncle Charles had told him, dealt with a wide variety of professional work and conducted audits ranging from well-known public companies through to small manufacturing and retail firms to one-man bands of self-employed persons in an alarming variety of occupations. And, of course, professional firms such as that in which Uncle Charles was a partner and where, for reasons of personal involvement, JJ would *not* visit on audit. The range of business experience and knowledge thus afforded to those fortunate enough to serve their articles with Harvey, Smith and Thomas was thus extensive, besides supplementing their studies for the Institute Examinations. The Saturday morning lectures arranged by the Students' Society, in which JJ duly enrolled and subsequently became very active, were useful, informative and/or amusing according to the merits of the lecturers and sometimes illuminated the correspondence course studies undertaken by every articled pupil.

Initially, JJ lodged with his uncle and aunt on Hagley Road but, as Uncle Charles tactfully pointed out, JJ's trust owned as much property as himself and, providing he paid the appropriate rent—which he could well afford to do from his first 'traunch' of inheritance—JJ could be independent whilst still being able to visit him and Aunt Charlotte whenever he chose. Their respective and still very desirable luxury apartments were, after all, within easy walking distance. As JJ suspected when the proposition was put to him, a suitable vacancy was about to become available—Uncle Charles was always ahead of the game—and thus JJ became a weekday resident of Birmingham. His weekend visits to Avonbridge and St Barnabas vicarage became rarer as the social activities of the Student Society and its members, plus his enrolment as a valued playing member of Moseley Rugby Football Club progressively claimed his attention and attendance.

It was on a home weekend in October 1965 whilst recovering from a sprained wrist that the opportunity of a further business venture with a Baker family involvement arose. JJ's liasons with Zoe Baker had long since ceased, but on the few occasions they had met there had been no awkwardness. Despite this arms-length amity, the initial approach came from Billy. Whenever JJ was due to return to Avonbridge he always telephoned Billy and they met for a few drinks in the Old Swan hotel bar. To JJ's surprise, Billy had abandoned his family's dedication to association football and become a playing member of Avonbridge Rugby Club— which used the old stables at the rear of The Swan as their changing rooms and were the backbone of the hotel's drinking custom. Billy had become a more than useful scrum half and had turned out for the first XV twice to replace the injured incumbent of that position. After initial talk of their mutual activities, sporting, amorous and otherwise, Billy broached the subject for which he had been preparing himself.

'JJ, you know my sister, Zoe, of course. She wants me to ask if you can advise her about a business matter?'

'Of course—if I can,' answered JJ. 'What's the problem?'

'I'd rather she told you herself, JJ, I don't know why she's nervous, but I said I'd ask you and then we'd talk to them. They're in the lounge bar, waiting,' said Billy—glancing towards the door that led to the lounge. 'OK if we join them?'

'Them?' queried JJ.

'Er, yes. You remember her mate, Janice?'

'Yes, of course. Be nice to see them both again. I'm intrigued, Billy. Let's join the ladies.' Saying which, JJ rose and, with Billy in close pursuit, strode into the lounge bar. Zoe and Janice, both smartly dressed, were seated at a table for four in the far corner of the lounge looking anxiously at the approaching pair. To offer to shake their hands in greeting, considering their past association, seemed silly in the extreme and JJ had no hesitation in giving each young lady a kiss on the cheek before offering to buy them another drink. They both refused and, making JJ even more curious, stated that they wanted to keep a clear head.

JJ and Billy sat down and, under Billy's urging, Zoe outlined their position.

It seemed that the hairdresser with whom they had trained and continued to work for the last four years had announced, to their astonishment, that he intended to retire and sell the business. A competitor from Stourminster had made what he considered a fair opening offer and, providing she was prepared to increase the offer, the deal would be sealed by Christmas. The prospective buyer had made it plain she would be staffing the business with her own people leaving Zoe and Janice particularly aggrieved and potentially unemployed. It seemed they had, in their own words and estimation been almost running the business over the last two years. Besides cutting and styling, Zoe had been making all the appointments and allocating work. Janice, the more numerate of the pair had, as well as styling, been operating the till; banking the takings; handing out the wage packets she had prepared for approval; and sharing the tips amongst the staff. The fact that neither of them had any respect or professional regard for the potential buyer and, in the unlikely event of her offering them a position, would not want to work for her anyway, only increased their bitterness. They felt they were being badly treated. JJ wholeheartedly agreed, of course, but felt he had to state that employment law was not his speciality.

'Oh no, JJ, that's not what we're asking you about. We've seen Mr Morton, the solicitor, and we know our position in that respect. What we wondered is whether we could buy the business. Mr Morton suggested we might try for a mortgage—he mentioned the Avonbridge Building Society based in their office—but we're not sure what we'd be getting into if we could get this mortgage thing . . .' Zoe trailed off as she looked imploringly at JJ.

Refocusing his attention, JJ looked at the two ladies, 'Firstly, and to the best of my knowledge, you are unlikely to get much of a mortgage unless you're in employment. As, and forgive me for saying so, that seems to be in doubt, forget building societies as an idea. Particularly the local one—Terry Morton's pushing his own cause as one of its directors. Any loan they might make to you would be costly, probably hedged about with all manner of difficulties and unlikely to be enough. A better bet would be a bank loan—but for that you would need a business plan and a cash flow statement covering at least two years.'

'I understand about a business plan,' interjected the practical Janice, 'but what's a cash flow thingy?'

'It's something the banks always insist on but, more often than not, the income aspect in many of them is pure guesswork. Compiling one is a long and often complex job and even a small local accountancy firm would charge you more than, in my opinion, it's worth.'

'Could you do one, JJ?' asked Janice.

'Yes, is the answer to that, Jan—but bear in mind what I've just said. Strictly, as an employee, I should only do such work for my employers. The firm I'm with in Birmingham would charge a lot more than any local firm so I wouldn't be doing you any favours if I prepared anything for you.'

Both girls looked downcast.

'Oh well. We just wondered. Sorry if we've embarrassed you, JJ,' said Zoe.

'We'd better go now, but thank you all the same, JJ,' added Janice.

Both girls began to get up.

'Whoa, there,' said JJ, 'Don't be so quick to take offence or to give up. Sit down, please.'

The girls looked warily at JJ. Billy, knowing his friend better than they, smiled.

'It's not funny, Billy,' snapped Zoe, noting his expression.

'No, Zo, but you are. Sit down, please, and listen. I think JJ's got more to say.'

The girls sat down again. Zoe was still glaring at her brother, but JJ was quick to note that Janice was rather calmer as she sat herself closer to Billy and, for a moment, they touched hands and locked eyes. JJ made a mental note to enquire into this should the opportunity arise. Meanwhile, he had composed his own thoughts.

'Sorry if you misunderstood, ladies. I didn't say I wouldn't help you, I needed to make it clear, however, that I need to clear any work I might do for you that involved a third party—such as the bank or building society— with my employers. However,' he smiled at them, 'what I would like to do, subject to going into details and looking at figures, etc., is to make you both a private loan for the purchase and improvement of the business. If I did that I'd be working for myself and no charges would arise.'

There was a stunned silence. The two girls looked in amazement at JJ who, a little embarrassed, gathered up the glasses and, carrying the tray one handed went to the bar for a round of drinks.

'Is he serious, Billy?' asked Zoe in a whisper.

'Oh, yes, sis, he's perfectly serious.'

'But,' asked Janice, falteringly and equally quietly, 'does he have the sort of money we would need?'

'Yes, love, he certainly does. Don't worry about that,' said Billy, quietly. 'But, let me warn you, please don't ask him that. Take my word for it; he's got more than enough money to help you. But, as you're about to find out, he'll need a lot more information than you've given him so far. And whatever happens it'll all be fair, legal and above board. Here he comes.'

And, as Billy had forecast, JJ proceeded to outline what he would need from the girls and what they would, possibly, then get from him. He was not surprised to find that Janice, besides producing a small pad and pen from her handbag, confirmed that she felt herself able to obtain almost all the information very quickly. The four agreed to maintain confidentiality until they met the following week.

Janice was as good as her word. Billy had been able to confirm the hairdressing salon's ownership was solely held without encumbrance or debt. JJ had not been idle either and, within a month, not only had the girls been financed but, to their employer's amazement, proved it and had their offer accepted. The legal matters were attended to, at JJ's insistence and cost, by his Uncle Charles—thereby killing two birds with one stone as his trustees were thus made aware of this latest activity—albeit it was using JJ's own money. The new name of the salon arose from Billy's use of the shortened form of his sister's name and, raising JJ's opinion of her commercial and marketing ideas, Janice's inventive thought. ZoNice Hair and Beauty salon opened in early December 1965 in time for the pre-Christmas beautifying rush.

JJ's student popularity was ensured due to him being one of the few possessing a car. The second-hand MG—C Series—purchased from his early inheritance took him, and often more than the intended single passenger, to all parts of the Midlands on many weekends. JJ had, under his mother's tuition, proved a capable and natural driver who passed his driving test at the first attempt. His first attempt to win the Combined Students' Societies annual motor car treasure hunt proved less successful due to undue haste incurring the need for costly repairs. The garage mechanic's opinion that attention to some mechanical aspects could have saved the cost of recovery and maybe allowed progress in the event persuaded JJ that having his friend Billy Baker—already working as a car mechanic in Stourminster—as passenger and co-driver might ensure a better placing. So it proved the next year when they only failed to win by a few points.

Billy blamed their loss on the 'escape' of the live fish they had surreptitiously scooped from the pond of a posh residence. 'It was worth five points in the treasure hunt, JJ.'

'Maybe—but what was it worth to the deprived owner?' replied a worried JJ.

'Come off it, JJ,' answered the ever practical Billy, 'D'you think he goes out and counts his fish every night? He'll probably think a heron's had it—if he even notices.'

They remained a good team—one that could easily have won the event the following year had they so wished. The chastening realisation that one of the rewards for winning was becoming the organiser of the ensuing year's event decided JJ and Billy that an unscheduled delay in a pleasant country public house incurring penalty points for late arrival and denying them the win was the easier alternative.

Another team for whom JJ found himself much in demand was the Chartered Accountants' Student Society Rugby XV. By the time he was in his third year of articles he had been elected secretary of the student society and captain of the students' rugby team. As was customary, JJ passed on the secretaryship before his final year in order to concentrate on his studies, and he was glad to be relieved of the time-consuming duties. He had, conscientiously, marked his twenty-first birthday with two very small celebrations: one with six close friends (Billy Baker included) and one with his trustees and Claude after he had come into possession of his second instalment of inheritance. His natural abilities had been rewarded with a distinguished result in the intermediate examinations—third in England and Wales and first in the company law section. Consequently, he did not relish the onerous expectations placed on his broad shoulders for the final examinations. JJ disappointed neither himself or his principal. He gained the best Midlands result of May 1970, once more beat all others in the company law paper and, for good measure, added the taxation prize to his achievement.

News travels fast, and obeying the summons to the office of his principal, William Burroughs, he found a large contingent of the firm, lead by Arthur Hill—now senior audit manager—gathered to cheer him as he entered reception. He even received the extremely rare, almost unknown accolade of a kiss from Thelma. He was then directed to the senior partner's office.

'Jolly well done, JJ,' said Mr Burroughs—or as JJ had become accustomed to referring to him, WJB—warmly shaking JJ's hand. Even allowing for prior acquaintance, it was rare for the senior partner to address any staff member by other than their surname in the office and, for once, JJ was embarrassed. He had, of course, met WJB and his other trustees regularly and, particularly, when becoming entitled to an even greater sum at the age of twenty-one than he had inherited at eighteen. On that occasion they had debated the investment and other dispositions of his wealth, but trustees' meetings, for reasons of tact and convenience, took place at Uncle Charles' office—with Sylvia travelling up to stay with Charles and Charlotte. WJB now invited JJ to sit down—something else which had been unprecedented since he had signed his articles—and began an entirely unexpected frank assessment of a possible future for the firm's most promising examinee since his own success many years ago.

'You are now not only a chartered accountant, JJ, but you are, as a consequence of your results, what I might call a marked man. The big firms will be after you as a catch and, though it pains me to say so, they can pay you far more than we can. In your case, salary is not a prime concern, you and I know that, but they don't, and, frankly, there is no reason for them to know. Everyone has a certain worth in the jobs market and yours, I regret to say, is rather higher than we can afford. I would love you to stay with us, of course, but the big boys can offer you greater opportunities—both in terms of work experience and, if you wanted, overseas posting.'

'At the moment I'm happy here, sir,' interjected JJ.

'It's nice of you to say so, JJ,' replied Burroughs. 'As senior partner, I would be delighted, as I said, if you stayed with us; in this envelope is the firm's bonus for your success and our formal offer of ongoing employment. If nothing else, it will serve as a benchmark for you to calculate your market worth. Don't open it now, the increased salary starts on the first of next month.'

WJB shifted in his seat, removed his glasses and continued, 'With my other hat on as one of your trustees, I must urge you to consider carefully your professional future. In the next month or so you are likely to be approached, formally and informally, by more than one other firm; you're already well known locally due to your activities with the Students' Society, and you can take it from me that every other worthwhile firm in the Midlands is, or soon will be, aware of your exam results. You're not obliged to accept any offers and I would deem it a personal favour and compliment if you chose to discuss your career path and any offers made to you with me. Be sure that anything you are inclined towards is offered in writing before committing yourself—some firms are, I regret to say, not as professional as they should be—no names but, I think you follow.'

JJ did follow. He had felt for some time that some members of the student body were ill-served by their employers. And, corroborating what WJB had said, the bigger, international firms offered, even to those still under articles, enviable experience and opportunities. He had always been loyal to Harvey, Smith and Thomas and he was aware that he owed them a great debt of gratitude; at the same time he appreciated WJB's sage advice.

'I'll think about what you have said, sir,' said JJ, 'and I will certainly discuss whatever might be offered with you. Thank you for being so frank—if I may say so.'

WJB smiled. 'You may certainly say so, JJ. We've known one another sufficiently long to avoid any misunderstanding, I hope. One last thing, and I'm sorry to state the obvious, but any future employer should, before you commence with them, be made aware of your other business ventures. I took the liberty of checking the files earlier, the printing firm is more than paying its way, and the hairdressing salon is doing remarkably well—good judgement of yours, there. Anyway, the ultimate decision as to where you go—or if you go—must lie with you and I would only counsel you to take your time coming to a decision.'

'I will, sir. Can I suggest that I come to see you again in a month's time?'

'Canny as ever, JJ,' answered a smiling WJB. 'Give it at least a month—more if you like. I'll tell my secretary to fit you in any time next month. But you're still working for us and time waits for neither you nor I. Off to wherever you are detailed today and have a good party tonight— but not too good, mind.'

Again they shook hands. JJ had already determined to have a good party and, before returning to the pile of company tax computations that he knew awaited him in the tax department, he sneaked into a vacant manager's office and, with the laughing complicity of Thelma, he telephoned the Grand Hotel to book a dinner on Friday night for at least thirty. He'd make a list at lunchtime, he determined, better than repairing to The White Horse and downing more pints than were good for himself or his work.

It was a good list and was a good party within the parameters JJ felt WJB had suggested.

CHAPTER THIRTY
JJ A.C.A. AND BILLY A.M.I.MECH.E.
ALL CHANGE, 1970

JJ was not the only person from Avonbridge to be successful in the examinations of 1970. Billy had attended night school, applied himself diligently to both practical and theoretical matters, obtained his City and Guilds proficiency as a motor mechanic easily and, deciding he liked learning, qualified as an associate member of the Institution of Mechanical Engineers. Billy had also become what his employers considered an indispensable employee of Paddy Collins's Worcester Road garage. Besides his skills at repairing and servicing customers' vehicles, he could successfully sell a car in the absence of showroom staff.

The August 1970 celebration of Billy's latest success, held at The Swan, was well attended and the local taxi firm derived more than the usual Friday night trips and tips transporting the inebriated to their homes. The biggest surprise was not Billy's qualification—a foregone success in the eyes of most—or even that he should choose to flaunt his success, but the announcement of his engagement to marry Janice Jones. Even JJ, despite being aware that they had become an item, was surprised. Billy re-assured him that there was no ulterior motive or pregnant purpose in the engagement before being particularly—and unnecessarily—insistent that JJ should be his best man. A radiant Janice added her insistence— similarly without necessity.

'I'd be honoured, of course, Bill—but what about your brother?' was JJ's reply.

'Ah—perhaps you don't know—you being in Birmingham. He's been nabbed and this time taken inside. Damn fool—it's not a long stretch, but quite when he'll be at liberty again depends on his good conduct. Anyway, I'd rather have you than him even if he was at liberty,' answered Billy.

The two friends shook hands on the arrangement. Janice gave JJ a warm, lingering kiss. JJ's intention was to purchase more drinks, but Billy had retained hold of his hand and Janice had taken his other hand in hers. JJ gave them enquiring looks.

'Can we sit down a moment, please, JJ? I've an idea we'd like to run by you if you don't mind?'

'Seems I don't have any choice,' said JJ good-naturedly. 'Fire away.'

They all sank into an unoccupied corner seat where Billy and Janice—mostly Billy—outlined the increasing demand for motorcar spares arising from more and more people doing their own car maintenance and improvements.

'Half of them bring the job to us to finish off, or put right, of course. But it's the other half I'm interested in. There's a good margin of profit on most of the parts. If you add in the usual motoring ancillaries—seat covers, floor mats, de-misting cloths—even the silly stickers and dangling decorations that ought to be against the law—there's an expanding market ripe for exploitation.'

JJ could see an opportunity when it was presented and thus began yet another of his successful business investments—Karbitz. Whilst Billy was opening accounts with potential suppliers, a suitable premises became available. Not only did it have a ready made retail outlet, but it backed onto a disused warehouse and tract of waste land that both friends agreed would be an ideal car lot, so B & J Cars ('honest and straightforward second hand car deals for the discerning motorist') was added to Karbitz.

By installing inspection pits in the warehouse they created car repair spaces for rent wherein keen owners could tinker with their beloved motors whatever the weather and, for an additional charge, seek the skilled advice of the proprietor—Billy. In the first year the venture had covered its capitalisation, besides providing Billy with better take-home pay than he had been receiving at Avonbridge Motors.

J & B Printing was functioning well under the guiding hand of Peter Hordern—an experienced printing-press operator formerly with a Black Country printers who, being both dissatisfied and ambitious, had eagerly accepted the offer to manage the small firm for a share of profit and guaranteed salary. ZoNice Hair and Beauty salons had just opened their third establishment.

Janice's book-keeping and business records venture, established under JJ's guidance and—at her suggestion—named 3J's Business Books was also prospering. She and JJ tried to meet every month to review the progress and status of every business. Initially, Janice had operated from the spare room behind ZoNice, but expansion of both ventures created the necessity of acquiring premises and staff for 3J's Business Books. A small shop at the end of the High Street became vacant and, after some hard negotiation and acquisition of planning consent 3J's Drop-in Business Books opened for business. The small flat above the shop—lounge, bedroom, bathroom and kitchenette—became Janice's private office and domain. The shop was imaginatively converted to an open plan office space where the two staff members occupied a desk each. Not only the books and records of less numerate traders were maintained here, but help with basic personal tax returns was given at JJ's suggestion—and after he had tutored the employees—which became a profitable development. In their third month in the new premises, JJ managed to be early for his monthly meeting with Janice. The usual reviews were all satisfactory and quickly dealt with. Janice had organised the small flat into both office and interview room—the latter complete with refreshments from the small kitchen, couches and low coffee tables. As they had time in hand she opened a bottle of wine and they toasted their mutual successes.

'Who'd have thought we'd come to this twelve years ago?' said Janice reflectively.

'Twelve years ago, Jan,' we were far more intent on loving than living, if I remember aright,' replied JJ. 'You and Bill,' seem to have carried on with both, bless you.'

'Not entirely, JJ, We had a few years when we each went our own ways and, well . . . did our own things—and persons, if you'll excuse me saying so.'

'Yes, of course you did. I wasn't forgetting. But now you've got together with a vengeance, it seems. No regrets, I hope?'

'Gosh no, JJ,' said Janice. Emboldened by the wine and their proximity she smiled as she said, 'Well, only one, really and that's—'

'Go on,' said JJ—intrigued as he was intended to be. And knew he was so intended.

'Well, JJ, when we were all at it in the little garden house, I always lusted after you as well as Billy. Your . . . immensity intrigued me, if I'm honest.'

Janice stopped speaking and blushing a little added, 'Sorry, JJ, it's probably the wine talking.'

There was a pause whilst the two business partners looked at one another.

'If you'd said—' began JJ

'There was never an opportunity, JJ, I couldn't suggest a swap now, could I? Zoe was rightly adamant she drew the line at having sex with her brother. So . . . '

'Exactly,' said JJ.

Another long pause.

'Of course,' they both said together and then laughed.

'You first,' said JJ.

'Don't get me wrong, JJ, I love Billy and we're going to get married and be happy.'

'I sincerely hope so, Jan.' I love the pair of you and I'd not do anything to upset either of you. You know that . . . I just . . . don't like you having regrets . . .'

'Me neither,' said Janice and with no more ado she stood up, led a willing JJ to the small bedroom where she swiftly stripped off and helped JJ to a similar state of nakedness and arousal.

Later, they lay together covered only by a large tartan rug. Janice was the first to state that tonight had been a once and for all and must be their secret.

'Goes without saying, love,' said JJ, 'I'm happy so long as you have no regrets.'

'None at all . . . now,' replied Janice, hugging JJ tenderly and giving a last grasp at his immensity before discarding the rug and getting dressed.

True to their word, neither Janice or JJ ever mentioned their single evening of lust again, nor was there any intention or suggestion they should repeat the experience—joyful though it had been. They remained the best of friends and closest of trusting business colleagues.

JJ's only problem remained his personal income tax liabilities—despite such preventative measures as were legally available to maintain the 'burden' as bearable as possible. Time and a costly residence in Guernsey would eventually allay that problem; but that was a long time in the future.

JJ, with Mr Burroughs's blessing and regret, accepted an attractive offer from the Birmingham office of Price Waterhouse to join them as an assistant manager and, the most interesting aspect, to be number two in the administration of a forthcoming major prospectus investigation for the acquisition of several firms under a new holding company being financed by a major share issue. It was not only fascinating work that took him all over the Midlands, but gave him an insight into aspects of commerce hitherto unsuspected. The resultant agglomeration of several seemingly disparate firms into one large combine proved, to the astonishment of JJ and his manager, Peter Jameson, to be startlingly successful. JJ's own mother, Sylvia, had ignored her son's advice and purchased a large block of shares in the new conglomerate that, to her own and Claude's delight, she sold at considerable profit within six months. JJ was doubly pleased for them, Claude had, belatedly but deservedly, been offered and had accepted the prestigious post of dean at Hereford Cathedral and, with a mixture of regret and happy anticipation, they were preparing to leave Avonbridge in mid January, 1971.

As the St Bartholomew's vast vicarage was tied to the Church and owned by the Church commissioners, JJ would find himself from January 1971 solely based in Birmingham with no Avonbridge base. With so many personal business investments and involvements in the town, this was not satisfactory and he began to entertain ideas of purchasing a small property for weekend use; ideas abandoned when Billy telephoned to ask if he would be interested in the joint purchase of Avonbridge Grange. It stood just beyond the town boundary in its own grounds and was available at a reasonable price for a quick sale. Billy and Janice, by Janice's calculations, could raise 75 per cent of the asking price from savings and a mortgage. The imposing house comprised a central section with east and west wings—the former wing suitable for a live-in housekeeper and gardener, whilst the west had already been converted into a self-contained luxury flat.

'Nearly as posh as your Hagley Road place,' said Billy as both friendly taunt and persuasion. JJ, as Billy well knew, was aware of the property and rushed across for a very satisfactory evening inspection. A deal was discussed whereby Billy and Janice had both independence and a better loan arrangement than previously envisaged. JJ had a new Avonbridge base.

The Old Vicarage had been kind to Sylvia and Claude. It's garden and garden buildings had been both meeting place, love nest and an initial business base for JJ and Billy. Sylvia and JJ decided that Christmas 1970 should be not only their last, but their best, in the old place. The dining room had rarely, if ever, seen such a gathering and festive celebration as occurred on 23 December that year: Charles and Charlotte arrived with William Burroughs and his wife; Billy and Janice with Zoe and her new husband, Gareth; Arthur and Jenny Hill travelled over from Birmingham with, to even her own surprise, Thelma and her 'hidden' husband; and they were joined by many of the local and loyal congregation. Sadly, Linda and James Brown were unable to be with them, they had taken early retirement after having inherited a North Wales property and, on the strength of the rest of James's late uncle's accumulated wealth, had booked a Christmas cruise. Sylvia's other regret was that JJ had no steady lady-friend. A confidential chat with Billy and Janice confirmed that they knew of no lasting liaison, but were sure that JJ would still enjoy Christmas. In which certainty they were proven correct. Out of a perverse sentimentality, JJ decided to occupy his old room for the Christmas and New Year before his mother and Claude left for deepest Herefordshire. Sylvia was delighted—and said so. Almost everyone attended Claude's last Christmas Eve service — St Barnabas had rarely been so crowded—and they heard an emotional but nonetheless excellent sermon before returning to the vicarage for punch and an early Christmas breakfast of kedgeree and white wine.

It was also the occasion of JJ's innocent late acceptance of Billy's invitation to join his party at the rugby club's New Year's Eve dance at The Swan. Billy was rather apologetic about it as JJ would have to make his own way to the dance since Billy, as a recent recruit to the club committee, would be attending a pre-dance dinner for committee and wives hosted by the president—builder Freddie Wells. Waving aside this minor problem, JJ was happy to accept; an acceptance that would have an unexpected and lasting effect on his life.

CHAPTER THIRTY-ONE
Freddie Wells
1924 TO 1946

Frederick Wellington Wells—his mother was a great admirer of the Iron Duke—was known as Freddie from an early age. He was, in every sense of the expression, a self-made man sprung from humble beginnings. Walter Wells, an itinerant bricklayer, had wooed, bedded and then wed the pregnant Agnes Clara Hollings when in the eyes of many both were too young and impoverished to be respectably married—let alone be parents. Percy and Gertie Hollings reluctantly allowed the young couple the use of their back bedroom and shared facilities, such as they were, in a Handsworth, Birmingham, two-up two-down terraced back-to-back. Freddie's arrival in this constricted world on 15 June 1924 made an already uncomfortable life almost intolerable. This proved to be the spur Walter needed and, to the surprise of everyone—himself included—he secured a contract to restore the stables at an almost stately home in nearby Smethwick. The acceptance of, and payment for, the first part of the work enabled he and Agnes to rent a small cottage in the almost adjacent Bearwood. Young Freddie was, thus, removed from central Birmingham. Walter's successful restoration was advertised in the cheapest and best manner—word of mouth—and led to further contracts increasingly far removed from Agnes's roots and parents. Young Freddie's childhood was spent at so many locations that he might have been considered a gypsy had he not been housed in successive rented cottages and semi-detached houses. The continual movement of home—usually within the West Midlands—made Freddie's schooling a random process. His practical education began at an early age—as soon as Walter deemed him strong enough to mix cement and carry hods of bricks and tiles. By the age of fourteen he was at least as good a bricklayer as his father. In order to avoid problems associated with employing an under-age boy who should have been in school, Walter had begun representing his strapping son as at least two years older than his actual years, a deception that back-fired on him when conscription began in 1939.

In early 1939 Walter and Freddie were working at Stone Manor near Kidderminster for a wealthy family of butchers and, primarily, sausage makers. In the October of that year, war having been declared, Walter was conscripted. He joined the local regiment and, after some swift and rather rudimentary training, found himself in France with the British Expeditionary Force. He was one of the many killed before he could even arrive at the Dunkirk beaches. Agnes, marooned in a rented cottage in the hamlet of Mustow Green—close to Stone Manor—was, initially, reliant on the earnings of her only son, earnings soon replaced by army pay when the authorities, believing him to be eighteen rather than sixteen, forced Freddie to follow his father into uniform. Agnes, in common with many women at the time, took work where she could find it—in her case at the Hartlebury supply depot of the Royal Air Force. She and three lady workmates were fortunate to find a small house adjacent to the railway level crossing at Hartlebury that, by splitting the rent and overheads four ways, became affordable.

Correspondence between mother and son was almost non-existent; neither being well-lettered. Consequently, Agnes knew little of Freddie's war service. When queried, she replied with the usual veiled care of the time that he was 'doing his bit for his country.' As it happened, Freddie did very little for his country—any conflicts he engaged in were within barracks and were more a question of self-defence rather than defence of the realm. His strength and adaptability allied to a loud voice and quick reactions soon brought him to the attention of those in command. In 1941 he was awarded one stripe; swiftly had a further added, and by 1942 was promoted from corporal to sergeant. Due to the lack of letters and his mother's ignorance of his whereabouts (a mutual lack of knowledge) her marriage to an American soldier—ladies so espoused were referred to as G.I. Brides—remained unknown to Freddie until his demobilisation in 1945. By which time he had become a quarter master sergeant and his mother a resident of the United States of America. They never again communicated.

Having used every trick he could manage, Freddie Wells left the army with rather more than a demob' suit. He had learned to drive—he had a piece of paper to prove it. He had money in the bank—another piece of paper proved that. He had sufficient money to buy himself a small truck and, having returned to the West Midlands in search of his now Transatlantic mother, rent a small builder's yard in Avonbridge. Work was plentiful for a good tradesman—and Freddie was a good builder. A 'Wells Builders' sign appeared above the yard entrance and was written on each side of the trusty truck. Before two years were out, two further trucks clearly designated as property of Wells Builders were not only apparent in the locality, but necessary for the volume of work Freddie's firm attracted.

Freddie was forced to become an employer in order to meet the demands made of his growing firm, he gave preference to ex-servicemen and, as he had in the army, drove them hard. He took every job that was offered—providing he was guaranteed payment. His reliable reputation rapidly grew and, in early 1946 he found himself asked to quote Mr Anthony and Mrs Constance Belshire for the maintenance contract on Avonbridge Hall. It was a massive job and one that would keep he and many others gainfully employed for years to come; the problem was with the gainful aspect. Local sources tipped Freddie that the Belshires, although county folk were not as solvent as they wished everyone to believe. Freddie was on the point of declining the work when two events persuaded him otherwise. The first was Mr Belshire's suggestion that, as he might be working at the hall for some time to come, he might find the disused stables useful for 'storing things, ye know. Wouldn't cost ye anything, of course. We don't use 'em—don't ride any more, ye know. You could do with them as you wanted—more or less.' Free storage would save Wells Builders the cost of another yard—Freddie was already outgrowing the original premises—and the presence of more men would make the hall more secure. The second factor that led Freddie to undertake the ongoing task was his chance meeting with the unmarried daughter of the house.

CHAPTER THIRTY-TWO
DOREEN DE VERE BELSHIRE
1923 TO 1946

Doreen deVere Belshire was a full fourteen months older than the well-muscled and confident young builder whom she discovered walking around the old stable block at her home. Due to her grandmother's tight hold on the strings of whatever purses remained to the family, social life for Doreen and her parents had become a distant memory. Someone—almost anyone—to talk with outside the family was a welcome distraction, and she did become distracted by this ambitious and not altogether bad-looking young man. As Freddie had been unable to ascertain much real detail concerning the estate from her vague father, he found this posh-spoken lass a mine of useful information on the extent and general state of the land and buildings known since 1828 as Avonbridge Hall. There was, despite the disparity in age and class, a mutual attraction; besides which, as they became better acquainted and began to verge on intimacy, each saw a definite personal advantage to a future relationship. For Doreen it could be a form of escape from the dictates and constriction of her parents and grandmother; Freddie saw the possibility of a considerable improvement in his own social standing. He also, having raised the delicate matter of his being regularly paid for work done at the hall, discovered that the rumours of pecuniary distress in the Belshire family stemmed from the fact that Doreen's aged grandmother—the honourable Mrs Cecily deVere and the last in direct line of the revered family who had built the hall—still controlled the family fortune, which Doreen was sure was certainly sufficient to fund any necessary repair to and restoration of the estate. Having disapproved of her daughter's choice of husband, the old lady was loath to part with any money that might benefit Doreen's mother and father. She was, however, inordinately fond of her granddaughter and still retained pride in the hall and its lands. Once Freddie had managed to secure an audience with the honourable old lady and his best manners and charm had, despite herself, impressed Mrs deVere, he was assured of prompt settlement of his firm's future invoices. He also became determined on two things: he would restore the hall to something like its former glory; and he would marry Doreen and, eventually, become master of Avonbridge Hall. His expectations were fulfilled far sooner than even he might have imagined.

Whilst Freddie Wells epitomised the self-made man of humble origin, his future wife was almost the opposite—an opposite that attracted. Doreen was a maid by herself in far from humble surroundings—she had been a lonely child since the premature death of her elder brother Tristan. Despite being separated by five years, she and Tristan had been boon companions, playing together in the vastness of Avonbridge Hall and, when they were allowed, in its surrounding parklands. Doreen had been devastated when Tris had been packed off to boarding school in far-off Devon; it had been no consolation to her to be told that in five years time she, too, would be sent to a good school with other girls. Her brother's letters arrived regularly every week for almost a year from which she learned of his distaste for lessons, games and, most of all, the school army cadet force. Attempting to share her concern for his misery with her parents, she had been forcefully told that Tristan would 'come to like it' and that it would 'make a man of him.' The prophecy proved false as Tristan failed to live into his teen years: posted as a marker in the Cadet Corps' shooting butts, he misheard the order 'duck' as 'look' and naively standing to peer over the parapet became a mark instead of a marker; the .303 bullet hit the dead centre of his forehead. The marksman subsequently suffered a nervous breakdown and was transferred to an asylum for life. Tristan's body was returned to Avonbridge with a letter of deep condolence from the school for the aggrieved family. Fortunately for the school, none of the family wished to view the body and the twelve-year-old boy remained in the coffin supplied (as a form of apology?) that was buried in the family plot. The accident became an accepted tragedy and Mr and Mrs Belshire determined to resume their former life of hunting and socialising; in this they were disappointed as Mrs deVere, tired of their wasteful ways, reduced their allowance in the hopes that it might force that wastrel Anthony to obtain gainful employment. Her hopes were dashed against Anthony's complete inability to persuade any prospective employer of his abilities—this being due to his having no abilities. The hall's horses were sold and the stables fell into disuse. Over the ensuing four years, despite the fate that had befallen her beloved brother, Doreen increasingly looked forward to being sent away to school.

The school to which she was sent was run by a former acquaintance of her grandmother and, since grandmother was paying, no one else was permitted an opinion on Annalie Drummond's Academy for Girls in Overbury. The likes of Mrs Cecily deVere were unlikely to overhear such cynical observations as those that made the mnemonic apt: ADAGIO being 'a slow movement'. Jealous critics also observed that at Drummonds the traditional 3Rs of reading, writing and arithmetic were replaced by unReal Righteous aRrogance. Doreen survived her schooling due to her intelligence and a latent ability to dominate her fellow pupils by power of voice and personality. Academically, she shone in the first two of what outsiders considered the neglected Rs as well as history and art. The latter was not a subject in which National Examiners of the 1930s felt inclined to award diplomas, so that talent remained unrewarded until Doreen had left the despised academy in possession of three top graded School Certificates of Education. Unlike her parents, still mired in misery and passing their time playing games of patience and walking around the deteriorating estate, Doreen was determined to become financially independent. Her doting grandmother was delighted by her ambition and equally pleased to fund any worthwhile venture.

Mrs deVere's first capital outlay on behalf of Doreen's desires was, despite feeling it an 'unladylike manner of conveyance', the purchase of a Raleigh ladies bicycle, on which conveyance Doreen daily descended into Avonbridge in search of gainful employment. Charming her way into the confidence of the clerk in charge of advertising at the *Avonbridge Gazette,* she chanced upon an impending opening for a 'person of artistic abilities' to assist Blackband and Greenlee the local chartered surveyors' practice. The applicant must be 'willing to learn and adapt.' Presenting herself at their offices even before the local newspaper had arrived, she found Steven Blackband admiring of her initiative and enthusiasm; in less than two weeks from acquiring transport, Doreen had obtained a job. Technical drawing, whilst rather tedious, posed her no problems. Her willingness to research and master photography, on which the practice felt they were spending far too much with Frank Fortune's Photographic Studio, ensured her acceptance on a three-months' trial period. B & G regretted their lack of space in which to establish their own photography department. Doreen, hoping grandmama would be willing, boldly offered to provide premises. Grandmama was willing and, unknown to her pathetic parents, Doreen set about establishing herself an art studio and photographic laboratory in the small house adjacent to the stables that had been the former home of the stable master. She learned quickly and within two years Blackband and Greenlee wondered how they had ever managed without her. From her studio and laboratory she supplied not only their requirements but, with their cognisance and grudging assent, provided regular service to other local establishments.

In visiting her clever young protégé's conversion, Cecily deVere could not fail to notice the sad state into which both the exterior of the hall and it's outbuildings had fallen. Thus it was that she instructed Anthony and Constance to find a suitable person to effect repairs and conduct ongoing maintenance of the entire estate.

Consequently, Doreen, on taking a breath of fresh air after an hour of developing photographs, found a curious, strong and forthright young man inspecting the stable block. They found instant attraction to and for each other, Freddie was fascinated with Doreen's studio and laboratory and was quite honest with her as to how her talents could complement his own work and ambitions. Neither had had much close experience with a member of the opposite sex, yet they found no awkwardness or embarrassment with each other. Within a month Freddie had proposed marriage.

CHAPTER THIRTY-THREE
FREDDIE AND DOREEN WELLS
1946 TO 1970

Doreen deVere Belshire accepted Freddie Wells's proposal and became a
May bride. At the suggestion of the controlling Mrs deVere, her grand-
daughter's new husband left his rented lodgings in the town and the newly-
weds took the recently renovated (by Freddie) west wing as their home. The
wing had three bedrooms, two reception rooms, a properly modernised
bathroom, kitchen, scullery and laundry room; in other words a self-
contained home for the newly-weds. And with almost indecent haste, Mrs
Wells became pregnant. The delighted grandparents and great-grandparent
in waiting were, however, never to see or hear the newborn heir to the hall.

During the war, the family's motor vehicles had been left untouched,
but properly protected in the hall garage—a cavernous space capable
of holding three times the pair of cars therein. As a little petrol
became available—Freddie was able to inflate his 'essential' business
requirements—the 1938 Standard 12 was again shod with wheels and the
engine tested and found sound. The interior had been the latest thing
in car fashion when it rolled from the factory: leather seats and drop-
down picnic tables behind the front seats. Mrs deVere could resume being
transported in something approaching the luxury she felt to be her due.
The first regular journey resumed was to church every Sunday morning
after which she and her daughter were driven to the best restaurant
in the area for lunch. No chauffeur having been retained, the driving
duties fell to Mr Belshire whose abilities as a chauffeur matched his other
practical shortcomings. Apart from his inability to drive with any great
competence, Anthony Belshire felt it demeaning to his self-deceiving
dignity to sit alone in the front seat grinding gears whilst his wife and
mother-in-law sat in the rear seats.

One dull August afternoon, the car did not return from the Sunday
outing. Anthony Belshire, his never very swift reactions dulled by an excess
of wine with lunch, swerved to avoid a horse and cart and, panicking,
pressed his right foot hard down on the accelerator instead of the brake
pedal. The pre-war steering failed to accommodate Anthony's frantic

wheel wrestling as the car veered off the road, crashed through a feeble fence and continued down a grassy bank into the river: a river swelled by summer rain. By the time help arrived in the form of an aged farmer and his boy—neither of whom could swim—Mrs deVere had breathed her last gulp of river water, Mrs Belshire was knee deep in the shallows and a hysterical Mr Belshire was running up and down the river bank yelling for assistance. Mrs Belshire survived her mother by less than a week— immersion in a cold river after being deprived of wholesome food for five years having brought on a fatal bout of pneumonia. Anthony Belshire walked alone behind two coffins at two funerals held on successive days. Jennifer, her pregnancy not yet apparent, was supported by her husband of a few months. Attendance at either last rite was sparse.

The senior partner of Ivens, Ivens and Horton, solicitors to the deVere family for generations, felt it more suitable and sympathetic to defer reading the wills of the deceased until after the second funeral. Accordingly, a weakened Anthony Belshire, racked by constant coughing, was joined by his only daughter and her husband in the seldom-used drawing room of the hall at 11.00 a.m. on one of the few sunny days in late August, 1946, to hear what Anthony certainly hoped would be something to his advantage—in which hope he was to be disappointed.

Ivor Ivens cleared his throat, adjusted his spectacles further up his nose and began, 'I'll start, if I may, with the will of the late Mrs Constance Belshire. She leaves everything of which she died possessed to her husband Mr Anthony Belshire. Sadly, she was possessed of very little, Mr Belshire, there will be no incidence of estate duty arising in this case.'

Belshire suppressed his coughing for sufficient time to enquire how his late mother-in-law's testamentary dispositions would affect his late wife's estate.

Ivor Ivens regarded him with a more mournful countenance before continuing, 'The late Mrs Cecily deVere revised her will annually, as you may know. Her last will and testament, made following Mr and Mrs Wells's wedding, is little changed to previous provisions. After a few small gifts to former family retainers—one of whom has since died, and whose share therefore reverts to the principal beneficiary—she left Avonbridge Hall, its lands and contents, together with a considerable sum invested in Gilt Edged Securities and several thousands of pounds held at Lloyds Bank,' he paused—the small audience held its collective breath—'to her granddaughter, Mrs Doreen deVere Wells. She expressed the hope that she and her industrious husband will restore the family home to its former glory.'

There followed a short pause before Anthony Belshire burst forth with indignant expostulation interspersed with pitiful fits of coughing. Doreen sought to calm her inconsolable father with assurances that he would be looked after. Freddie tried his hardest to subdue the near proprietary smirk that constantly threatened to invade his features. So upset did her father continue to be that Doreen felt it best to take him upstairs and to summon a doctor.

'Please explain any further details and what happens now to my husband, Mr Ivens,' Doreen instructed as she left the room. Left in peace with the aged lawyer, Freddie quickly ascertained that something called probate would be applied for and that a valuation of the hall and its lands and contents would be necessary before fixing the amount of estate duty payable. Ivens felt this might take a few weeks after which, unless Mr Belshire chose to challenge the will—something he had a right to do—Mrs Wells would become the sole owner of Avonbridge Hall and all within and in the near beyond. Ivens's own estimate, to which he stressed Mr Wells was not to rely upon at this early stage, was that Mrs Wells net inheritance would be worth close to half a million pounds.

Anthony Belshire did not contest the will since, within days of learning that he was now reliant upon his daughter and her bombastic builder husband, he succumbed to bronchial pneumonia—thus necessitating the return to the hall of undertaker Christian Harley to arrange a third family funeral. As he supported his weeping wife behind a third coffin, Freddie Wells reflected that the vagaries of fortune were, indeed, strange and that it behoved him to build—in every sense of the word—upon the unexpected wealth of which his still new wife had suddenly become mistress.

Ivor Ivens's unreliable valuation of the Estate of Doreen's grandmother proved to be cannily accurate. The liquid assets were more than sufficient to fund the restoration of not only the hall but the various outbuildings pertinent to it in as gracious a style of living as could be achieved in the austere post-war days. The rental income from the two farms and five habitable cottages in the extensive grounds seemed, to Freddie, a poor return on even the low valuation accorded them in the settlement of the estate. His accountant, Stanley Roberts of Edward Chamberlain and Silk, agreed and recommended the services of estate agent Stanley Kempice—known locally as Honest Stan—in the removal and relocation of existing tenants. Farmers Jim and Gerald Lloyd were only too pleased to cease tilling the land and retire with what they felt to be a generous severance, the younger Patrick Parker proved more reluctant to quit his inherited tenancy and, in what proved a compromise favourable to both parties, agreed to surrender one third of his land—that adjoining the Lloyd lands—and retain the profitable pig and poultry rearing portion and the fine family farmhouse. Freddie's part of the compromise involved restoration of the farmhouse and the retaining walls of the reduced tenancy. As long as the pig portion remained down wind he and Doreen were content with the arrangement—particularly the provision that their Christmas turkey and pork joints would be supplied as a rental supplement.

The residents of the five cottages, all being long past the first flush of youth, were content to be transferred to the nearby home for the elderly—built, of course, by Wells Builders. After restoring some of the surrounding walls of the estate, Freddie and Doreen agreed that she should finance the diversion of the remaining walls in order to separate the former farm land and the soon to be demolished cottages. The deVere estate of fashionable, affordable homes designed by Doreen deVere Design and built by Wells Builders Limited, supervised by Blackband and Greenlee, were sold with amazing pace by Kempice and Oldacre and established Freddie as the 'builder of choice' in the West Midlands. He repaid his doting wife in both cash and shares in Wells Builders Limited.

Now that Freddie, Doreen and their daughter were the only residents of the hall, and the restoration was no longer inhibited by the needs of others, the work proceeded apace after completion of the deVere estate. Doreen, Freddie, Jenny and the new nanny moved into the suite of rooms in the main hall leaving the west wing available for visiting friends and dignitaries—they were both convinced that important persons would wish to visit—and the east wing as staff accommodation. Entertaining was only distantly recollected by Doreen from her early childhood. Nevertheless she persuaded Freddie—he needed little persuasion—that dinner parties, soirées and the once annual Avonbridge autumn ball should be revived. They could well afford such hospitality as business for both of them continued to expand. Freddie, detecting the beginnings of the DIY boom, opened Avonbridge's first combined builders' merchants and DIY shop on Avon Road North; it did a roaring trade. He moved his yard and business garages from the hall stables in order to afford unhindered access to Doreen's art and photographic studios, further small craft workshops were made from the remaining space and were swiftly taken up by talented tenants. The offices of Wells Builders remained in the two end stables—now made one, of course.

All work and no play can, as the old adage indicates, make for dull persons. Doreen joined the Avonbridge branch of the Women's Institute and, finding them losing their tenuous tenancy in town, persuaded Freddie that the large room at the rear of the old cricket pavilion could easily be restored for use both in and out of the cricket season. The cricket pitch was mown, marked out and after a few trial charity matches was pronounced better than the old council pitch for the local eleven.

Freddie found himself elected honorary president of the Avonbridge and District Cricket Club. He had never played and never did—deeming it a dangerous sport due to the hard ball. Perversely he had, whilst in the services, played and enjoyed rugby football. He had no great skill or aptitude for the game, but as a stalwart front-row forward of considerable strength and aggression he maintained a regular place in the town's 4th Fifteen with occasional games for the 3rds over four or five seasons before the need to train took too much of his time and energy and he 'hung his boots'. He never lost touch with the social side of the rugby club and, as a man known to willingly stand his corner, he soon became a member of the committee. By 1970 he was chairman of the rugby club and president of the cricket club, whilst Doreen was a twice past president of Avonbridge Women's Institute and an active member of the W.I. County Executive.

Any neglect of their dear daughter was entirely unintentional . . .

CHAPTER THIRTY-FOUR
JENNIFER DOREEN WELLS—CHILDHOOD AND EDUCATION
1947 TO 1964

It was no fault of Jennifer Doreen Wells—for ever known as Jenny—that her birth followed so closely upon the triple tragedy of the deaths of those who would have been her only known grandparents and great-grandmamma—the latter honourable. Her christening was a muted affair—not that she was aware of that. During her early years the apparently frenzied daily activity around her home of builders, decorators and other noisy and sometimes noisome workers imbued her with a child's inner fear of the world beyond her nursery and her beloved nanny. Physically, she grew to resemble the physical traits of her parents: a tall, well-built mother and strong, stocky father. Those parents' increasing wealth and indulgence of her appetite led to the description—only uttered behind her back—of Big Jenny. It was not entirely apposite, a figure of 44"-33"-42" could be said to resemble an hour-glass—albeit one standing at five feet and nine inches in stockinged feet. Her parents' loud confidence and occasional even louder rows added to Jenny's nervous disposition and her repressed lack of speech at home. Initial education at the local convent preparatory school only caused the young Jenny to withdraw further into herself—the intimidating Sisters of (little) Mercy and their compulsory worship frightening her into her only vigorous daily exercise of cycling home as fast as her sturdy legs could manage. Academically, she was far ahead of any fellow convent pupils—something else that contributed to her solitary existence. Jenny's greatest joy as a child was her bicycle excursions on fine weekends into the country where she treasured the sound of birdsong and the peaceful silences between. She became a self-taught authority for her age on both birds and botany.

Everything changed when she left the convent and, at her father's insistence ('teach her what the world's about') moved to Grove Street School, a mixed secondary school. Here she mingled with a cross section of Avonbridge children under the tutelage of enlightened men and women overseen by an immensely tall and universally respected headmaster. Jenny soon discovered that attempting to hide away made her an unwanted outsider. Wanting to be inside the activities, she gradually learned to make friends with her fellow pupils, of whatever background. She became a happier, more outgoing child.

Doreen Wells, with any possible opposition from her grandmamma now far removed, was determined her daughter would not be a victim of what she considered the inadequate standards of education and attempts to create superior snobs to which she herself had been subjected. She remained, however, convinced of the value of independence from parental indulgence offered by boarding schools. The Women's Institute monthly magazine gave a glowing report on the fine facilities and distinguished alumni of what, although Doreen did not appreciate it, had been the editor's alma mater. By such random means can the formative years of a young person's life be decreed. Jenny was transported in the recently acquired Rolls Royce to the imposing halls of residence in the Surrey Downs where she was, holiday time excepted, to spend almost the next five years. Again she excelled scholastically and, despite her size and initial reluctance to participate in physical activity, found she enjoyed hockey. Her bulk allied to some lack of speed over the ground persuaded the popular and insightful games mistress, Miss Gasson, to train her as a goalkeeper. Concentration, practice and an acquired feel for the game made Jenny good enough to represent the school and, in her final year, Surrey. The school's fine facilities sharpened her intellect and earned her excellent grades.

CHAPTER THIRTY-FIVE
JENNIFER DOREEN WELLS—VICTIM AND ESCAPER
SUMMER 1964

In even the best establishments it is possible for evil to develop unseen. In Jenny's year a gang of bullies had been recruited by the daughter of a well-known minor peer. Cruel of face and nature, the honourable Cynthia Cholmondely-Price and her cronies shamelessly manipulated the rules and their fellow pupils. They were also crafty enough to avoid stricture and punishment since none of their victims were prepared to face the physical consequences of blabbing.

Jenny was popular amongst both staff and pupils—something infrequently experienced by those at the top of the form. She also had, despite hockey and compulsory sessions in the gymnasium, exceedingly big breasts—such that without proper restraint by brassiere she may have been in danger of incurring a blow in the face. It was not a blow to the face she received from Cynthia and her malevolent mates, but several violent blows to her ankles with hockey sticks. Jenny limped, in great pain, to the school sanatorium. Whilst the school matron Mrs Bell was still applying cold compresses, Miss Gasson rushed in—deeply concerned both for Jenny and for the school team who would be without their first choice goalkeeper for the morrow's match. She also suspected how Jenny had become lame; for some months the staff had sought in vain for a credible informant against Cynthia Cholmondely-Price and her cohorts. Being a big girl and her father's daughter, Jenny was not intimidated by threats and willingly told Miss Gasson and, following her, the headmistress how and by whom she had been attacked. To the disappointment of Jenny and numerous previous victims the gang members, on their own assurances that they were sorry and would not transgress again, were only lectured and made to serve a few hours detention.

After gym it was compulsory for all girls to shower. It was during one such unsupervised ritual laving that the cruel creatures sought their revenge on the informant. As Jenny wrapped a large towel around her she was seized by three of the naked 'we'll not transgress again' gang, who dragged her to the toilets at the end of the shower room and forced her to sit on a toilet. After a prolonged tug of war that, being one against four, Jenny was never going to win, her towel was torn away and Cynthia and her lieutenants, all considerably less well-endowed than Jenny, told her that she was to be punished as a fat freak. After some chanting of Jenny's gigantic titties and painful squeezing of poor Jenny's aptly styled breasts, Cynthia announced their intent of removing her bosoms to their own bony frontages. Two of them held Jenny back on the toilet whilst others held her strong legs down and Cynthia roughly seized her breasts. Knives were produced for the unlikely transfer of flesh: one was thrust into her upper left breast and another carved a long gash along her right. Jenny had an inherited vocal power of which many an operatic diva would be proud, she screamed in agony.

'Shut up,' yelled Cynthia, 'or you'll be burned as well. It's what they did to witches.'

Jenny screamed even louder. Before her cries brought two school mistresses and a senior prefect—all of whom were shocked witnesses of the assault—lighted cigarettes had been pressed around her wounds. Jenny was rushed to the school sanatorium and the best balms Mrs Bell and a hastily summoned and appalled doctor could find were applied. Jenny was gently told that whilst they were sure the wounds would heal, she was likely to be left with considerable scarring. She wept.

Later that evening she received a visit from the deputy headmistress, Miss Batty, known behind her back as 'Bony Batty'. Displaying a hitherto unsuspected kind and sympathetic nature, she assured Jenny that 'the evil perpetrators of this outrageous assault' were being expelled forthwith. Jenny generously replied she was pleased others would be spared their cruelty. Miss Batty then, hesitantly, advised Jenny of her duty to inform Jenny's parents about the assault, whilst the incident was quite unprecedented it was 'only right' that they should be given the option of removing their daughter from the school. Jenny was enjoying school life. With the bullies gone she had no wish to be removed.

To Miss Batty's apparent surprise and, she honestly had to admit, relief, Jenny firmly asked, 'Please, Miss Batty, will you leave my parents out of this, if you can? They'll only fuss and . . . well, it wouldn't be good for the school, would it?'

The deputy head praised Jenny's magnanimity, fussily tucked Jenny her into bed as far as the dressings allowed and actually kissed her on the forehead.

'Sleep well if you can, dear,' she said gently. 'I'll try to pop in when I can.'

Jenny did sleep, albeit fitfully. Mrs Bell carefully tended Jenny's wounds every day. The sanatorium was one of the school facilities not greatly used and for most of her time there Jenny was the sole occupant—certainly during the evenings and night. There was what Mrs Bell described as 'the usual cuts and bruises' during the day and every patient expressed sympathies to and for Jenny. She also received updated tuition from several sympathetic teachers. Miss Batty 'popped in' as she had promised most evenings—each time giving Jenny a goodnight kiss. Jenny didn't object to the kiss, but it was with smiling stoicism that she suffered the deputy head's tobacco-tainted breath, which was also sometimes supplemented by stale alcohol.

After ten days the breast dressings were removed. Jenny was still in some pain but, she supposed, it was progress. The doctor and Mrs Bell spoke of the possibility of plastic surgery to remove the ugly scarring in a year's time, but Jenny, whilst expressing gratitude for their advice, was fully aware that she alone could not meet such an expensive bill; telling her parents would be necessary and she still dreaded her father's re-action. Miss Batty made her usual visit that evening and, rather to Jenny's surprise, asked if she might see the wounds. It was ingrained in all pupils that they should obey the staff at all times so Jenny succumbed to Miss Batty lifting each of her breasts to examine the damage. She was gentle but also, it seemed to Jenny, eager, and the handling bore a close resemblance to fondling. She said nothing. That evening's kiss was on her cheek.

For the next week the deputy head continued her evening visits—always arriving shortly after Mrs Bell had left. Her inspection and handling of Jenny continued—always with solicitous enquiry that she wasn't hurting Jenny there. As the regular ritual gave her little pain Jenny could do little but offer her assurance that it was alright. On the Saturday Miss Batty, for the first time, brought biscuits and a bottle of sherry with two glasses.

'I thought a drink might cheer you up, Jenny,' she said—hesitantly adding, 'You do drink wine, dear?'

It seemed odd—alcohol was strictly forbidden on school premises. But as Jenny had never been forbidden alcohol at home she had to be honest and admit that she did drink and enjoyed a good sherry. The Batty bottle did not contain a good sherry but, feeling it was a kind gesture, Jenny sipped and forced a smile of approval. The deputy head seemed determined to stay and chat whilst they emptied the bottle and it was obvious to Jenny something was worrying the deputy head. After the third glass Miss Batty confessed her concern.

'Jenny, dear, I'm afraid a parent of one of the expelled girls is threatening to sue the school. After your generosity in keeping this business from your parents it's so unfair that we could still receive adverse publicity.'

'Oh dear, Miss Batty. Am I likely to be dragged into it?'

'It's very likely, I fear, Jenny. But,' she looked firmly at Jenny, 'the head and I feel there might be a way to avert legal action and we feel you should approve before we implement such a strategy.'

'I'll do what I can to help the school, Miss Batty, but I can't see how I can help.'

'What we thought we could do to counter his unwarranted action and avoid the adverse publicity it would attract to the school, would be to inform him that your father was very close to suing his daughter for assault. We could suggest that trying to have his horrible daughter reinstated would certainly make Mr Wells take action. Would you mind us doing that, Jenny?'

'I wouldn't—just so long as father isn't actually involved—or even knows.'

'Thank you, dear. I can't guarantee it will stop any action against the school, or that it won't get to your father's attention—but it seems worth a try.'

Jenny sat and thought. Miss Batty replenished their glasses.

'Alright. If the school is willing to take the risk, I'll do the same,' said Jenny.

'Oh, thank you, dear,' said the smiling deputy head. 'You are a kind, generous girl, you know. You have borne your suffering very bravely.'

'What I can't understand, Miss Batty, is why they should do . . . what they did.'

'Some people are sadistic by nature, Jenny. And, of course, they were very jealous, you know.'

'That's silly, though, Miss Batty. I can't help how I am. Why should they resent it?'

'Well, dear, it may seem strange to you, but for those of us who have not been as well-blessed physically as you, it is easy to resent your splendid . . . development. I can well understand it myself.'

'*You*, Miss Batty?'

'Oh, yes, dear,' answered Miss Batty. 'How would you feel if these were all you had?' And before Jenny's shocked gaze the older woman removed her blouse to expose a small pair of breasts with hard, thrusting nipples. Whilst Jenny sat stupefied at this sudden wantonness by someone who should be an example to her, Miss Batty seized Jenny's free hand and placed it over one of her eager little breasts. Jenny tried to remove her hand but it was held firmly clamped to the small bosom. She put down her sherry glass preparatory to making a two handed move to free herself.

'You can feel the other one, as well, dear,' leered Miss Batty.

'Well, actually I was——'

'Go on, Jenny—feel it,' ordered the deputy head.

Hesitantly, Jenny did as she was ordered. The older woman was smiling at her.

'The tobacco breath's still at some distance,' was Jenny's strange thought, which was of little comfort. Comfort was not on Miss Batty's agenda. She became more dictatorial and Jenny became more confused, embarrassed and ashamed.

'Move them about, Jenny,' she commanded, 'Like this,' and, suiting the action to the word, she began vigorously squeezing and massaging the younger girl's breasts with little of her previous concern for any hurt to the recipient.

'This is nice, Jenny,' she stated as a fact not to be argued against. 'Haven't you done this with anyone else in the dorm, child?'

'No, Miss Batty,' said Jenny. It was a lie as she and Sally from the next bed had had quite a few furtive fumbles together, but she was intent on being released from the older woman's clutches.

Before Jenny could say more Batty spoke again, 'It's lovely, child. You'll come to love being with me.'

Jenny could think of no reply that would help her to be free. Her tormentor was now utterly absorbed in seeking and, as she thought, giving sensual pleasures. Temporarily released from bosomy bondage, Jenny's relief was short lived as the now naked, foul-breathed, bony woman flung back the sheet and laid herself atop of Jenny.

'Should we be doing this, Miss Batty?' she blurted out.

'Of course not—but we must enjoy ourselves when we can, my dear,' came the breathy reply. Before Jenny could say more she found her hand being firmly placed between the deputy head's legs and the demanding woman's bony hand thrust between her own thighs. She gasped.

'See, Jenny. You like it. Don't you?' The latter was definitely a command.

Jenny felt ashamed, alarmed and, despite herself, aroused. She lay holding the older woman's wet crotch and wondering when and how this sexual nightmare would end.

It ended rather more quickly than had seemed possible as they heard the sound of the outer door opening and Mrs Bell's voice calling to whom she believed to be the only occupant.

'It's only me, Jenny . . . Forget my head one of these days, I will.'

If Jenny had been surprised at Miss Batty's swift strip she was now amazed at the celerity with which the older woman assumed her clothes and composure.

'Not a word, young one,' she whispered threateningly before throwing the sheet over Jenny and greeting matron with the assurance that she was just tucking Jenny in after having a lovely, long chat.'

'Goodnight, now, dear Jenny,' said Miss Batty rather too loudly. 'Sweet dreams.'

As she bent to plant a kiss on Jenny's forehead she whispered, 'We'll continue tomorrow, love.'

'Time we left Jenny to get her beauty sleep, Matron,' she then barked in her best authoritarian style.

'Quite, Miss Batty,' replied Mrs Bell, gathering up her forgotten shopping from the vestibule. 'See you on Monday, Jenny.'

The outer door slammed. Jenny wiped away her tears and ran to the shower room where she tried to scrub away the feelings of shame and disgust. She slept little and whenever she dozed woke with a start of revulsion at remembered images of the brazen predator she had once known only as the deputy headmistress. She spent Sunday morning in a constant state of dread—sometimes alleviated by the unfulfilled and unworthy hope that another pupil would be taken seriously ill and consigned to the next bed. After a lunch brought by the duty prefect for which Jenny was grateful, but for which she could summon no appetite, she put on the biggest, thickest pair of panties she possessed in the hopes of deterring further advances.

At five o'clock her worst fears were realised. The door opened and an eerily smiling—leering would have been more accurate—Miss Batty arrived, locking the door behind her. There were no preliminaries. The lecherous woman stripped off her clothes and tore away the sheet to which Jenny had been vainly clinging for ineffective protection.

'Oh, you little tease,' cooed Miss Batty. She seized hold of the front of Jenny's panties and with strength surprising in one so slight, tore them away—physically lifting Jenny from the bed as she did so. Jenny was terrified. The terrible woman had a sort of harness about her lower parts that sported a profusion of coarse hair hiding her own sparse pubic growth. Instead of instantly climbing in beside Jenny, Batty bent down, exposing a most unattractive rear, and extracted something from the large handbag she had placed on the floor.

'I've a proper treat for us, tonight, Jenny,' she gasped—almost slavering with anticipation. 'Look at this.' She waved a stiff, reddish-pink model of a male sex organ at Jenny before inserting it to protrude from the elasticated strapping.

'Right, my dear, let's get to it, shall we?' urged the repulsive creature.

Jenny was frozen with fright and horror. Again the passionate strength of the older woman proved too great for poor Jenny and, despite vainly trying to resist, her legs were forced apart and she lost her maidenhead, her dignity and her self-respect.

Having satiated herself, the beastly Batty climbed from the bed, divested herself of the dildo and energetically played awhile with herself whilst looking at the naked and devastated schoolgirl she had so violently abused.

Eventually she spoke—and there was no tenderness in her tone now, 'I can see it was your first time, Wells,' she said. 'You'll enjoy it more the next time, though. Tell Mrs Bell you had a sudden period. She'll have to believe it. I'll see you again tomorrow night after lights out, Jenny Wells of the big breasts.'

This time there was no parting kiss.

Again Jenny spent ages under the shower. She could not bring herself to lie on the bloody bed of shame, but wrapped herself in blankets from other beds and sat in the chair where she cried until it seemed she could cry no more.

Exhausted as she was, sleep would not come. As the night wore on some clarity of thought began to emerge. She knew that her word against that of the deputy head would be dismissed as unfounded vilification. She knew she could not endure another bout with Batty and her simulated sex act. She reached the only possible conclusion: she must escape. Determining on that she began to plan how it could be successfully accomplished.

'Good morning, Jenny,' trilled Mrs Bell making her usual prompt arrival at 8.30. Then, observing that her only patient was out of bed, had stripped the bed as was usual on a Monday and, presumably, had already put the sheets in the laundry basket, she asked how Jenny had slept. Hoping her lie would go undetected Jenny replied that she felt so much better that all she really wanted was to go for a walk in the fresh air. And, the whole purpose of her deceit, could she have her daytime clothes, please?

'Certainly, Jenny,' was the prompt reply. Followed by the jolting statement that, 'The doctor and I wanted to send you out last week—but Miss Batty felt you should have a few more days rest and recuperation.'

Having thus unconsciously damned the deputy head, Mrs Bell unlocked the clothes room and, hers being the only set of clothes currently retained, Jenny was easily enabled to dress for the first time in many weeks.

'Take as long as you like—but don't exhaust yourself,' cautioned the unsuspecting matron as her patient set forth on her rehabilitating walk.

'You'll have to sleep another night here before the doctor can sign you off to the dormitory,' were Mrs Bell's last words to Jenny.

Desperately though Jenny wanted to thank Mrs Bell for all her care and kindness, she dared not trust herself to say more than a brief, 'Yes, thank you,' before walking, painfully due to the pain she still felt at the juncture of her legs, towards the main school. By now, as she knew and had counted upon in her nocturnal plans, all pupils and staff would be in morning assembly. Indicative of the poor security of a trusting, insular establishment, there was no one in or near the personal lockers. Opening her own locker Jenny took out her accumulated pocket money—more than she remembered—thrust a few portable belongings into the leather travelling case her mother had gifted for her seventeenth birthday before, the while hoping not to be seen, walking away across the playing fields. Her hopes were fulfilled. On the far side of the fields, out of sight of the main buildings, she slipped through a gap in the hedge into a lane leading, as she knew, to the main road. Her luck continued as a kindly service bus driver stopped in response to her waving arm and pleading face. An hour later Jennifer Doreen Wells alighted in the nearest town and, as she had planned and also dreaded, telephoned Avonbridge Hall, reversing the charges, from a public telephone box. Her mother accepted the charge, listened to her distressed daughter's tale of physical bullying to which she had been subjected (Jenny had decided it would be easier to relate only the earlier 'ankle' incident) and reluctantly agreed to collect her truant daughter from a Brighton Hotel where the family were known and where Jenny would be allowed to pledge her mother's credit until Doreen arrived. Jenny's great escape had been successful.

CHAPTER THIRTY-SIX
Jennifer Doreen Wells—a Career, a Friend and a Future
1964 to 1970

Fortunately, Freddie was concerned with yet another big building contract when Jenny arrived home and left Doreen to deal with their unexpectedly returned daughter. Doreen contacted the school and, to her surprise, the deputy head waived any outstanding fees and agreed to forward Jenny's just released Certificates of Education. Doreen attributed her daughter's 'Yes, I suppose,' response to her branding Miss Batty as kind and obliging to teenage attitude. She surrendered to Jenny's plea for a few weeks' quiet rest to recover from the traumas of being bullied.

'Little does she know,' thought Jenny, who was still certain that giving her mother a true account of her reason for abandoning education was as likely to be believed as her having achieved unassisted flight. To Jenny's surprise, Dr Peter Young seemed to believe her and, in response to her pleadings, agreed to respect her confidence. She wondered how much blame he attributed to herself rather than Batty—particularly in light of her insistence that her confidences should go no further—but the kind doctor prescribed painkillers and soothing ointment for her damaged breasts. There was little he could do for her state of mind. He chose to ignore the state of her vagina. Over the next weeks, cycle rides being too painful to contemplate, long walks in the fresh air whether rain or shine gradually restored some semblance of mental balance for Jenny. She knew, as she had for many months, what she hoped for in her future.

After three weeks of having their proven intelligent daughter mooning about, as Freddie termed it, Mr and Mrs Wells agreed enough was enough and that the girl should make some decisions about her future. In his usual manner—or lack thereof—Freddie confronted the issue over Saturday morning breakfast. His blunt question, 'What do you want to do with yourself then, Jenny?' received a prompt reply.

'I want to be a florist.'

The elder Wells were surprised and a little relieved. After a moments pause, Freddie posed the next obvious question, 'And how is that to be achieved?'

The well-detailed response impressed both parents. They learned that the top society florist in the country, Mrs Constance Spry, had established an exclusive two-year training course at her exclusive floristry shop off Park Lane in London. Although Mrs Spry had now passed to the great flower bed in the sky, the course continued and a place was still available beginning in mid September. The cost was not inconsiderable, but Jenny was confident she would, in the fullness of time, be able to repay her parents. As she had hoped, any question of a loan was instantly dismissed and, after a few telephone calls to London, Freddie 'Wealthy' Wells forwarded the first half-year's non-refundable course fees. On an exploratory trip to the nation's capital, a small but nonetheless expensive second-floor flat in Porchester Gardens, Bayswater—close to but definitely not overlooking Hyde Park—was viewed, disapproved of by Doreen, but insisted upon by Jenny, and her tenancy secured for two years. The landlord was even more delighted than the tenant. Jenny Wells departed Avonbridge for what was to become the happiest two years of her life so far.

Her aptitude in her chosen career delighted both herself and her tutors/employers. The pace of London life wherein she had to walk and often run—even up and down the Underground escalators—did wonders for Jenny's waist and hips. The initial need, to eat out also contributed to her reduced inches since the café food she could obtain in and around Bayswater was not conducive to either completion or digestion. Her small flat comprised a tiny lounge, two bedrooms—one single, one double, a tiny bathroom and toilet, and a surprisingly spacious kitchen with an almost new modern cooker. Aided by the purchase of some books on cooking, including Mrs Spry's, and a few hints from fellow workers—'If you can read, you can cook!' was the most apt—Jenny became adept at cooking. She enjoyed the creative aspect as well as the resultant dishes. After two months exercising her new-found culinary talent she was emboldened to issue a return invitation to Terri Buchanan, a fellow student whose hospitality she had accepted and enjoyed. Terri—'the vicar named me Theresa, but I've always been known as Terri'—was as tall as Jenny but, in contrast to Jenny's full figure and mousy brown, hard-to-control hair, Terri was, whilst still full-breasted, slimmer of frame. She had long, lustrous black locks, tied back in a pony-tail for work, but let loose in the evening. Her parents had secured her a shared flat in far-off Ealing, meaning Terri did a great deal more travelling than Jenny. They had more in common than a love of floral art and botany and, for the first time in her life, Jenny found she had a real friend of her own age.

Lingering long and talking together after supper in Jenny's little flat Terri suddenly realised the tube station was closed and she would have to spend more money than she had with her on a taxi cab ride to Ealing.

'Gosh, I'm sorry, Jenny. Could you lend me a few pounds until tomorrow, please?'

As she searched in her purse another solution occurred to Jenny. Tentatively she turned to Terri, 'Look, why don't you just stay the night here? I can make up the spare bed for you—it's a bit small but it'll save you travelling tonight and in the morning.'

'Well . . . if you really don't mind?' Jenny shook her head. 'I'll help you with the bed,' finished Terri.

As Terri moved her outdoor coat and scarf from the bed to the tiny hanging cupboard, she giggled.

'What's the matter?' asked Jenny.

'I was just thinking it's been a long time since I slept in the altogether.'

Jenny joined in the giggling—before adding to the hilarity by proposing that Terri was welcome to one of her nighties—even if it might be somewhat large on her.

'Better than being too small,' said Terri.

The outcome of the solution to a too-long evening was that Terri, who disliked her Ealing flatmate, took up residence in the second bedroom of the Porchester Gardens flat. Jenny now had a close personal friend. Since they shared the costs of the small flat, each girl had more spending money than previously. Having agreed a rota, they alternately cooked and rested in the evening. Despite both girls having been boarding school pupils, there was some initial domestic modesty and almost too-considerate permission of privacy in the tiny bathroom; youth and occasional oversleeping soon swept this away and the usual careless familiarity of flatsharers became normal for both girls. As a result of these familiar habits, Terri, wandering half-asleep into what she imagined to be the vacant bathroom clad only in brief knickers, first saw Jenny's scarred bosom.

As recommended by the school doctor and confidentially confirmed by her Avonbridge GP Jenny had, since the first bout of healing, regularly applied a proprietary cream to the affected areas. It was whilst she was conducting this Sunday salving, having overlooked locking the bathroom door, that the near naked Terri was confronted by her friend with one big breast and a tube of something in one hand whilst the other applied cream to an ugly, disfiguring bosom scar. Terri had never seen Jenny without a bra before. Both friends stood immobile for several seconds—frozen in shock and shame respectively.

Terri spoke first, 'Oh, gosh, Jenny dear. I'm sorry . . . I didn't realise you were . . .' she became lost for suitable words with which to continue. She also realised that she had, even whilst offering her apology, been staring transfixed at her friend's mutilated mammaries.

'Oh, dear,' they both said in unintentional unison. It somehow seemed to ease the situation as both smiled at their united utterance. Jenny sank down on the side of the small bath and dropped the precious tube of ointment onto the bath head.

'Look, Jenny, I really am sorry. I know I shouldn't have intruded. But . . . its . . .'

'Not very nice?' answered Jenny.

'Well, no—particularly for you, dear, but, I mean, well . . .'

'How?' said Jenny, tears by now coursing down her face and dropping onto her still naked chest.

'In a word, yes,' replied Terri. Quickly adding, 'Only if you want to tell me, of course. I know I've no right . . . but . . .'

Terri joined her weeping friend by sitting on the bath-side and putting an arm around her. After an awkward moment, Jenny responded by enfolding Terri to her and giving vent to great sobs of shame and self-pity. After a few uncomfortable moments Terri suggested their current cold 'perch' could be bettered. The friends moved themselves to softer seats on the side of Terri's bed where Jenny Wells recounted the horrors of jealous taunting and the assault on her chest to which she had been subjected. Terri wisely heard her out, only speaking to offer sympathy and surprise in short utterances. When she had finished, Jenny looked Terri full in the eyes for the first time since she had intruded upon her in mid-treatment, 'Thank you for listening, Terri. I've never been able to talk properly to anyone about it before. The school matron was—well a grown-up. And our doctor at home was very kind and sympathetic— but he was a man. You're a friend so it's different . . . if you see what I mean?'

Terri sort of did.

Jenny suddenly looked at her near-naked friend and, with a giggle, said, 'Do you realise if anyone could see us they'd think we were a couple of lesbians?'

'I think if we were, Jenny dear, we'd not even have our panties on.'

'Which we do . . . Have our panties on, I mean.'

They sat looking at each other awhile before Terri, being practical, suggested that perhaps Jenny should complete the interrupted application.

'Oh, gosh. The cream's still in the bathroom,' said Jenny.

'Which is where I was going earlier and where I now need to go quite urgently,' said Terri.

'To the bathroom, then,' said Jenny.

Laughing, they walked into the bathroom where Terri sat unashamedly on the toilet watching Jenny apply her ointment. Although Terri's naked knee was against her own lower leg, Jenny realised she felt no trace of embarrassment or self-consciousness.

'Does it hurt at all?' asked Terri.

'Sometimes—but I'm used to it now,' answered Jenny.

'You really ought to have something done, Jenny.'

'I know there are people who do wonderful things. Of course I do,' said Jenny, 'but they charge an awful lot, I'm told. My parents could certainly afford it but . . . it would mean I'd have to tell them both, you see?'

Terri stood to flush the toilet—an old-style chain pull—and due to the cramped conditions left her panties around one ankle as she reached in front of her friend to wash her hands whilst Jenny screwed the cap on to the tube of ointment.

'You could have those beautiful breasts restored you know, Jenny. A friend of my uncle is one of those who do wonderful things, as you put it, in the field of plastic surgery and if you ever decide to have your wonderful tits made even more super, then let me know and I'll introduce you.'

'Thanks, Terri. I'll bear it in mind,' answered Jenny. Looking down at her chest she rather shyly asked, 'Do you really think they're . . . "wonderful"?'

'Gosh, yes, Jenny. And so should you. Scarred or not, you should be proud of them.'

Jenny had never felt any pride in her over-sized body. To find someone, especially someone of her own age and sex, expressing 'wonder' at her generous form gave her a joyous feeling of fulfilment. She turned to Terri with tears in her eyes.

'Thank you again, Terri. You make me feel better about myself.'

Looking at her friend and now naked confidant she said, boldly, 'I think yours are wonderful, as well, Terri.'

'Aaah. Come here,' said Terri. And the two friends joined themselves in a warm, loving embrace.

Jenny giggled.

'What's so funny?' queried Terri.

'You know what we said in the bedroom . . . ' she began.

'We both said quite a lot in the bedroom, Jenny.'

'Yes. I mean about being lesbians . . . Well, you haven't got any panties on now.'

'No,' answered Terri. 'D'you want to take yours off?'

Terri playfully grabbed and began to pull down the front of Jenny's only item of clothing. To Terri's surprise Jenny stiffened and stepped back—alarm in her wide open eyes.

'Sorry, love,' gasped Terri. 'Gosh, I was only fooling, Jenny.'

'Yes, sorry. I realise that. It's just . . . Oh gosh . . . I've never told anyone . . . I didn't tell you everything that happened at school before I . . . ran away.'

Terri gaped at her frightened friend, 'Don't tell me they cut and burned you . . . down there?' she asked in horror.

'Oh, no. No, no . . . But . . .' Jenny looked pleadingly at Terri. 'Can we go back to the bedroom and sit down, please, Terri? This is very difficult.'

To regain her friend's confidence, Jenny removed her panties to demonstrate the lack of any cutting or burning. Then, haltingly at first, Jenny recounted being raped by Bony Batty and why Terri unexpectedly grabbing the front of her pants had evoked the re-action it did. Terri was, of course, horrified. They discussed the impossibility of successfully suing a deputy head whose word would be believed before that of a pupil.

For the rest of the afternoon Jenny lay in the comforting arms of Terri. From then onward only one bed—the double—was occupied in the Porchester Gardens flat. To help cure Jenny of her bodily modesty they instituted nude Sundays, dressing only for dinner, and Jenny became entirely happy in nothing but her own skin.

At the end of their training, both Jenny and Terri were invited to join the full time workforce at Spry's and happily accepted the option of a further two years in the capital in the so-called Swinging Sixties. If asked for an honest appraisal of the time, both would have admitted the 'oscillation' was not all it was reputed to have been.

They attended a few 'wild' parties—at one of which, totally inebriated, they joined everyone else jumping stark naked into an outdoor swimming pool. Having 'taken the plunge' and been swiftly sobered by the temperature of the water they rapidly regained dry land and their clothes. In order to protect themselves from the advances of aroused males for whom they had no corresponding feelings, they lasciviously dried and caressed each other until they were left alone to dress and depart.

During one of their exchanges of confidence, Terri confessed she had willingly surrendered her virginity to her long-term boyfriend, Gerald, who was currently at Sandhurst Military Academy. It was tacitly agreed they would marry when he was commissioned, but in the meantime they had both agreed to be free agents. Jenny envied her friend her openness and sexual freedom, but still shied away from the approaches of young men.

In early 1965 Terri announced Gerald had a long weekend pass. He and his friend Jeremy had four tickets for *Oliver* and wanted to treat Terri and her friend to dinner at their hotel and the show. Dinner at the Carlton was sumptuous in the extreme and afterwards all four enjoyed Lionel Bart's long-running musical before returning to the Carlton for more drinks. After a while, Terri and Gerald asked to be excused and, as Terri had told Jenny would be the case, crept away to Gerald's room for the night. Jeremy was a delightful man with whom Jenny found herself entirely at ease. He insisted on escorting Jenny back to Bayswater by taxi at his expense.

'What will you do for the rest of the night, Jeremy?' queried Jenny in the taxi. She was aware that he and Gerald had booked a double room.

'Oh . . . wander about. Read a magazine and doze in a lounge chair, I suppose. Old Gerald'd do the same for me if my lady was in town.'

'Oh . . . you've got a steady girl friend, then?' asked a slightly disappointed Jenny.

'Sort of, I suppose. We have an understanding—as the saying goes. She's at finishing school in Switzerland for the next year . . . probably reaping a few Continental wild oats, if I know anything about her. . . . Oh, sorry, Jenny—didn't mean to be coarse or offensive.'

'Don't be silly, Jeremy. This is supposed to be Swinging London, you know,' answered Jenny. And, surprising herself at her boldness, she added, 'I don't like to think of you wandering about and dozing in a lounge all night.'

'And what alternative might there be, young lady?' said Jeremy—turning towards his fellow passenger with a shy smile.

'Well . . . there is a spare room in our flat. It's not the Carlton by any stretch of imagination, but the spare bed would be more comfortable than a chair—even a Carlton lounge chair.'

'Well—if you don't mind me using Terri's bed . . . She won't be sleeping there tonight, as I think you know,' ventured Jeremy.

'It is really a spare bed, Jeremy . . . Terri and I share a double . . . It's the only one made up as a matter of fact.'

'Well . . . I wouldn't want to put you to any trouble making up a bed,' said Jeremy.

They exchanged anticipatory looks. Their taxi drew up to Porchester Gardens, deposited both passengers and was paid with a generous tip. Jenny found, as Terri had told her, that there was pleasure and no pain in mutually accepted sex. From that time onwards both friends enjoyed themselves where and when they chose—although they were discriminating.

As Christmas 1966 loomed, both girls admitted to one another they were becoming bored with the slightly unreal world in which they lived and worked. They had, during occasional long weekends, visited each other's provincial homes. Both had been offered the chance of their own flower shop by a generous father.

After not very lengthy discussions the two friends decided to return to their native heaths, accept their fathers' offers and become self-employed florists and shopkeepers. In March of 1967, Terri opened Flowers for All in Lichfield. The following month, Freddie having secured the freehold of a site on Avonbridge High Street, Jenny opened Jenny's Flower Patch. Both businesses were instant and ongoing successes. The two friends remained in constant communication with one another and in the June of 1969 Jenny stood proudly and happily as chief bridesmaid at Terri's wedding to the honourable Gerald Anstruther.

CHAPTER THIRTY-SEVEN
JJ AND JENNY
NEW YEAR'S EVE 31 DECEMBER, 1970

Dances at The Swan were an ever popular feature of the Avonbridge social scene. The presence of the rugby club changing rooms downstairs and the players' happy insistence upon attending Saturday night dances ensured a galaxy of hopeful young ladies were always in attendance. In those days a dance needed to be sponsored in order that a late-night licence could be granted. Whichever local organisation was successful in securing attachment of their name to a Saturday dance at The Swan had no need to sell tickets, Saturdays were always full. The resident band, George Cookson and his Merry Men, always ensured a good time was had by all—particularly themselves, the sobriquet *merry* being a certainty. Tradition decreed that the ever present rugby club were always the named sponsors of the New Year's Eve dance. The members of the committee and their wives, Mr and Mrs Billy Baker included, dined downstairs before mounting to the festivities with music. The elders amongst them had conveniently forgotten their own inebriated excesses of the past and enjoyed paternally appearing to disapprove of the present crop of jolly playing members in their cups, the younger ones were pleased to join the jollity.

The present chairman of the committee was a former front row forward, the noted local builder Freddie Wells. Freddie had, as ever, wined the committee, their wives and families right royally. He had reserved the chairman's table at the bar end of the ballroom where he; his wife, Doreen; and his daughter, Jenny, ensconced themselves with the vice chairman, solicitor and former full back Terry Morton and Mrs Sally 'Bubbles' Morton. Freddie Wells was not one for ballroom dancing; his activity on the dance floor being exclusively with Doreen and consisting of an early shuffle-round to something slow and a 'smoochie', the last waltz—'more smooch than waltz' as Doreen was fond of saying. Any dancing his daughter felt she was likely to do would be with a slightly embarrassed Terry Morton and any man who felt sufficiently bold to approach the top table. In her new ball dress, enhanced with an orchid she had carefully chosen—as she had similar flowers for her mother and Mrs Morton—Jenny Wells sat resignedly at her father's left prepared for a boring, provincial evening. She sipped her wine and forced a smile in answer to the excuses of the rest of the top table as they left her for 'this slow one, I think' as described and—it was understood—commanded by her father. Fate had a better night in store for Jenny Wells than she could possibly have dreamed of as she gazed in boredom at her nearly finished drink.

'May I have the pleasure of this dance?'

A tall, handsome, fair-haired young man smiled down at her; she looked into his clear, blue eyes. He returned the gaze. Wondering whether she was in a waking dream, Jenny rose and together they drifted on to the dance floor. He moved beautifully. Jenny had been taught the finer points of ballroom dancing at her expensive school—mostly partnered by Miss Gasson the games mistress whose ill-disguised moustache did little to console Jenny for her not being of the male species. As with many large persons, Jenny was light on her feet.

'I'm known as JJ,' her partner confided.

'Jenny,' she replied.

Suddenly the evening had become a good one. When true love dawns it excludes all around, they danced on as if alone on the floor. They collided with none of the clumsy fellows of the club, nor did they interrupt the middle-aged staggering of their elders. JJ steered effortlessly and their closeness was not entirely due to the correct posture required for dancing. Neither of them were inclined to return to their respective seats between dances: they tripped tirelessly through every waltz, foxtrot and quickstep—only looking dubiously at each other when jolly George announced, 'one of your favourites—the Gay Gordons.'

'Shall we have a drink and sit this one out?' suggested JJ.

'I think we ought,' replied Jenny—secretly delighted that this Adonis seemed to have no immediate intention of abandoning her for the gaieties of Gordon or, worse, for another girl. As they made their way toward the bar, Jenny was aware of her parents staring in ill-disguised curiosity. Mr Morton was smiling—perhaps relieved that he might be excused an obligatory dance with his host's daughter and little realising the relief would be mutual.

'I'd better get my handbag,' said Jenny.

True to form, her father leaped in where any angel might fear to tread, 'Who's yer feller, then, Jenny?'

Before his embarrassed daughter could stammer a reply—she suddenly realised that she had no idea of this wonderful man's surname—her *feller* suavely advanced on Freddie Wells with outstretched hand.

'JJ Whitehouse-Martin, sir. Please forgive me depriving you of your charming daughter for so long.'

'Nothing to forgive, young man. Freddie Wells, local builder,' replied Freddie, shaking JJ's hand. 'My wife, Doreen Wells. Mr and Mrs Terry Morton.'

'Mr Morton and I are acquainted,' replied JJ, smoothly. 'Pleased to meet you, ladies.' Then, to Jenny's consternation, he added, 'May I get you each a drink?'

He appeared to memorise their order with consummate ease and, smiling at Jenny as he moved to the bar, this new man she wanted in her life seemed able to attract the attention of the barman far more swiftly than others.

'Get him a chair, then, our Jenny,' whispered Freddie Wells. And as she hastened to do so he leaned towards Terry Morton. 'Who's the smoothie, Terry?' he asked quietly. Doreen Wells was amazed at the discretion this handsome young man seemed to have created in her noisy husband.

'Very clever chartered accountant. Rising star in his profession, I'm told. Just bought part of Avonbridge Grange—shouldn't tell you that, though,' answered the slightly mellow and consequently indiscreet solicitor.

'Word to the wise,' answered Freddie Wells, tapping his forefinger to the side of his nose.

'Put his chair here, Jenny. Here he comes.'

Here, indeed, came JJ, holding high a tray loaded with drinks to avoid the roistering rugby players still Gay Gordoning. As before, he only had eyes for Jenny—due to which he failed to see the folded carpet, lost his balance and, desperately trying to avoid hurling alcohol at the object of his affections, her family and the local lawyer, fell heavily. His head struck the solid back of a chair before being buried, sideways on, in shattering glasses. His left hand, with which he had attempted to stabilize the tray, and the right side of his handsome face were badly gashed by breaking glass. Blood bubbled freely forth.

The sound of the crash brought everything to a silent halt, even jolly George Cookson and the already Merry Men temporarily ceased their joviality and merriment. A concerned George spoke for everyone through his microphone, 'Everyone alright?'

Freddie Wells was not a man to be quelled by an accident. He was, as he had always been, calm and competent in emergencies—however slight. Standing in his place he yelled at the querulous band leader, 'No problem. Carry on, George,' before stooping to examine the bloody JJ.

'Ought we to send for an ambulance?' asked the alarmed Terry Morton.

'Probably needs hospital attention. Ambulance will take forever tonight, though, Terry. Nip downstairs and tell Bennett, me chauffeur, to bring the car to the front entrance.' 'You,' Freddie summoned a gawping, strapping young lock forward, 'help me get this young man downstairs. And be careful.'

Glancing around at the still curious who had ceased being Gordons of any persuasion he added, imperiously, 'Carry on everyone. No need to panic.'

Freddie and the forward conscript carried JJ towards the stairs, a distressed Jenny following in their wake. As they neared the stairs, JJ, recovering consciousness, said—not very distinctly due to the glass in his mouth and lip:, 'I think, sir, it will be easier if I walk down the stairs. My legs are alright.'

'Good thinking, young feller,' replied Freddie, still in man-of-action mode.

'Support him on that side,' he commanded the bemused lock forward—who was now wondering why he wasn't at the dance or the bar—and together they helped a still slightly concussed JJ down the stairway. Jenny faithfully followed with tears flowing down her cheeks. Bennett had been, as his employer expected, quick to re-act and now stood at the foot of the stairs. The Rolls Royce, engine running, awaited its bleeding passenger. They helped JJ into the car.

'Hospital A&E with him, please, Bennett. Then take him home if they don't keep him in. Keep me informed through hotel reception. If you're not back when this ends we'll get a taxi.'

To Freddie Wells amazement, Jenny stepped into the car alongside JJ.

'I'll go with him, Dad, and see him home. I'll ring you at the hotel when I know something.'

It was said with such finality that, recognising some of his own determination in his child, Freddie concurred with his daughter, shut the car door and patted the roof of the car as the signal for Bennett to move on. Bennett moved on.

Billy, Janice and the rest of their party had been pleased to note JJ's apparent attraction to the large young lady with whom he had danced for nearly fifteen minutes. They were sure he would return to their table sooner or later. The disturbance at the other end of the ballroom seemed to have been resolved, the stentorian tones of the club chairman assuring everyone that all was well had served to keep Billy, his guests and fellow players away from whatever it was that had happened. It was only later in the evening when, concerned as to JJ's whereabouts as there had been no sighting of him on the dance-floor or elsewhere for over thirty minutes, Billy made enquiries. The strapping lock forward slumped over the bar cleared his befuddled head sufficiently to inform Billy, 'Oh, yesh. Ole JJ wash taken to hospital in a Roller,' before returning to the drowning of his sorrows.

The club chairman more clearly confirmed the lock forward's information and assured Billy, 'He'll be alright, Bill. Me daughter's with 'im and she'll keep me informed.'

Later in the evening, little short of another calendar year, he was able to tell Billy his friend had been taken home to his parents and tucked up in bed. Billy and Janice's welcoming in of the new year was a little subdued.

The reverend Claude Eustace Martin and Mrs Martin, having had more celebration than they usually did in a year during their memorable pre-Christmas party, spent New Year's Eve in preliminary packing prior to their impending removal to Hereford. By 11.15 p.m. both of them had had enough of sorting and packing. Sylvia's suggestion of a sherry had just been actioned when the unusual sound of the front door knocker echoed through the house.

'Too early for letting in the year. Too late for carol singers,' said Claude. Together they made their way up the little used hall and, for the first time in many months, unbolted the front door. With some difficulty, Claude eased the door open. To their amazement, Sylvia and Claude saw a bandaged and blood-spattered JJ leaning on a large young lady in an evening gown and, beyond them, a Rolls Royce with liveried chauffeur standing beside the driver's door. JJ's left arm was wrapped in a voluminous sling.

'He's alright. The hospital say he must rest—he was a bit concussed. I'm afraid,' said the young lady as she helped a bemused JJ over the little used threshold.

'He needs to get to bed, of course,' she continued as she and JJ moved along the hall towards the light. Uncharacteristically becoming the action man but, characteristically caring, Claude gently took JJ from the domineering young lady and, avoiding touching the arm in a sling, steered JJ toward the stairs.

'I'll take him from here,' he said.

'Oh. Yes . . . yes, of course. Sorry,' answered the begowned one. She turned to Sylvia. 'Please excuse my rudeness. It's been a bit upsetting—and JJ's welfare was the most important thing. I'm Jenny Wells. You must be Mrs Whitehouse-Martin.'

'Just Mrs Martin, actually,' answered Sylvia—confusing Jenny. 'What happened?'

'He tripped and fell carrying a tray full of glasses. He tried to keep the glass and drink away from us, bless him, and he fell onto a chair back and then into all the glass. He was concussed, as I said, his arm was dislocated and his face was badly cut. But the hospital say if he rests he'll be alright in a few days.'

'Thank goodness,' said Sylvia. 'And, of course, thank you Jenny for looking after him.'

The large but lovely young lady was already making her way back up the hall towards a front door about to be opened twice in the same hour—something unprecedented for many moons.

'Sorry to rush in and rush out,' said Jenny, 'but I'm supposed to get daddy's car back to The Swan . . . Can I come and see JJ tomorrow, Mrs Wh . . . Mrs Martin?'

'Yes, er, yes, of course, if you want to,' said Sylvia. 'I'll see you out.'

Jenny passed through the rarely opened front door. Holding the door open Sylvia decided to avert any potential embarrassment the following morning, 'As you might have noticed, Jenny, we don't use the front door much. Well, not at all, really. Could you come to the side door in the morning, please?'

'Oh . . . yes . . . Oh dear—sorry again. See you in the morning,' said Jenny.

She walked toward the impressive car. Sylvia had never seen a Rolls Royce at the vicarage—indeed she was just wondering whether anyone had ever seen a Rolls Royce in this drive when Jenny turned and added, 'Oh, yes. Happy New Year.'

'Happy New Year,' echoed Sylvia. After bemusedly waving to the departing limousine Sylvia closed and bolted the door and hastened upstairs. Claude had managed to help JJ remove his blood-stained clothes, get into his pyjamas and bed.

'Sorry, Mum,' muttered JJ, a little indistinctly. 'Did Jenny get away to the hotel?'

'Yes, darling,' answered Sylvia. 'You get some sleep, now.'

'I will, Mum . . . Jenny's alright, isn't she?'

Both Sylvia and Claude interpreted this as more a statement of the young lady's acceptability than a question as to her well-being, but before they could seek clarification, JJ had fallen asleep with a contented smile on his bandaged face.

Sylvia and Claude closed JJ's bedroom door and stood on the landing looking in bewildered wonder at one another.

'Happy New Year, Claude.'

'Happy New Year, Sylvia.'

CHAPTER THIRTY-EIGHT
New Year—New Love
January to June, 1971

The dawn of another year makes little difference to the hours of waking in a conscientious vicarage. On 1 January 1971 it was as well that this was so since Sylvia and Claude had hardly finished breakfast before the side door bell sounded. Expecting a distressed parishioner or the church treasurer—it was his day—Claude opened the door. Shock was mutual. Claude saw the generously proportioned young lady of last night smiling behind an enormous bunch of flowers; Jenny saw only a clerical collar. The nice man who had relieved her of the burden of JJ last night had been in an open-necked shirt with rolled-up sleeves and, not having taken much notice of his face, Jenny was uncertain whether this was the same man or if JJ had suddenly deteriorated and a vicar been summoned. The slight impasse was relieved by Sylvia appearing behind Claude and, recognising Jenny, inviting her in.

'You didn't really meet one another last night, did you?' said Jenny with a laugh.

'Not really—we had our hands full—as it were,' answered Claude. 'Jenny, isn't it? I'm Claude Martin,' and he extended his hand to shake before realising that both Jenny's hands were again full, this time with flowers. Sylvia covered the embarrassment by both admiring and taking the flowers.

'Oh, thank you,' said Jenny. 'I felt I should apologise again for interrupting you last night—and coming to the wrong door. But, of course, I wasn't to know, was I? And I didn't realise you were a vicar, Mr Martin. I'm so sorry for gawping at you when you opened the door.'

Jenny ran out of breath and, temporarily, anything to say.

'You probably didn't realise this was St Barnabas Vicarage, I expect?' said Claude—compounding poor Jenny's embarrassment.

'No . . . no, I didn't I'm afraid. . . . Gosh I'm not doing anything right, am I?' she said.

'You're not doing too badly, Jenny,' said Sylvia. 'Why not sit down here in the kitchen and have a cup of tea with us? JJ's still asleep and we'd still like to know a bit more about what happened and, if you don't mind me asking, about you as well.'

Having little option but to obey, Jenny took a seat at the Martin's kitchen table and, over what became several cups of tea, elaborated on the events of the previous night at both The Swan and the hospital. They had all became better acquainted before Claude was despatched to JJ's attic room to ascertain, in very particular order, that JJ was awake, was at all hungry, and whether he would be prepared for the young lady from last night to see him in his night attire. The answer to every question being affirmative, Sylvia, with bowl of cereal in one hand and cup of tea in the other, led Jenny up the two flights of stairs and into JJ's attic room. Whilst Sylvia arranged the cereal and tea on JJ's bedside table she realised that the young couple were simply gazing at one another, seemingly rapt in wonder that last night was not a dream.

'Can you manage the cereal, JJ?' asked Sylvia.

'Yes . . . I think so,' was the vague reply.

'I can help him,' offered Jenny, tentatively. 'If it's alright?' she added.

'Well I——' began Sylvia.

'Oh, Mother. I'm in no fit state to sully the house by seducing our guest. It's neither the time nor the place,' burst forth JJ.

Jenny suppressed a giggle. Sylvia could think of no polite reply. A short pause followed.

'Sorry, Mum. Sorry, Jenny,' said JJ. 'But you know what I mean?'

'I know what you mean,' replied Sylvia. 'But it might have been better put, dear. I'll find you somewhere to sit, Jenny,' she added, removing JJ's bloody evening suit and shirt from the only chair in the room to a clothes hanger.

'This will have to be dry cleaned, JJ,' she added—really for something to say and to ease her own unexpected embarrassment.

'I think at the least the shirt's a write-off, to be honest,' said JJ. 'Thank you, Mum.'

Feeling herself dismissed, Sylvia departed in as much dignity as she could muster with the sanguinary shirt and dress suit suspended from her free hand. As she left she noted that the cereal remained untouched, the young couple were simply holding hands and looking in wonder at each other.

As Sylvia and Claude were beginning to consider whether they should, despite JJ's gauche assurance to his mother, disturb the apparently besotted young couple in the attic, the side door bell rang and, before it could be answered, the familiar voice of Billy Baker assured them it was, indeed, only he and Janice and could they, as they were doing, come in. Whilst Janice took the third chair at the breakfast table and prepared to sample the third pot of tea brewed that year, Billy, as instructed by a relieved Sylvia and Claude, mounted to JJ's attic room where he was introduced to Jenny and given accounts and assurances concerning last evening and JJ's health.

Jenny's little red Triumph TR3 car was a daily, sometimes twice daily visitor to the vicarage throughout the next week—as, of course, was its owner. By the end of the week, Dr Lurring had pronounced JJ fit and well and on an unseasonably warm Sunday afternoon, he was returned in Jenny's sporty little MG to the west wing of Avonbridge Grange. Despite his having described it to her, Jenny realised JJ's self-effacing manner had radically undersold his local base. She was greatly impressed. Before JJ could stop her she was tidying and polishing things—to the amusement of JJ. They sat awhile in the lounge before exploring the bedroom and each other. Whilst willing and absorbed by her love for JJ, Jenny winced at his first touch to her bulging breasts. They both apologised in unison.

'If you don't want me to . . .' ventured JJ.

'No, darling, it's not that. It's . . .' And, to JJ's acute embarrassment, Jenny burst into tears.

With sympathetic application of a handkerchief JJ calmed her— re-assuring her that he would do nothing to offend or upset her. And then, in a hushed voice, slowly at first and then—as she realised how understanding he could be—in rushed, staccato sentences, Jenny recounted how some girls at her school, probably inspired by jealousy, had held her arms and legs, exposed her breasts and applied knives and lighted cigarettes to them. The school doctor had tended to the cuts and burns and the culprits had been expelled. JJ asked what, to him seemed the obvious question. He learned that Jenny had not asked for plastic surgery to repair the unsightly damage because she was afraid to face the embarrassment of telling her parents the expensive school for young ladies they had insisted she attend allowed the sort of barbaric behaviour inflicted upon her. She now had unsightly scarring to each breast and if they were handled unexpectedly or at certain angles it still hurt.

'Must be awful for you, darling,' said JJ.

'I've got used to it,' replied Jenny. Impulsively she added, 'So should you.'

And with no more ado, to JJ's surprise and delight, she proceeded to remove her blouse and brassiere to facilitate his familiarity by inspection. It was a close inspection. Being assured that gently handling the largest female breasts he had ever been close to was not painful, a tender physical exploration . . .

If she had been impressed by his flat, Jenny was astounded by the Whitehouse penile characteristic. She was both flattered and embarrassed in equal measure by JJ's insistence that it was only right she should retain her chaste state until they were man and wife.

'I'm actually not 'unspoiled', JJ.'

'Oh,' Jenny noted the disappointment on his face and, being a clever and tactful girl recounted the further degradation she had undergone at school after the assault on her breasts.

JJ was aghast.

'Surely you sued the school?'

'Who'd have believed me? I just ran away before anything more happened. Anyway I'm over it now, thank goodness,' she said. Quickly adding, 'Please don't try to make a fuss or talk about suing—mummy and dad don't know—and I don't want them to. Not now—or ever.'

'Yes . . . OK,' replied JJ. This was turning out to be the strangest seduction he had ever made. If he actually 'made' it, he thought. He couldn't suppress his curiosity, however. 'Have you never told anyone, before, though?' was his next question.

'Yes, JJ, I told Terri—and it made me feel better to have told someone who was understanding and sympathetic.'

'Who's Terry?' interrupted JJ—not without a pang of jealousy.

Jenny laughed at him, 'Terri was my flat mate in London—and, before you leap to any more conclusions, her real name is Theresa. Everyone calls her Terri and she's my best and dearest friend so, please, darling, let's have no jealousy or silly questions. We've established that you can't deflower me—much as I would have loved you to have been the one. We're sitting here almost naked and, if you feel as I do, we ought to do something about it.'

Some time later they became unofficially engaged.

'What say we have a drink to toast our future?' said JJ getting to his feet and walking, still entirely naked, to the lounge.

'What drink would you like, darling?' he called.

'What have you got?' asked Jenny, following JJ out of the bedroom in a similar unclothed state. As she walked towards JJ, the door opposite the bedroom swung open to admit a smiling Billy. He stopped in his tracks and the smile turned to a mixture of shock and admiration.

'Oh, gosh. Look, I'm sorry. I didn't know. I was looking for JJ.'

The laugh of the said JJ interrupted Billy, by now looking at the carpet, who looked to his right where, not for the first time, of course, he saw JJ totally unclothed.

'We forgot to put the "Do Not Disturb" sign up, Bill,' said a completely unfazed JJ. 'Jenny, I don't think I told you, Billy owns the other half of this place and we do tend to barge in on each other.'

'Yes. But sorry anyway, Jenny,' said Billy and, the smile returning, he was unable to resist adding, 'Nice to see more of you.'

Jenny by this time had grabbed a cushion from the settee that was proving totally inadequate to conceal her breasts.

'Steady, Bill,' said JJ, we've just got engaged.

'Oh! You mean?'

'Yes, Bill. Jenny's the woman of my dreams and, if her father gives us his blessing, we'll be fixing a date for her to become Mrs Whitehouse-Martin. And, even though you're a married man now, I insist on you being my best man.'

'Of course, JJ. Congratulations. I hope you'll both be as happy as we are.'

Billy warmly shook hands with his friend before, unthinkingly, turning toward Jenny.

'Gosh, this is difficult—I ought to give you a kiss,' he stuttered whilst Jenny continued with her unsuccessful attempt to convert a small cushion into a large bra.

'Yes, thank you, Billy,' echoed Jenny who, seeing how at ease JJ seemed and deciding she may as well display a similar composure herself, flung the inadequate small furnishing back onto the settee.

'Oh, heck. You saw everything as you came in,' she said, and briefly allowing her finest features to again become visible to his wide open eyes, she gave an amazed Billy a friendly kiss.

'Please excuse me now, though,' she said, turning to leave for the bedroom.

'I think you should buy some bigger cushions, JJ,' was her parting remark. Billy could not fail to note and admire her undulating pink and surprisingly firm buttocks as Jenny left them.

There was a short pause.

'There's a phrase about being knocked down with a feather that sort of applies to me,' said Billy. 'That's some woman you've got there, JJ—if you don't mind my saying.'

'Of course not, old friend. But, look, Bill, you're the first to know—which is quite right as far as I'm concerned—but please don't tell anyone until Jenny's parents have blessed us and, er, well, made an announcement and all that. It wouldn't be right.'

'Yes—I understand—of course I do. But I'm going to have to tell Jan.'

'Oh, of course, Jan knows how to be discreet and keep secrets,' said JJ—with more confidence than Billy realised. Then, impetuously, he added, 'Look, Bill, why don't you and Jan join us for a premature celebration drink?'

Raising his voice he enquired towards the bedroom, 'Jenny—it'll be alright if Billy and Jan join us for a drink, won't it?'

'Providing we're properly dressed, darling,' came the reply.

'Super. It's a date. I'll give you a bit of time to get dressed,' laughed Billy, still reeling at the momentous news that old JJ had fallen for and was to marry an amazing woman. He shot out into the hall.

'Back in about an hour,' he called from beyond the door.

'About right, I should think,' answered JJ as he returned to the bedroom.

'Sorry about that, darling, but he is a great friend. . . . And you don't mind me asking them in?'

'You're forgiven,' replied Jenny. 'He gave us plenty of time to get dressed, though.'

'You're right,' said JJ. 'We could make good use of, say, thirty minutes?'

'Come on, then, big boy. I've never done it against the clock, as it were.'

Fortunately for Jenny, JJ, in his eagerness, either missed or chose to ignore her careless admission of previous copulatory experiences.

Forty-five minutes later they were back in the lounge and in their clothes. And twenty minutes after that Janice rushed in, and to Jenny's slight surprise, gave JJ a great big kiss, full on the mouth before congratulating him. And turning to Jenny started to say, 'And you're the lucky lady who's——' before they both realised that they were acquainted.

'You come into my shop every week.'

'You're that lady with the super flower shop.'

They had both spoken at the same time. Their laughter broke any figurative ice that may have been waiting to be broken. JJ popped real ice into four glasses.

To Freddie Wells's surprise, JJ insisted on calling on him formally to ask his blessing on the engagement. Freddie effusively gave JJ his consent and, within moments, a large whisky and soda. Doreen Wells gave JJ a lingering kiss on his unscarred cheek. Later, as planned, JJ and Jenny motored into Birmingham.

Jenny had been expecting to visit one or more smart jewellers' shops in the city centre. The better informed and connected JJ took her to a small workshop at the rear of an unimpressive, small terraced house on Vyse Street in the city's jewellery quarter. He knew it from his days at Harvey, Smith and Thomas when he had conducted the audit and found he got on well with the owner. From the vast selection offered, Jenny selected and JJ bought an expensive diamond and ruby cluster engagement ring. Whilst they waited it was correctly sized and the happy pair were wished well in the broadest Birmingham accents Jenny had ever heard. Before they left the workshop JJ, ever careful, telephoned his insurance broker and arranged insurance on the ring.

Later that week, Freddie and Doreen Wells gave a lavish dinner party to mark the engagement of their adored daughter. In a hastily tailored new evening suit and shirt, JJ made his first of many guest visits at the magnificent Wells mansion—Avonbridge Hall. Experiencing similar feelings of happiness mingled with well-concealed relief—as did their hosts—Sylvia and Claude, who had made an unexpectedly early return visit to Avonbridge, sat to the left of the Wellses. To Sylvia and JJ's surprise, Claude and Freddie appeared to have made each other's acquaintance before; the invitation to attend Chandlery Lodge ladies' night the following October clarified matters for Sylvia and Doreen—but further confused JJ—especially as he and Jenny seemed to be presumed as amongst the party for nearly nine months time.

The next celebration—the Wells loved celebrating—was for the birthdays of Jenny and JJ. They had quickly discovered, to mutual delight, that they had been born on successive days—JJ being a whole day older than his fiancée. Freddie, being fond of making little speeches, insisted on proposing their joint health. Responding with commendable brevity compared to his future father-in-law's expansive toast, JJ formally announced the date for their wedding—Saturday 19 June.

The new vicar of St Bartholomew's had graciously—and with some relief due to his newness—agreed to his predecessor, Claude, performing the service. The best man would, of course, be Billy Baker. Jenny had been equally insistent that her friend Mrs Terri Anstruther should be her matron of honour and she happily accepted the joint offer of Zoe and Janice to dress her hair for the big day. Jenny and her mother became regular customers of ZoNice Hair and Beauty. And, to complete a combined circle of friendship and business, Billy shook hands with Freddie on a deal for the future servicing and maintenance of all Wells Builders Ltd vehicles. Billy was wise enough to avoid mention of the

Rolls-Royce—such cars being best cared for by specialists in that superior marque.

Over the next months the combined talents of JJ and Billy were tested by the bombastic exuberance of the father of the bride-to-be who wanted to arrange every little detail of what he felt to be the wedding of the year. His extravagance clashed with the more modest wishes of his daughter—supported, with a little reluctance, by her mother—and the two friends found their new experience as mediators an amusing challenge. As they had formed the habit of doing, they prevailed. Jenny was able to anticipate a day which she had privately never thought possible with pleasure. The one fact over which neither she or Billy had been allowed any control or input was their honeymoon venue; it remained JJ's secret until the wedding day.

Jenny was delighted when her friend Terri told her that she was three-months pregnant. Terri also honoured the long-standing offer to introduce her friend—and JJ—to Sir James McMaster, plastic surgeon. The secret kept by Jenny and JJ from everyone except Terri, was the extent of the plastic surgery carried out in a discreet private practice in Cheshire. Ostensibly, their trip to the North West was for the sole purpose of restoring JJ's scarred face—Jenny accompanying him merely as company and consolation. In fact, the principal purpose of the expensive exercise was the restoration of unscarred skin to Jenny's breasts—such skin being taken from other delicate parts of her body. The operations were the work of a day; the recovery period before removal of bandages sorely tried the patience of each patient. Eventually, the pair returned to Avonbridge where JJ displayed an unscarred face to the world at large, and Jenny at last felt able to publicly display more of what were now her pride and joy.

CHAPTER THIRTY-NINE
AVONBRIDGE MASONIC HALL
SUNDAY 24 JANUARY 1988, 6.30 P.M. AND ONWARDS

Still clad in black, the deliverer of the three summons to attend later that evening walked casually past the entrance to the Masonic hall and, glancing around to ensure he was unobserved, unlocked but left in place the padlock securing the gates to the former boatyard and chandlery. He then returned to the Masonic hall, admitted himself, switched on the outside light over the door and climbed the stairs to the temple where he donned the black robes of a Knight of Malta, his black balaclava and the cheap mask he had, so fortuitously, found and bought in London. It may have been premature, but he realised that Jeffries had a habit of arriving early— the reason he had been asked to attend first. As expected, it was ten minutes to seven o'clock when the sound of the outer door below opening and closing presaged the arrival of the first victim. Jeffries tried to open the dining room door and, finding it locked, rattled it in annoyance. Then, noting the lit staircase and lights beyond, he ascended the stairs as intended.

'What's going on?' asked Jeffries as he entered the temple. 'I thought meetings took place downstairs?'

'Not this one,' said a strange, squeaky voice from behind him. Jeffries turned sharply around and found himself confronted by a tall, black-clad person with, where the face should have been, a white skull. He stood temporarily transfixed in horror as a pad was pushed over his face. Chloroform assailed Jeffries's nostrils and system and he fell, insensible, into the arms of his tormentor. He was part dragged and part carried to the large chair furthest from the door and divested of his clothing—not, as expected, an easy disrobement, but by tearing off the shirt—buttons being difficult in gloved hands—and failing to treat any garment with care, it was accomplished. Jeffries was sat on an incontinence cushion and secured by his arms and legs to the similarly named parts of the chair with strong canvas webbing. Next, a half lemon was inserted into his mouth and a gag securely but carefully applied so as to allow him to breathe through his nose. His still closed eyes would, when he awoke, be able to see the other victims in a similar state to himself. All as planned. It being still only 7.10 there was time to press one of the sharpened daggers into Jeffries's right hand and impress his fingerprints on the handle. The dagger was then replaced on the secretary's table alongside the other.

The sounds of the door below warned of the arrival of Maurice Fisher. At just five feet and four inches in height, the nervous, socially inept Fisher had been amazed at the tolerance of the Brethren who had allowed him to complete his progress through the various offices of Chandlery Lodge. He had joined the lodge since attending his mother lodge in Cheshire involved travelling and, more importantly, taking time from work. He was only a Craft Freemason—never having wished to, or been asked to, proceed to any other order or degree. He was proud to be a past master and wished to remain precisely that; none of the senior offices of the lodge usually occupied by past masters interested him. He had only completed his year as master with the assistance of nerve tonic and the fear of failing—not in the eyes of the lodge, but in the opinion of his wife. Caitlin Fisher had been delighted with her position as master's wife—particularly what she perceived as the rapturous reception of her speech at the Ladies Festival. Standing five feet ten inches in her stockinged feet, her statement that she never failed to overlook her dear husband drew laughter from all save her 'dear' husband, and one other vertically challenged brother. Her further attempt to elicit laughter at the worshipful master's expense by stating that he 'taught me almost everything I know' passed above the heads of most—they being unaware or uncaring of Maurice's former status as a teacher of science. It was not Maurice's scientific awareness, but fear and native cunning that had led him, ever since becoming a past master, to arrange their holidays abroad to coincide with the lodge past masters' night, thus neatly avoiding any possibility of him being called upon to assume the duties of any office of the lodge for the evening. In his craven single-mindedness, he regarded this small victory as a stroke of genius. Caitlin was so little interested that she failed to attach any significance to the late autumn vacation other than her own enjoyment.

The diminutive brother crept warily into the temple. Seeing Jeffries as he was—and as he had never before seen him—he started forward in what could have been an attempted rescue, but was more likely reflex curiosity.

'Leave him alone,' said a squeaky voice from behind him.

Fisher turned. He had recently treated his niece's children to the latest must see film Star Wars and now, for a moment, he imagined himself confronted by Darth Vader. His little eyes focusing upwards saw, in place of a human face, a skull. Fisher obliged by fainting.

His task made easier, the man in black picked up the small, inert Fisher, carried him to the central of the three large chairs and subjected him to the same treatment as Jeffries, the only variation being that instead of impressing his fingerprints onto the handle of a dagger, Fisher's fingers were made to grip the larger tyler's sword. The sword was then placed beside Jeffries's right foot. Two down and one to go, thought the tormentor as he returned to the seat by the door. Many a slip . . .

At 7.35 the closing of the lower door was accompanied by the unnerving sound of two persons conversing. As their footsteps mounted the stairs, he recognised the unmistakeably stentorian voice of the director of ceremonies, Raymond Hughes, and the broader accented, but equally carrying tones of Frank 'Floury' Fallowfield. Floury, as everyone referred to him though none but the unwise addressed him, was the local baker and pâtissier, a past master of Chandlery Lodge and a former lodge director of ceremonies. His accompanying Hughes was an unforeseen factor that would have to be dealt with, the tormentor braced himself for a struggle with two rather large men. Fortune favoured him. Floury announced his intention of 'going for a Jimmy Riddle.'

Raymond Hughes was a self-made man and proud of it. His brash furniture emporium at the end of the High Street was well known to the majority of Avonbridge inhabitants and carefully avoided by the more discerning. One could not fail to know when Ray Hughes was present; his overbearing manner and voice to match were not sought out by many. His wife, Doris, was equally, if not more, vociferous and she was rarely still. It was the opinion of the more discerning that it was she who was the brains behind the commercial success of Hughes Fine Furniture. The fortuitously unaccompanied Raymond Hughes bounced into the temple uttering a similar query as that voiced by Jeffries, but stopped in his tracks on seeing the two trussed, unclothed brethren.

'What the——' was all he managed to say before the chloroform fumes weakened and felled him. The pad was held to his face a little longer since not only was he a large man, but it would now be necessary for him to remain unconscious a little longer whilst the innocently intrusive Floury one was similarly rendered limp and harmless.

'What's goin' on, Ray?' queried Fallowfield from across the landing where he had been relieving himself in a toilet void of light bulbs. He bustled into the temple with his usual bluff heartiness; spotted Hughes on the floor and, as he advanced to right the recumbent Hughes, he saw Jeffries and Fisher. His shock enabled the sleep-inducing pad to be applied. Now, concluded the man in black, not only did he have two large men to seat, but one had no prior reservation. No time to waste on self-recrimination he thought as, not unexpectedly, he failed to lift Hughes easily. The overweight director of ceremonies was dragged to the last chair and denuded whilst on the floor, before the hernia-inducing effort of lifting him into the chair was accomplished. After regaining his breath a little—he should take more exercise he thought—Hughes was bound, half-lemoned and gagged. He then re-arranged the plastic covering the floor that had been disturbed by dragging the heavy Hughes.

Muffled sounds of protest and fear signalled Jeffries's recovery to consciousness. The secretarial eyes, when they focused, grew wide with disbelief. His bonds allowed him not only to look to the side where his two brethren in the buff sat slumped, but downward to observe his own naked state. He watched in further disbelief as the junior deacon's chair was moved from its usual position to the right of the senior warden until it stood on the warden's left and behind the temple door. Worshipful Brother Fallowfield was then hoisted into the chair and his limbs secured. Floury, it seemed, was being spared full exposure. Only his frayed check jacket and striped tie were removed before he was secured to the chair. He was then half-lemoned, the man in black being thankful for the fact that he had brought two lemons that allowed for four halves. Floury was then gagged.

The next moment Jeffries felt as Fisher had done when the sinister figure undid the buttons of Fallowfield's shirt, folded back the left half of the shirt and appeared to plunge a knife into the baker's chest. No blood spurted forth, although the knife remained affixed to the baker's breast, which puzzled the watching, wincing lodge secretary. He was even more bemused as their faceless tormentor returned to Floury with a small pot in his hand. When he moved aside, Jeffries could see blood in plenty staining the baker's breast and shirt; so, in a brief moment of consciousness, could Fisher before he lapsed into his second faint of the evening. Perhaps as well for him, thought Jeffries, watching the skull-faced one approach him with the same pot in hand. Jeffries's head was forced back and he felt wetness across his throat. He watched in horror as Hughes, still not recovered, had both his throat and chest painted as though bleeding. Finally, the frightened Fisher was decorated in blood red on his throat and chest before the addition of a seemingly deep cut across his scrawny body. The mysterious figure returned to the secretary's table where he took up the two daggers. Jeffries was sure his end was nigh in this strange ritual—yet now the tall, black-clad man carefully placed one dagger beside Hughes right foot before closing Hughes's fingers over the handle of the second, which he then carefully placed on the floor beside Fisher's foot.

Jeffries was beginning to feel a call of nature similar to that satisfied by Fallowfield. The black figure placed a large, high-sided bowl at his feet and, in an unexpected utterance said in a strange, squeaky voice, 'That's the place to do it.' He provided Fisher and Hughes with similar pissoirs before leaving the room—only to return after several moments with a washing up bowl to serve Fallowfield's calls of nature. He seemed almost apologetic in unfastening old Floury's trousers and positioning him so that he could make use of this rudimentary convenience. Jeffries watched the sinister figure move to the secretary's table where he packed things unseen into a large, black luggage bag. He then systematically searched the pockets of Jeffries's, Fisher's and Hughes's clothes. Everything he removed from the pockets, with the exception of car keys, he carefully put into small plastic bags placed on top of their respective clothing. He then tightly tied each parcel of clothes and belongings together. He took great care labelling the three sets of car keys before setting them aside. The three bundles of clothing were then stuffed into another canvas bag and the car keys pocketed beneath the black robes. After a final glance around, their black-clad tormentor left the temple. Jeffries and a now recovering Hughes heard his steps recede down the stairs. They were left with an occasionally fainting Fisher and a muttering Fallowfield in the still fully lit temple. Mercifully, they felt, the heating seemed to remain fully functional. Eventually, after each had struggled without success, they sank into naked misery.

In the hall below, the man stowed the black robes, skull mask, balaclava and other things in a black bag, last to be stowed were the black Wellington boots. The tormentor unlocked the outer door, extinguished the outside light and noting that he was unobserved, unlocked the correctly identified cars, and placed the appropriate apparel on the front passenger seat. Still no one about, he was pleased to see. He was nervous about the next part as he had no control over whether he would or would not be seen or, worse, questioned. Donning the large workman's cap, especially brought for this part of the venture, and assuming a limp as he walked across the road to the old chandlery gates, he removed and pocketed the unlocked padlock and opened the gates. He then limped quickly back to the Masonic hall car park where, it being the smallest car, he started up and drove Fisher's battered, old, split-screened Morris Minor out of the temple forecourt, through the chandlery gates and down to the parking area he had scouted earlier. His luck continued to hold whilst he similarly transferred and parked Jeffries's immaculately preserved Austin Devon alongside Fisher's Morris. Lastly came Hughes's pride and joy—an almost vintage Armstrong Siddeley. It was a large car, for longer journeys it would doubtless have been a joy to drive, for the quick trip of a few hundred yards it was singularly ill-suited. He drove it slowly, and as he parked the last car out of sight of the little-used road, he heaved a huge sigh of relief. He had been so careful with Hughes's big car that he had failed to notice the passing, with dipped headlights, of a late-returning Versey Street resident. By the time he had driven the old van, which he had left on his previous visit for just this purpose, back to the gates, the local night-owl was parking his truck behind his wife's B&B. The black clad and be-capped one secured the gates with the original padlock and drove calmly away along Avon Street.

As the clock ticked relentlessly on towards 10.30, the Mesdames Jeffries, Fisher and Hughes were, in their different ways, becoming increasingly concerned. Before the half hour struck, Mrs Fisher telephoned Mrs Jeffries in the faint hope that the wife of the lodge secretary would know why what her husband had told her would be just a little meeting was seemingly stretching further into the night than did some full-fledged lodge meetings. Judith Jeffries was no comfort. She, too, had been advised of a little meeting. She promised the irritated Caitlin Fisher to report anything she could discover as soon as she could; she had no idea of how or when she would make any discovery, but hoped that the empty re-assurance would calm the notoriously domineering Caitlin Fisher. As she pondered what, if anything, she was able to do, the telephone rang again. She snatched it up only to hear the rather indignant tones of Doris Hughes seeming to blame her and George for her husband's failure to return at a decent hour. Judith explained that she and Caitlin Fisher were as puzzled and worried as Doris. They had a concerned discussion at the conclusion of which the all-action Doris undertook to drive round to the hall to see what they were doing. Twenty minutes later, she telephoned Judith to report that the hall was all in darkness and that there were no cars parked there. They decided that if no husbands had returned by 11.00 o'clock they would, separately, telephone the police. Judith made the difficult call to Caitlin Fisher and told her of Doris Hughes's journey of no discovery and that she and Doris had agreed to leave matters until eleven o'clock before calling the police.

'I've already rung them,' said Caitlin Fisher. 'They say they can do nothing for twenty-four hours. A Sergeant Bagnall it was; very short with me he was.'

The three wives spent a sleepless night interspersed with telephone calls to the powerless police and each other. No worried wife was aware of Floury Fallowfield's absence from home, he being a confirmed bachelor living alone. Had Station Sergeant Ernie Bagnall been aware that his good friend Frank was an absentee from his home he might have taken more note of the undetected connection between his old friend—a long-time Freemason—and the other missing men.

Dave Morris was often late home—especially when his work took him far from his comfortable home at number 31 Versey Street. He had been forced to complete the last job on a Sunday due to delays during the week, but was pleased to be back with his wife, Molly. As usual, she had a fine supper awaiting her man. After hearing about the problems Dave had overcome to effect completion before another deadline, she shared his puzzlement as to why there had been a big car being driven into the old chandlery as he drove by. From time to time maintenance men would come by in the week and drive in and out of the old place. But never on a Sunday night.

'Ain't nothing there to pinch, is there?' stated Dave.

'Not that we know to,' replied Molly.

'I'll take a look-see later; take Rags that way for 'is walk,' decided Dave.

As there were, as was often so on a Sunday, no guests enjoying one of their several beds before breakfast, Molly's curiosity drove her to accompany her man and his dog. They examined the now re-secured padlock. The three of them looked into the dark night beyond the gates and saw . . . nothing. Rags marked the gatepost and they returned home.

CHAPTER FORTY
A LOVELY WEDDING
SATURDAY 19 JUNE 1971

As those who have meticulously planned weddings—and, indeed, other functions—well know, the one imponderable over which there is no human control is the weather.

It was, therefore, with relief and pleasure that at various times between 6.30 and 8.00 a.m., the families Wells and Martin particularly—and many others besides—regarded a sunny morning and heard a favourable forecast for the day ahead. The most anxious and subsequently relieved participants in the wedding day were in Avonbridge Hall where Sylvia and Claude Martin, Terri and Gerald Anstruther, Charles and Charlotte Whitehouse, William and Elsie Burroughs, and others awoke from sleep of differing depths following the more than usually lavish dinner party bestowed upon them by Freddie and Doreen Wells. The bride-to-be insisted on having a light supper in her own room. The male residents of Avonbridge Grange and their far fewer guests had done their celebrating the previous Saturday at one of the best stag dos in their hazy memories. Their female counterparts had also enjoyed Jenny's less lavish, but equally memorable, hen do on the same Saturday. Almost certainly the clearer heads on the morning of Saturday 19 June were those regarding a cloudless sky from the windows of the grange. Those looking somewhat blearily from the casements of the hall could see the sunlight reflected from the enormous marquee set in the grounds. Already, hired caterers and flower arrangers from far and wide were to be seen moving in and out of the impressive canvas reception venue. More local floristry artistes were busily weaving their decorative magic in St Bartholomew's Church—recently re-decorated and restored to glory at the expense of Messrs Wells and Whitehouse-Martin.

At 9.30 a.m Janice Baker and the recently wed Zoe Connolly left the grange to take the 'tools of their profession' and their combined skills to the hall where they, Terri Anstruther, three other excited bridesmaids and the mother of the bride coiffed, dressed and pampered the surprisingly calm bride to be. The father of the bride's nervous allusion to his daughter being prepared for the altar drew the merely polite hollow laughter reserved for the jests of one's host. Of all the principal participants in the ceremony and reception, Freddie Wells was undoubtedly, and uncharacteristically, the most nervous; used to being the controlling force, he harboured a strange feeling that, despite footing the bill for his daughter's nuptials, the arrangements—splendid as they were—had somehow been taken out of his hands by his son-in-law to be and his cheeky best man. Quite how this had been accomplished still bemused Freddie. A knowing observer in the person of the Reverend Claude Martin's wife, Sylvia, was quietly amused by the practised machinations of her son and his friend. The reverend himself was flattered to be returning to his former church and eager to officiate at the wedding of his now reconciled stepson. The ladies' hats and dresses, carefully chosen for an optimistically anticipated fine day, were donned over thrice the time taken for the men to don their morning suits. The groom, best man and most of the younger males were less accustomed to wearing striped trousers and tailcoats than the higher ranked Freemason's present—each giving the other the familiar looks of those in-the-know.

By 10.55 a.m., the many guests were gathered together with the groom and his men awaiting the arrival of the bride. At 11.05 precisely—she had been determined on being only a little late—Jenny and her proud father alighted from the beribboned Rolls Royce and, watched by a large crowd of well-wishers, walked toward St Bart's.

The verger blew his nose loudly and, taking the signal, organist Timothy Andrews's fingers and feet caused the church to be filled with Richard Wagner's stirring music that has heralded brides for as long as many remember. The disrespectful comment of a member of the rugby club that 'we're off' was heard by only a few, as one hundred admiring guests rose to admire and greet the radiant Jenny Wells in a stunning ivory silk dress bearing a bouquet of white, yellow and red roses. Her never-so-proud father bore himself with pride and dignity. Her mother wiped away her tears—an ongoing exercise throughout the service. The groom beamed in admiration of his beautiful bride.

The Reverend Claude Martin had rarely been so emotionally involved in a service he had conducted—yet experience enabled him to direct what everyone present felt to be both a dignified yet happy and joyous wedding. Sylvia glowed with pride in both her son and her husband. The happy couple spoke their vows and responses clearly and with sufficient volume for all present both to hear and feel involved. Those of the rugby club who had wagered on the bride promising to obey won their bets and the losers paid up with little rancour before the familiar strains of Mendelsohn's 'Wedding March' heralded a lengthy procession of bride and groom, best man, Billy, and matron of honour, Terri, followed by Freddie and Sylvia, Claude and Doreen, and three grinning groomsmen escorting three glamorous bridesmaids in eye-catching pink and yellow creations. Curious lady guests were later informed that the dresses and, indeed, the photographer all originated from the nation's capital where both the bride and her matron of honour, in their time with the West End's finest florist, had acquired more than useful contacts. Local wedding guests admired the organised celerity with which David Armstrong and his assistants despatched the obligatory photographs, including some unusual yet charming shots outside and beside the church, before the newly weds, liberally showered with confetti, were driven away to the hall in an open topped, vintage Rolls Royce.

Marquees can be a risk for wedding receptions should the weather be either wet or, at the other extreme, too hot. The combined brains and contacts of the father of the bride, the groom and best man had anticipated every exigency and extractor fans maintained a comfortable atmosphere—despite the cigarettes and at Freddie's insistence cigars—in both large adjoined tents—one for receiving and drinking and one for dining, speechifying and drinking. Billy, to the delight of Janice and the amazement of his sister, Zoe, excelled as best man and master of ceremonies. He and JJ had attended two weddings, that of Terri and Gerald had featured a red-coated toastmaster who had conducted proceedings. They had concluded that, whilst expense was little object, with application and some imitation they could avoid the intrusion of someone who, however skilled, was a stranger to most present. Freddie had, rather reluctantly, been guided by the two friends and would later congratulate Billy and agree the decision had been the correct one. Freddie's own speech was, as everyone expected, lengthy, but he was also humorous and none resented his self-indulgence in proposing the health and future happiness of his daughter and her 'fine, upstanding, talented and bloody lucky husband.' JJ's response was shorter, wittier and utterly apposite. He referred to the many enquiries as to the honeymoon destination and assured everyone that not even his wife was aware where they were headed, and to disclose where they would be for the next two weeks would, indeed, be silly. Surprisingly, no one, not even Jenny, saw through his straightforward hint. He ended with a traditional though sincere tribute to and toast of the matron of honour and bridesmaids and, to their surprise, he departed from tradition by including in the toast the best man and groomsmen. This left Billy to improvise part of his response but, again, Billy was equal to the challenge and managed to draw even greater laughter than the previous two speakers before evoking more mirth reading a host of telegrams from which he had cleverly saved the ribald and ridiculous to the last. Everyone was happy, some very much so as Freddie had not skimped on the champagne. After an hour during which JJ and Jenny endeavoured, without complete success, to speak to everyone, they managed to slip quietly away for Bennett and the attendant Rolls-Royce to whisk them the quarter mile to the hall where they changed into their going-away outfits.

Whilst the happy couple were changing, members of the rugby club, surprised at how easily detected was JJ's car, effected the usual decoration of and attachment of tin cans to what they were certain was the honeymoon transport. Only Billy, excusing himself due to his position, failed to join in the jollification of daubing the car with silly slogans. The Rolls-Royce returned Mr and Mrs Whitehouse-Martin to the marquee where they bade fond farewells to their nearest and dearest before, laughingly, climbing into JJ's 'decorated' car and driving away down the drive. Several cars extracted themselves from the parking with the intention of chasing the honeymoon chariot. They were, to their surprise, frustrated by the sudden appearance immediately behind JJ's slowly moving car of a large breakdown recovery lorry that took up the entire width of the drive. The procession did not travel far. The attention of the pursuers was drawn to the helicopter that suddenly appeared—summoned by JJ's telephone call as he had left the hall—and which landed on the outfield of the hall cricket pitch. Bride and groom speedily left the decorated car and ran, bending low, to the helicopter. With the cheery smiles of those who had outwitted their tormentors, they boarded the whirlybird and were whisked away to none knew where. As the disappointed pursuers, who were nonetheless admiring of the initiative displayed by the couple, returned to the marquee and more consolatory wine, the driver of the recovery lorry—one of Billy's trusted mechanics who was being well paid for his services—drove JJ's car onto the flat-bed of the larger vehicle, secured it and drove to the pre-booked car-wash and valeting service.

Jenny was aware that their honeymoon luggage had already been forwarded to wherever she was being taken, but she had only been appraised of the escape plan whilst she and JJ changed. She remained in ignorance of their final destination—having only been told that she would love it. Again JJ promised her that it was all for her and asked for her patience and trust. The helicopter whisked them to Birmingham airport.

JJ had invested a great deal of time—and money—in the operation and a small plane awaited them for a short flight to Newquay airport.

'So we're spending a fortnight in Newquay?' queried Jenny, endeavouring to hide some disappointment.

'No, darling. There's another two helicopter rides, yet,' replied a smiling, although inwardly apprehensive JJ.

'But——'

'But me no buts, Mrs Whitehouse-Martin. It *will* be alright. . . . And if it's not to your absolute delight then, I promise you, we'll come straight back and go wherever else you would like to go.'

Jenny held her peace and her stomach for yet more helicopter journeys. They flipped to Penzance heliport, changed helicopters, and soon saw, nestling in a (for once) calm blue Atlantic, the Isles of Scilly.

They did not make an immediate return from the Scilly Isles. The luxury hotel on St Mary's Isle became their base but, as JJ had imagined and expected, they spent a great deal of time on the smallest inhabited island of the Scilly's—Bryher—population fifty-seven. Noted for flower gardens and wild flower meadows, Bryher was, as JJ had known it would be, a heaven on Earth for his botanical wife. In between gazing at and extensively photographing flowers, they lazed on and swam in Rushy Bay and other sandy beaches. It was a thoroughly relaxing fortnight and, having very few others with whom to talk, they grew even closer in spirit. They wrote and despatched only four postcards: one each to their respective parents, to Billy, and Terri. The St Mary's postman was proved correct in his forecast that the cards would only narrowly beat them back home. That journey was staggered due to distance as, by prior arrangement, JJ's car had been cleaned and delivered to Penzance. The Whitehouse-Martins made a leisurely, tourists' journey through the West Country staying one night each in the maligned-by-Jenny Newquay, Plymouth, Torquay, Exeter, Bath and Cheltenham.

CHAPTER FORTY-ONE
CHANGES OF DIRECTION
JULY 1971 TO MARCH 1972

On his return to Price Waterhouse on 12 July 1971 after an agreed extended holiday, JJ was delighted to be told that he was being immediately promoted. He would be the youngest manager in the firm's UK offices. He was less than pleased, however, that the post involved him spending time away from the Midlands, initially in London and thereafter in whichever regional offices required his skills in bringing to the market new companies, and effecting amalgamations and acquisitions. He was expected to assume his new duties on the following Monday—allowing a week of preparation. The increased salary was of little financial importance—his other interests were all profitable despite needing little of his time. The irony of Jenny having spent her time in Swinging London and returned to the calmer region of her birth, whilst he was now expected to move himself and, by implication if not direction, his new wife to the capital was not lost on either of them. It would be churlish to refuse promotion—but nor would it be agreeable to Jenny or JJ to instantly remove themselves from not only their family and friends, but their respective businesses in the Midlands. After long discussions between themselves and consultations with Billy, Janice, Zoe and Freddie, it was agreed that their home would remain at the grange and JJ would commute between Avonbridge, London and wherever else he was required to be for the next year. After which they would review the situation. It was not the start to their life as a couple that JJ and Jenny had hoped for.

Nor would their desire to be parents be fulfilled. It had been their intention to start a family of their own as soon as they were married. Since this seemed not to be happening despite energetic and enjoyable bouts at bedtime (and other moments when both so wished) they agreed to consult a Harley Street gynaecological specialist—Jenny's trip to London being excused as necessary to inspect JJ's small flat in Fulham. The resultant diagnosis that the internal trauma of Jenny's rape had rendered her infertile left them both devastated. They sat together in the

Fulham flat in deep despondency. Despite the constant hum of traffic and humanity around them, they felt utterly alone.

Two sensible, intelligent and practical people can, as did Jenny and JJ, accept even sickening disappointment. After a disturbed night and over an early breakfast, they discussed adoption and fostering; neither found favour. Such adopted children as Jenny had known were either miserable or disturbed. JJ recalled, with sadness, his own hostile reception of Claude as a stepfather. As was too often usual, arrival at London offices was not the prompt-at-nine habit of the provinces, so JJ accompanied Jenny to Euston Station for her 9.25 train. As he stood on the platform awaiting Jenny's departure, the beginnings of what might help them occurred to JJ, 'Jenny . . . when you get home could you ring Uncle Charles and Auntie Charlotte to see if we could go and talk to them on Saturday or Sunday?'

'Yes, I could, darling. . . . But why them?'

'Because, Jenny, they've been childless all their married life—so far as I know—and a more level-headed, happy and contented pair of people I couldn't hope to meet. They're discreet and sensible. I think it might help us to talk to them . . . if you agree?'

Jenny stood and thought. Her acquaintance with the elder Whitehouses was, obviously, of far less duration than JJ's, yet she could not but agree with JJ's logic.

She agreed to arrange something for the weekend—JJ wished she'd not used that phrase, but he let it go in the circumstances—and let JJ know by telephoning the London office once the proposed meeting was in place.

The meeting with Charles and Charlotte included separate talks between Jenny and Charlotte, and Charles and JJ before all four sat down to a civilised Saturday lunch and openly spoke of their feelings and, in the younger pair's case, future. As JJ had hoped, the frank exchange of views did help both him and Jenny. Mr and Mrs Whitehouse-Martin returned to work on the Monday more settled persons determined to broaden the scope of their already busy lives by involvement with betterment for others.

Jenny joined the local Women's Institute that one of her best customers had been advocating for months. Subsequently, she judiciously selected three local charities with whom she felt her interests and abilities best suited. She took charge of the flower rota for St Barnabas' Church and, largely due to her dexterous selections, the church looked a more welcoming place of worship than before. Jenny's flower patch continued to be both popular and profitable—in some measure due to the young assistant Jenny had engaged. In March 1971, Jenny travelled to Lichfield to stand as godmother to Terri and Gerald's first born—Samuel George.

JJ found the pursuit of outside activities more difficult. Uncle Charles had spent some of their discussion time outlining the pleasure and other intangible benefits he himself had reaped from Freemasonry. He had not been insistent upon JJ joining the fraternity, but had simply indicated that, in his opinion, it would both interest and benefit JJ. Should he so wish, Uncle Charles would be only too pleased to assist his application. Obviously time and lack of availability during the working week did, for the time being, discriminate against JJ pursuing any interest Uncle Charles had engendered in the Midlands and, despite becoming aware of opportunities that could be available to him in London—he discovered there was a chartered accountants' lodge in the capital—he knew his future lay with Jenny in Avonbridge and tying himself to obligations beyond business in the capital would be unfair to all concerned. As he felt he should, JJ applied his best efforts to his new working responsibilities. He managed to return to Avonbridge almost every weekend. It was the almost aspect that posed a problem, since such Saturday and Sunday absences as were unavoidable always seemed to coincide with the need for him to join with Billy or Janice or Zoe—or other senior colleagues—in decisions concerning their joint interests. He had also, in token of gratitude for his father-in-law's wedding gift of shares in Wells Buildings Limited, become involved in the organisation—or in too many cases lack of such attribute— of Freddie's businesses. To properly institute the changes he deemed necessary for improved efficiency and fiscal savings, he really needed to be in or around Avonbridge full time—initially in order to persuade the bull-headed Freddie of the logic in his suggestions.

One year as a London-based Price Waterhouse manager was the time-line Jenny and JJ had initially agreed and both were, without speaking of it to the other, impatient for that time to pass and a decision to be reached. Yet it was Freddie who initiated the change for which, in different ways, his daughter and son-in-law had been longing. Bluffly interrupting their precious time together one April Sunday morning, Freddie barged into their lounge at the grange and, as was his usual style, came straight to the point with no preliminaries or polite introduction.

'See here, JJ—oh and you, too, Jenny—I've been thinking about all this modernisation you've been suggesting and so on. It seems to me that not only is there a lot of sense in what you say but, as you said last week—or was it the week before? don't matter—as you said, you ought to be here to get things done properly. And I agree with you. I'm out of touch with some of these things—never heard of some of 'em as it happens and . . . well, anyway I feel—no Doreen and I feel—you ought to join the board. Be a director, you know? Jenny as well. What d'ye think?'

Freddie paused for breath. He looked quizzically at the young couple who returned his gaze with a mixture of surprise and delight on their faces. Jenny had thought of making such a suggestion, but had not liked, as she saw it, to interfere. Similarly, JJ had been sure it would be a solution, but felt it would be best should the suggestion come from Freddie; now that it had, he knew there were details to discuss and agree but, knowing Freddie as he did, he was sure he should agree instantly and negotiate his own conditions later.

'Well . . . yes, Freddie. Thank you. I would be pleased and honoured, of course——'

'No need to make a speech about it, JJ. Firm can afford it, as you well know. We'll work out the details in the week—or whenever you can be around. Consider it settled. Best not take up your time any more for now, though.'

And, with his usual brusqueness, Freddie Wells left as sharply as he had arrived.

JJ and Jenny looked at one another and, feeling Freddie was out of earshot, burst out laughing. They then moved into the study, sat down at their respective desks and, since they both knew Freddie would not give any more thought to the details, began to do some working out.

JJ gave notice to his employers that, with regret but for personal reasons—a motive he and Jenny felt would be both diplomatic and deflect discussion—he would leave their ranks at the end of July 1972. At a June 1972 weekend meeting of the small board of directors (Freddie, Doreen and Terry Morton) both JJ and Jenny were appointed and welcomed as directors with equal voting rights unless a poll (number of shares held to decide) should be demanded. It never was.

CHAPTER FORTY-TWO
More Changes of Direction
July 1972 to March 1974

Billy and Janice, the latter six months pregnant, were the first to be told of the forthcoming changes. JJ had always confided in Billy and, since they had become engaged, with Janice too. Whilst JJ had been absent in London, Jenny and Janice had seen more of each other than previously and were now almost as firm friends as JJ and Billy. Janice and her efficient 3J's Business Books staff now maintained the business records and calculated and distributed wages for Jenny's Flower Patch; the (now five) hairdressing salons of ZoNice Hair and Beauty; Karbitz and B & J Cars; and J & B Printing as well as numerous local firms in which the friends had no direct investment, but who had been sufficiently impressed by Jan and her staff to enrol. JJ felt it better to keep some of his affairs to himself and the administration and records of his Birmingham properties remained with Harvey, Smith and Thomas in the second city. In June 1972, the Ministry of Transport tests for older cars became mandatory and, with commendable speed, Billy obtained the first test station licence in the area. He also, with warnings to conform, engaged his half-brother, Bobby, in the motor workshop.

Having served two years of his three-year sentence, Bobby Baker was determined not to return to incarceration at the pleasure of Her Majesty—or anyone else minded to remand him. He was grateful to his successful younger brother (half brother to be accurate) for immediate employment and applied himself diligently. One lesson Billy had swiftly learned from experience, JJ and Janice, was not to waste talent. Bobby had a talent for entering without permission not only locked cars, but locked premises. After three months of exemplary conduct and definite usefulness, Billy and Janice, now a new mummy, felt more certain of Bobby's intent to tread the straight and narrow. Aware, from an earlier episode of lost keys, that Avonbridge lacked a locksmith they initiated discussion with Bobby. Subsequently, with as many safeguards to their invested finances as Jan and Billy could devise, Bobby was established in an offshoot venture, Avonbridge Security. Although he maintained a low profile and was more diffident than he should have been, it proved the making of Bobby Baker. What had previously been but nefarious skills, he could now exercise legally. The business prospered, as did Bobby Baker, whose attitude towards the Establishment altered accordingly. JJ's involvement in Avonbridge Security was minimal, but he certainly gave the venture his blessing and a little financial backing. He would, in later years, not only utilise the firm, but confidentially charter Bobby Baker's skills. As would others.

Billy and Janice's son, William Arthur, was born in the of August 1972. Jenny, now working harder than ever for St Bartholomews, accumulated a portfolio of godmotherships. She stood Christian surety for William Arthur Baker in September, and in the next month similarly tied herself to the lives of Terrri's daughter, Jean Buchanan Anstruther, and Zoe's daughter, Jenny Marie Connolly.

JJ began full-time work as financial director of Wells Builders Limited on 1 August 1972. By mid-September his first wave of changes had been implemented with the formation of Wells Holdings Limited tying together several subsidiary companies whilst effectively keeping the disparate parts of Freddie's empire separate and self-regulating. A few foolish ventures that had never succeeded and in which Freddie had lost interest as swiftly as it had arisen, were dissolved and such able staff as had been frustrated or coasting with their fruitless tasks either transferred elsewhere in the organisation or generously dispensed with.

It was at this time, too, that the Whitehouse-Martins began a twelve-year dedication to cruising—primarily on the oceans of the world, but also on those major rivers that had begun to float passenger vessels bearing eager, curious tourists on their navigable waters. Jenny and JJ's first cruise was of two weeks duration and visited the Canary Isles and Madiera, they fell in love with the latter and alternated their water-born holidays with stays at the island's prestigious Reids Hotel.

Whilst the Bakers were well aware of the allure of holidays away from their native shores, the demands of parenthood and their own insularity persuaded Billy and Janice to vacation in the UK. Finding hotels too intolerant of their child and dogs, they purchased themselves a small property at Aberdovey on the southern edge of the Snowdonia National Park. There young William Arthur and his subsequent sibling could play happily on the sandy beach whilst their father indulged himself with the small sail-boat he maintained on the town slip and sailed on the Welsh waters. Janice's talent for organisation soon arranged their seaside home not only to their holidaying advantage but, by leasing it when they were not present, to their financial benefit. Over the course of each year, even allowing for the local agent's maintenance and letting charges, their holiday home cost little or nothing.

Since his talk with Uncle Charles, JJ had pondered whether or not to seek involvement with Freemasonry. He had been aware, well before Charles had openly spoken of it to him, that both of his male trustees and his stepfather were members. Uncle Charles and Mr Burroughs were, he reasoned, in lodges that met in or near Birmingham, Claude had absented himself from the vicarage on many winter Monday evenings, whilst he and JJ's mother were in Avonbridge but, since it seemed to be a confidential matter, JJ had only guessed where Claude had gone (he was correct, of course). After moving southwest, JJ was uncertain whether Claude's duties in Hereford were compatible with a continued involvement in a lodge (they were . . .). There had been ladies' nights which it had been suggested he might attend with a suitable lady friend, but the absence of such mandatory partners and other entertainments more attractive to JJ had ensured such suggestions were deflected until the impossible to refuse bidding to Freddie's lodge ladies' festival. The forthright manner of his father-in-law left JJ—and anyone else to whom he spoke at any length—in no doubt of Freddie's fraternal affiliation. JJ was actually surprised that Freddie had made no mention of JJ's joining him in the Masons during the first three months of his return to living locally and working daily alongside him. Freddie's reticence on the subject ceased as soon as JJ and Jenny returned from their first cruise. JJ was cornered in the office as soon as no other staff were present where Freddie's opening salvo informed JJ that he was presently junior warden—whatever that was—of his lodge and that, all things being as they should be, he would be master of the lodge in January 1974. As part of his programme, Freddie very much hoped that he could initiate JJ.

'The lodge would love it!' he said—apparently believing this would prove convincing to JJ, a belief in which he was, at least temporarily, disappointed. JJ said he would think about it—silently resolving to talk with Uncle Charles before making any commitment. At the time, Charles and Charlotte were holidaying in Portugal and not due to return until October. This left poor JJ subjected to constant queries from Freddie as to what he was dithering about; eventually JJ firmly stated that he needed to talk to Uncle Charles before he could make any binding commitment.

'Oh, old Charles will be in favour. I wouldn't do you without him present,' was the challenging reply. JJ persisted in his intent to speak to his uncle.

'Charles's lodges are in Warwickshire, JJ, you don't want to be doing all that travelling back and forth,' replied Freddie.

The pluralisation of lodge further bemused JJ. He decided he must be firm with Freddie and insisted that he would not make any decision until he had seen Charles. Whilst Freddie sulkily accepted his decision, it did not deter him from bringing the matter into conversation as often as he could. JJ found himself inventing reasons to be away from the hall and offices of Wells Holdings and subsidiaries and wishing his time away until October. At long last, Charles and Charlotte returned to Hagley Road and, as he was now semi-retired, JJ's uncle was happy to see him any time. What ensued relieved JJ greatly. Charles first assured him that he was under no obligation to be beholden to him due to their previous talk. He next, with the delicacy JJ had always admired in him, enquired to what examination Freddie had subjected him.

'Well . . . none really, Uncle Charles. Not sure I understand the question,' replied JJ.

'Oh dear,' laughed Charles, 'typical of Freddie, I'm afraid. Thinks he can ride roughshod over everything. Excuse me a moment, JJ.'

Charles left the room for a few moments and returned with a small, blue book in his hand. He consulted the early pages—list of contents—before turning the book to two pages headed 'What a Candidate Should Know' and handing the open book to JJ.

'Read that carefully, please, JJ,' he instructed.

JJ did so. When he had finished reading he looked up at his uncle.

'Anything there you disagree with?' queried Charles.

'No,' replied JJ.

'Any questions?'

'Not really . . . should I have?' replied JJ.

'It's not mandatory—or unusual, JJ, I'm sure you realise that there's a lot you don't know—and won't know until the time is right. Trust is essential. Now you need to make a decision or two. Since you telephoned I've made a few calls myself. I'd be more than happy to propose you into one of my lodges—yes, I am in more than one—but in none of them is there, presently, anyone who knows you well enough to be your seconder. More relevant, however, there will be no available place for an initiate until at least 1975. Fortunately for us, we're quite popular at the moment. Anyway, and perhaps just as important, travelling to and from Birmingham just for lodge meetings would add a lot of time to any commitment you enter into. If Freddie can get you in during 1974 then that and the local and family connection persuades me that it would be best for you to accede to his invitation. I suppose he's got a seconder in mind, but that's really no business of mine.'

'He did say there would be no problem about me being accepted,' said JJ.

'No doubt he did. Let's take him at his word—you're pretty well known in Avonbridge after all. There is just one thing I'd like to have your assurance on, though, JJ.'

'Of course, Uncle Charles—if I can.'

'Oh you should be able to,' laughed Charles. 'I'd like to be present when you go in and for at least your third degree. You won't know what that is, yet, of course. But if you give the secretary of Freddie's Lodge . . . Chandlery isn't it?' JJ nodded. 'Yes. If you give the lodge secretary the details I'm about to entrust to you when he informs you— and it will be in writing—of the date of your initiation, that will ensure you have two prestigious guests present. You are allowed to invite suitable guests. You're also expected to pay for their meals but, being aware of your finances, I don't see that as a problem.'

Uncle Charles took a piece of his personal notepaper from the small desk beside him and spent a few minutes writing. He then sealed the piece of notepaper into an envelope, addressed it to the secretary of Chandlery Lodge and handed it to JJ.

'Keep that safe until they write to you and then when you reply, as you must do, enclose this as it is. I needn't tell you not to open it. Good luck . . . but I'll see you before then, I hope.'

'So do I, Uncle Charles. And, well, thank you. I'll be able to make Freddie's day.'

And make Freddie's day he did.

He and Jenny duly attended Chandlery Lodge ladies' festival night on a Friday in October. The venue was familiar since The Swan seemed the only hostelry in Avonbridge capable of accommodating from eighty to 140 diners and dancers. Jenny, of course, had been persuaded to attend the Ladies Nights in 1969 and 1970, and despite feeling lonely, she had been, as she remained in 1972, impressed with the dignity and old-fashioned courtesies of the occasion. JJ was coming anew to such events. He shared his wife's admiration of the conduct and general tenor exhibited, but was slightly—and only slightly—resentful of the patronising attitude of one or two elderly brethren who constantly assured him how much he would enjoy being one of us. He preferred the jocular approach of those nearer his own age who expressed jolly hopes that JJ would be 'alright riding the goat', he felt he would enjoy their future company. He did just that at the 1973 ladies' night and, with a select few, found sufficient rapport to spend leisure time with them and their wives. Eventually, Freddie placed a very large form—conspicuously labelled 'Form P'—before JJ and asked him to complete the section relating to himself. Having done so, JJ was surprised and pleased to see that his seconder was his stepfather, Claude. After his name Claude had added 'Prov. G. Chap. H'ford & Glos'. JJ deemed it discreet not to enquire.

Wells Holdings Limited and its several subsidiaries continued to prosper as did JJ's various local business interests and Jenny's Flower Patch. The Hagley Road, Birmingham, properties of JJ and his Uncle Charles had been held in several property companies and, as had often been discussed, both principal participants now felt it time to re-organise and consolidate their interests. Through Charlotte's family trusts, Charles had other sources of income in addition to a well-funded personal pension and, conscious of the damaging effect of taxes on the estates of the wealthy, he felt it time to cede his interests in the luxury flats, apartments and houses. He and JJ carefully drafted a programme of disposals, amalgamations and gifts. To be certain, they jointly funded the cost of counsel's opinion. That approval being favourable, they implemented changes during 1973 resulting in JJ's net worth being considerably increased, Charles's net estate being reduced and several grateful Charities receiving unexpected donations. At the same time JJ, aware of the advisability of equalisation of estates between spouses, bestowed several parcels of shares upon Jenny. As they had always done, with no regrets and ultimate benefit to themselves, Billy and Janice, Zoe and her husband, George, and Peter Hordern and his wife followed JJ's example and advice—similarly re-arranging their affairs and shareholdings. They would never regret so doing.

To Freddie's disgust (he remained chairman of the rugby club) the residents of Avonbridge Grange decided, being honest with themselves, they had outgrown the jovialities of the New Year's Eve dance at The Swan. For New Year's Eve 1973 and 1974 they held small and select dinner parties in the little used salon of the grange. Sixteen adults sat down to a six-course repast cooked by the best chef-for-hire Jan could find. Before this, the children of the diners were similarly, though not so opulently or alcoholically accompanied, catered for with the two hired nannies before being put to bed—but not to sleep. At midnight they all saw and heard the televised image and sonorous chimes of Big Ben from London. There were hopeful toasts and friendly embraces. The seemingly forced gaiety of various entertainers well known and enjoyed north of Hadrian's

Wall were dismissed with the off-switch of the television and each grange guest and resident began New Year with a far earlier retirement to bed than had been their custom in earlier years. The following morning, as instructed, the well-paid hired chef, who had been accommodated for the night, served a running breakfast of kedgeree and rich coffee.

The imminent arrival of the second Baker baby—to be named Jonathan James or Jennifer Janice—and the oft-repeated invitation from Freddie and Doreen to Jenny and JJ to join them at the hall prompted a residential change at the grange. Billy and Janice converted JJ's flat to playrooms and offices for 3J's Business Books. JJ and Jenny moved to their own private wing of Avonbridge Hall bringing JJ closer to his administrative work with Wells Holdings and subsidiaries. It also enabled Freddie to travel, in the Rolls Royce, of course, with his initiate to the Avonbridge lodge rooms in March 1974.

CHAPTER FORTY-THREE
Avonbridge Hall
Monday 25 March 1974

Having spent a pleasant Sunday with Jenny visiting a four months pregnant Terri and Gerald and Jenny's godson Sam in Lichfield, JJ began the last Monday of March 1974 as he usually greeted any other working week—with expectant equanimity. Entering Wells Holdings' offices at 8.30 a.m., he automatically checked his diary, only then did he remember he had an evening engagement. (After tonight, the last Monday evenings of September, October, November and January to April inclusive would be reserved in his diary for Chandlery Lodge Number 5591.) No sooner had JJ consulted his diary than the booming voice of his father-in-law greeted him.

'Today's the day, then, JJ.'

JJ smiled and returned a meaningless, 'Oh . . . yes.'

Realising Freddie expected a more animated answer he added, 'Better not make any long trips, had I?'

The attempt at jocularity failed lamentably.

'I should b——y well, think not, indeed, lad. Try to have a quiet day and be ready at five o'clock. We need to be early—or I do. And its only right that I take you and bring you back tonight of all nights, so you'll have to wait about a bit. . . . But I've told you all this before, JJ. Sorry and all that.'

JJ smiled indulgently—he had concluded during previous lectures *his* evening had great significance for Freddie—and proceeded to sort the post and deal with what could quickly be despatched .He then made his usual telephone checks with the operational sites of Wells Builders, followed by more relaxed conversations with Billy, Jan, Zoe, Peter and other contacts with whom he always spoke at the start of a working week. At 11.00 a.m. he declined coffee to quickly nip home where he carefully made ready, as he should have done earlier, the specified dress for the evening: dark suit, black tie, white shirt, black socks and shiny black shoes.

On his way back to the offices, he met Doreen in the hallway of the hall. JJ's relations with his mother-in-law had always been at least cordial and more usually friendly—there was certainly no music hall characterisation involved. This particular morning, Doreen was more than usually friendly and confidential, 'I hope everything goes well for you tonight, JJ,' she said. Then, speaking conspiratorially, she confided, 'Freddie's in a bit of a state about it. It means a lot to him, you know. The trouble is, as it's always been with his Masonry, he can't remember the right words every time. Try not to notice, JJ, please—he does want tonight to be special for you.'

'I'll do what I can, Doreen,' replied a slightly bemused JJ, 'but it's all new to me so I'm not sure what I can do to help him.'

'I know, dear,' answered Doreen. 'Hope you enjoy it, of course. But'—she can't resist making her point again, thought JJ—'do be kind to Freddie.' With which parting shot, his mother-in-law bustled to her car and, without a wave, as usual, drove away in a shower of gravel and dust.

Back in the offices he was immediately hailed, 'Phone call for you, JJ, your Uncle Charles.'

Wondering what Charles could want of him in the middle of a Monday morning, JJ picked up the receiver and greeted his only uncle.

'Just thought I'd wish you well for tonight, JJ,' said Charles. 'Remember, we've all gone through exactly the same, so just relax and enjoy it.'

'Yes. Thank you—I intend to as far as I can.'

'Good, good. That's all . . . unless there's anything bothering you?'

'No. Not really . . . oh, well my dear mother-in-law buttonholed me earlier on and told me to be good to Freddie. Apparently he has problems getting the words right—or that's what I think she was trying to tell me. Should I do anything about it, Uncle?'

Charles laughed and assured JJ that there was nothing for him to worry about.

'If Freddie's in any difficulty there'll be lots of help for him— maybe too much. Think no more about that—just Doreen doing her usual fussy-wife routine. As I said—enjoy it. Cheerio.'

JJ was left listening to the dialling tone before returning the receiver to its rest and his concentration to the matters in hand.

At 4.00 p.m., as JJ put the 'finishing touches' to a quotation for a promising new customer he was commanded to, 'Leave that, now, JJ. Time to change.'

Wondering how a change of clothes warranted an hour devoted to nothing else, JJ decided this must be part of Freddie's state to which Doreen had alluded.

Ignoring his father-in-law's impatiently audible sighs, JJ, as he always did before leaving the office, tidied his desk before following Freddie back to the hall.

'See you back here at five to five, JJ,' said Freddie as they went to their separate wings of the hall.

'I'll be here—boots blacked,' replied JJ. He reflected how unlike his usual confident self Freddie appeared, if that's what this Masonry does to one, JJ thought, I might not stick around for long. In years to come, JJ sometimes wryly reflected on this early judgement.

At 4.50 p.m. JJ observed the ever-faithful Bennett drive the ever-present Rolls Royce to the usual boarding space opposite the hall front door. He made his way to the hall's hallway where he found only Bennett—surprisingly not wearing his driving uniform, but clad in a black morning coat and striped trousers over his usual white shirt and black tie. Smiling knowingly at JJ, he looked him up and down, 'Big night for you, then, sir.'

'So I'm told, Bennett.' Before he had chance to confirm Bennett's knowledge stemmed from Freddie, the said Freddie appeared dressed exactly like Bennett. Freddie was now more flustered than before—as usual any nerves or uncertainty over-ridden by bad temper at his own, as he deemed it, weakness.

'Come on then, JJ. Never be late for lodge—eh, Bennett?'

'Not if it can be avoided, sir.'

CHAPTER FORTY-FOUR
Avonbridge Masonic hall
Monday 25 March 1974

Bennett drove in to the Masonic hall car park and parked the Rolls in a place conspicuously specified by a large sign for 'W.M.' Alighting, Bennett opened the car's rear doors for Freddie and JJ and then, instead of driving away as he usually did after delivering his employer, he locked the car and followed them into the strange portals.

'I'll leave you with Brother Bennett now,' said Freddie. 'He'll take care of you until we need you.'

So saying, Freddie turned away and, Masonic case in hand, mounted the stairs. Bennett took JJ gently by the arm and guided him from the hallway through double doors into a large downstairs room where tables were already set for dining. In a smaller room beyond were casual chairs and a bar. As they walked towards the smaller room, Bennett hastened to put JJ at his ease.

'It seems Worshipful Brother Wells failed to explain I'd be looking after you, sir?'

'All he said was the tyler would take care of me and see I was properly prepared—whatever that means.'

'Oh, dear, sir. Typical, I'm afraid. Too much secrecy. Right, Mr JJ—I'm the tyler of this lodge—and two others as it happens. Part of my duties is getting you ready for the ceremony—exactly as everyone's prepared on their first night. After the lodge is opened at six o'clock, I can take you upstairs. Until then sit here, please. I don't recommend much drinking but, if you feel so inclined, a small brandy or whisky won't hurt.'

'I wouldn't mind a whisky, please, Bennett. How much?'

'Don't worry about that, sir. It'll be my pleasure to buy you a drink tonight.'

So saying, the chauffeur-turned-tyler slipped behind the bar and served a double Scotch that he handed to JJ with a jug of fresh water.

'I need to leave you now, sir. I have to make sure everyone's properly attired and so on. It'll be an hour or so before we need to go up, I'm afraid. I'll bring one of the brethren in to meet you when he arrives, but otherwise no one will disturb you. Just stay calm. You'll be alright, sir.'

So saying, Bennett left JJ with his Scotch and water—and his thoughts. As time passed, JJ began to wish he'd brought a book to read. Bennett re-appeared with another familiar face above an unfamiliarly morning-suited body.

'Hello, JJ.'

'Gosh—hello, Alan.'

'I obviously don't need to introduce the two of you,' said Bennett. 'Parade in about twenty-five minutes, Brother Simmonds.'

Bennett left JJ with the former captain of the town second XV rugby team. As often happens, their paths had diverged and they'd not seen one another for at least three years, but any attempt to catch up would obviously have to wait—as Alan Simmonds made clear.

'Can't be long, JJ. I'll be looking after you in the ceremony, tonight.'

As with his father-in-law, JJ detected an unexpected nervousness in Alan—unlike anything he'd observed on the occasions they had played rugby together. Again, he wondered whether he was embarking on something he might regret. 'If it's good enough for Uncle Charles, it's good enough for me,' he thought.

Alan Simmonds stood beside JJ and took his left hand in his before crooking their arms. Had JJ been told he would be blindfold? He had.

'OK then. I'll be leading you like this. You'll be asked questions, but only answer what I tell you to say—except for one time when I'll say "answer" and by then you'll know what to say, believe me. Above all, enjoy it, JJ. Super to have you with us. See you later.'

After warmly shaking JJ's hand, Alan Simmonds walked away, then paused, 'Nearly forgot. You don't wear glasses at all, do you, JJ?'

'Good Lord, no,' replied JJ.

'That's good. See you soon.'

JJ finished his whisky. Should he serve himself another, he wondered. No. Old Bennett had implied one would be enough. It had been good of him to buy JJ that one. He decided to wash and dry his glass and, once behind the counter, couldn't resist checking the bar prices on a printed tariff, very cheap, was his first conclusion. The second surprise was finding that the tariff had been printed by his own (and Billy and Peter's) firm. Small world, he thought, resuming his lonely seat. From beyond the dining room doors there had been sounds of men greeting each other. Above him, JJ had heard sounds of people moving, but then there had been someone calling for and getting silence, a voice seemed to be making an announcement and then there came organ music, banging and voices raised in song. And . . . even more banging followed by near silence. To JJ's relief, Bennett re-appeared.

'Come along, then, Mr JJ. Time to get you ready.'

JJ followed Bennett up the stairs to a small landing on which stood a small desk and a big book with 'Chandlery Lodge No. 5591' printed on its cover, and when opened up, the date handwritten at the top of the page. There were also a lot of signatures, but JJ felt he ought not to examine them closely.

'Can you just sign the book, please, sir,' requested Bennett—pointing to a space against which had been written, 'After initiation.' For the first of many times, JJ signed the attendance register of his lodge. Bennett then politely, but firmly, instructed JJ to remove his jacket and tie and undo the top four buttons of his shirt.

'This is traditional, sir, so that it's obvious to everyone that you're a man,' he patiently explained, folding back the shirt to expose JJ's left breast. Next, he asked JJ to remove his cuff-links from both sleeves, turn back the left cuff and roll up his right shirt sleeve. He examined JJ's hands and patiently explained that all candidates had to be without any metal.

'No belt, JJ?'

'Not yet, Bennett,' smiled JJ. To his own surprise he felt quite relaxed.

Lastly, Bennett turned his attention to JJ's lower body. He rolled up JJ's left trouser leg and asked him to remove his shoes and left sock and place his bare foot into a heel-less slipper he secured with an elasticated fastener.

'What's that all about?' queried JJ.

'You'll be asked to kneel on your left knee. Symbolically your knee will be directly in contact with a representation of hallowed ground. A lot of Freemasonry's symbolic; as you'll find out as you progress.'

JJ began to feel there was something to all this—he wanted to 'progress' and started to say so. Bennett motioned to him to be quiet as he went to a door with a knocker and, at eye level, a sliding panel. Bennett eased the panel aside and listened intently. Closing the panel he led JJ towards the door before gently placing a blindfold over his eyes and securing it behind his head. He also placed something else around JJ's neck that hung down his back—but no explanation was offered. Instead Bennett said, 'This is it, JJ. As everyone else has probably said—enjoy it. Just pay attention and do as you're told.'

JJ heard a loud knock just in front of him and a voice inside saying something inaudible. Eventually, he heard the swish of the door being opened.

A voice with a strong Worcestershire accent asked, 'Whom have you there?'

Bennett answered giving JJ's full name, '. . . a poor candidate in a state of darkness, who has been well and worthily recommended and wants to partake of the mysteries and privileges of ancient Freemasonry.'

There was another question and answer and then the accented voice said he would report to the worshipful master and the door was closed.

JJ heard a further distant exchange of words before the door re-opened and something cold and hard was pressed against his left breast. The accented voice asked if he could feel anything.

As JJ was about to say yes, Bennett whispered in his ear, 'Say, "I can."'

JJ dutifully said, 'I can,' the cold thing was removed and his hand was taken.

The familiar voice of Alan Simmonds asked him to, 'Come with me, please.'

They walked forward a few steps and Alan whispered, 'Stop there.'

His hand was released and a re-assuring hand, presumably Alan's, held his elbow. Then there was Freddie's loud voice, speaking slower than usual—as if he were reciting—asking JJ if he were free and over twenty one.

Alan whispered in his ear, 'I am.'

JJ, resisting the temptation to reply that Freddie should know, and remembering what he had been told, repeated, 'I am.'

Then, in a formal language, JJ had never heard him use before, Freddie requested him to kneel (in his own words, Freddie would have commanded him to kneel) Alan whispered there was a stool in front of him and JJ was lowered to a kneeling posture. There was more 'banging' and sounds of people moving before another voice—this one almost inaudible—recited something that seemed, from what little JJ could hear, to be a prayer. At the end of the prayer, the organ burst forth and lots of voices intoned something that sounded like 'somo tit bee'.

Freddie, still formally addressing JJ as Mr Whitehouse-Martin, asked who he trusted, Alan whispered the reply which JJ repeated at greater volume, he was beginning to get the hang of this blind adherence. Freddie said he could 'safely rise', so JJ began to get up, but Alan held him down, perhaps he wasn't getting the hang of it after all. Freddie finished his laboured sentence and JJ was helped to his feet. Freddie said that JJ would pass in view for them and, unnecessarily in JJ's opinion, said he was 'a fit and prosperous person' to be made a Mason.

Alan took hold of his right hand as he had in the room below and said, 'Step off with the left foot . . . right.'

Despite the contradictory instruction they both put forth their left foot and walked slowly forward and around, using staccato stops and starts to change direction. They then stopped and, obeying Alan's whispered instruction, JJ was led, shuffling, sideways. Alan pulled JJ's right hand forwards and pumped it up and down on what seemed to be another person.

That other person—if it was he—said, 'Whom have you there?'

Alan stopped whispering, and in his normal voice, said what Bennett had said outside the door—contradicting Freddie, JJ noticed, by saying he was a 'poor candidate'. The other person, who had a very mellifluous voice, bade him 'enter'. Instead of, as he expected, going into somewhere JJ was, again, shunted sideways before starting the slow march with the 'left foot, right' instruction. Again they stopped and shuffled sideways for the same procedure of hand-banging on someone and a further enquiry as to who Alan had there. Alan was further questioned, gave clear answers and they were, again, bidden to 'enter.'

JJ was moved around a short distance, his right hand placed into that of another before his arm was almost torn from its socket as the last examiner announced, 'Worshipful master, I present to you Mr Johnson Whitearse-Mitton probably prepared to be made a Mason.'

'This is *it*,' thought JJ, suppressing a giggle as he sensed it was Alan beside him. It wasn't. Freddie said he was going to ask some more questions, he trusted would 'be answered with camphor.'

JJ, rightly, assumed there was forgiveness for Freddie's confusion of linament and integrity. Three long questions, laced with spoonerisms and mispronunciations, followed, to each of which JJ gave the required answer supplied by the attentive Alan. Then, as instructed, he was to be 'advanced to the pedestal' an advance accomplished by means of slightly complicated steps—all with the left foot followed, as instructed, by the right.

Worshipful Master Freddie now seemed very near to and somewhat above JJ, booming forth about his duty and, with a few more unintentional errors, telling JJ about Freemasonry that, apparently according to Freddie, possessed, 'great and immoral privileges.'

It was obvious to JJ that Freddie had learned—or memorised as best he could—what could be a rather fine spate of language. He recalled Doreen's words of the morning and understood her concern. Freddie was asking him if he was willing to take, 'a solemn obligation to keep in violence the secrets and miseries of the Order.'

Instead of dictating a reply, Alan said, 'Answer.'

Recollecting what Alan had told him earlier and the tone of previous answers, JJ said, 'I am.'

He was told—this was more like the Freddie he knew—to kneel.

Alan whispered, 'Pedestal at knee height right in front of you.'

Freddie was given JJ's right hand and gently placed it down flat on 'the volume of the sacred law.' JJ was given some cold and pointed compasses to hold against himself and told to, 'repeat your long name and repeat what I say.'

More knocking—the first very close to him. The feeling he was the subject of something very special and meaningful to those around him was very strong. JJ repeated what Freddie diligently dictated in staccato phrases (he was corrected or prompted from time to time and JJ, with commendable quick thinking, chose to correct the phrase 'wilfully purged individual' to 'wilfully perjured individual.')

He was asked to seal his obligation by kissing the volume and then he was, with loud and simultaneous applause, relieved of the blindfold and able to see the large Bible before him on which his hand still rested. Not only his hand, but a Square and a set of Compasses in shiny metal that Freddie proceeded to laboriously explain before tightly seizing JJ's right hand and telling him to, 'Rise, newly obliged brother among Masons.'

Freddie was smiling with pleasure and relief. Alan was given JJ's hand again and led him to Freddie's right. As they moved around, JJ saw his Uncle Charles wearing an impressive collar with lots of gold, before he again came face to face with the worshipful master. He too, wore a big collar, his had silver crests attached to it. Freddie smiled at him—obviously pleased with not only himself, but with JJ as well.

Freddie's smile waned as someone behind him prompted the start of further explanations. It was obviously a great strain for Freddie to master the language required of him, but he struggled on and JJ joined the general sympathy for him. Somehow, with increasingly frequent prompting, Freddie continued before, with evident relief, he arrived at a point where, once more, Alan was telling JJ what to reply to the mercifully short and, therefore, better recollected questions the worshipful master posed. He was told to pass and Alan walked him away on a course he felt he had previously traversed in darkness and ignorance. He was examined by the same brethren as before and, now that he could put a face to the voice, he identified the man with the mellifluous voice as W. P. Hilton, a retired solicitor of the town who had been a member of a Charity Committee JJ's mother had embraced. The man addressed as senior warden was a bluff, red-faced fellow whose thin, reedy voice ill-matched his appearance. It later transpired he was a market-gardener from a village on the Worcester Road, in years to come his gardens were marketed as building plots and he retired to the English Riviera.

The examinations were an extension of that already gone through with Freddie. After the last one, JJ was taken to the opposite side of the senior warden where a further attempt to dislodge his right arm from its socket preceded another, equally inaccurately named, presentation. The senior warden was marginally less nervous and accomplished than Freddie—despite which, JJ felt pleased and honoured to be clad in a Masonic apron. He was escorted to the centre of the room and then, to the surprise of many in the room—JJ included—Freddie proudly and with evident relief announced, 'I now request Worshipful Brother Whitehouse, our newly made brother's uncle, to assume the master's chair.'

Uncle Charles was clad in regalia far more magnificent than anyone present except the brother sat beside him who, JJ now realised, was his former principal and trustee, William Burroughs.

What Uncle Charles said was far more fluent than anything Freddie had uttered. After an interesting few minutes during which Alan Simmonds asked him to contribute in the cause of charity and another brother dictated answers in a long form of negatives, Uncle Charles explained very clearly what had just occurred before—another surprise for JJ—calling upon Worshipful Brother Claude Martin to present the working tools of an entered apprentice.

Claude, also clad in quite impressive regalia—not as big or as golden as Uncle Charles or Mr Burroughs, but still impressive—was also fluent, comprehensible and sincerely friendly in first giving JJ a wooden ruler, a wooden hammer and a metal chisel, before taking them back with cogent explanation as to their different symbolic interpretations for Freemasons. After that, Uncle—now Worshipful Brother—Charles presented JJ with a small collection of books and pamphlets on behalf of the worshipful master and asked Alan—Brother Junior Deacon as he addressed him—to conduct JJ to his proposer and seconder to be congratulated. Freddie and Claude both shook JJ's hand warmly and Claude presented him with a small book which, he said explained the recent ceremony of his initiation.

Uncle—Worshipful Brother—Charles then told JJ he was, 'at liberty to retire, and on your return you will hear a charge, usually given by the junior warden but'—and here he drew gasps of surprise and expectation from many—'to be given this evening, by kind permission of the worshipful master and the lodge, by myself and Worshipful Brother Burroughs.'

Alan escorted him down the lodge room with a small library in his right hand. As they halted, he was quietly advised to transfer that lot to the other hand before being more audibly told to salute the worshipful master. Which he did, before being escorted to the door and returned to the care and attention of Brother Bennett, the tyler.

As JJ dressed himself again—he liked the apt phrase Uncle Charles had used, 'restore yourself to your usual comforts.'

Bennett told him if he had questions about the recent ceremony he would answer if appropriate but that, 'No one can take it all in when they're the candidate. The best way to make sense of it is to see someone else being done. Very likely someone will invite you later.'

JJ did want to know—it being the most recent thing to mystify him—why there was such surprise when his uncle had said he and Mr —sorry—Worshipful Brother Burroughs were 'giving' something when he returned.

'Ah—now there I can help you. What is to come is known as the charge. In this lodge—in fact in most lodges I know—it's usually given by the junior warden only. Tonight the appointed junior warden isn't able to be here due to a long-standing business arrangement and Worshipful Brother Hilton is "sitting in" for him. In the circumstances, and as I understand they have both known you a long time, you are to be charged by two grand lodge officers. Never been done before that I know of. Probably never be done again. So you're a lucky young man, Brother JJ. Enjoy it.' He looked JJ over.

'Almost ready, brother. One last thing, if I may, JJ. Please accept these as my gift to you on your initiation.' He presented JJ with a pristine pair of white cotton gloves.

'Put them on now, brother. I'll announce you.' Bennett knocked three times on the lodge door and informed the man, whom JJ came to realise was the inner guard, 'Our new made brother, now restored to his comforts, requests admission.'

'Wait whilst I report to the worshipful master,' replied the inner guard and closed the door. A gloved JJ turned to look at old Bennett with further admiration.

'Gosh thanks, Benn . . . Brother Bennett,' gasped JJ.

'My pleasure, brother,' replied the tyler. He solemnly shook JJ's hand.

The door opened and JJ saw Alan—Brother Alan Simmonds—smiling and holding out his hand to escort him in. Again he was asked to salute. Again he concurred. He was then taken to the centre of the room where Brother Simmonds told him to, 'Stand firm and listen. I'll be back for you later.'

Freddie was again in the worshipful master's chair. To his right sat Uncle Charles and William Burroughs who both rose to their feet, saluted the master and stepped forward to stand almost together. JJ again quietly admired their magnificent and slightly opulent regalia.

Uncle Charles began, 'After you were initiated, I ensured that you were first congratulated by your proposer, the worshipful master, and your seconder, Worshipful Brother Martin—one being your father-in-law and the other your step-father.'

Worshipful Brother Burroughs then continued, 'The congratulations are not upon your own conduct, excellent though it has been, but for you choosing to be, and being admitted to, Freemasonry. And now, we are privileged to add our personal congratulations to you on the occasion of your being admitted a member of our ancient and honourable institution.'

They continued to speak alternately for what was actually twenty-five minutes—although for JJ it passed almost too quickly. Having been mentored by both of these fine men, whom he respected immensely, for large parts of his formative life, it was easy to listen to the words of wisdom they were imparting and a sort of second nature to remember and resolve to abide by all that they had to say. When, later in the evening, it became clear to him that what the two grand officers had said was, in fact, part of the ritual and had been learned and remembered for recital by them, it came as a mild shock. So natural had been their delivery, and so used to listening to their advice had JJ become, that he had assumed them to be speaking freely from experience.

When they finished they signified this by bowing their heads to him before saluting the master and sitting down. Everyone slapped their aprons loudly—JJ assumed this was the manner of applause in a lodge. Brother Simmonds appeared at his right, took his hand and, swinging him around, took him to a chair near to the door. As he let go of JJ's hand he whispered, 'Remain standing and nod your head at me when I nod at you.'

JJ did as he was told and, to his surprise, was rewarded with several 'apron-slaps'. Brother Alan then shook his hand and said quietly, 'Welcome, Brother JJ,' before gesturing for JJ to sit. He did so with some relief—he had been standing for some time, he now realised.

The brother whom he sat next to shook his hand and muttered his name—sadly inaudibly. There followed what seemed to be a business and correspondence session with Freddie in the master's chair banging his gavel and jumping up and down before the secretary did likewise and read out things of which JJ understood little. Then a lot of men—Masons—mostly on the master's right, stood in turn and offered greetings from their lodges. Freddie thanked them and assured them of a warm welcome at the festive board.

'What's that?' JJ quietly asked the brother sat next to him.

'It's the food and drink and speeches, of course,' was the muttered reply.

Then Freddie asked them to help him to close the lodge; everyone rose to their feet and the muttering one unnecessarily helped JJ up. The lodge was closed with more banging and some quite impressive exchange of words before a precession was formed. The brother at the door crept forward and moved JJ to a prominent position, this mystified him until everyone began to file out and, as they passed him, each one shook his hand and said either 'congratulations' or 'welcome', or variations of one or both. As JJ was finally escorted through the door—again by Alan Simmonds, but less formally than before—Bennett relieved him of the plain white apron in which the senior warden had clad him. He assured JJ he, or another tyler, would always find him an appropriate apron.

'Thanks again Benn—Brother Bennett,' said JJ. 'Where do I go now?'

'Downstairs, JJ. The bar's open. The D.C.—sorry, director of ceremonies—will look after you when dinner is ready—should be in about twenty minutes.'

The number of people—now brethren—eager to buy him a drink could have seen JJ intoxicated in a very short time. He was surprised at how many of those present he already knew from social and business contacts. Having heeded Freddie's advice, mysterious though it had been when given, he had his pocket diary with him—which was as well since he received several invitations to see an initiation at their lodges. He was able to accept three of them during March and April, two at lodges meeting in the Avonbridge premises, and another in Bromsgrove to which his host promised to transport him. The chatting was interrupted as the big, florid man who had been pointed out as Floury Fellowes the D.C. banged yet another gavel (JJ had discovered the wooden hammers were called gavels) and asked everyone to take their places at the festive board.

Everyone began to file towards the dining tables.

'Sit where we like?' enquired JJ naively.

'Grief, no!' expostulated a short man in a morning suit. 'There's a table plan.'

Only then did the exasperated speaker realise to whom he was speaking and, clearing his throat to cover up embarrassment, added, 'You sit by the master tonight, of course.'

JJ felt that there was no 'of course' in light of what he knew. He had no chance to reply as a large brother took him by the elbow, introduced himself as, 'Ray Hughes, A.D.C. I'll show you where you're sitting tonight.'

JJ was, to his surprise, seated at the top table next to, if the place card was to be believed, the worshipful master. He had no chance to read who would be at his right as worshipful brother Hughes pushed him, not too gently, against the wall saying:

'Leave them room to enter.'

At the far end of the room the D.C. banged a staff on the floor and announced, 'Brother wardens and brethren, please receive your worshipful master accompanied by grand officers.'

Everyone began clapping in unison as a piano played 'Hail to the Chief' and Freddie swaggered in led by the D.C. carrying a wand and followed by JJ's former trustees. Freddie walked past JJ and stood by his seat at the table. Uncle Charles, for it was he who was placed to his right, beckoned JJ forward. Freddie banged his gavel which was answered, as it had been in the room above, by two other gavellings before Freddie ordered, 'Pray silence for the chaplain—who will say grace.'

The same semi-audible brother as in the room above delivered a short grace after which everyone made the same response as JJ had heard before, and which was now interpreted by Uncle Charles as, 'So mote it be', an elongated version of 'amen'.

The meal was very good, as was the company. JJ asked questions, but swiftly appreciated that for many answers he must be patient and trust his new brethren. He was told, after Uncle Charles had checked with Freddie, that there would be 'more enlightenment later.' During cheese and biscuits, Uncle Charles explained to JJ the traditional manner of honouring toasts at Masonic table—known as 'firing'; the small, thick glasses—known as 'firing glasses' to everyone's right were for that specific purpose. Despite the explanation, the 'fire' proved difficult at first, but by the time the first five formal toasts had been drunk—Uncle Charles and William Burroughs sat down during the third and had glasses raised to them, then they, Claude and others remained seated for the fifth—JJ was becoming sufficiently adept at the manoeuvres to avoid embarrassment. The next toast was to the worshipful master and a pleasant, well-spoken old brother wittily flattered Freddie before everyone stood and drank to him. JJ expected Freddie to reply straight away—indeed he did shuffle a few notes around. Instead of which another younger brother stood up and, with piano accompaniment, sang rather a jolly song with three verses and chorus in which everyone joined. Again, they all toasted Freddie and, after being announced by the director of ceremonies, who pulled back Freddie's chair as he rose, his father-in-law finally responded. JJ was used to hearing Freddie make lengthy 'little speeches' as Doreen called them. Here, he was pleased to note, the Wells penchant for interminable oratory was subdued. Freddie sat down with a sigh of relief and, to JJ's surprise, leaned across to ask Uncle Charles if his speech was alright? It seemed to be approved of although the quiet, smiling exchange between the two grand officers might, had it been audible, have belied the assurance.

'You next,' said Freddie, nudging JJ. 'Remember how to address everyone?'

Having had it drilled into him at every opportunity for the last week or more JJ, could scarcely have been expected to forget, but he gave a restrained affirmative and sat back with the best appearance of relaxed comfort he could assume.

'Worshipful Brother Claude Martin will propose the next toast—to our brother initiate.'

Claude, who was seated several chairs to Freddie's left, though still at the top table, rose to his feet. He was sincere, amusing and managed to avoid giving JJ cause to blush; he clearly explained to JJ why he was seated at the master's right hand for tonight only and why he would shortly receive Masonic fire in his own right tonight and not again until he became master of a lodge (he actually said 'succeed to the chair of King Solomon', and said it in such a sincere manner as to imbue JJ with a desire to eventually do just that).

Freddie's constant nagging and Uncle Charles's gentle hints had prepared JJ for his reply. He had been on his feet as secretary of the Students' Society many times and after dinner speaking held no great terrors for him. But he was not called upon to respond straight away. As they had done for the worshipful master, the brethren now sang a song for him, only this time there was a different soloist for each verse. For the first time—and he hoped the last—JJ heard his father-in-law attempt to give vent to musical voice. It was as well, he felt (as did everyone else) that each three lines were repeated by everyone. After six verses, JJ wondered what was happening as everyone rose and, with much shuffling and suppressed laughter, formed a circle around the room. Everyone extended their arms and joined hands. As JJ was wondering what was going on the florid-faced director of ceremonies inserted himself into the circle at the far end of the room facing JJ.

'Brother initiate,' he began as everything went quiet, 'with open arms we receive you into Freemasonry.'

What he said, and the manner in which he said it combined with everyone swaying gently, made as much, if not more, impression on JJ as had the ceremony in the room above. It was sincere, meaningful and the more impressive for being utterly unexpected. When, at last, the final verse of the song had been sung and everyone had sat down again, JJ was announced as pleased to respond to his toast.

Pleased he was. Respond he did—although not with his usual ease and fluidity. The emotional impact of what he was told was known as 'the chain' robbed him of his well-rehearsed spontaneity and he abandoned the attempt at humour he had, against all advice, intended to introduce. He did, as he had been told, thank his proposer and seconder for their trust in him adding that, in either case, it was not the first time they had accepted him since he was, respectively, their son-in-law and step-son. He expressed his hope that he would, in time, prove a sufficiently good Mason to justify their continued confidence and sat down to enthusiastic banging of the tables in appreciation as he packed his unused speech notes into his jacket pocket.

The remainder of the evening passed in a blur. Eventually, he arrived home to find Jenny and Doreen enjoying a good wine and the television. All JJ wanted to do was sit quietly and talk to his wife. Freddie may not have realised this—but Doreen, recollecting the night when Freddie himself had been initiated, wished JJ and Jenny goodnight and dragged her husband away to their part of the hall.

Somewhat later, the younger pair finally went to bed.

CHAPTER FORTY-FIVE
JJ and Jenny: Business, Freemasonry and Tragedy
April 1974 to December 1983

Having accepted they would remain childless, the Whitehouse-Martins settled into a busy life of business and 'good works'. Jenny had only her Flower Patch as a direct business involvement; directors' meetings of Wells Holdings being monthly affairs she attended with only passing interest since her father and husband had everything neatly arranged. She found outlets for her energies with the church, the Women's Institute and several charities whose committees she enthusiastically attended. Due to his several businesses, JJ had not spread his leisure wings so widely until the advent of Freemasonry into his life opened a fresh avenue of opportunity for his talents outside work. He began to absorb the basics of Masonic protocol and history—mostly gleaned from conversations with Brother Tyler Bennett that began during the next Chandlery Lodge meeting in April when JJ was asked to leave the lodge room whilst a higher degree was worked. He took the opportunity to ask questions of the knowledgeable old Tyler who was only too pleased to have an interested and intelligent listener. JJ visited other lodges to which he was invited where, watching and listening as others were initiated, he began to understood more and more of the ceremony. His own lodge—his mother lodge as he was told to refer to it—did not meet in the summer but there were social events to which he and Jenny were invited and which they enjoyed. A garden party at the hall found both JJ and Jenny very involved since the use of hall staff seemed to be *de trop* for Masonic dos. That and a summer lunch at a delightful hostelry were the principal events of what JJ heard referred to as the close season. The lodge meetings resumed in September but, again, JJ found himself asked to retire to talk with and learn from Bennett.

In October 1974, the second degree in Freemasonry was conferred on him. It was a shorter ceremony than initiation and was followed by Brother Alan Simmonds giving a lengthy explanation of what was referred to as the second degree tracing board. Alan was praised for his work and JJ did appreciate that Alan must have taken time and trouble to learn the twenty-five-minute long description delivered to he and two others

who had also never seen or heard the explanation previously. Again JJ
was invited to other lodges to witness others undergoing their second
degree—referred to as 'passing'—and thoroughly enjoyed meeting
more brethren and seeing how other lodges conducted their meetings.
During one such visit, he found himself seated next to a brother of his
own age with whom he found instant rapport. Kenneth Hugh Knowles
was an independent financial adviser of greater probity than others of
his profession with whom JJ had had contact. Over the next two years
they became better friends, and in May of 1976, using some of JJ's vast
available funds, they bought a small building society in Stourminster
from the ailing firm of solicitors who, with little success, had been trying
to maintain its solvency. An office block in the old professional quarter
of the town was acquired and, after refurbishment by Wells Builders, was
formally opened by the mayor. The ground floor was occupied by the
building society; offices on the first floor were proclaimed on the sign-
written windows as 'Knowles-Martin: Financial Advisers' and on the
top floor, with more discreetly styled windows, was a firm of chartered
accountants new to the town. The partners were two keen and well-
informed chartered accountants JJ had known from his Student Society
days, plus the senior partner who appeared on the notepaper, but very
little in the offices: Jonathan Justin Whitehouse-Martin. The firm was
named Whitehouse, Butler & Rock.

The first business JJ and Ken Knowles concluded, to mutual
satisfaction, was a complete revision of the pension and life assurance
arrangements for the Whitehouse-Martins, the Martins, the Wells,
Billy and Janice Baker, Zoe and Gareth Connolly and every senior,
administrative person in JJ's business empire. The re-hash of life policies
for Freddie and Doreen were to prove tragically timely.

In the September of 1975, JJ was raised to the third degree in a long
and impressive ceremony in which Freddie took a small but significant
part. When the ceremony ended, JJ was presented with a ritual book
in the temple, and afterwards, in the robing room, with a smart new
Masonic case in which to carry his master Mason's apron, his gloves
and whatever else he deemed relevant; all gifts from his proposer and
father-in-law. His seat in the lodge was now, he was told, behind the
steward's. He had no official duties, but he was more often than not
both selling raffle tickets and acting as a steward serving wine and any
other table drinks requested by more senior brethren. It was an easy way
in which to become acquainted—or in some cases better acquainted—
with brethren ahead of him in Masonic experience. Naturally, their long

friendship continuing, JJ spoke of Freemasonry as he understood it to Billy and in late 1976 a completed Form P evidenced the application of William Marston Baker for initiation into Chandlery Lodge. His proposer—Freddie—and seconder—JJ—were surprised to learn or be reminded respectively of Billy's full name. At Billy's initiation in March of 1977, three years behind JJ, Brother Whitehouse-Martin first delivered Masonic ritual when he proudly presented the working tools of an entered apprentice to Brother Baker.

As JJ had been, Billy was surprised and pleased with Bennett's status and the depth of knowledge that the old chauffeur seemed willing to impart. In the same way that JJ had done, Billy set aside some of Freddie's rambling reasoning in diplomatic deferral to the wisdom of the tyler. Being unaware, Freddie was happy. He had had a satisfactory year as master of the lodge, had introduced two promising young men to Freemasonry, and was confident enough in his son-in-law's conduct of the firm and its subsidiaries to enjoy life outside of business.

On a 1973 holiday, Freddie and Doreen discovered and fell in love with the historic Devon town of Salcombe. Despite a burgeoning number of non-residents' holiday homes, there was little of the usual plethora of tourist attractions; the principle reason for many continuing to visit the ancient town being sailing, almost every resident had their own boat or boats, and boats for hire were legion. Although they had never sailed, Freddie and Doreen loved the quiet old town and immersed themselves in its history, and by 1975 they had become so enamoured of this hideaway that they became another pair of in-comers and purchased a second home there. During 1976 they spent several weeks in Salcombe and were willing though not very adept pupils on courses designed to impart the necessary skills of handling a boat under sail. Before leaving Salcombe in September 1976, the Wells purchased a small sailing boat, re-christened it *Fredeen* and pre-paid berthing and maintenance for a year ahead.

The day following the April 1977 meeting of Chandlery Lodge, Freddie and Doreen left Avonbridge to spend a few late spring days—or weeks, depending on their mood—in their Devon holiday home. Freddie had told anyone willing to listen they intended to 'sample the peace of the sea under sail'.

One of the maxims both mature Wells pupils failed to heed in their few maritime pursuit lessons was to always be aware of the weather and the warning signs displayed in and around the harbour whenever it was considered difficult or dangerous to sail. On the second day of their stay, having provisioned the boat, they blithely set forth into a stiffish breeze. Freddie's habitual bull-at-a-gate attitude, which Doreen tended to encourage and which JJ had managed to somewhat tame, swept aside the counsels to caution muttered by old salts on or near the waterside. With Freddie at the tiller, Doreen cast off. Their blissful ignorance of matters maritime gave no cognisance to the fact that a stiffish breeze in the lee of the land is likely to presage a howling gale once away from the shore. Several concerned persons waved at them as the offshore wind carried them from the harbour. The Wells waved back and sailed on in majestic bliss and oblivion. As they cleared the shelter of the land, the strength of the wind increased. The waves loomed larger. Doreen's eyes grew round with apprehension. Freddie's barked command to trim the sail was whipped away on the wind even as his cowering crew of one failed to cower sufficiently low and had her head hit heavily by the swinging boom. Freddie's commendable concern for his wife overcame sense or reason—deserting his presence of mind and the tiller, he began crawling to Doreen's assistance. The little boat, totally uncontrolled and at the mercy of the elements, with its occupants clinging desperately to its deck, was swept away from glorious Devon into the far reaches of the English Channel.

Container ships of many tons are not stopped in their 'tracks' for anything. A small sailing boat with a Midlands builder and his semi-conscious wife aboard would be an unexpected sight in the shipping lanes at any time, in the teeth of a near-gale the small vessel would not even be sighted from a bridge high above. The collision that reduced the *Fredeen* to matchwood and shredded canvas was not even felt by the officers of the container ship as it continued its imperious progress up-Channel.

Alderney is the third largest of the Channel Islands which, despite their proximity to France, remain stalwartly British. Corblets Bay is the beach most popular with surfing enthusiasts, and it was here that a pair of early morning board-riders discovered a bloated and bloodied male body. Later his dried documents became faintly legible and identified one Frederick Wellington Wells with an impressive address in Avonbridge, Worcestershire. Fatalities on a small holiday island whose external measurements are only three and a half by one and a half miles are rare. The discovery on the following day of a second drowned person—this body female and much mutilated by offshore rocks—in Arch Bay, which was adjacent to Corblets Bay, caused even greater distress among the residents and holidaymakers. The remains of the lady's sailing jacket yielded only a leather purse containing—besides money—credit cards in the name of

Mrs Doreen Wells. The bodies were taken to the small room used for emergency medical treatments by the local doctor. Communication with the mainland authorities was made via the Jersey Police and Avonbridge Police Station was asked to contact the family of Mr and Mrs Wells to request someone to identify the bodies and make the appropriate arrangements.

JJ had spent a few days in Jersey and Guernsey shortly after qualifying to research the viability of establishing company bases there in order to reduce the burdens of taxation. Some clients had moved their registered offices to one or other of the islands, but JJ's personal preference had been for the similar facilities available on the Isle of Man where he frequently made flying visits. Neither he nor Jenny had changed their vacationing islands preference from the Scillies, and although Jenny had never been to the Channel Islands, and despite her distress, she insisted on accompanying JJ to Alderney. Billy drove them to Birmingham airport from where they managed, at short notice and at considerable cost, to obtain tickets to fly via London Gatwick to the small Jersey airport. From there, JJ pre-booked a fast, private charter boat to take them to Alderney. Although they were both immensely distressed at the state of Jenny's drowned parents, they controlled their emotions sufficiently to make positive identifications and, after greater delays than he would have thought possible, JJ was able to set in train arrangements to transport the bodies to the mainland and on to Avonbridge. The delays could not be blamed on Harleys, undertakers of Avonbridge—indeed Christine Harley, who now managed the firm established by her late father, Christian—could not have been more helpful and sympathetic. St Bartholomew's was crowded with standing room only for the joint funerals. Claude travelled from Hereford to conduct a moving service and, steeling himself to it, JJ read the portions of the Bible that each of his late parents-in-law had selected in their recently re-written wills and last wishes.

Avonbridge Hall had not hosted a wake for over thirty years—the last being the hastily arranged and poorly attended post-funeral affairs for Jenny's grandparents and great-grandmother in 1946. Whilst the time frame for arrangements was similar to the post-war wakes, financial circumstances were vastly different, which was as well since the attendance was far greater. The many business and social activities of both of the deceased ensured that so many persons wished to celebrate the lives of the dear departed, after having paid their last respects, that even the little-used ballroom failed to accommodate everyone at the time of peak attendance. The local caterers, Browns Riverside, proved equal to the challenge and JJ and Jenny agreed they should add 10 per cent to Russell and Pam's invoice. The hall bedrooms were full and The Swan was grateful to the memory of the late Doreen and Freddie as all their rooms were booked for at least one night. It was 11.00 p.m. before the last guests, Billy and Janice, left. As Janice strapped the sleeping William Arthur into the rear seat of their car, Billy gave a just and correct judgement on the day, 'Well, we gave them a good send off.'

The following morning, as arranged, Terry Morton arrived to formally read the wills. Freddie and Doreen's shares in Wells Holdings Limited passed to Jenny and JJ as did ownership of the hall, its estates and properties. Other bequests were divided amongst the various local charities and other interests in which they had been involved. The property in Salcombe and the boat, or whatever they could get from the insurers, as a mournful Terry Morton said, were left to the astounded Billy Baker who kindly drove us to and from our Devon retreat. After consulting with JJ, Billy subsequently sold the property and, adding the proceeds to the poor monies of the insurance claim, made a large donation to the almost overwhelmed Salcombe Sailing Club. Chandlery Lodge received £500 'to be utilised for purchase of good wine for consumption at festive boards and, should it be so wished, to drink my health.' For the next few years, the lodge gratefully toasted Freddie's memory. Billy, who was surprised to even be invited, was assuming his unexpected legacy involved only a cottage in Devon and a lost boat when he heard himself bequeathed the older Rolls Royce from the hall garages—the later model being willed to Percy Bennett 'our faithful chauffeur in the hopes he will enjoy owning the car and make its use available to our daughter and son-in-law at any mutually convenient time they may require it.' Old Bennett, as on the previous day, wiped away more than one tear.

Life goes on: JJ assumed the title of managing director—the duties of which he had been performing in Freddie's absences for more than a year. Jenny was seen less in the Flower Patch as she was content to leave the shop in the efficient and enthusiastic hands of Annie Tennant who had been with her since shortly after the opening when Annie was a keen sixteen-year-old fresh from school. As JJ had gathered a capable company of fellow directors in Wells Holdings and his other businesses (most were titled executive directors—thus saving them the expense of acquiring shares) he and Jenny increased their cruising to two, and sometimes three, trips during the year. They always included at least one river cruise— repeating the Rhine voyage every other year—and one ocean outing.

They particularly enjoyed their cruise around the Norwegian fjords in 1983 and made a provisional repeat booking for 1985.

As JJ proceeded in the progressive offices of his lodge, they had to arrange some of their holidays around lodge meetings—something Jenny mildly resented. On some cruises JJ and Jenny joined other cruising Freemasons and their wives in a lodge meeting and social that raised funds for worthy charities nominated from a list issued by the cruise line. Billy was also rising in the lodge hierarchy and, due to some brethren 'in between' not accepting promotion for business or personal reasons, he had moved up to a position only five behind JJ. Janice felt little resentment similar to Jenny since the Bakers still resolutely and happily vacationed in Aberdovey from where Billy could commute, should it prove necessary, to the lodge. In November of 1983, JJ was made master elect and, with great mutual pleasure, asked—actually insisted—that Billy be his inner guard for 1984. They looked forward to a good year in the lodge.

CHAPTER FORTY-SIX
Worshipful Brother JJ
January to April 1984

JJ and Jenny welcomed 1984 in at home. JJ had resisted the pleas to succeed his father-in-law as president of the rugby club and they had no compunction declining attendance at the New Year's ball. Billy and Jan were, likewise, at home with their children when 1984 dawned. Amongst other ambitions, they all shared anticipation of a good year with the eager brethren of Chandlery Lodge; an old adage about travelling hopefully to a disappointing arrival never crossed their minds. Every one of their businesses were, if not booming, doing far more than break even.

JJ's invitations to take office in Chandlery Lodge for 1984 had all been accepted and his programme of ceremonies indicated a full and satisfying Masonic year. The only disappointment for both JJ and Jenny had been the perverse refusal of the lodge committee, forcibly persuaded by Worshipful Brothers Jeffries and Hughes, to change the format of the October ladies' festival from one night at The Swan to a weekend abroad. Amongst English lodges there had been a growing trend in the late 1970s to gather brethren and their ladies at welcoming hotels in fashionable resorts for a full weekend of celebration—rather than the previous habit of a one-night festival—which allowed the wives to be relieved of domestic duties for two or three days. To JJ's and Jenny's acute disappointment, the commitment of the stick-in-the-mud traditionalists on the lodge committee to doing what they had always done prevailed—albeit by only a slim majority—and Chandlery remained steadfastly traditional. JJ's pleading that failing to move with the times would, ultimately, prove detrimental to the lodge and Billy's urging that 'we've always done it that way' was the worst reason for almost any course of action, fell on more deaf than understanding ears. One night at The Swan it would be.

JJ and Billy—the old firm—were not so easily daunted. Having recently acquired a struggling coach hire firm, injected capital and expanded the fleet, they and the young, ambitious driver John Robinson, who they appointed managing director, were anxious to expand the newly named JBR Travel. Prior to the lodge committee's 'nay' vote, a provisional booking had already been made in Bruges, Belgium and a deposit made with the best Bruges hotel. Demand was such that the presumption was driven by necessity to secure accommodation. JJ and Billy, sensing there was sufficient interest to ensure a good time for all, decided to offer the overseas weekend as an additional event for those interested—Chandlery members or not. Embarking on such Continental ventures was daring and unusual in the early eighties—most lodge weekends were spent on the south coast of England—but young Robinson had driven coaches all round Europe, was amazingly knowledgeable on the routes and could more than get by in several European languages. He was also well connected with cross-channel ferry operators. The second festival was arranged for 10–12 November inclusive. JJ, Billy, John Robinson, and their wives sketched out detailed plans for the first Continental ladies' weekend. Little did they realise their well-laid plans would accord with Robert Burns's oft quoted prophecy and 'gang agley.'

Such planning as the two old friends could do for JJ's installation as worshipful master was restricted by their ignorance of those parts of the ceremony mysteriously referred to as the inner workings (they refrained from poor jests concerning the digestive system). The lodge rehearsal—always called a 'practice'—did not promise well. JJ's predecessor, Maurice Fisher, had been a rather petty and perverse master prone to pretend his failings of memory could be blamed on others and/or changed circumstances. His attitude toward installing his successor was no different and a well-meant offer to assist by performing part of the ceremony was petulantly dismissed in a not too Masonic manner. He was nearly twenty years JJ's senior in age and felt any suggestion JJ made an impertinence, as old Floury Fellows opined quietly (he could be quiet if the mood took him) to JJ, 'Fisher's never really left the classroom despite being retired.'

Fisher's stuttering, staccato delivery was frequently interspersed with Ray Hughes's booming corrections and prompts. The part of the rehearsal JJ and other brethren below the rank of an installed master could attend was anything but dignified or impressive. They hoped for better on the night.

Despite Fisher's shortcomings—a cruel pun since the poor man stood a mere five feet and four inches—the evening had its impressive moments; mostly due to the large numbers attending. At seventy-nine, Uncle Charles was still upright and dignified in his grand lodge regalia. Alongside him, William Burroughs, although four years

Charles's junior, had aged badly and was bent of back and racked with rheumatism. All together, there were six brethren present who had been accorded grand lodge office in addition to the team from the provincial grand lodge, including not only the provincial grand master, but one of his assistant grand masters together with the usual quota of provincial wardens and the director of ceremonies. At the festive board, JJ was assured by the provincial grand master that, but for calls upon their resources elsewhere in the province, every ruler of the province would have attended in tribute to 'the outstanding promise' JJ had shown prior to tonight and which he had 'liberally endorsed . . . tonight in the room above.' As praise had also been accorded—although certainly not heaped—upon Maurice Fisher, JJ did not feel embarrassed. He had, despite Fisher, been impressed by the ceremony in the lodge room, even though the physical act of placing him in the chair was not primarily successful or comfortable due to Fisher's over-eagerness in pushing JJ onto an arm of the chair. (JJ managed to slide, awkwardly and with little dignity into the part of the master's chair intended to accommodate his posterior). JJ's appointment and investing of officers was much admired, he was perfect in the ritual, but also made verbal tributes to each brother—most were sincere, although he did feel hypocritical giving even slight praise to Worshipful Brothers Fisher, Jeffries and Hughes. Billy was the only one who fully realised how JJ felt concerning those three ultra-conservative brethren and his well-concealed amusement was overwhelmed by the sincere tribute JJ paid to himself as his 'oldest and dearest friend and colleague whom he was particularly delighted to have as his inner guard.'

Whilst the men were busy at 'whatever it is they do', Jenny, assisted by Janice, happily hosted a dinner party at the hall for the wives of most of the officers—Mesdames Fisher, Jeffries and Hughes declined attendance as they felt it was 'not appropriate . . . we've never done that sort of thing before.' Jenny and Janice were not greatly disappointed by their absence. All things considered, the Whitehouse-Martins were happy with JJ's installation night, an opinion shared by most save the Jeffrieses, Hugheses and Fishers who, wisely, expressed no opinion beyond their customary grumbling to each other.

In February and March, JJ passed brothers Paul Miller and Edwin Harris to the second degree in Freemasonry. At each ceremony there was a departure from what is known as emulation working for the talented junior warden, Colin Old, to deliver the charge after passing. Each evening was completed in the temple by Billy and Brother

Graham Weir jointly explaining the second degree tracing board; they were complimented not only for their delivery, but also for not having prolonged the evening or shown off by giving the extended version. In April, JJ initiated one of his executive directors, Cecil Georgeson, before the lodge broke for the summer recess.

For many years it had been the custom for lodges in their various geographic groupings to invite masters of other local lodges to at least one meeting during the Masonic year. As a consequence, and also because he had acquired a deserved reputation as an after dinner speaker, JJ had found his evenings too much occupied with Freemasonry for his own and Jenny's comfort. Despite which he felt obliged to honour a pledge made to Terri's husband, Gerald, to visit Spireton Lodge, Staffordshire, for their May meeting. One of the fascinations for many Masons is the small and not always subtle differences in the manner of lodge conduct. JJ had not previously visited in Staffordshire and was, therefore, a keen observer of the lodge workings. The food at the festive board was far better than he was used to in Avonbridge and the company was enjoyable. Particularly pleasant for JJ was meeting Brother James Whiteman who, as Gerald had previously indicated with amusement, bore a remarkable physical similarity to himself. Not only did they look alike and have similar surnames, but they seemed to hold remarkably congruous views on almost every subject they broached. A firm friendship was forged.

The two new friends and brothers' circumstances in life differed vastly. James and his wife lived in a small cottage at the end of an unmade, unlit lane with few adjacent properties. They had their own small business: making and supplying cakes, jams, savoury sauces and chutneys to local shops and restaurants to whom they also supplied fresh vegetables and flowers, the bulk of which was grown on the smallholding to the side and rear of their cottage. James's contribution to the business had been growing and selling, he had no culinary skills, nor needed any until recently when his young wife had contracted Huntingdon's Chorea—a distressing and progressively debilitating disease from which there seemed to be no cure. She now required almost constant care, the cost of which, allied to the lack of home-made cakes, etc. and less time spent on the land, was draining away the couples' few resources. James was outwardly cheerful and optimistic—although to JJ's eye it was obvious that beneath the social exterior the good fellow was a worried and distressed man approaching financial and possibly physical breakdown. Travelling to Gerald and Terri's—JJ's hosts for the night—after the meeting, Gerald confessed to similar fears for James and admitted that he was nursing hopes for JJ's ingenuity to discover some way in which, without insulting James's pride and independence, the Whitemans could be helped. JJ had no immediate thoughts, but promised to give the matter more consideration.

CHAPTER FORTY-SEVEN
A MONTH OF PORTENTS
MAY 1984

Jenny found herself in receipt of unexpected and unwelcome visits. Annie Tennant, her able assistant, had met and married the man of her dreams. Their nuptials and ensuing honeymoon on the Scilly Isles—a present from Jenny—took place in early May, ensuring that Jenny would, for a fortnight, tend the Flower Patch full time. Annie had told her of a recently-arrived, free-spending, but unpleasant customer named Mrs Marriott whom Jenny had not as yet met and so had been unable to confirm Annie's judgement of. Although forewarned that Tuesday morning was the first regular visit of the week for Mrs Marriott, it was almost predictable that just as Jenny had prepared and was preparing to enjoy her mid-morning mug of coffee in the small rear office someone entered the shop calling imperiously for service. Jenny abandoned her coffee.

Mrs Cynthia Marriott and Mrs Jennifer Whitehouse-Martin stood face to face staring in disbelief. Jenny saw the never-to-be-forgotten cruel face of her school tormentor, the small, mean eyes and the thin-lipped, down-turned mouth of Cynthia Cholmondely-Price—erstwhile leader of the pack who had so grievously assaulted her and begun the series of events Jenny tried never to think about. Cynthia saw the girl who had sneaked and caused her to be expelled from school. The tormentor was the first to speak, 'What the hell are you doing serving in a flower shop, then, fatty?' she queried.

'Since it's my own shop,, I please myself when I do and don't attend to customers,' replied Jenny—determined to maintain her dignity and self-control.

'Oh . . . Well I usually deal with Annie—she seems to know what I need,' said Cynthia—obviously not inclined to talk of old times or even be pleasant.

'Annie's on honeymoon, Cynthia. She told me to expect a Mrs Marriott today, so I assume that's you?' Cynthia nodded curtly. 'She also told me what you liked and disliked,' continued Jenny. She was unable to resist adding, 'We like to keep our customers happy by all being aware of their likes and dislikes.'

Cynthia tossed her head, causing no disturbance whatsoever to her tightly permed hair, and ordered exactly what she had purchased the week before according to Annie's notes.

'Since you know me you can open an account for me,' ordered Cynthia.

Jenny calmly continued wrapping the flowers. 'We don't give credit to individuals, Cynthia. . . . Perhaps Annie didn't tell you?'

The Marriott purse was angrily extracted from Cynthia's handbag. She flung several notes onto the counter before snatching the two bunches of fresh blooms from Jenny.

'Keep the change, then, fatty. God knows why, though, you owe me for having me slung out of that school, Jenny Wells. Now I know where you are I can arrange pay back for that.'

Before Jenny could retort that her own actions had resulted in Cynthia's expulsion, her unpleasant customer had left, slamming the shop door unnecessarily hard behind her.

Jenny sank on to the counter stool and blinked back tears. She recalled a saying about one's past returning to haunt one. Quite what Cynthia Marriott, née Cholmondely-Price, was doing in Avonbridge was a mystery. Whatever it was, Jenny devoutly wished it was otherwise. As to the threats she could, surely, ignore those. She tried to put Cynthia's visit from her mind—but it kept returning. Curious as to why her school nemesis should return to haunt her, she looked into the shop customers' address book. Annie had, as Jenny expected, recorded Mrs C. Marriott with an address and telephone number. It told her little save that the Marriott's lived in the outlying village of Dunnington. That evening she asked JJ as casually as she could if he knew of anyone called Marriott recently arrived in the area. He had heard of him and, after a moment's thought, remembered that it had been Billy who had mentioned Marriott.

Still curious, Jenny telephoned Billy. It seemed that Jeremy Marriott was a rich industrialist from north of Birmingham who, late in life, had taken a wife and, in response to her wishes, moved to the country. Billy had supplied him with a second-hand four-wheel drive vehicle to deal with the muddy roads around his outlying property. Marriott had also purchased a new car for his wife. In Billy's opinion, it was the wife who wore the trousers and drove everything except his business. 'Why are you asking, Jenny?' continued Billy.

'She's a new customer. Came into the shop today,' answered Jenny.

'Word to the wise,' replied Billy, 'be careful of that one. Not a nice person.'

'That's how I felt, Billy,' was Jenny's reply. For reasons she could not fully justify to herself, she chose not to disclose her former acquaintance with the abhorrent Mrs Marriott to either Billy or JJ. The nurturing of secrets can be the beginning of obsession and mental torment. Over the next few months, Cynthia Marriott seemed to haunt Jenny. Whenever she was in the Flower Patch, Cynthia would arrive with either another order or, more often, a complaint. Having sprayed her husband's money into their funds, Cynthia had been co-opted onto the committees of two charities of which Jenny had been a long-time member. Despite being but a recent member, Cynthia had, somehow, inveigled herself into the office of president of Dunnington Women's Institute—a part of the group of institutes to which Avonbridge W.I. belonged—and began attending Jenny's W.I. as a visitor.

'I'm sure no one minds,' Cynthia would announce as she swept in— Jenny and her fellow members were too polite to differ.

Whatever exchange of words took place between the two former school adversaries was initiated by Cynthia; and was both terse and capable of interpretation as either social banter or, as intended and so interpreted by Jenny, veiled threats. This constant veiled venom began to undermine Jenny's confidence. She re-acted oddly to harmless sounds or remarks. Despite the solicitous and puzzled queries and offers of help from her friends and husband, she remained obdurate as to both the cause and even the effect of Cynthia's insidious insinuations. She assured everyone that she was perfectly alright and, as is often so with such things, responded to their well-meant sympathy with requests to be left alone. JJ was worried about her, but with Wells Holdings and subsidiaries still expanding, and the time he was spending on Masonic activities, he was little at home. On one of their rare evenings together, Jenny began to wonder if this might be the moment to confide her irrational fears to JJ without being ridiculed; whilst she wondered, JJ decreed they should discuss the details of the lodge ladies' night presents. Jenny was sure that attempting to divert the subject would not be welcome, the moment had gone, but agreement was reached concerning the ladies' presents. The venue would be, as it had been for many years, The Swan. The format was to be exactly as it had ever been. Jenny had attended more Chandlery ladies' nights than JJ as she had also been a guest of her father's—and needed little reminding of the staid set formula that so appealed to the ultra-conservative brethren who, in her opinion, had so stupidly rejected JJ's suggested change. One tradition peculiar to Chandlery and instituted by the founders of the lodge did meet with JJ and Jenny's approval. Rather than, as in other lodges, the master and, ostensibly, the lodge presenting the master's wife with a grander present than was accorded other ladies, the immediate past master presented the master's wife with a ladies' night jewel—a brooch purchased from and for one of the national Masonic charities. She was expected to wear this at all subsequent ladies' nights—a fact that annually accounted for the sudden return home to search their wives' dressing tables of more than one brother with a forgetful wife. The ladies at Chandlery Lodge 1984 would receive, JJ and Jenny agreed, a tasteful Stourbridge cut-glass vase.

Also in May, JJ discussed with the lodge almoner, Worshipful Brother Terry Cox, what might be done to assist Brother James Whiteman. Terry was one of the past masters of the lodge and was entirely supportive of JJ—welcoming his suggestions as a breath of fresh air. He was, as JJ had hoped, understanding but practical. Whilst he could not, and would not interfere with anything concerning another lodge in another province, he promised to contact the provincial almoner for Staffordshire, whom he knew personally, in the hope of easing some grants from the grand lodge charities and, if possible, physical assistance with nursing Mrs Whiteman. JJ advised Gerald Anstruther what it was hoped might be accomplished. Later, Gerald was happy to tell JJ how grateful James was for the assistance; he failed to mention that he had also told James of JJ's role as instigator and it was, therefore, somewhat of an embarrassment to have a very grateful Brother Whiteman telephone JJ at work.

CHAPTER FORTY-EIGHT
Passion and Compassion
June 1984

Jenny and Janice were looking forward to the two ladies' festivals: one standard night in Avonbridge and three nights in Bruges. In early June, as they discussed dresses, Jenny wondered aloud whether the excellent little shop in Covent Garden to which she and Terri had delivered flowers and from where they had both purchased their wedding gowns was still open. She telephoned Terri to find that only the previous week Terri had visited the shop and purchased dresses for, amongst others, the two ladies' festivals. Disappointed they were unlikely to meet in London in the near future, Jenny thanked her friend and relayed the substance of the conversation to Janice.

'You know, Jen,' I wouldn't mind a short break in London. If we went together, you could show me the shop and we could both get dresses and other things. What d'you think?'

'Let's do just that,' said Jenny.

'Super,' replied Janice. 'I'll sort the kids—they enjoy nights at Auntie Zoe's.'

Diaries were consulted, dates decided upon, and Jenny telephoned the Bonnington Hotel in Bloomsbury—another destination to which she had delivered and arranged flowers twenty years previously.

'They've only got a double room available, Jan. Is that OK?' she asked holding her hand over the telephone mouthpiece.

'Alright with me, Jen,' answered Janice.

Two weeks later, they were delivered to Birmingham International railway station by one of Billy's drivers and departed for London. From Euston Station they took a taxi to the Bonnington. Jenny had explained that whilst it may not be the best hotel in London, it was reasonable and, more to the point, very convenient for Covent Garden. So it proved. Janice was impressed by the old-fashioned service at what she termed Jenny's shop, they could try on various dresses, make their selections and then return the following afternoon for a final fitting following necessary alterations. Jenny was very taken with a black and gold creation.

'It looks absolutely super on you, Jen,' enthused Janice.

'Not too low-cut at the front for Avonbridge, is it?' asked Jenny anxiously.

'Gosh no; you've got 'em—flaunt 'em,' replied Janice.

After visiting several other shops they returned, happy but footsore, to The Bonnington and, feeling disinclined to venture forth again that evening, they ordered dinner and took the lift to their bedroom. Their room had been described by the porter who brought up their luggage earlier in the day as the best in the whole place. Not having toured the establishment, they had no means of verifying his statement, but were content with the firm comfortable bed and a bathroom boasting the strange facility of a double whirlpool bath. There being no shower, they decided they may as well avail themselves of the unusual, shared double tub with whirlpool jets. Having so decided they discovered that the double bath took more than twice as long to fill with sufficient water for immersion as a normal, one-person tub. They sat on the side of the bath clad only in hotel dressing gowns waiting.

'Are there many of these double baths in London, Jen?' asked Janice.

'If there are, I've never encountered one before,' said Jenny.

Then, losing patience and hoping their combined presence in the tub would raise the water level to a reasonable height, Jenny stood up, flung the dressing gown aside and stepped in. Janice, feeling she had no other course than to do likewise, shed her dressing gown and lowered herself into the large tub alongside Jenny. Although the water was warm enough and the pressure jets squirted water at their sides, they both began to wonder whether they were missing something.

Janice spoke first. 'I've not done this before, Jen, but I'm not sure whether we're supposed to be thrilled or excited by this double tub, pressure jet experience?'

'To be honest, Jan,' I think it's rather a disappointment. It was more exciting to share an ordinary single bath—as Terri and I used to.'

'Did you, really?' said Janice—filled with curiosity.

'Gosh, yes,' replied Jenny. 'When we were living down here it was the Swinging Sixties and almost anything went, as we used to say. Anyway, we couldn't afford to heat two lots of bath water.'

'That makes sense. There's hidden depths to you, Jenny Whitehouse-Martin.'

'Maybe—but there's not much depth to this bath, is there?' said Jenny, sitting up.

'Even less when you take your big beautiful breasts out of the water.'

said Janice, also sitting up and soaping herself.

Jenny looked down at her chest and back at her bathing companion, 'That's what Terri used to say about them . . . twenty years ago. Thank you, Jan.'

Janice was surprised by Jenny's re-action, false modesty seemed far removed from the Jenny she had come to know and admire.

Both thoroughly dismayed by the double tub and its whirlpool jets, they finished washing, clambered out, and grabbed a large hotel towel each to dry themselves.

Janice remained puzzled by her friend's reaction to her favourable description of her breasts which she had intended as a no more than a sincere compliment. Although they had been friends for some years, Janice had never before viewed Jenny's naked bosoms and her comment had been entirely honest and a little inspired by jealousy. Having dried herself, she dropped the towel onto the rail from whence it had come and, facing Jenny, confronted her friend and what might be a problem of misunderstanding.

'Look, Jen, I didn't mean any offence mentioning your boobs. I just think they're super—in fact I'm a little bit jealous, if I'm honest.'

Jenny discarded her towel and stood, stark naked, staring at her similarly unclad friend, 'Jan, my dear. We are all as we are. I used to be a bit shy about these but, due largely to Terri, I got quite proud of them and, as Billy no doubt told you the night JJ and I got engaged, I used to parade them around shamelessly. I'm glad you like them because . . . well—I like yours . . . and . . . oh heck, come here.'

The two friends embraced. Janice hadn't been this close to another female since her teens when she and Zoe had been what they privately referred to as adventurous trollops. She cuddled and stroked Jenny until Jenny, taking the lead despite being younger, suggested they might be more comfortable in the other room. Laughing, they tumbled together onto the bed and resumed their bathroom familiarity.

A while later they lay quietly together on the bed. Each knew they should, by some peoples' standards, feel guilty. Neither did.

Jenny was the first to speak. 'You know, Jan, much as I dearly love my husband, it's nice to be with another woman. I'd almost forgotten. . . . It must be London.'

'Did you and Terri often . . . ?' queried Janice—not sure how to end her sentence.

'Oh yes. To be honest with you, if it weren't for darling Terri, I'd probably be a fat, frustrated, sex-starved spinster.'

'Wow,' said Janice, raising herself up on an elbow to look down at Jenny, 'that's quite a tribute. And, if I'm not being too nosey, requiring a little more detail, please.'

Jenny smiled up at Janice. It would be a good thing, she thought, to have more than one confidante. She turned to face Janice, 'How long do we have before dinner?'

As Janice consulted her discarded wristwatch, the telephone trilled. The receptionist asked if Mrs Whitehouse-Martin could speak with a Mrs Annie Belmont.

'Annie?'

'Jenny—I'm sorry to pester you, but I'm worried and don't know what to do . . .'

'Tell me about it, Annie.'

'It's that Mrs Marriott, Jenny.' Jenny's heart sank. 'She came in an hour ago and asked for lots of flowers to be delivered to her house and several other houses. And then she said I should put it on her account. I told he we didn't have credit accounts for individuals, but she said you'd authorised her as a special case because you were at school together. It's nearly seventy pounds, Jenny. What shall I do?'

Janice, still laid on the bed, heard Jenny sobbing and Annie's voice on the telephone saying, 'Hello, Jenny?' over and over. She prised the telephone from Jenny's tight grip and, as calmly as she could, asked Annie to tell her the problem.

Having listened she turned to her distraught friend and quietly asked, 'Did you authorise a credit account for Mrs Marriott?'

'Never,' sobbed Jenny.

'Annie,' said Janice, now the administrator, 'have the flowers gone out, yet?'

'No, Mrs Baker. They're on the van, but I was just nervous and wanted to check.'

'Alright, Annie,' said Janice, 'give me Mrs Marriott's telephone number, please.'

Janice used the pad and pencil supplied by the hotel.

'Thank you, Annie. Wait to hear from me again before you do anything about this. Jenny's very upset about it, so I'll take any flak.'

Despite Jenny's weeping protestations, Janice dialled nine for an outside line, telephoned Cynthia Marriott and calmly informed her, as finance controller of the Flower Patch, she could not authorise despatch of her order until settlement had been made for the flowers ordered, plus a £20 delivery charge. If Mrs Marriott so chose, she could accept a charge to her credit card on this one occasion, but future purchases must be paid for with the order. After arguing and being advised by Janice of the Flower Patch's legal representatives, a furious Cynthia Marriott—née Cholmondely-Price—dictated her credit card details to Janice. Janice thanked her and telephoned Annie with instructions and thanks for her patience and care. She then turned to her still crying, distressed friend who was muttering, 'What will she do next?'

Janice wrapped a hotel dressing gown around Jenny, donned one herself and telephoned reception to have their dining room reservation cancelled and a light supper for two with white wine, coffee and brandy delivered to their room at 8.00 p.m. After which she quickly dressed and persuaded Jenny to do likewise before sitting her down and, with the aid of two miniature whiskies from the room's mini-bar, persuaded her to talk. Over the rest of the evening, before, during and after supper, Jenny recounted the saga of her school days: the horrific Miss Batty; running away; going to London; meeting Terri and their swinging times; and, finally, how the awful Cynthia had suddenly come into her life again. Jenny had another confidante. Even better, she felt, she had support in any future conflict with Cynthia

CHAPTER FORTY-NINE
Just Compassion
July to September 1984

JJ's summer was less traumatic than his wife's. In July he visited James Whiteman at home and, with a carer attending Mrs Whiteman, took James out to lunch, whilst—unbeknownst to James, a Wells Building surveyor inspected the Whitemans' property and land, the latter of which covered more acres than JJ had expected. Later, the surveyor, Eric Carter, made a local records search and enquired discreetly about the possibility of development, he was used to such assignments—Freddie Wells had never been slow to find suitable sites for new estates. The report to JJ was comprehensive and more favourable than anticipated. Mrs Whiteman was declining fast and transfer to a hospice was expected soon.

In early August, James Whiteman took delivery of a bulky package, it contained details of the possible development of his land into a small estate of exclusive homes. If the initial information came as a shock, the price offered him for his house and land made him glad he had been seated when he read it. There was also a short, confidential memo promising him either one of the new houses or, should he so wish, a home of his choice elsewhere as part of the package. Only the previous week, his dear wife, who no longer seemed to recognise him, had been transferred to the local hospice. James sat, alone, and wept. His pent up sorrow and relief took a long time to flow away in tears. He tried to pull himself together. He needed to look into this offer from a firm he had never heard of—but who could he talk to? He telephoned Gerald Anstruther.

Gerald was away, his charming wife informed James, but she would be happy to help him if she could. Haltingly, he explained his problem, if indeed it was a problem. Terri had better breadth of thought than her husband and, as James talked, she perceived the influence of JJ Whitehouse-Martin in this. After asking a few searching questions, to which James replied, she suggested James contact JJ.

'After all, he's in building and development—amongst other things,' she said.

JJ was not entirely surprised to hear from James. A meeting at James's cottage was arranged for that very evening, and after a long discussion, and whilst despatching half a bottle of good whisky brought by JJ, the two friends shook hands and fell asleep in the cosy armchairs.

Planning permission was eventually granted and James moved to a small country house with two acres of land on which he cultivated flowers and, in suitable hothouses, orchids. His principal customer was Flowers for All—Terri Anstruther's select shop. Development of the Whiteman estate by a subsidiary of Wells Builders began in the summer of 1985 and was yet another profitable success.

CHAPTER FIFTY
AROUND AVONBRIDGE
MONDAY 25 JANUARY 1988

The Masonic hall, 9.30–10.00 a.m.

Off-duty nurses Greg and Phil were having as difficult a time with Mrs Scarlett Jones as they expected to have with problem patients at work. Neither had any pain-killers on their person with which to calm the poor woman.

Asked what she would like, Mrs Jones replied, 'I reckon I'm due a free drink from *them*.'

To Greg and Phil's surprise, she then indicated the bar keys on her key ring. In the continued absence of Mr Fawner and at Mrs Jones insistence, Greg opened the bar and poured the patient the stiff whisky she specifically and persistently requested. Evidently, Greg's perception of stiffness did not match Mrs Jones's since the whisky was despatched in two swift gulps and a repeat dose ordered; both nurses suspected this might not be the first time Mrs Jones had sampled the Masons' bar spirits—more so when she assured them, 'Mr Fawner won't mind—'e owes me, 'e does.'

The mantra of 'bodies and blood' began again as, to the considerable relief of Greg and Phil, two young men appeared introducing themselves as, 'D.S. Horseman and D.C. Peters. Someone called for the police?'

'Yes, indeed,' answered Phil, 'I did.'

Indicating Mrs Jones he and Greg gave a swift, concise account of their street encounter with the still babbling lady. Greg also stated he had asked Mr Fawner, secretary of the Masonic hall, to join them at the request of Mrs Jones. The senior of the two new arrivals who, despite his apparent youth, seemed very authoritative, asked Mrs Jones if she could tell him what she had seen. After a rambling reprisal of ''orrible bodies and blood up there,' he asked Greg and Phil to keep Mrs Jones calm as they would need to question her again.

'Best if we take a look upstairs,' said the authoritative one. 'Come on, Derek.'

They disappeared up the stairs.

Once at the top it was obvious from the light filtering through to which room they needed to direct their exploratory steps. Standing in the doorway, David Horseman instantly perceived what the incoherent Mrs Jones had been trying to convey. Whilst he had a nose for a good story—and this seemed a very good story—he was also sufficiently aware of police procedures not to disturb the crime scene. Scribbling on his pad he backed away and, apprehensive that he might be sensitive to the sight of blood, summoned Derek to the doorway.

'Get several shots of this, quick, Derek. We need to be on our way ASAP.'

To Horseman's relief, young Peters showed no signs of fainting and, setting his camera to flash, snapped away—to the wide-eyed distress of the three elderly nudes. After the second flash he became aware of muffled cries from behind the door and, not as aware as Horseman of the need to leave the scene untrampled, he stepped further into the room. Behind the door was yet another gagged and bloodied old gentleman—though this one was at least partly clothed.

'Dave,' hissed Peters, 'there's another one here.'

'Where?' queried Horseman.

'Behind the door—look'

Look Horseman did—through the crack between the door and it's frame.

'Get a shot of him, too, Derek, and get out of there. No more footprints.'

Poor old Floury Fallowfield became as goggle-eyed as his fellow Masons had been for the two flash photographs young Peters then took of him. He also became angry as he heard the young men, whom he had thought to be their rescuers, walk away and descend the stairs. In his ire he tried to move his chair by swaying from side to side—the result of which was that the chair and its captive occupant fell heavily against the open door causing it to close. Worshipful Brother Fallowfield had landed himself—quite literally—in greater discomfort, lain on his side, still inexorably attached to the chair and with a view of his fellow captives he found more repulsive than previously.

Back in the hallway, Greg informed Horseman—whom he still imagined to be a policeman—he and his colleague needed to leave.

'Of course,' replied the wily journalist. 'If you could leave your names and contact details with my colleague, please.'

Whilst Phil was adding his name, address and telephone number to that of Greg on young Peters's notepad, Greg confided to Horseman his professional opinion that Mrs Jones should be moved away from the building in which she had suffered such distress and trauma.

'Would it be possible to take her home and get a statement from her there?' he naively enquired. This posed Horseman a problem. It also seemed to pose Mrs Jones a problem, which she vociferously expressed, demanding her wages and cards from Mr Fawner. Greg, attempting to be helpful and proving anything but to Horseman and Peters, quietly told her that Mr Fawner was hardly likely to have her wages and cards with him, but would, surely, deliver them to her as soon as he could get them ready.

To Horseman's distress, Mrs Jones agreed with Greg and promptly began beseeching Horseman to take her home.

Caught between exposure and expediency, Horseman agreed. He told Peters to bring the car around and, with the two male nurses' assistance, squeezed Mrs Jones onto the rear seat of Peters's small sports car.

As they drove out of the Masonic hall car park, Douglas Fawner's car turned into Avon Street.

At the *Avonbridge Gazette*, 9.45–10.15 a.m.

Whilst Fawner was chatting to and paying his newsagent and the intrusive young pressmen were photographing the disrobed and distressed brethren, the elder pressman of Avonbridge, Gilbert Williams, grudgingly agreed to take an anonymous telephone call. The obviously disguised voice of his caller urged him to get down to the Masonic hall as quickly as he could with a photographer.

'What am I supposed to find there?' asked Williams.

'Some local dignitaries in a very undignified state.'

'What's that supposed to mean?'

'It means they're not dressed for any ceremony, in fact, they're not dressed at all.'

'How do I know this isn't a hoax?'—Gil Williams had been had before.

'Because that's how I left them last night. And they're not able to move yet.'

The line went dead. Gil Williams sat thinking for a moment. Local news was scarce at present. It was worth a quick look. Any story about the Freemasons always sold papers. He yelled for David Horseman.

'He went out with Derek Peters, earlier, Gil,' came the voice of Dotty, the receptionist/typist/tea-maker and general assistant of long-standing.

'As b——y usual, I have to do everything myself,' muttered Williams. 'Where's the f——ing camera?'

'They took it with them, Gil.'

Muttering testily, Williams found the old, spare camera, checked there was film inside, and shrugged himself into his overcoat.

'Hold the fort, Dotty. Shan't be long, I hope.'

With his battered trilby on his head, Gil Williams walked toward Avon Street. He'd not driven since his early twenties when he had drunkenly directed his one and only car into a pair of prams parked on a pavement; the perambulators were unoccupied at the time, but the horror of what might have been never left him. The car did—for far less than its worth.

The Masonic Hall, 10.30–11.00 a.m.

Fifteen minutes later, Gil Williams arrived at the Masonic hall. There was only one car in the large car park. He entered the building, somewhere he had never been before, but a story was a story he thought, walking through the unlocked door. The entrance hall was empty. Williams looked about him.

No sign of any undignified dignitaries here, he thought. As he wondered whether to venture upstairs, a flustered and distressed man with white hair, moustache and complexion came almost running down the stairs. He grabbed for the telephone, then, seeing a stranger standing expectantly regarding him, replaced it.

'Who're you?' asked Douglas Fawner.

'Press,' replied Williams. 'I was told there was something newsworthy to be found here.'

'No . . . oh no, no, no, no,' said Fawner, rather too quickly, confirming to Williams there certainly was a story, and one, moreover, this fellow didn't want told. Good job it's me, thought Williams; Horseman would have been too keen and got nothing except denial. The canny approach of an experienced pressman was needed here.

'Oh dear,' said Williams. 'My apologies. I must have been misinformed.'

He turned toward the door—although he had no intention of leaving. Looking back he detected the relief on Fawner's face—Fawner had again taken up the telephone, but paused as he saw Williams still in the building.

'You look a bit troubled, if I may say so,' said Williams. 'Is there anything I can do to help?'

'No, no. Oh no, thanks,' gasped Fawner. 'Just got to make a phone call, that's all.'

The two unacquainted adversaries stood for a moment facing one another.

'OK then. Sorry to have troubled you,' said Williams. He opened the door, passed through and, having determined it would not lock, shut it noisily behind him. The art of this was, as the wily Williams knew, to lull the unwilling source into a false sense of security. Any door will, unless the lock is activated, easily re-open on a rebound if pulled hard enough— the eavesdropper's ploy being to ensure it only opens sufficiently to allow what is being said to be heard without the speaker becoming aware of the hearer. As Williams intended, Fawner now resumed his telephone call. Every word was clearly heard and noted in shorthand by Williams.

'Good morning. I need to speak urgently to Chief Superintendent Rex Raymond, please. Yes. My name is Douglas Fawner.'

Williams underlined it on his pad.

'Please tell him it's a matter of Fraternal concern and criminal acts that he will want to know about.'

Williams smiled as he wrote—yes, this was a story.

'Rex. Yes, yes. I'm sorry, but I don't know who to tell and . . . no it's not about your lodge . . . or mine but . . . well, I'm at the lodge rooms. The cleaner found three men here bound and gagged, without any clothes on and all smeared with blood. . . . There's another one with clothes on, but he's bloody as well. . . . In the temple. . . . I was telephoned—an off-duty nurse called who asked me to come down, but he didn't say—well I don't think he knew what was upstairs, but the cleaner. . . . No—your chaps took her home and the nurses . . . a sergeant and a constable, the nurse said. . . . I didn't see them. I think the nurse said one was called Houseman.' Gil Williams almost dropped his notebook. What the hell was Horseman up to? Whatever it was, he needed to hear the rest of Fawner's side of the conversation.

'No, no, they're alive and they can talk . . . I took the gags off to . . . Oh! . . . I didn't think of that. . . . Yes, yes. I went in and helped them as much as I could, but I couldn't undo the knots . . . Rex . . .'

Even from outside, Williams could hear the chief superintendent berating Fawner.

'I'm sorry, Rex, but your chaps had been here and then gone. Oh dear, and a man from the press was here, but I got rid of him. Well, I know two of them . . . yes, they are . . . but not my lodge. . . . Yes. Alright, Rex, I'll wait here.'

Fawner dictated the telephone number and disconnected. Obviously the chief superintendent intended to call back. Time for another crafty old pressman's ploy, Williams pushed open the door, at the same time dropping a glove onto the hall floor.

'Hello, again. Did I drop a glove here, by any chance? Ah, yes, there it is. Finished your call, I see?'

Before Fawner could answer, the telephone rang, making him jump. Obviously his nerves were not in a stable state, thought Williams. The phone continued ringing.

Gill Williams continued standing inside the door, watching Fawner who stared back.

'Shouldn't you answer it, sir?' said Williams with the practised, innocent expression only a cynical old pressman chasing a story can muster.

'Er, yes. Of course. Was there anything else?' asked Fawner— hoping to be left alone.

'Just wanted to confirm a few things, sir. No hurry. Take your phone call first.'

Douglas Fawner knew he had no choice. He picked up the telephone receiver, 'Hello, Masonic Ha . . . Yes, Rex. . . . No, I said I didn't see them. They . . .

'What? . . . Oh dear, oh dear, oh dear. Who do you think? . . . Oh, yes, of course I'll wait here for them. No, no, Rex, I won't go upstairs again until they get here . . . of course, yes, a statement . . . Inspector Gorman, a sergeant and two constables, yes, yes. . . . Listen, Rex, I wasn't to know. . . . No. . . . Sorry, Rex. Thank you, Rex, I . . .'

Several things were obvious to Williams: the police superintendent had ended the telephone call before Fawner had thanked him; Fawner had interfered with a potential crime scene; some police were about to be despatched to the Masonic hall; and, somehow, that wretched David Horseman had been here and left with a material witness. Quickly weighing up his options, Williams decided he needed to find Horseman as soon as possible—and before the police did. First, though, he could give Fawner a quick grilling.

'Well, sir. I think my information was correct and there is a news story here. It would be easier if you told me rather than leaving us to, shall we say, speculate?'

Williams left the implied threat hanging and stared hard at Fawner.

'No, no. None of your business, this.'

I'm sorry, sir, but from what little I heard, the police seem to be involved, and there's something rather interesting upstairs. Perhaps I could just take a look?'

'No. No, you can't go up there. It's private. Please leave,' said Fawner.

'Very well, sir. But could I ask for your name and how I might contact you later. I'm sure the police will release details later. I may need to question you when you're feeling calmer.'

Reluctantly, Fawner gave Williams his name and telephone number. Having scrawled this down, Gil Williams decided this was a good time to withdraw and try to trace his errant, but enterprising, young reporter. Having no idea where else to go, he retraced his steps to the offices of the *Avonbridge Gazette*.

At the *Avonbridge Gazette*, 11.15–11.30 a.m.

The way in which Williams burst through the outer door warned Dotty that her boss was in one of his rages.

'Horseman in?' he barked at Dotty.

'Yes, Gil, he's in the reporters' room with Derek Peters.'

Williams stalked on until Dotty's summons to, 'Wait, Gil,' halted him.

'Well?'

'He's on the phone to the *News of the World*, Gil.'

'Is he now?' replied Williams, propelling himself through the inner door.

Horseman was, indeed, on the telephone talking excitedly. As he heard and then saw his boss join him in the room he hesitated—looking both excited and anxious.

'Don't hang up, David,' said Williams in his icy, calm voice. 'Ask them to hold on a moment, would you?' It was neither plea nor request, but an order demanding instant compliance. Horseman duly asked them to hold on a moment.

'Got yourself an N.H.S., then?' said Williams. Seeing young Peters with an incredulous look on his still innocent face, he snapped an interpretation, 'Shorthand for National Headline Story, Derek. Well, David?'

'Yes, I have,' came the half defiant reply.

'Publishing next Sunday, then?'

'Yes.'

'You got pictures?'

'Yes,' replied both Horseman and Peters in unison.

'They're being developed by Debbie Pycock as an urgent job, Mr Williams,' added Peters.

Williams continued to talk rapidly to Horseman. 'I suppose you offered them an exclusive?'

'Well——'

'You can't, young man. You're employed here.'

'But I——'

'No, you didn't, David. You thought you'd cut us out and scoop the fee. Who're you talking to?'

'The deputy news editor.' There was almost a *so there* tone to Horseman's reply.

'Give me the phone, David.'

Horseman hesitated.

'Hang on to it and you won't have a job at all.'

The telephone was handed over; Horseman still glared at Williams; Peters cowered—hoping to become invisible. Williams explained his position and then, politely, asked to speak to the editor. He gave his name and assured the deputy news editor that on hearing his name he would be spoken to. He was. Horseman clearly heard the voice from London greet his boss with a booming, 'Gil, you old bugger. How're things out there in the wild provinces?'

'Probably quieter than in the sleazy capital, Jerry.'

The obvious familiarity caused Horseman's heart and hopes to sink. The ensuing exchange made him admire and respect anew Gil Williams. Within a few minutes a deal had been struck whereby the *Avonbridge Gazette* had the initial rights to the story and pictures after which, for a far higher fee than Horseman had dreamed of, or dared to request, the rights passed to the *News of the World*. The story and pictures would be published in the *Avonbridge Gazette* on Thursday evening and nationally in the *News of the World* the following Sunday. Similar priorities for subsequent developments and revelations were also agreed. The local and national byline would include David's name—Horseman was almost delirious. The next condition deflated his ego, 'Fees payable to the *Avonbridge Gazette*; contracts in the post tonight.'

Williams exchanged a few more vulgar pleasantries with the national editor and replaced the telephone. He turned to regard a rather pale and somewhat indignant Horseman.

'That, David Horseman, is how you deal, as fairly as the newspaper business allows, with a scoop. Like a lot of things in this world, it depends on who as well as what you know. I suppose you're looking so down in the mouth because you've lost a big fee? How much were you asking for?'

Horseman told him.

Williams snorted, 'You'll get double that at the end of next month. Now get back down to the Masonic place; see what happens and get as many follow-up angles and interviews as you can. Take this with you.' Williams handed over the spare camera. 'Any problems ring me—try to use their phone if you can. If that pompous clod Fawner refuses to let you use it, find another.'

A rejuvenated, relieved and better informed David Horseman needed no second bidding. He said a heartfelt thank you to Gil Williams, which the old pressman waved away in annoyance or embarrassment. Derek Peters moved to follow him.

'Derek, get back to young Miss Pycock's lab and wait for the photos. I want at least three prints of each. Bring back the negatives and an invoice. Dotty will give you a cheque to take straight back.

'Oh, and Derek, learn from this. Off you go.'

The Masonic Hall 11.00–11.30 a.m.

Had Douglas Fawner been aware of developments at the *Avonbridge Gazette*, he might have contemplated moving home. Or worse. Complacently feeling he was rid of the press, he awaited the arrival of the promised police presence. He did wonder who the previous persons apparently posing as police could have been, but naïve conceit convinced him it was nothing to worry about. He needed to get a new cleaner for the building, of course.

It suddenly occurred to Fawner that tonight was Chandlery Lodge's installation of a new master. That mess upstairs would have to be removed, and it dawned upon Fawner that at least two, if not all four, of the brethren upstairs were members of Chandlery Lodge. Should he go up again and talk to them about it? What could he say? Fawner decided to wait for the Police as he had been told.

Stourminster Police Station, 10.45–11.15 a.m.

Detective Inspector Steve Gorman was surprised, to say the least, to be personally summoned with all haste to Superintendent Raymond's office.

'Bring the best investigative team you can get together, Steve,' he was told before the internal line went dead.

With Detective Sergeant Paula James, Detective Constables Alan Hughes and Harry Carter-Knight in his wake, Gorman knocked on the superintendent's door.

'Come.'

Come they did. The six-foot-six superintendent was seated behind his desk. Not being invited to do likewise, the detectives stood in an awkward, expectant line. Raymond was not known for mincing words or beating about bushes, true to form, he came directly to the point.

'We have a potentially problematic situation at the Masonic temple in Avon Street, Avonbridge; could be attempted murder or just an elaborate, tasteless prank for all we presently know. Whatever it is, the press seems to have got wind of it and, from what I have learnt, we could be embarrassed. I want a show of force, a quick resolution and then you can all return to normal duties.'

Gorman and James had experience of murder investigations, for the two constables the mention of even an attempted murder induced a frisson of excitement. All four were taken aback by the superintendent's next query.

'Any of you know anything about Freemasonry?'

Raymond's steely blue eyes regarded them in turn. It was obvious that none were any better informed than the mythical man-in-the-street.

D.S. James was the first to speak. 'My father's a Mason, sir. My boyfriend and I've been to two ladies' evenings at the Edgbaston Winter Gardens with him.'

'Thank you, sergeant. You can, at least, assure your colleagues that we're not a bunch of nutters.'

He noted the raised eyebrows and one smirk, 'Yes, Gorman. Smirk if you must, but I *am* one of them—and proud to be.'

He paused to let what he had said sink in before continuing. 'Tread carefully on this case—if case it be. A lot of influential citizens could be either involved or affected. Report directly to me at least twice a day.'

Raymond was pleased to note all four now had notebook and pen in hand. 'Information so far is that at 8.45 this morning a call came in from a Phil Carlton advising of a hysterical woman discovered in Avon Street and babbling about bodies and blood in the Masonic rooms. The young constable who took the call foolishly filed it "for attention".'

'I'd just found it in my in-tray when you called, sir,' interjected Gorman. 'Uniform were sending someone along.'

'Thank you, Steve. Now it's your urgent matter of the day. God knows what some uniformed plod could be doing there—if anyone's there yet—but try to keep whoever it is outside, repelling reporters and nosy-parkers. Try not to appear as if it's a crime scene, if you can. I've had a personal call from a Mr Douglas Fawner—secretary of the hall—who confirms that there are four blood-spattered bodies, three unclothed, in the upstairs room known as the temple. They're all very much alive. Unfortunately, Fawner seems to have trampled all over the scene—I've already told him off, so go easy.'

Raymond gave a rueful smile 'But not *too* easy. . . . It seems the cleaning woman who discovered the scene has been removed from the building. Where to and by who, we don't know, but, apparently, two men gained entry posing as police officers. One called Houseman. The cleaning woman needs to be found and interviewed. Fingerprinting should be in Avonbridge soon and I've asked Henry Lamb, the on-call doctor, to be there soon as. He knows the premises well, being—yes, he *is*, Gorman—one of us. Any press pester you give a, "no comment"—and say I'll call a press conference, if need be, as soon as we know anything.'

'Sir,' unwisely interrupted Carter-Knight, a recent Hendon Police College graduate, 'Do we know who any of the . . . injured parties are?'

The unfortunate young constable found himself the recipient of the steely gaze that had affrighted many felons.

Raymond continued. 'Fawner tells me he knows two of the victims are Freemasons, but he didn't name them when we spoke. However, in last night's call log, Sergeant Bagnall received several persistent and distressed calls between 10.25 and 2.30 from three ladies with missing husbands. . . .' Here Raymond paused to consult notes on his desk, 'Mrs Francis, Mrs Jeffries and Mrs Hughes. Addresses on here,' he handed the notes to Gorman.

'Mrs Hughes is certainly the wife of Raymond Hughes, the furniture retailer in Avonbridge High Street and he is a member of Chandlery Lodge—which is one of the lodges meeting at the Avonbridge temple. You need to establish identities as soon as possible and let me know. If, as I suspect, the bloodied men are the husbands reported missing, I'll see that the wives are informed and brought to Avon Street with clothes for the victims. Get statements before you release them, of course, Steve. I don't need to tell you there's something odd about this one so, as I said, tread carefully. Questions?'

There were few queries other than to establish transport and communications. The four slightly bemused detectives departed *en route* for Avonbridge.

The Masonic Hall, 11.30 a.m.–1.00 p.m.

As two unmarked police cars carrying respectively Gorman and Hughes, and James and Carter-Knight drove along Avon Street, the location of the Masonic hall was glaringly obvious. A double row of yellow crime-scene tape stretched across the car park entrance in the centre of which stood a uniformed constable.

'So much for a low profile,' muttered Gorman as he pulled up facing the stolid, uniformed one. He lowered his car window and waved his warrant card at the self-appointed guardian of the hall. To his extreme irritation, the stupid flat-nose insisted on examining it closely before raising the tape to admit the two cars. He was told, not too gently, to remove all yellow tape and take position at the door to the hall—not at the car park entrance. The two police cars drew up alongside the only other parked car. Gorman, rightly, assumed it belonged to Douglas Fawner—whom they found waiting in the entrance hall.

The detectives curbed their differing levels of curiosity concerning the various glass display cabinets containing aprons, badges and, in one instance, inscribed drinking glasses. Fawner, though eager to help, constantly urged the inspector to relieve and release the 'poor chaps upstairs'. Gorman confined his initial questions to basics and after only a few minutes—although it seemed longer to Fawner—all five mounted the stairs and entered the outer room.

'Is this the door to where the gentlemen are?' asked Gorman.

'Yes. . . . But you can't go through there,' replied Fawner.

Gorman's eyes grew hard. He glared at Fawner, 'Mr Fawner,' he said in his best official tones, 'we're here to investigate what may or may not be a crime. If you're refusing to allow us access to the scene, that could count as impeding a police officer in the conduct of his duty. . . . As an afterthought, he added 'sir' with little respect in the single syllable.

'Oh, no. No, no, Inspector,' said a flustered Fawner. 'No, what I meant was, the door is blocked by one of the Brethren who's lying inside.'

'Well, can't he roll away?' asked a still irritated Gorman.

'No, Inspector. He's tied to a chair . . . a big, heavy chair. I couldn't lift it on my own, you see. . . .' Fawner's voice trailed off as he realised he was, again, admitting to having disturbed a crime scene.

'For the moment, I don't see, Mr Fawner. Would there be another way into this room? I understand you've already been in, so——'

Gorman was interrupted by a strong voice at ground level behind the door, 'That you, again, Fawner? About bloody time. When you going to get us out of this confounded mess, man?'

'Yes, yes, Frank,' said an obviously cowed Fawner. Approaching the door and lowering his voice to a conspiratorial whisper that everyone except Fallowfield heard, he confided, 'I've got the police with me, now, Frank.'

'What're you saying, Fawner?' came the answering angry bellow.

Gorman took charge, 'This is the police, sir. We'll be with you as soon as Mr Fawner shows us how to gain access.'

'About bloody well time, too, if I may say so,' came the reply.

Fawner realised all four detectives were looking at him.

'If you would follow me, Inspector,' he said.

Fawner was concerned not that there appeared to be a lot of detectives, but that one of them was a woman.

Realising Fawner's meaning, Gorman was more determined than before that his entire team should view the crime scene—if, indeed, it was a crime.

'Come along . . . team,' he said firmly, stressing the 'team'.

All four followed Fawner along a narrow corridor. They passed a room in which could be glimpsed colourful banners and gold-inscribed boards. At the end of the corridor, another partly open door led to the main temple—similarly beset with banners and boards. Fawner again attempted to preserve his interpretation of decencies.

'Inspector, the breth . . . the men in here are naked.'

'So I have been given to understand, sir,' answered Gorman in a flat voice.

'Well . . .'

'Well, what?' bellowed Gorman.

'The . . . er, the young lady, sir.'

'The young lady, Mr Fawner, is Detective Sergeant James. She's seen worse sights than naked men. Correct, Sergeant?'

'Certainly, sir,' replied Paula.

'You'll not be upset by Mr Fawner's naked friends?'

'Not in the least, Inspector,' answered Paula—enjoying Fawner's discomfort almost as much as Gorman. The two detective constables suppressed laughter.

Fawner reluctantly pushed open the door. The detectives did not, as Fawner expected, immediately enter. Thrusting him aside, they surveyed the scene one by one. Then, following their leader, they filed into the temple and stood before the three white-bodied and red-faced men. As might have been expected two—those on the outside—objected loudly to the presence of Paula James, the little man in the middle, who had the most bloody markings on his poor old body, slumped down into his chair.

'Is he alright?' queried a concerned D.S. James—trying to make herself heard over the stentorian demands for her to leave.

The more composed, only partly undressed and still recumbent Fallowfield answered her, 'Mr Fisher's fainted again, miss. He's made a bit of a habit of that these last few hours, I'm afraid.'

Having seen all he needed to see, Inspector Gorman now took full charge.

'Is there anything with which we can cover these gentlemen up to keep them . . . warm and . . . so on?' he demanded of Fawner.

'Well, not in here, of course, but——'

He was loudly interrupted by the gentleman still on the floor, 'For pity's sake, Fawner, go and get some chapter gowns from the cupboard.'

To the surprise of the police, Fawner meekly departed.

''Bout time he used his head, that one,' added the man on the floor.

'Now, perhaps, you could put me upright, if you please, officers?'

'We'll do that, sir, as soon as Constable Carter-Knight has taken photographs.'

All three conscious old gentlemen's voices tumbled over each other to tell Gorman they had already been photographed. This was one of those times, Steve Gorman knew, when thinking on his feet and evasive 'verbals' were needed.

'Just a further set to be certain, please, gentlemen,' he said. 'Harry . . .'

The keen young detective was already focusing the camera on the gentleman by the door whom he rightly judged to be the most uncomfortable—posturally. As soon as he had taken a couple of pictures of Fallowfield, and at her suggestion, he passed the camera to Paula James who quite enjoyed photographing the embarrassed and uselessly objecting naked old men.

With more effort than they had imagined would be required, the two detective constables hauled the partly-clothed old gentleman's chair upright. It was obvious that during his ordeal he had, despite, or because of, the ineffectual bowl, soiled himself.

'Sorry about the mess and smell, lads—it's been a long and damnably uncomfortable night for us,' he apologised. Admiring the old gentleman's composure, the young constables heaved his chair upright. The old gentleman heaved a sigh of relief.

'Thanks a lot, officers. Be nice to be relieved of the perishin' restraints next.'

The inspector was trying to quieten the two conscious, complaining nudes.

'Sir,' queried Carter- Knight, 'would it be alright to let Mr . . . er——'

'Fallowfield,' interjected that gentleman.

'Mr Fallowfield out of his chair?'

'We've got photos of the scene,' answered Gorman, 'so, in the circumstances, the sooner these gentlemen can move around and get their circulation going, the better. Alan, you release Mr Fallowfield. Harry, note Mr Fallowfield's details and then, if they'll be quiet,' he glared at the two still protesting old men, 'get the same from these gentlemen while Alan releases them.'

'I'll need a knife, sir,' said D.C. Hughes.

'Don't use those on the floor,' said Gorman and James in unison.

The Hendon-trained Carter-Knight calmly produced a Swiss army knife from his back pocket and handed it to his colleague. It was at this stage that the observant Detective Sergeant James called the inspector's attention to the strange fact that, although the four bound men appeared to have been cut and had blood on their bodies, there was no blood on the floor. They pondered this for several minutes.

Stourminster Police Station, 11.30 a.m.–1.00 p.m.

Superintendent Raymond impatiently awaited a call from Inspector Gorman. It was tempting to telephone the three ladies who had so frequently pleaded for or ordered (depending upon who was calling) searches to be implemented for their missing husbands, but caution and experience made him wait until Gorman had confirmed the identities of the bound brethren. Quite why they should have been denuded mystified him, he hoped Gorman's team could discover a reason.

Gorman's telephone call confirmed the men's identities to be as suspected—but why four old men should be bound and left in the temple, three as nature made them, remained a mystery. Gorman confirmed the telephone numbers of the parties who had all been examined by Dr Lamb and, apart from Mr Fisher, pronounced no worse for their experience. Raymond steeled himself. He decided to telephone the ladies in alphabetical order. Fallowfield having no wife, this initially condemned the superintendent to the far-from-tender tones of Caitlin Fisher. Eventually imposing his message between her accusations and denunciations, he forcibly forbade her to telephone the other wives, but to gather clothing for Mr Fisher and await the car he was sending for all three ladies. His subsequent telephone calls were infinitely easier. Each wife complied with his requests.

Gorman's next report to Superintendent Raymond advised him that statements had been taken from Fawner and the four brethren forced to spend a naked, or near-naked, night away from home. D.S. James and

D.C. Hughes would deliver Worshipful Brother Fallowfield home to, as the latter had succinctly said, 'restore meself to me usual comforts,' (the superintendent smiled) before going to interview the cleaner—address courtesy of Fawner. Gorman was remaining on site whilst fingerprinting and other investigations took place and Carter-Knight had been despatched to do a door-to-door of which Gorman expected little or less.

After looking at the uninviting pile of paperwork still to be dealt with, the superintendent decided to visit the crime scene himself.

Avon Street and Versey Street, 1–2.00 p.m.

Henry Alan Carter-Knight, known since infancy as Harry, had no illusions about the tedious tasks required for the routine resolution of a crime. It had been impressed upon him at Hendon and he was intelligent enough to appreciate such time-consuming and repetitive tasks would, for a time at least, fall to him. Reluctantly, he left the strangely interesting Avonbridge Masonic hall to begin yet another round of door-to-door enquiries.

Cynically surveying the surrounding streets, he felt there would be few doors behind which he would find anyone who had been in a position to observe anything out of the ordinary last evening or night. He ignored the queries of a rude, intrusive young man who stated he was from the press. It took little time to confirm the shops in Avon Street all closed before the earliest time at which the old gentlemen were summoned to attend the Masonic hall. One cynical shopkeeper informed him, gratuitously, that 'We'—whoever *we* might be—'takes no notice o' them in their dark suits'. Harry turned his attention to Versey Street—at least this was dwelt in and not devoted solely to commerce. The press man watched him start these enquiries and, becoming more bored than Harry, returned to the hall car park. The terraced cottages on Harry's left proved to be inhabited by lonely and unobservant souls who, whilst having nothing useful to impart, were eager to talk with and, if only he would enter, entertain him. Harry maintained a courteous manner, but was relieved to reach the end of the terraces. Approaching the last house he was sorely tempted to take any tea if offered; the odour of cat urine and unwashed humans emanating from the opened door dispelled temptation and hastened him across the street.

On the opposite side, every other house offered 'unrivalled' bed and breakfast for the weary traveller. Harry worked his enquiring way patiently downhill towards the Masonic hall; Harry would far rather have been inside that strange, fascinating building than endlessly asking the same questions and endlessly hearing the same variations of denial of any useful observation. 'Persevere—you never know when someone will supply information of importance' had been one of the many mantras impressed upon him in training. With commendable perseverance, Harry rang the bell of number 31.

Not only did Harry accept the invitation to enter number 31, Versey Street, and take tea, he eagerly took statements from Dave and Molly Morris and, after visiting their downstairs, accompanied the helpful couple and the overjoyed Rags to the padlocked gates they reliably advised led to the old chandlery and wharf. It was obvious to the trained eye that a car—or cars—had recently entered the deserted premises. To Harry's annoyance, the obvious was being observed by that press chap. Harry ignored him and counselled his informants to do likewise. Other than the wheel tracks, nothing of interest was visible. Dave Morris was certain the car he had seen disappearing inside was 'a big 'un' but as to its make or registration number he could be of no further assistance.

Thanking the Morrises for their valuable assistance, Harry watched them trudge toward their home, pursued at a distance by the reporter. Feeling certain Inspector Gorman would want to know what he had discovered as soon as possible, he postponed enquiries at the remaining Versey Street doors. The absence of the old gentlemen's cars had been a problem his boss had voiced before Harry left the hall, according to the nudes, their three cars should have been parked outside the hall. Gorman was pleased with Harry's information. He was less pleased to be told that 'some chap from the press was hanging about'.

Douglas Fawner had complied with Mr Fallowfield's instructions, the three unattractive companions, having attempted to cleanse themselves at the small hand basins, were now clad in white surplices. The two larger and more vocal men were walking tentatively around the outer room—it was difficult for the officers of the law to suppress their smiles at the weird and awful sight. The small gentleman, for whom the doctor had expressed concern, sat miserably mute in a corner.

Fawner had no idea who held the keys to the old chandlery gates, 'I've not seen them opened in the last few years, although before the business closed . . .

Gorman halted Fawner's less than useful reminiscences.

'Let's take a look, Harry,' he said to the young detective. 'Be so good as to remain in the downstairs vestibule, Mr Fawner'—he requested the disappointed secretary and manager—'in case the ladies arrive. Don't let them go upstairs, of course.'

'But, Inspector, they'll want to see their husbands——'

'No doubt, Mr Fawner. But I doubt they'll want to see the other husbands in their present state. Keep them down here and take the clothes up yourself. Come on, Harry.'

So saying, Gorman hastened from the building.

'Come with us, Constable,' he ordered the uniformed officer.

Welcoming a change of scenery, the uniformed constable pursued them—it was a wise precaution in light of a loitering reporter. Gorman was relieved to be away from the constantly complaining, still malodorous and unclothed old men and out of the unpleasant atmosphere that was now permeating downstairs. Even the air of Avonbridge smelled sweet as he crossed the road with young Carter-Knight.

Avon Street and Chandlery Wharf, 2.15–2.30 p.m.

Gorman glanced at the obviously recent wheel tracks before—noting the reporter was out of earshot—saying quietly to Harry, 'Don't suppose you tried the padlock, did you, Detective?'

Holding the inexperienced detective's gaze, he took from his pocket a bunch of strange objects.

'Er, well, I actually——' began Carter-Knight.

'No, Harry. Didn't think you did,' said Gorman. 'You never know, with these things,' he continued, before waving the now unfastened padlock before him, to the young detective constable's amazement. Then with one hand he returned the lock picks to his pocket.

'If you unravel the chain carefully, Harry, we might be able to see what entered Chandlery Wharf last night.' He turned to the uniformed constable, 'No one follows us into here until I say, OK?'

The constable stolidly took stance. Privately he was pleased the reporter photographed him standing guard.

Together, the detectives walked down the slope, carefully avoiding the wheel tracks.

'Bingo,' muttered Gorman as they reached the flat area beyond the buildings. The three missing cars were neatly parked, the ignition keys still hanging inside. On each passenger seat was a bound pile of clothing.

'Well done, young Harry,' said Gorman. But for forensics we could have saved the wives the trouble of bringing fresh clothes. I bet the impatient old so-and-sos will want their wheels back immediately and won't like having to wait.'

As they walked back, an excited mongrel with wagging tail jumped up at Harry.

'Oh, no! Down, Rags,' said Harry.

'You know this animal?' asked Gorman.

'Yes, sir, it belongs to'—with sinking heart he saw his informants at the top of the slope—'those people.'

The curious Morrises were asked to remove themselves from a potential police crime scene. Their dismissal, though politely requested, thoroughly disheartened them and they felt less proud of having assisted the police. Knowing there was nothing they could do about it, Gorman and Carter-Knight furiously watched the eager reporter walking alongside the retreating Morrises. Harry's earlier euphoria faded and he was not in the least surprised to be ordered to guard the gateway until they could get another uniform.'

Followed by the bored uniformed constable, Gorman stumped toward the Masonic hall. His mood was not improved as he observed Superintendent Raymond and a discomforted Fawner standing on the hall steps. Raymond was regarding him and, he assumed, his absence with considerable disfavour.

The Masonic Hall, 2.30–3.30 p.m.

Having offered what, even as he said it, seemed a lame excuse for leaving the scene, Detective Inspector Steve Gorman cautiously regarded his superior. He had always found Raymond fair—deserving any fairness in this instance was, he felt, unlikely. He received a stern, disapproving look as he followed the superintendent inside the Masonic hall and was surprised to be ushered into the large room opposite the stairs.

Raymond, curtly but politely, asked Fawner to remain in the hall to wait for the wives. His expression softened, 'Odd business, this, Steve,' said Raymond once they were alone.

'Very,' answered Gorman, relieved to have the matter of his absence undebated.

'Have you seen the three gentlemen, sir?'

'Oh yes, Steve. I'm acquainted with two of them—more's the pity, between you and me. They're in the upstairs toilets getting dressed. They managed to wash off the body paint—or whatever it was. It's certainly not blood, of that I'm certain. Tests could show what it is, but I doubt we'd be able to trace the source.'

'Why were they painted or whatever, sir?'

'The way they were marked would have significance for other Masons, Steve. But, whatever, it's no longer important. I've discussed things with the three of them upstairs and I managed to get old Fallowfield on the phone, they don't want to court publicity and they're all refusing to make any official complaint or pursue prosecution. Fawner thinks he can make a small claim on insurance for any minor damage to the premises. So, all we can do is remove ourselves and leave whoever's going to do so to tidy up. It would be good policy, I don't need to tell you, to see the erstwhile naturists restored to their homes. I'll leave that to you. Then we can all return to normal policing.'

'Right, sir,' replied the inspector. 'There's a reporter hanging about, I'm afraid——'

'I'll deal with him, Steve,' said the superintendent in a resigned tone.

Superintendent Raymond left a bemused Inspector Gorman to gather his team together whilst he dealt, as diplomatically as he could, with three wives bearing men's overcoats, before being confronted by:

'Horseman—Avonbridge Gazette, sir. Would you like to inform our readers of the matter of concern here, today?'

Raymond looked hard at Horseman. The over-zealous reporter, eventually realising what else was required, added a grudging, 'Please?'

Having bought himself time to think, Raymond replied, 'What has occurred here today is a private dispute that, initially, was mistaken for a possible crime. No formal complaint has been made concerning the incident and, to the best of my knowledge, there will be no further proceedings of either police or civil concern. That's all, thank you.'

The superintendent walked quickly to his car, ignoring the familiar protestations.

Douglas Fawner had, as suggested by Raymond, locked the outer doors to the hall.

Detective Inspector Steve Gorman was confused and annoyed. None of the old gentlemen seemed inclined to talk to him, there had been tired, almost conspiratorial talk with Fawner about 'tonight', but no satisfactory reply had appeared to be forthcoming. So far as he knew, none of the victims had spoken to the insistent reporter who still haunted the car park. Now, restored to their own clothes and wives, they were transported home. The only dissident had been Mrs Fisher who, outspoken as ever, had persistently insisted, 'Someone ought to be locked up for this.' She had been, almost as insistently, hushed by two of the old gentlemen—her husband remained mute.

When they eventually emerged from the hall, Horseman recognised Raymond Hughes from the furniture shop and made a note to interview him elsewhere as soon as possible. From Derek Peter's photographs, his astute editor identified the others.

When, finally, the old Masons and their wives had been taken home and accepted assurances that their respective vehicles would soon be returned, Steve Gorman, deciding honesty was the best policy, gathered his team together. He could, at least, hide beneath the skirts of the superintendent's orders. D.S. James and D.C. Hughes had returned with a carefully interpreted statement from Mrs Jones. They and the man of discovery Carter-Knight regarded Gorman with ill-concealed amazement.

'One of the oddest and shortest cases I've known, Steve,' opined Paula James.

'Those poor old men stripped and left tied up all night and they don't want to make a complaint or prosecute anyone?'

'It may be the wrong place to say this, sir,' added Alan Hughes, 'but, well, have we stumbled onto a Masonic secret? Or what?'

'I just don't know, Alan,' answered Gorman. 'To be honest, I don't think so. But what puzzles me, and I think all of you if you stop to think about it, is *why*? Why strip three old chaps; leave another partly dressed; tie 'em all up; paint 'em with bloody (and I'm not swearing Paula) odd marks; and then . . . just . . . leave 'em there all night? It's a puzzle.'

CHAPTER FIFTY-ONE

The Banqueting Suite of The Swan Hotel, Avonbridge
Chandlery Lodge Ladies' Festival, Friday 19 October 1984

Dear Lady,

On behalf of Chandlery Lodge, it is my pleasant duty to express the pleasure we feel welcoming you for your festival. It is our sincere wish that you enjoy this evening and leave with only happy memories.

J. J. Whitehouse-Martin
Worshipful Master

Laugh and be merry together, like brothers akin,
Guesting awhile in the rooms of a beautiful inn,
Glad till the dancing stops, and the lilt of the music ends.
Laugh till the game is played; and be you merry, my friends.
(John Masefield)

Officers of the Festival
Director of Ceremonies: W.Bro. Raymond Hughes, P.P.G.Reg.
Assistant Director of Ceremonies: W.Bro. James J. Russell, P.M.
Festival Secretary: W. Bro. Alan Simmonds, P.M.
Chief Steward: Bro. Paul A. Miller

There's different ways of doing things
As everyone supposes
Some turns up their sleeves to work
And some turns up their noses.
(Anon)

The unchanging format of Chandlery ladies' nights had been set for many years. It always took place on the third Friday of October. The invitation to apply for tickets always stated: 'Reception 6.00 p.m.; Banquet 7.30 p.m.; Dancing 10.30 p.m. to midnight.'

As ever, the programme for the night of 19 October 1984 gave no further indication of times.

Since it was JJ and Jenny's ladies' night, application for tickets was brisk and the capacity of The Swan was reached by mid-September. Having been grudgingly told he could use whom he liked as festival secretary, JJ had ignored the broad hints of Worshipful Brother Jeffries and asked Alan Simmonds to assist in that capacity. Although he would have wished otherwise, JJ had been advised it would be Masonically incorrect not to have the lodge director of ceremonies in that capacity for the evening, consequently the planning meetings were little fun due to the unbending dictates of Worshipful Brother Ray Hughes, and the attendance of his all-action/all-knowing wife, Doris, added little joy to proceedings. After their departure, the remainder of the festival committee relaxed. Following two such meetings, JJ scheduled the start for 6.00 p.m. and manipulated proceedings so that the Hughes left at 7.45 enabling the Whitehouse-Martins to sit down to a sociable supper with Billy, Janice, Alan and Julia Simmonds.

JJ had cleared his business diary for the whole of the festival Friday. In the morning, he and Jenny, in their respective cars, set out for The Swan—Jenny travelling by way of the Flower Patch where she confirmed with Annie arrangements for the late afternoon and evening. The shop van, kindly driven this one time by Annie's husband, Fred, would transport floral table arrangements; bouquets for Julia Simmonds and Doris Hughes and carnation button-holes for festival officers and stewards to The Swan at 5.00 p.m. and, to save time changing, Fred would drive the van in his evening suit. Jenny confirmed numbers with Annie and they agreed when to meet and oversee the arrangement of table flowers. Jenny then joined JJ, Alan, Julia, Billy and Janice at The Swan where they made short work of distributing place cards in accordance with the impressively displayed table plans—courtesy of J. & B. Printers. In the dining room vestibule, despite the five-course menu they were due to eat later (page four of the table cards, again by J & B Printers) they all sat down to a jovial one-course pub lunch in the midst of which Ray Hughes arrived with much bluster and few apologies for lateness. Despite being assured everything was ready, he insisted on just checking before he departed with disapproving looks at the young, lunching upstarts.

As had always been so, anything organised by JJ and Billy—either solely or in association with others—proceeded smoothly and as intended. Ray Hughes's stuffy announcements of attendees were neatly contrasted by JJ and Jenny welcoming each and every one as if they were the only guests they wished to see. Both of them were surprised at the uninspired and repetitive utterances of so many—the relaxed manner of less inhibited guests contrasted favourably—and, a poor reflection on Chandlery Lodge, most of the outgoing attitudes were exhibited by their many personal guests. Uncle Charles and Auntie Charlotte, despite approaching octogenarian status, were full of joy and laughter. The evening for Jenny, however, was, as she had feared when she saw the table plan, doomed. Worshipful Brother Hughes announced, 'Mrs and Mrs Carl Marriott.' Jenny smiled through her hatred and JJ, sensing her discomfort, ensured the two women did not speak together for long.

'Jenny and I were at school together. Weren't we Jenny?' said Cynthia—cynically.

'Oh, really? How nice,' replied JJ, gently ushering the Marriotts away.

'Is she the one who . . . ?' asked JJ quietly.

'Yes, she is, damn her eyes,' answered Jenry equally quietly.

'Well, we don't have to talk to them again tonight, darling,' said JJ gesturing to Ray Hughes to announce the next couple.

'Or any other night as far as I'm concerned,' said Jenny, forcing a smile for the next arrivals.

The reception over, Ray Hughes requested—it sounded more like an order—the ladies, gentlemen and brethren to take their places in the banqueting room where they were asked (ordered?) to receive with acclamation the Worshipful Master and Mrs Whitehouse-Martin. Jenny and JJ entered to thunderous applause and a few undignified cheers. In the absence of the lodge chaplain, JJ was delighted to call upon Worshipful Brother the Reverend Claude Martin for grace.

Claude gave a witty, sincere and apposite grace and everyone sat down to soup; goujons of plaice; roast duckling; and peach melba. The management of The Swan were making every effort for this occasion, the volume of business JJ, Billy and their associates brought to the establishment deserved every attention at any event with which they were involved. Cheese and biscuits with fresh celery was swiftly followed by coffee and mints and, right on time—as planned—JJ asked everyone to rise and honour the loyal toast to Her Majesty the Queen. Before most had resumed their seats, the booming voice of Ray Hughes informed everyone that there would now be a ten-minute comfort break. Please return to your seats by 9.30.'

The majority present knew that proceedings never resumed until nine forty, but hope always dictated a request for an earlier return.

Before JJ could leave the table to chat to those with whom he had been unable to talk earlier, he was confronted by George Jeffries sourly telling him how incorrect some parts of the printed programme for the evening were.

'Your choice of quotes is, if I may say so Worshipful Master, not the sort we usually have, you know?' he gloated. JJ regarded him with tolerant disdain.

'I do know that, George. I'm sorry they're not up to your literary expectations. As the programme is now printed we can't change them, I'm afraid. But I'll announce an alternative selection if you've got any suggestions?' He looked quizzically at the pompous lodge secretary.

Jeffries glared back, made no response, turned about and left JJ outwardly smiling and inwardly seething. From behind JJ, Charles Whitehouse, having heard every word despite his age, patted him on the back and advised JJ to ignore such pomposity.

'Easy to say, Uncle Charles. Not so easy to do. Nice of him to wish me well for the rest of the night, wasn't it?' They both laughed which relaxed JJ.

Jenny, Auntie Charlotte and Sylvia took advantage of their top-table position to be first into the ladies. As Jenny checked herself in the mirror, Terri came in and gave her a big hug before taking a vacant cubicle. Jenny decided to wait for Terri and excused herself to Charlotte and Sylvia who, having plenty to talk about between themselves, left. To Jenny's dismay Cynthia Marriott entered the room.

'Done well for yourself, fatty,' said Cynthia. 'I'm looking forward to your little speech. It will be little, won't it? Not like you, of course.'

Terri, emerging behind them, heard Cynthia taunting Jenny. Seeing Terri glaring at her, Cynthia turned and entered a vacant cubicle.

'Who the devil's that?' asked Terri—not even bothering to modulate her voice.

'We were at school together,' answered Jenny, gesturing Terri to hurry. Terri was having none of it.

'She's not one of those who . . . ?' she asked, horrified.

Jenny nodded. 'Let's get out of here, Terri. Please,' she pleaded.

'Come on then,' said Terri, 'But I'd like to teach her some manners.'

As they were leaving, they met Janice and Zoe on their way to the ladies. Janice only had to take one look at Jenny to realise all was not as it should be.

'What on earth's the matter, Jen?' she asked.

'It's nothing—I'll be alright' said Jenny. Janice looked enquiringly at Terri.

'Rude bitch in there making snide remarks,' said Terri. 'They were at school together, apparently.'

'She's not one of those who . . . ?' said Janice to Jenny.

Jenny nodded. Then realising that both Janice and Terri were looking rather awkwardly at her, she said to both of them, 'She knows . . . well, you both know. Sorry, Zoe, it's something from the past.

Jenny gathered herself together as best she could and, assuring her three friends that she was alright and begging them to all have a good time, she took Terri's arm and walked towards the dining room.

'Please don't say anything about Cynthia to JJ, Terri.'

Having secured Terri's reluctant agreement, Jenny returned to the top table.

Tradition never relents. Despite the best endeavours of Ray Hughes and his few assistants it was, as it always had been, nine-forty before everyone re-assembled at the tables. The order of events had been unchanged for as many years as the lodge had existed: firstly the immediate past master would present the master's lady with a ladies' festival jewel, after which a brother selected by the master would propose the toast to the ladies, a brother with an acceptable singing voice would lead the brethren and gentlemen in the ladies' song, and lodge stewards dashed or dawdled around presenting every lady except the master's with a gift. It was only then that the master's wife had the opportunity to make response to the toast to the ladies —often having to raise her voice above expressions of pleasure or otherwise at the nature of the gifts.

Over years of attending ladies' nights, firstly as her father's second lady and then as JJ's only lady—Jenny had heard numerous variations on the ladies' toast and a similar number of responses. Some were memorable for their wit and expert delivery; some were memorable for a total lack of such talents; others were utterly unmemorable. Jenny had taken time to craft what she felt to be a response to be remembered. Since Brother Billy Baker was proposing the ladies toast they had dovetailed their respective addresses to avoid the need for late bursts of spontaneity. Neither had cause for, or entertained, many nerves, neither could have known that their carefully crafted wit and wisdom would not fall on any ears that evening.

'Worshipful Master, ladies, gentlemen and brethren,' boomed Brother Hughes, fully in his element as director of ceremonies, 'in accordance with the tradition of Chandlery Lodge the immediate past master, Worshipful Brother Maurice Fisher, will now present the Worshipful Master's Lady, Mrs Whitehouse-Martin, with a ladies' festival jewel.'

Sotto voce—his sottos could be heard at some distance—Ray Hughes urged the little fellow, 'Now, Maurice.'

Jenny stood. Maurice Fisher took the new jewel from its presentation box and, as tradition dictated and he had been made to practice with his wife, held it in such a way as to enable him to insert the long vertical pin into Jenny's dress. The disparity in height between his five feet four inches and Jenny's five feet nine inches, supplemented by three-inch heels, should have been no impediment to the task since Mrs Fisher stood five feet ten inches and wore two-inch heels. The two women's physical proportions were a different matter, Mrs Fisher's evening dresses— indeed any of Mrs Fisher's upper body vestments—never disclosed more than an inch of flesh below her well-lined neck, some spiteful opinion had it that her breastbone was tattooed with a Welsh dragon, but none of the spiteful had, as yet, questioned Brother Maurice on the subject. This evening, timid Brother Fisher found himself confronted by a vast vista of female flesh, but little dress material upon which to impale the proudly poised pin. Jenny, feeling Fisher may be hesitating due to nerves stepped forward. In the same instant Maurice Fisher summoned his little courage and similarly proportioned legs and also stepped forward—onto the front of Jenny's dress. As the Fisher foot descended so, too, did Jenny's dress. Fisher, losing balance and gazing with wonder at a sight his eyes had never beheld, decided to complete his task and, without taking aim, thrust the pin downwards from his upraised right hand. Despite resistance, he forced the pin onward and downward. Jenny found herself losing balance and toppling forward—her already low cut dress descending to the point of exposure. JJ, seeing his wife falling forward, grabbed the back of her dress. Something had to give: the hook at the back of Jenny's dress departed its parent garment and flew, with considerable force, into the Worshipful Master's right eye. With no restraint at the back of her dress and a panicked little man clutching the front in a vain attempt to prevent himself falling into the depths of her cleavage, Jenny found her breasts exposed, the left punctured and spurting blood. Behind Fisher, his wife's thin, mean face appeared. In her panic, Jenny mentally transported back to her school with bloodied breasts and the ghastly Miss Batty tearing at her nightdress.

She began screaming very loudly and incessantly. Maurice Fisher fainted. The swift exposure of the master's wife and her terrible cry briefly brought stunned silence and incredulous immobility around the room. A few interminable seconds later, action erupted. Janice and Terri, realising Jenny's mental nightmare, decided to hasten to her aid; Janice spurned the long way round, mounted a chair and stepped onto the top table; Terri, further from the top table, followed her example, as did Nurse Julia Simmonds who, seeing blood erupting from Jenny's breast, was propelled by her professional duty of care. The arrival onto the top table of the three friends coincided with the two wives of the past masters deciding to use the top table tablecloth to cover Jenny's embarrassment, and seizing the tablecloth, upended the precarious, temporary balance of the three younger women, who fell as one. The dining tables of The Swan appeared presentable when covered in white linen: beneath were old trestles supporting stained boards. The angle at which the ladies landed disturbed the trestles. The top table collapsed—glasses, wine and water scattering in all directions. Caitlin Fisher, busily endeavouring to extract her collapsed little man from the fallen folds of Jenny's dress was showered with red wine. Maurice, recovering consciousness, looked up to see two enormous breasts—from one of which blood dripped onto his sweaty little forehead. He fainted again. Angry, Caitlin, ignoring the part her man had played in her denuding, decided to tell Mrs Whitehouse-Martin exactly what she thought of her disgraceful behaviour. With the thin, earnest face thrust before her and stripped of frontal garb, Jenny's confused mind saw only a re-incarnated Miss Batty. Her screams died to a whimper of fright and she collapsed.

Away from the top table an unprincipled man (no brother, surely?) took a flash photo. Gerald Anstruther, incensed by this breach of decency and consideration, seized the camera from its owner and tore open the back to retrieve and ruin the film. The erstwhile cameraman remonstrated. His more physical friend swung a punch at Gerald that missed its intended target and landed flush on Zoe's cheek. Zoe fell senseless into the arms of another lady. Zoe's husband, Gareth, man of action and amateur boxer, who had been seated opposite Zoe, vaulted onto and over the table and proceeded to knock six or more bells out of his wife's assailant. By now, blood was running high, alcohol had been consumed and inhibitions were abandoned. Fights broke out. Tables tumbled. Glasses, bottles and chairs were broken. Wine flowed in an unintended manner. Chaos reigned.

Two of the calmest persons present were Charles Whitehouse and Claude Martin. As their wives rushed to attend to Jenny and JJ, Charles and Claude hastened to the telephone in the hall of The Swan and dialled nine-nine-nine. Charles requested an ambulance. Claude, seeing the free-for-all erupting, prompted him to also ask for a police presence. The manager of The Swan, temporarily elsewhere in the hotel, heard the commotion and Worshipful Brother Hughes bellowing for order as he searched, vainly, for his gavel. As he ran towards the banqueting suite, a fleeing waitress screeched, 'It all flared up, Mr Costins,' as she ran past. Misinterpreting her, Costins activated the fire alarm that automatically summoned the fire brigade, setting deafening bells ringing and adding to the escalating panic.

As her husband steered her from The Swan ballroom, Cynthia Marriott voiced her opinion, 'That's just what that Jenny Wells deserves.'

Gerald Anstruther overheard her sour judgement. He would later report it to his wife.

Returning to the function room, Charles and Claude surveyed a scene reminiscent of a Hogarth print. Charles calmly and correctly observed, 'I rather fear the party's over, Claude.' It was a fitting epitaph to the evening.

CHAPTER FIFTY-TWO
AFTER THE BALL THAT NEVER WAS
LATE EVENING ON 19 OCTOBER 1934 AND BEYOND

The small accident and emergency department of Stourminster Hospital was prepared for the usual Friday night selection of drunken rowdies who habitually arrived for attention to their cuts and bruises before being released into the far from tender care of the local constabulary. The arrival from ten o'clock onwards of a succession of ladies and gentlemen in evening dress and varying states of medical need may have been a variation on the usual Friday theme, but the number deposited upon the staff of one doctor, two nurses and three auxiliaries was certainly not a welcome distraction. Doctor Peter Harper and Senior Nurse Edna Drew needed all their accumulated experience to sort the urgent from the not so needful cases. In this they were not helped by the loud insistence of a tall, thin lady, spattered in what was swiftly detected as red wine rather than blood, continually ordering their attention to her diminutive husband who constantly lapsed in and out of consciousness.

There were few really serious cases. First to be examined was the large lady with the big bleeding breast and terrified expression. (Surely she's from that flower shop?). Her torn evening gown was being ineffectually held up by her friend Mrs Baker. Mrs Baker herself had a swelling eye and glass cuts to her face and arm. The terrified and topless large lady was also assisted, Doctor Harper and Nurse Drew were glad to see, by a bruised and slightly cut Nurse Julia Simmonds. In consultation with Julia, they felt that Mrs Whitehouse-Martin, (yes, she *is* from the flower shop) needed treatment for shock. Attempts to tend her wounded left breast not only caused her immense distress, but she physically resisted the approach of anyone towards her chest. So, in order to examine the wound, it was necessary to sedate poor Jenny. Before and after her own treatment, Janice stayed with her friend—privately agonising as to how much of Jenny's history might be relevant to the situation and how much she should disclose to the doctor. Whilst the emergency department was so busy, Janice felt she ought not to detain them, but she still agonised. After her wounded breast had been dressed, Jenny remained semi-conscious, she whimpered and desperately clutched the sheet to herself. Janice quietly gave Doctor Harper a modified version of the assault on Jenny at her school. The doctor listened, conferred by telephone and told Janice that her friend would be admitted to the hospital's D Ward for psychological assessment.

The next serious case was the gentleman with a bleeding eye. The gentleman—Mr J. J. Whitehouse-Martin—had a metal hook embedded in his right eye and was examined and swiftly despatched by ambulance to the prestigious Birmingham Eye Hospital. The only other serious case was Mrs Zoe Cutler—she who regularly tended the locks of Nurse Drew—who had suffered concussion; she was detained overnight in a short-stay ward. By twelve thirty Saturday morning, all the posh patients had been dealt with and the familiar attendees—more drunk and less well attired—could be patched up and sent on their way. The department returned to normal.

At The Swan, returning to anything resembling normality was proving more problematic. The principal organisers of the evening, Mr Baker and Mr Simmonds, had accompanied their wives to the hospital. The genial, retired solicitor, Mr Whitehouse, paid off a not-so-jolly George Cookson and his far-from-merry (old) men who had been rendered redundant through no fault of their own. The Reverend Martin, formerly of the local church, seemed to be everywhere, offering advice and comfort to the many distressed ladies and angry gentlemen whom he urged to depart in peace. The local taxi drivers, summoned far earlier and at a less profitable tariff than anticipated, were not at their happiest. The only remaining member of the organising committee was Mr Hughes from the furniture store, Costins approached him to broach the question of damages and was brusquely dismissed—it was none of his affair and the others would have to sort it out. Hughes and the pompous Mr Jeffries left with their wives and without another word. Malcolm Costins silently determined never to book any Chandlery Lodge dos in future. The Saturday morning's apology and generous offer of compensation from Mr Baker caused Costins to revise his resolve.

Billy and Alan Simmonds decided, after discussion with their wives, that the following month's outing to Bruges was now a non-starter. Billy negotiated a costly settlement with the Belgian Hotel. John Robinson was more financially successful with the ferry firm. Billy and Alan, with the kind and unsolicited assistance of Ken Knowles and his staff, contacted all those who had so eagerly enrolled for the Continental outing. Refunds would be made from the lodge festival account.

The Meeting of Chandlery Lodge on Monday 29 October was a strange, short affair. It should have consisted of a second degree ceremony followed by Brothers Baker and Wear explaining the second degree tracing board. The candidate had a black eye and felt unable to attend, rendering the ceremony of no practical purpose. The worshipful master had been counselled to rest after an operation on his injured eye and the immediate past master—according to his wife—was in no fit state to attend lodge. Reliable old Floury Fellows took the chair for what was a very low-key, restrained lodge night from which those who attended arrived home far earlier than usual to variations of the question as to why this could not always be their time of return.

JJ wore an eye patch for a few weeks and thereafter had to become accustomed to permanently wearing glasses; characteristically he was more distressed for Jenny than for himself. Jenny was pronounced beyond the scope of the local hospital and transferred to a neurological unit for further assessment. The experienced consultants informed JJ his wife had suffered severe trauma and they could make no determination as to when she might return to normal. When pressed, they admitted she may never recover. Jenny continued to resist attempts to treat her injury and continually sedating her in order to treat the now infected wound was counterproductive to her mental recovery. JJ desperately insisted on further treatment at whatever cost and was firmly told this was not a case where money could buy recovery. Trying to control anger and frustration affected his concentration; his business judgements became hasty and unsound. Co-directors and managers in turn approached both Billy and Janice (now a full director of almost everything) to persuade JJ to leave work well-alone until Jenny recovered and he could be more rational. Old friends are the best friends. The Bakers persuaded JJ to leave his able fellow directors to manage. The Whitehouse-Martin's February booking for another cruise was cancelled.

Uncle Charles frequently telephoned and, despite his age and at Billy's request, he visited the hall to discuss JJ's Masonic situation with him. Listening to his uncle and lifetime mentor settled JJ's mind on the remainder of his year as master. He arranged for co-operative Brethren Alan Simmonds and Terry Cox to cover the November meeting. Telephoning George Jeffries to advise him of the arrangement, JJ met the expected lack of understanding, listened to Jeffries's thoughtless dictates on duty to the lodge, etc. and responded by quoting the portion of ritual declaring duty to the lodge to be 'without detriment to myself or connections' before disconnecting. There was no December meeting.

JJ was obviously not going to attend the lodge Christmas party—indeed very few attended. Spurning further telephone calls, JJ wrote to Jeffries assuring him that, accidents permitting, he intended to be present at January's lodge practice and meeting to install his successor.

JJ's Christmas was not a merry one. Throughout December he made daily visits to Jenny—though she still failed to recognise anyone, himself included. He also attended the funerals of William Burroughs and Percy Bennett. At the former he was one of many mourners saddened by the passing of a kind and generous gentleman and brother. Bennett had been a long time employee of the Wells family, and in his last twenty years had lived in the flat above the garages at the hall so, in the absence of any known relatives of the old chauffeur, it fell to JJ to arrange the funeral service, cremation and disposal of ashes. It was also assumed he was the one to pay tribute to the faithful old retainer and he was afterwards complimented on a heartfelt, dignified eulogy. Hosting Bennett's wake at the hall, JJ wondered anew at the immense respect the old man had commanded in Masonic circles whilst otherwise remaining a humble servant and worker. Senior brethren from the province attended and took time to talk with JJ, express sympathy for his wife's predicament and confidently state they were sure she would be well again soon; sentiments JJ received with a fixed smile whilst inwardly wondering how stupid intelligent people could sometimes be.

'How the hell do they know she's going to recover?' he bitterly asked Billy later. 'They've not seen her. They mean well, I know, but they just don't think, Billy.'

Billy, conscious that his suffering friend had imbibed too freely, quietly agreed and, with the assistance of Janice, got JJ to bed where, after some moaning and crying, he slept soundly until 6.00 a.m. Later that morning, his apology to Billy was waved aside. Terry Cox was acting as mediator between JJ and George Jeffries and Ray Hughes—whose well known zeal for the conduct of the lodge superseded all personal concerns and caused some tempers to flare un-Masonically. Terry's duty of care as almoner of the lodge included checking on the health and well-being of Maurice Fisher and his wife; he had only once mentioned them to JJ since the doomed ladies' night and the angry response, 'What the devil do I care about that little runt and his miserable Mrs?' ensured Terry never mentioning their names to JJ again.

JJ took the January installation of his successor in his stride and was praised by the provincial ruler attending. Between the close of the lodge meeting and the start of the meal, that same ruler, the provincial director of ceremonies and surprise attendee the provincial secretary manoeuvred JJ to a quiet corner of the lounge bar, enquired anew about Jenny, before posing questions about what time JJ might have available for Masonic duties in the future. He assured them that apart from needing to constantly attend to his wife's condition, he was entirely master of his own time and could do with it as he so wished. The three provincial dignitaries nodded sagely, looked knowingly at each other and suggested they return to the bar.

'What was all that about?' JJ asked Uncle Charles much later over a late brandy at the hall, where his uncle was staying overnight rather than driving back to Birmingham in the dark.

'What it means, JJ, is that they are sounding you out with a view to your being a future provincial warden. It would be a great honour for you and for the lodge but, particularly in this province, it would also involve an awful lot of your time.'

'Oh,' said JJ lapsing into thought. Unlike most Masonic provinces, every Worcestershire installation of a master was attended by a provincial ruler—plus two provincial wardens and a provincial director of ceremonies—it had never occurred to JJ he might be appointed a provincial warden.

Charles, feeling the need for rest and a comfortable bed, wound up the discussion, 'Don't worry about it, old chap. You won't be given provincial rank for another five years. Plenty of time for Jenny's situation to resolve itself.'

JJ loved the delicate way in which Uncle Charles avoided expressing any certainty or otherwise about Jenny. They both knew only time would resolve her case. They had no idea how soon that resolution would come to pass.

CHAPTER FIFTY-THREE
INTERLUDE
EARLY FEBRUARY 1985

Jenny's condition had not improved and, more in hope than expectation, JJ had had her moved to a private nursing home outside Farford. Neurological consultants, although assuring JJ that only time could effect a recovery, continued, at JJ's insistence, frequent visits to examine Jenny. They felt, and in one instance stated, they were taking fees to no purpose. JJ visited daily. Business continued as usual in his almost constant absence. The economy continued to boom and JJ's net worth grew daily without his assistance. Billy became concerned about JJ's increasing consumption of alcohol and struggled to find valid reasons for nightly visits. He feared JJ was heading towards depression and sought to distract JJ from thoughts of Jenny's traumatic state. To Billy's surprise, mention of lodge practice on 18 February and the present worshipful master's problem of something to fill the evening stirred JJ into positive thought.

'I've had an idea for a Masonic paper, Billy,' he said. 'It might fill the gap if it's OK with the W.M.'

'I'm sure it would be, JJ,' answered Billy. 'I'll ring him now and check.'

Suiting the action to the word, Billy called Roger Bloomer, JJ's successor in the chair of Chandlery. Still holding the phone in his hand he turned to JJ, 'He's delighted. What's the title of your paper?'

Having resolved to present his first Masonic paper, JJ devoted himself to the necessary research, consequent composition and production in readable form. He found it harder than anticipated and the concentration required definitely distracted him from worrying about Jenny. Everyone, with the sour exception of George Jeffries who groused about having to insert slips in the lodge summonses notifying the new inclusion, was delighted at the change in JJ and his return to almost his former self. At lodge practice he contented himself with assuring the brethren that he would not exceed twenty minutes unless interrupted. On the afternoon of the twenty-fifth, he confessed to an unhearing Jenny that he was quite nervous about tonight, an uncharacteristic concern which he repeated to Billy who had insisted on driving him to the Masonic hall. JJ had worried without cause, his paper was received with acclamation. A visiting brother asked JJ if he would deliver the paper at his Kings Heath Lodge the following month and, since he could think of no good reason to refuse, JJ agreed and diaries were annotated. Billy drove JJ home and, for the first time in ages, they both drank only coffee. JJ went to bed sober.

CHAPTER FIFTY-FOUR
ANOTHER NIGHTMARE AND ANOTHER ESCAPE
MONDAY 25 FEBRUARY 1985

Vivienne Mortenson felt herself destined to be a medical person. Although only an orderly, she was convinced she should be a state registered nurse or, more fittingly, a doctor. Her appeal against the unjust suspension imposed upon her for exceeding authority had, due to her brother Simon's advocacy, been reduced from six months to three. She returned to her duties at Hillside Nursing Home on Monday 25 February 1985 to re-commence her duties—she preferred career, but Simon's warning to agree with authority kept her silent on the matter—on the night shift. She was, to her annoyance, serving a period of probation. At least, she consoled herself, she was with Nurse Karen Jorgenson who always allowed her to take responsibility. The truth was that Nurse Jorgenson preferred to read romantic novels when not slipping outside for a cigarette, Vivienne was welcome on her shift as she willingly shouldered the work.

After the 6.00 p.m. takeover from the day team, the odd pair settled down for a quiet night. Occupancy was low and Nurse Jorgenson looked forward to the conclusion of the torrid affair recounted in the pages of her latest Mills and Boon. Vivienne would have preferred to chat but, conscious of her probationary term, she sat quietly. At ten o'clock they walked the corridors. In each occupied room they turned off the television, settled the patients to sleep for the night and extinguished all lights apart from a low night light. Quiet reigned. Jorgenson departed with her pack of Capstan full strength and lighter to the rear porch. Vivienne moved to the small illuminated patch allowed under Karen's reading lamp to read the latest edition of *The Lancet*—she knew where the doctors stored these—mostly unread—and had never encountered any queries as to the absence of one or more issues. Karen returned. Time passed slowly. No sounds emanated from the patients' rooms. The two shared the pool of light and little conversation. At midnight they reluctantly put down their respective reading matter.

'Better check round, Viv, although it's all quiet,' said Nurse Jorgenson.

'Shall I do it?' queried Vivienne, looking pointedly at her colleague's cigarettes.

'Why not?' answered the addicted nurse 'Let me know if there's anything.'

Nurse Jorgenson departed to the back porch. Vivienne, pleased to be left in charge, walked briskly along the corridor. Room one was empty. In Rooms two and three elderly patients slept soundly—only one emitting slight snores.

The large lady in room four was, according to Karen, a difficult case, she was the wife of a wealthy man and was to be treated as special. She seemed to be asleep, but in the dim glow of the night light, Vivienne could see there seemed to be blood on the patient's upper left side. Vivienne switched on the bedside light. It was blood—she touched it— still wet. She remembered Karen saying this lady had a wound to her bosom that was not healing well; there was something else, but Vivienne couldn't recall. Obviously this lady needed her wound re-dressed—a straightforward task she could accomplish without Karen. Fetching the trolley from the hall, Vivienne prepared a new dressing.

The lady woke. Her wide open eyes stared at Vivienne.

'It's alright, dear,' cooed Vivienne in her best bedside manner. 'Here's a nice, new dressing. Let's get to you.'

Vivienne extended her thin left arm to fold back the sheet. The woman stiffened and held tightly to the top of the sheet—staring wide-eyed at her. Vivienne had dealt with awkward patients before. One had to be firm with them.

Jenny was having a recurring dream: she was in the school sanatorium; Mrs Bell in the daytime, but Jenny dreaded the nights. Opening her eyes she saw a thin woman who cooed at her. Jenny didn't like her. The woman started to pull away her bedclothes. In her tortured mind, Jenny saw the thin, evil face of Miss Batty. She clung tightly to the sheet. The woman smiled and tugged harder at the sheet.

'Right, my dear, let's get to it, shall we?' she said, seizing the sheet.

Oh no! Not again, thought Jenny. As the horrible lecher paused to change her grip on the sheet, Jenny lashed out. Her left forearm made forceful contact with the vile creature's head, the woman grimaced and moved determinedly forward. Jenny attacked with both arms and fists, even though it hurt her injured breast, she had to rid herself of this awful woman, however much pain it cost her. Her assailant lost balance; as she fell she banged her head hard on the solid wooden bedside table and slumped to the floor. Jenny regarded the insensible figure. She had saved herself. But—what if her tormentor woke? Escape! She must escape. She needed clothes. All she could find in the wardrobe were two silky dressing gowns. She put them on. Shoes, she needed shoes. The unconscious woman wore trainers, Jenny tore them from her and forced them onto her own feet. They were tight, but they would have to do. She opened the door and slipped into the corridor. At the far end was a light.

A voice quietly called, 'That you, Viv?'

Jenny walked in the opposite direction until she came to barred, double doors. Grabbing the bar, she pulled upwards, the doors opened and Jenny emerged into a dark, damp night, and ran as best as she could in the ill-fitting trainers across a well-kept lawn to a hedge. The opening in the hedge wasn't where it should have been. In confusion she ran along the hedge until she reached a gate. She stepped through onto an unlit pavement. To her right she heard a passing motor vehicle, which meant that the main road was over there. She could catch a bus and make good her escape. Jenny walked towards it.

[290]

CHAPTER FIFTY-FIVE
A BIZARRE RESOLUTION
LATE MONDAY 25 FEBRUARY 1985

Johnny Garside was one of many chancers residing on the Dean Grimes
Estate, Farford, three hundred desirable dwellings, two churches and four
public houses contained in a poorly drained hollow between hills to which
roads of differing degrees of steepness provided access. A high proportion
of the male population were regular claimants at the local benefit office—
their wives and partners providing food and occasional copulation. Most
of the women had ill-paid work as cleaners or factory workers. Many homes
supplemented their income by crime and/or cash-in-hand work. Johnny
Garside's dearest wish was to better himself and move up the hill. How to
accomplish this was only ever clear to him as he began each new venture.
None of his 'can't fail' schemes had yet yielded more than beer money, but
Johnny was an incurable optimist. His poker skills were not great, but in
the drink-sodden period after Christmas they had proved superior to those
of the more drunken Rob Harris, and on the turn of the cards Johnny had
found himself the owner of a fifteen-year-old Volkswagen camper van. He
collected it the following morning from the rear of the Harris house before
any of the occupants had risen to greet the day. Johnny knew Harris would
not report the loss of the van or make an insurance claim—there being no
insurance.

It wasn't in too bad a state, thought the new, unregistered, owner.
He cleaned out the inside and his ever tolerant mother produced some
nice, strong material of dubious provenance with which she upholstered
the side mounted seats—one of which converted, with considerable
difficulty, into a bed. Johnny was good with engines and after fitting a
new exhaust pipe, the old van sounded almost as good as new. The tyres
resembled Yul Bryner's dome, but when he had earned something from
the van, Johnny would remedy that. Fred down the road, in return for
a past favour, effected a re-spray in red and blue. Johnny had himself a
good set of wheels. His mother imagined that, at last, her well-meaning,
but ultimately useless son would treat her to a holiday; but vacationing
with his mother was far from Johnny's mind. If he offered the van for

hire with himself as driver he could make a good profit. He crafted a handwritten advertisement, 'Camper van for hire with driver,' and paid a month's fee for display in the local newsagent's window.

As he was leaving the shop, Florrie, the large, loud proprietor, yelled to him, "Ow many can yer get in this van of yourn, Johnny?'

'It's a camper, Florrie. Sleeps two—or four if you'm friendly.'

Sensing success at the start, the ever hopeful Johnny turned back toward Florrie, 'Where d'yer wanna go, Florrie und when?' he asked.

'What I wants, young Johnny, is someone to take me and my five mates to a 'en party in Yardley, Birmingum next Munday night. Can yer get us there?'

Johnny thought about it. It could seat three each side, so why not? It seemed like a good start. He proposed a price and, after the usual Dean Grimes haggling, a cash deal was agreed. Florrie extracted half the agreed cost from the till and agreed to pay the balance as her party arrived in Yardley. Johnny Garside was in business. Again.

At 5.30 p.m. on Monday 25 February 1985, six raucous matrons clambered aboard Johnny's van outside Florrie's 'closed for party' shop and driver Johnny Garside drove them up the steepest hill out of the Dean Grimes estate. His passengers were a noisy crowd, but their incessant chatter was amongst themselves and offered no distractions to Johnny. With Florrie's help, he found the large Yardley pub and, having disgorged his lusty passengers and, after some grumbling, been paid the balance of his fee, parked at the rear of the establishment. Whilst it troubled Johnny little that his van had no tax or insurance, he was almost perverse in abstaining from alcohol whist driving. He sat himself in the pub's snug, sipped his Coca Cola and studied the raunchy magazine Florrie had gifted him as a bonus. The hen party seemed to be slow in starting as there was little noise to be heard from the large function room. Johnny dozed.

He was woken by being roughly shaken. He opened his eyes only to gaze, unwillingly, into the watery, bloodshot eyes of his cousin Joe.

'It'sh you, Johnny, ishn't it?' slurred Joe. 'Wha' you doin' 'ere, Johnny?'

'I'm 'ere on business,' answered Johnny—trying to impress. 'What you doin' 'ere?'

With difficulty and after several leading questions, Johnny gathered that his errant cousin had been removed from his lodgings by an ungrateful girl who had tired of his services and demanded rent. Joe was without friends or funds, and in the last hour had again been rejected after refusing to buy the next round in the adjoining bar. All the poor

idiot seemed to want was to leave Birmingham and return to his mother
in Astoria Grove, on the Dean Grimes estate. Uncertain whether his aunt
would accommodate her roving son, but not wanting to offend family,
Johnny offered to transport Joe to his mother's house when his passengers
returned.

With difficulty, assisted by Joe's impecuniosity, Johnny managed
to restrict his cousin's consumption of ale to two pints whilst they
waited for his passengers. The screams and yells from the function room
indicated that the event was under way, and much to the liking of the
female audience. Enquiry at the bar elicited the information that Florrie's
'en party was actually a performance by a troupe of well-known and well-
endowed male strippers.

At ten thirty the snug bar ceased service and Johnny had to plead
with the truculent barman for some lights to be left on whilst he and
Joe continued to wait. They did not have long to wait. By 11.00 p.m.
Johnny had shepherded the giggling or raucously laughing ladies into
the seats behind him and, with Joe beside him, Johnny cautiously drove
towards home. It had been a profitable first trip, Johnny thought, all that
was left to do was get these noisy women back to Dean Grimes. He had
been concerned to note not one, but two bottles of vodka carried to the
van and hoped they were not intended for consumption on the journey.
A vain hope. As they left the outskirts of the city, both bottles were
circulating. With wider and less congested roads ahead, Johnny increased
speed—hoping to arrive before drink induced sickness soiled his van. He
feared it was another vain hope.

The roistering soon led to tuneless singing in which, ignoring
Johnny's attempts to silence him, Joe joined. Equally tunelessly. The
most boisterous of the women, realising that one of the males present
was with them passed Joe a part-consumed bottle of vodka from which
he took several long gulps. He was invited to join the party in the rear of
the van. In vain Johnny pleaded for everyone to sit down. The van swayed
about alarmingly with the vigorous movements of the women who were
now encouraging Joe to 'get 'em off'.

'Off. Off,' echoed their demands.

And off came the utterly intoxicated Joe's clothes.

Cries of 'Eeh, look at that!' and, 'Almost as big as the lads in the
show,' competed with yells of desire and Joe's slurred 'Come on then—
you get 'em off.' Johnny glanced into the rear of the van and wished he'd
not. His naked, drunken cousin was being joined by inebriated middle-
aged ladies competing to be the first unclothed. Johnny felt rather than

saw bodies slump to the floor of the van. He needed no visual aid to realise what was happening behind him. At least, he thought, I'm nearing home when they'll have to get dressed and out of my van. As he turned the van towards Bicton Hill for the run down to Dean Grimes, he was alarmed to be joined in the front seats by two semi-naked and very drunk women who made no secret of their intentions towards the sole clothed male present. Johnny loudly ordered them to behave and to get back in the back. This was getting out of hand, he thought. An eager hand grasped at his trousers with a slurred instruction to 'Gerrit out.' Johnny struggled. They were now on Bicton Hill and he needed to steer. The second woman, her large, pendulous breasts heaving with her efforts, was trying to join her friend in close contact with Johnny. Her heavy hip hit the gear lever and suddenly Johnny was trying to control a run away van and two erotically intentioned, near naked women.

Constables William Ian Boland—known to everyone as Bilbo—and Howard Williams—Howie—had not been best pleased when instructed to patrol Dean Grimes estate. In patrol car Red Three they negotiated the usual route through the estate noting, to their surprise and relief, no signs of unrest. Congratulating themselves as Bilbo drove Red Three up Bicton Hill, they saw ahead of them a large woman, apparently wearing only dressing gown and trainers, cross the road to the bus shelter. Deciding this warranted investigation, Bilbo parked a few yards beyond and opposite the concrete eyesore/bus shelter and cut the engine. As he climbed from the car, a camper van rounded the corner ahead and careered relentlessly towards them . . .

Johnny knew he was losing control of the van and the situation. The attentions of the two women intent upon exposing his person was affecting his concentration and his ability to depress the clutch and re-engage a gear. He just managed to steer the van round the corner onto Bicton Hill—but on the wrong side of the road. A man was alighting from a parked car—a policeman! Johnny leaned into two sweaty bosoms as he tried to turn the steering wheel and avoid—horror of horrors—a police car. The rear side of the van struck the police car a hefty blow. Its speed little diminished, the old van slewed away from the patrol car. Johnny stamped on the inefficient brakes as he vainly tried to disentangle himself from his fleshy assailant; the bald tyres skidded on the wet road. The policeman's shouts were drowned by the passengers' screams. Johnny looked through the windscreen; oh no, a woman in a dressing gown was standing ahead of him holding up her hand for him to stop. Johnny Garside felt the sickening thump as the woman disappeared beneath the front of the van before it mounted the pavement and ploughed into the concrete bus shelter where it crumpled and came to rest.

P.C. Bilbo Boland had only just managed to avoid being impaled on car Red Three. Recovering his balance he watched the careening camper run full tilt into and over the lady in the dressing gown before coming to rest in the almost unyielding bus shelter. Howard was already on the radio as Bilbo ran across the road. The sliding side door of the van had burst open, Bilbo could see the driver trapped between the steering wheel and his seat and beyond him a large, unclothed woman wedged halfway through the shattered windscreen. Another near naked woman lay in the well of the van moaning. More moans and screams came from within the broken van. With some trepidation, Bilbo looked into rear of the van. His shouted message to Howard echoed in the damp night.

'We'll need more than one ambulance here, Howie.'

JJ Whitehouse-Martin usually rose from his bed at 6.30 a.m. and after showering, breakfasted at 7.00. The morning ritual had not been adhered to since mid October 1984, but on 26 February the hall domestic staff were pleasantly surprised to find Mr JJ coming downstairs at 6.55 a.m. expressing an appetite for his scrambled eggs and bacon. Although he sat down to eat, it was a breakfast he never had; the telephone inserted its insistent tone into the day even as the plate of appetising eggs and bacon was placed before JJ. Grumbling about who could be disturbing him at such an hour, he hastened to answer the call. Doctor McFallon from the nursing home was not one to prevaricate with wasted words and came, at once, to the point.

'Mr Whitehouse-Martin. I'm afraid Mrs Whitehouse-Martin has gone missing from here, sir. It seems she attacked one of our staff last night before absconding. The night sister only advised me less than an hour ago. I have instituted a search of the grounds, but there is, as yet, no trace of Mrs Whitehouse-Martin. Perhaps you could——'

'I'm on my way,' interrupted JJ. 'I want this thoroughly investigated and my wife found without delay, Doctor.'

JJ slammed down the telephone and dashed from the hall. Had he delayed a further ten minutes he would have been present to receive a telephone call from West Mercia Police.

CHAPTER FIFTY-SIX
A Wandering Widower
March to August 1985

Despite the recent experience of old Percy Bennett's last rites, JJ found his emotions confusing his logic as he made arrangements for Jenny's funeral. First there was a necessary but annoying wait whilst the Coroner's Court deliberated and came to the rather obvious conclusion. Then a further delay due to the accident having taken place in a different county; Harts, the undertakers, handled that with their usual efficiency, but it was, for JJ, a further cause for suppressed anger at the inability to finalise his beloved's last rites. Eventually he was able to telephone Peter Hordern with a date for the front of the otherwise set order of service: Friday 8 April 1985. The other dates on the front of the service sheet reflected the distressing fact that Jennifer Doreen Whitehouse-Martin had died two days before her thirty-eighth birthday.

Claude officiated and he, Sylvia, Billy and Janice were invaluable to JJ both before and after the service. Once more the hall and The Swan were fully occupied for the night before Jenny's funeral. Terri insisted on coming down from Lichfield two days before the service to assist Annie with the floral tributes and decorations in St Bartholomews. JJ walked alone behind Jenny's coffin. There had been no question of viewing her remains—although there were still some morbid souls wishing to do so—as the collision with the uninsured van had rendered poor Jenny unrecognisable. The police and ambulance services had identified her from the nursing home wrist tag, and it was only JJ's intimate knowledge of the uninjured parts of her mutilated corpse that had enabled him to identify his deceased wife.

The driver of the van was eventually committed to a lamentably short sentence at Her Majesty's pleasure, but died of remorse before his release. JJ decided there was no point in pursuing action against either the driver or the four survivors from the unlicensed transport, 'their shame should be their penance' he told the investigating officers who, tactfully, refrained from advising JJ that the force of conscience was not strong on the Dean Grimes estate. Against Claude's advice, JJ insisted on delivering a funeral eulogy for Jenny. He did it with dignity.

It was only when the event was over and most of the guests had left the hall that JJ gave way to his despair and grief. The combined efforts of Sylvia, Claude, Charles, Charlotte, Janice, Billy and Terri were not sufficient to calm him, and eventually a doctor was summoned and drugs prevailed where his nearest and dearest had failed. JJ stayed in bed, taking pain-killers and sleeping fitfully for three days. To Billy's relief he did not, again, resort to strong drink despite a plentiful supply being readily available. After two weeks, Sylvia felt JJ sufficiently balanced for her to return to Claude in Hereford. Billy continued his nightly visits although, for the first time in their long friendship, conversation was stilted and sporadic. As the daffodils bloomed in the approaches to the hall, JJ returned to work only to announce that he was ceding authority to his capable fellow directors for an indefinite time. He took a late availability cruise to St Petersburg and remained in that city for four weeks, every day visiting the Hermitage Museum and immersing himself in art and culture.

Having, in a manner of thinking, re-established himself in Chandlery Lodge with his well-received paper, JJ was, obviously, absent from the March and April meetings of the lodge. On his return from abroad, he did attend other lodges. Firstly, in early May, as a guest of his Uncle Charles who, with Charlotte's approval, attended his Mother Lodge on the eve of his eightieth birthday before having another party on the day itself. JJ stayed in Birmingham for both . JJ's second fraternal visit was a week later as a guest of his friend James Whiteman, whose wife had eventually succumbed to her long illness. Although her death had not been unexpected, it had saddened James, who felt mutual grieving might help them both. Besides which, he wanted to discuss his affairs with JJ.

JJ spent a comfortable night in James's spare room after attending the lodge. The following morning, he and James took their post breakfast coffees into the small lounge and James, as he had determined to do, immediately came to the point.

'Look, JJ, I was more than grateful to you for your part in sorting me out when things were getting on top of us. The last few months have been emotionally difficult, but financially rewarding for me; with Terri Anstruther's support I've established a nice little line in flowers, particularly orchids.'

James paused.

'I sense a "but" coming on,' said JJ.

'You're not wrong, JJ,' replied James. 'What it is, is this—and please don't broadcast this—I've been diagnosed with cancer and advised to take it easy. Please don't start sympathising, JJ, I couldn't bear it. I've refused to have the chemotherapy treatment that the doctors are urging me to try, I don't want to walk around with a bald and unnaturally shiny head and skin. Two friends of my father had the treatment and it did little good save to prolong the end. They reckon I'm good for another three or more years if I stop cultivating orchids in a hothouse and then going out to the fields. So, although I'm grateful to you for helping to set me up—please don't deny it, JJ—I intend to sell this plot and business.'

'Do you have a buyer, James?'

'As it happens, I do, but I felt honour bound to let you in on the matter before I finalised the deal. I'll tell the Anstruthers tomorrow. I've found a nice little cottage to move to and end my days in. Due to you and the generous deal for the old place I'm financially secure so . . .'

James stopped speaking. He had said all he wanted to say. JJ sat for a moment before commenting, 'Doesn't seem much I can say, James. Thank you for telling me first and, almost needless to say, if there is anything I can do, please ask.'

'You've done more than enough for me, JJ. That's why I wanted to tell you first. Really I ought to be doing something for you if there ever is anything?'

JJ sat quietly. He had a thought and, almost to his own surprise, he suggested that the two newly widowed friends take a summer holiday together. They discussed it and, with James's insistence on paying his way accepted, dates and venues were agreed. During the July and early August of 1985, two rather similar looking gentlemen, usually taken—mistaken would be more accurate—for brothers, travelled around Scotland in a large hired car staying at the best hotels and shamelessly seeing all the best known tourist attractions they had previously only heard tell of. Both of them thoroughly enjoyed their holiday, at the end of which JJ returned James to his cosy cottage outside Lichfield before returning himself to the empty echoes and mixed memories of Avonbridge Hall. He admired James's bravery and sensible acceptance of his fate. His little cottage had also impressed JJ and he began to seriously contemplate finding himself an easier to manage home. There was, of course, far more business attenuated to the hall than there had been to the smallholding James had, so swiftly, disposed of, but nonetheless . . .

CHAPTER FIFTY-SEVEN
REVENGE OF THE FAIR SEX
AUGUST 1985 TO DECEMBER 1987

Billy and Janice were also reviewing their situation. The children were away at school and happy with their educational establishments, but whilst they were at home, their parents' busy lives left them wondering what happened to the happy times. William's late August question to his father who was preparing to dash out, set Billy thinking, 'Dad,' said William, 'why don't we go to Aberdovey any more?'

'No time, Will,' answered Billy. He paused to look at his son. The look on William's face kept coming back to Billy throughout the day. That night, as he and Janice lay in bed, he broached the subject and, particularly, its wider implications. Despite having had yet another hectic day, Janice listened. Before falling asleep they agreed to have a family conference and talk frankly with their children before reviewing their immediate and long term future.

The conference was a success: the Baker family indelibly marked the kitchen calendar for two weeks sailing and relaxation at their neglected seaside home for the last fortnight of the school summer holidays. JJ's near invisibility in his companies had increased responsibilities for both Bakers—particularly Janice as finance director—whilst they were not bitter, neither wished to continue working at the intensity of the last few months. They resolved to talk things through with JJ.

Billy, of course, had his lodge commitments to fulfil. He would become worshipful master of Chandlery Lodge in January 1989 and the year would need to be a good one. It was, he and Janice realised, early to make detailed plans, but they were resolved that whatever the past masters said, the 1989 ladies festival would be, as had been intended for Jenny and JJ's, in Bruges. Whilst exchanging confidences—swearing him to silence—Janice told Billy she and Terri had resolved to wreak revenge on Cynthia Marriott for her cruelty to Jenny; physical cruelty at school and mental torture since Cynthia arrived in Avonbridge. (She and Terri had also determined to inflict some suffering on Miss Batty, but their initial enquiries, posing as old girls of Jenny's school, found fate had beaten them to it as the former deputy headmistress had been murdered the previous year by another former pupil.)

'How're you going to wreak revenge?' asked Billy.

'What you don't know, you can't tell about,' answered Janice, cryptically. 'Just watch this space, as they say, or rather watch Mrs Horrible Marriott's space.'

'I'd rather not watch her, if I don't have to,' said Billy. 'But she deserves to be taken down a lot of pegs, Jan.' Just be careful, though, darling.'

'Aren't I always?' smiled Janice. Billy had to agree.

What Billy didn't know—and couldn't tell about—was the devious scheme his wife and Terri Anstruther evolved with the co-operation of his own elder half-brother's unlawful talents. Bobby Baker was now successfully managing Avonbridge Security. As much as Billy would have wished to appoint Bobby a director, his past record had not commended him to other directors in the group and Billy and JJ had not pressed the matter. Bobby was content. If his brother's wife asked him, as a confidential favour to her and her friend, to observe the comings and goings of a Mr and Mrs Marriott, reporting to her when Billy was not about, then he would. And later—when the Marriotts were definitely away—admit her and Mrs Anstruther into the Marriott home having disarmed the alarm (his own installation), who was he to argue? After all, Janice still controlled salaries.

If Bobby had been confused by the request to admit two smart ladies to an strange, empty house whose owners had been observed departing with more than a week's luggage, he was further befuddled by their insistence not to disturb or remove anything. He had abandoned petty crime with his clever younger brother's help, but breaking-in and just looking around was contrary to all his old instincts. Wearing gloves, his sister-in-law and Mrs Anstruther examined every room of the house—only pausing in the smaller of the two downstairs studies and the woman's dressing room upstairs.

In the small study, hardly hidden in a stationery cupboard, was a cheap safe.

'Could you open that, Bobby?' asked Janice.

'Easy, Jan,' he replied.

'How long would it take?'

'Two minutes, tops,' said Bobby scornfully, stepping forward.

'Not now, Bobby,' said Janice.

'Wait a minute, though, or rather two minutes,' interrupted Mrs Anstruther. 'Better see what she keeps in it, Jan.'

Bobby opened the safe in less than a minute. Both ladies looked inside the untidy little safe. In a drawer were papers and a passport, on the shelf above more papers and, in an elastic band, a bundle of banknotes—mostly Sterling but, mixed amongst the two-inch thick collection were a few foreign currency notes. Mrs Anstruther seemed delighted.

'That's good,' she said. 'Close it up, please, Bobby.' Bobby, still confused, closed the safe as he was bid.

In the dressing room upstairs, the two ladies poured scorn on a muddle of scent bottles, sprays and female accoutrements spread untidily over the dressing table top. In the right hand drawer they disgustedly discovered unwashed underwear mingled with clean, but not very fresh, nether garments. (Bobby silently recalled similar unsavoury finds in his past.) In the large central drawer was, judging from their expressions, what Jan and Mrs Anstruther were looking for, a selection of jewellery boxes untidily storing rings, bracelets, necklaces and ear rings—most of which were not cheap, as Bobby could have confirmed had he been asked.

Finding no more safes, the house was re-secured, the alarm re-activated and, with the ladies grateful thanks and a cash bonus, Bobby Baker returned to work little wiser than before, save that a repeat of the profitless break-in would be required at some future date to be advised.

Janice and Terri had resolved to find a way in which the awful Cynthia Marriott, nee Cholmondely-Price, could be punished for demoralising Jenny on that awful night in October and, of course, for her initial cruelty to their friend for whose recovery they had so fervently prayed. After Jenny's death they became even more determined to exact retribution. They debated planting drugs on Cynthia, but the problem of obtaining drugs without being discovered and making certain Cynthia was discovered seemed insoluble. It seemed appropriate, in light of Mrs Marriott's past history, to have her arrested for possessing for sale sado-masochistic sex toys: again acquisition of such things with no certainty of her being arraigned ruled out the idea. They kept thinking.

It was a pathetic attempt to snatch the takings from the Flower Patch—bequeathed by Jenny in her will to her 'dear friend and invaluable floral colleague, Mrs Annie Belmont'—that set Janice and Terri on the course they eventually pursued. After calming down Annie, ensuring she was uninjured and being told that the police felt it likely they would soon apprehend the sad young fool pictured on the shop's C.C.T.V., Janice telephoned Terri with a plan. In pursuance of the plan, Bobby Baker was recruited and surveys of the Marriott home began. Terri insisted they were to be thorough, efficient, and above all patient.

'This race is not to the swift,' she cautioned Janice.

'You're good at this, Terri,' teased Janice.

'Poor choice of reading matter,' replied Terri. 'Since I'm not local, more of the work will have to fall on you, Jan, so its only fair I contribute some of the plot.'

'True enough,' said Janice.

Over the next few months, thefts of money from the Flower Patch, two branches of ZoNice Hair and Beauty salons, and the Karbitz shop were reported to the police: all, by strange coincidence, comprising new banknotes with traceable consecutive numbers recently drawn from the bank. No perpetrators were identified and no arrests were made. Stourminster Police Station also recorded thefts of jewellery from Avonbridge Grange (Mrs J. Baker: three distinctive gold rings with sapphire and emerald stones, plus an antique brooch in silver and gold with yellow diamonds); 1 Poplar Drive, Avonbridge (Mrs Z. Connolly: four silver rings with diamonds and garnets set in geometric patterns and a sapphire pendant in the shape of a 'z'); 11 Avon Close (Mrs J. Simmonds: an antique gold ring inset with garnets; a brooch with diamonds forming the letters 'J. D.' and a necklace of cultured pearls with 'J. D.' etched on the two largest stones); and, during the owner's absence, the dressing room of the late Mrs Whitehouse-Martin at Avonbridge Hall (six gold rings inset with diamonds and sapphires; a gold amulet having 'J. D. W.' inscribed on the inside and a very distinctive platinum brooch featuring concentric circles of diamonds, pearls and emeralds surrounding a large ruby with 'To J from JJ' inscribed within). The usual fliers were distributed to retail establishments, jewellers and pawn shops, but no sightings were reported during 1985. Consequently, there were no arrests or even suspicions falling on any known thieves.

In March 1986, the proprietor of the Flower Patch, High Street, Avonbridge, telephoned the police station on a Tuesday morning to report one discovery and one definite sighting of a stolen item. One of the new notes with the circulated numbers had been tendered to her not a moment since by a woman who was wearing a brooch Mrs Belmont recognised as having definitely belonged to her friend and benefactor the late Mrs Whitehouse-Martin.

'Would Mrs Belmont recognise the woman again?'

Of course she would, she knew her name and her address.

'Police, Madam. We have a warrant to search your premises.'

'Don't be stupid, Officer. My husband and I don't want you trampling all over our home, thank you.'

'We have a warrant, Mrs Marriott. If you have nothing to hide, then you won't mind our looking,' said Detective Sergeant Morris.

The conviction of Mrs Cynthia Marriott at Worcester Crown Court in October 1987 for theft was widely reported beyond the circulation areas of the *Worcester Evening News*, the *Berrows Gazette* (the oldest newspaper still published and based in Worcester) and the *Avonbridge Gazette*. This was partly due to the consistent refusal of the accused to comply with court rules resulting in her being convicted for contempt of court besides theft, and in part because of the divorce proceedings brought against Mrs Marriott exposing her as a vicious husband-beater—comprehensively attested to by independent medical specialists. Much as they would have wished, neither Janice or Terri attended the court proceedings. Following the guilty verdict, they did treat themselves to a slap up dinner for two at a Sutton Coldfield Restaurant where they solemnly toasted the memory of their late friend Jenny. Later that week, Janice innocently enquired of JJ if he had read about Mrs Marriott's conviction.

'Wasn't that the one at school with Jenny who . . .' JJ stopped in mid-sentence.

'Who . . . cut her breasts?' continued Janice. JJ looked surprised.

'Yes, JJ, it was. Jenny told me about it. Terri knew as well.'

'I see,' said JJ.

'Did you know she turned up in Avonbridge and was taunting and threatening Jenny?'

'Was that what was upsetting her, Jen?' asked JJ—now thoroughly curious.

'Yes, JJ. She was at it on your ladies' festival night as well.'

'Gerald did tell me someone said after . . .' said JJ—again leaving his sentence unfinished.

'Well, anyway, she's been convicted of theft and contempt of court and put away for three years. She'll be inside for at least half that time, JJ, which is less than she deserves but . . .'

It was Janice's turn to leave a sentence in mid-air.

JJ smiled and looked keenly at Janice. Janice tried to look innocent, but JJ knew her too well.

'Revenge is sweet?' said JJ, raising his coffee cup to his finance director.

'As is this coffee,' replied a smiling Janice—raising her cup in returned salutation.

That night, JJ thought about the conversation with Janice. He admired Jan for her business acumen and her astute brain. It was unlike her to either gossip or gloat over the fate, albeit just, of someone they neither of them knew well. The memory lingered. JJ sat down at his desk, drew out a pristine pad of plain lined paper and began to write.

CHAPTER FIFTY-EIGHT
JJ Contemplates Semi-Retirement
December 1987

The smooth manner in which his business interests had continued during his long absences from work confirmed JJ's determination on a gradual withdrawal from Avonbridge. He had, for some years, retained a small base on Guernsey in the Channel Islands: aware of the taxation advantages a more permanent stay would avail him, his forward planning centred around removal from the UK mainland. Still being slightly disillusioned with Freemasonry, he reduced his memberships to a select few and his attendances to even fewer. Living alone at the hall was a lonely existence, despite the daily presence of staff and Wells Holdings employees in the former stable block offices. He examined anew plans of the hall drawn up many years ago by his late mother-in-law; though not falling into decay, many rooms were little used of late, the possibility of selling the entire estate to a hotel chain would realise a considerable capital sum. But JJ had no need of greater wealth. Building around the hall had, from time to time, been proposed by one or other of his executive directors, but JJ was determined, if at all possible, to maintain the old hall and its grounds intact. A chance remark during a telephone call from another Freemason set him on a more amenable course.

'Just got back from a business conference,' said Hugh Merry. 'Had to go all the way up to Yorkshire as the firm couldn't find a suitable venue any nearer.'

Hugh had babbled on about the facilities of the Yorkshire conference centre and how much it had cost his employers, but JJ was only half listening. The other part of his mind—the entrepreneurial side— was envisaging Avonbridge Hall as the Midlands Conference Centre. Concluding his conversation with Brother Merry, JJ again spread the plans of the hall on his desk and began making notes and calculations for a new, exciting project. The planning stage was the part of any venture he most enjoyed. He did have another project in train—but that was approaching fruition and would require initial preparatory action before Christmas . . .

Billy and Jan's children were insistent that Uncle JJ spend the three principal days of Christmas with them at the grange. Their parents were equally insistent, and on the morning of Christmas Eve, JJ arrived at his former home laden with parcels. The Bakers' Christmas tree became almost unapproachable due to the profusion of brightly wrapped gifts spread around its base. It was a good Christmas enjoyed by all of them. By tacit mutual agreement there was to be no talk of business until after Boxing Day lunch. Much as the Baker children loved their parents and Uncle JJ, almost three days of adult company is more than enough for any teenager. Both William and Jenny departed after lunch on 26 December to spend time with friends of their own age. The adults devoted the afternoon to serious business discussion. Frank views were expressed and acknowledged. Plans to delegate responsibilities were agreed. After discussing and making plans concerning existing businesses, JJ introduced the unexpected bombshell of an entirely new venture, the Avonbridge Conference Centre.

Billy and Janice saw the sense, both financial and emotional, of JJ leaving the hall and were amenable in principle to the scheme, whilst insisting their own involvement be purely nominal. They would take founders' shares in the new venture and remain shareholders and directors-without-portfolio for the first five years. Billy and Jan's hopes for a more relaxed future remained intact.

JJ had further surprises for his closest friends.

'I intend, in the next year, to move permanently to Guernsey. You'll always be welcome anywhere I am, of course. I've put in motion the purchase of a private plane and applied to take flying lessons. Although I never knew him properly, I'll be doing as my late father did. I can fly back for directors' meetings and most lodge meetings, but, for tax reasons, I have to limit the number of days I spend on the UK mainland. I'll miss seeing you two so often, but you'll be almost rid of me. All that said—and it won't happen overnight, of course—let's get to the happier part: this is the Christmas present for you both I didn't put under the tree.'

JJ withdrew a bulky envelope from his case and laid it on the coffee table.

'You know I've spent some time in London the last few months and it's not all been business. I've booked a three-week Caribbean cruise starting on 16 January. I can drive myself down to Southampton, Bill, so no need for a driver. But it seems unfair I should be the only one having a break, so I've booked you two into the Savoy hotel for three nights from

Thursday the twenty-first to Saturday the twenty-third—leaving Sunday morning.' Billy and Janice began to stammer thanks—they knew well of old not to object or reject JJ's generous gifts—but he held up his hand to stop them.

'That's not all, my dear, dear friends. In the envelope with the Savoy booking are two much-prized theatre tickets to see *Les Miserables*, the exciting musical at the Palace Theatre on the Friday night, and another two for the night before to see *The Mousetrap*—they're both considered must-see theatre and, having been to both, I know you'll enjoy them.'

There was a pause. Eventually, Billy managed a breathless, 'Thanks, JJ. You've excelled yourself in generosity again.'

'So long as you both enjoy yourselves, I'll be more than happy,' replied a smiling JJ.

Janice gave JJ a grateful kiss. As she sat down again, a thoughtful Billy said, 'You do realise you'll be away for the lodge installation, JJ?'

'Yes, Bill. I know that, but you're only going in as senior warden. I'll be there in 1989 to see you installed as W.M., of course. You'll have all of Sunday to get back from London in time for the installation—even if, as I think probable, you visit that pal of yours with the motor museum in the Cotswolds on the way back.'

'As usual, you've thought of everything,' said Janice, looking warily at JJ.

JJ returned her knowing look, 'I do hope so,' he said.

The emphatic way he said it, made both Bakers look quizzically at him.

JJ smiled enigmatically at his closest friends. 'Enjoy yourselves is all I ask and don't worry about me. I've booked a luxury cruise around the Caribbean and it will be one of my January pleasures to think about you two living it up in London.'

Before the two Baker offspring returned home, JJ had done likewise and was enjoying a nightcap in Avonbridge Hall. He enjoyed seeing his plans resolve.

CHAPTER FIFTY-NINE
Masonic Panic, Protection and Re-arrangement
Monday 25 January 1988

It was past 2.00 p.m. when Douglas Fawner telephoned William Pritchard, the assistant secretary of Chandlery Lodge. Will was only a junior member progressing through the offices of the lodge. To be suddenly informed that not only was Avonbridge temple not available for tonight's installation—scheduled to start in less than four hours' time—but that the secretary was unlikely to attend, left him dumbfounded. Recovering his powers of speech, he stammered a 'why' and received the odd reply that the temple was 'unfit for occupation'. He then heard the further disturbing information that George Jeffries and Ray Hughes were 'unwell', would not be in attendance, and ought not be contacted.

Fawner could offer no assistance. Brother Pritchard desperately needed some assistance; any assistance.

In turn, and in increasing desperation, he telephoned Jamie Burroughs, the lodge assistant director of ceremonies; Edward Smythe, the lodge treasurer; Sid Wear; and Alan Simmonds, the lodge charity steward. The two former were still at work and apart from telling Will that something would have to be done—a fact of which he was very well aware—they were of no practical help. Sidney Wear, the installing W.M. would be in class at his school and unavailable—as Will had discovered several times during the past year. He left a message for Sid to telephone him urgently.

Alan Simmonds, however, although shocked, did seem to realise the problems posed and appreciate swift, practical action was required. Knowing JJ was on a cruise, Alan telephoned Billy Baker, who dropped everything and was at Alan's consulting rooms within fifteen minutes. Attempts to contact provincial office were doomed as they closed at 1.00 p.m. Billy contacted Andy Thomas, secretary of Stourminster Masonic Centre who confirmed that their temple complex was not booked that evening and could be made available. Billy booked it. Andy doubted the caterers could or would accept such a late request, Billy contacted the Comberton Road Chippie—recent winners of chip shop of the year—and, to their delight, ordered fifty ('probably more') fish and chip suppers—numbers to be confirmed. Where Alan and Billy were at a loss was the Masonic protocol involved in such a crisis. Realising the obvious authority was old Floury Fallowfield, Alan telephoned him. The telephone rang for a long time and Alan was about to hang up when a very tired voice confirmed he was speaking to the retired master baker. Alan had not got far into telling the old past master of the unprecedented situation when old Floury suddenly came to his senses as Alan told Billy.

Floury seemed to know Avonbridge rooms were unsuitable and even why. He commended Alan and Billy on their action so far and said that what must be done was to obtain a dispensation from the province to change venue and inform the provincial team, as well as everyone else, of the change. He asked if Alan knew which provincial ruler was attending as presiding officer. Alan didn't know. Billy did. Taking the telephone, he told Floury it was the provincial grand master himself, the Right Worshipful Brother Mike Copper.

'That's good in the circumstances. I'll get in touch with him—know him of old—and see what can be done. Where're you based?'

Floury promised to join them as soon as he could. Alan and Billy busied themselves with the legion of other practicalities involved. A concerned and relieved at the same time Will Pritchard arrived to help with the list of attendees. Following the death of Percy Bennett, many local lodges were now served by Arthur Phillipson, who would have a key to the Avonbridge Rooms and could get hold of the lodge collars, Banner and Warrant. Alan telephoned Arthur who was out at a British Legion lunch, but expected back at any moment. Ten minutes later, a bemused Brother Philipson called.

'What the 'eck's going on, Alan?'

Arthur had been told the rumour that the Avonbridge premises were restricted for the time being and he mustn't go there. At this point, Frank Fallowfield arrived at Alan's rooms and took charge. Being told what Brother Philipson had been told, Floury took the telephone from Alan and, in basic Anglo-Saxon language, told the tyler that whatever he had or hadn't been told, he could—and would—enter the Avonbridge rooms with the tyler to collect what Chandlery Lodge needed. A time was arranged. Alan and Billy looked on in wonder.

'Probably that blundering clown, Fawner. Had enough of him today,' said old Floury. 'Now, where were we?'

By 4.00 p.m. the provincial grand master had telephoned Alan's rooms assuring them he had an emergency dispensation and would bring it with him; he had contacted the rest of his team. Alan's secretary had prepared, at his instruction, a notice to be affixed to the Avonbridge rooms door that Frank Fallowfield put in place as he and the tyler collected the lodge collars, warrant and other necessities. By employing a form of telephone tree—Billy's idea—lodge members and guests were being informed and numbers firmed up for the fish and chip supper that the Comberton Road chippie were providing. It would be collected by Billy and two others at eight thirty—Billy's cheque to be accepted in settlement.

Sidney Wear's installation of Hugh Kington as the fifty-fifth master of Chandlery Lodge was, against all odds, accomplished and remained memorable for reasons hitherto unsuspected. Despite his ordeal of the previous night, Worshipful Brother Fallowfield acted as director of ceremonies of the lodge and, having been briefed by both Alan Simmonds and Billy as to how old Floury had taken charge of the emergency, the provincial grand master, who had commended the installing master and the new master, waited until Hugh Kington had invested all those of his officers who could be present, before, as was his right, asking the assistant provincial director of ceremonies to conduct Worshipful Brother Frank Fallowfield to him.

Exercising his prerogative as master of the province, something rarely done, he instantly promoted Floury—he affectionately called him that—to past provincial senior grand warden. He instructed Brother Will Pritchard, nervously acting as secretary, to record in the minutes his appreciation of the sterling efforts this day by not only Worshipful Brother Fallowfield, but Worshipful Brother Simmonds and Brother Baker, without whom tonight's meeting would never have taken place.

Julia Simmonds, Janice Baker and Helene Wear, having intended to dine at The Swan, had cancelled the booking and, with three other wives, followed their husbands to Stourminster Masonic Centre where, in innocent emulation of their husbands, they donned aprons before finding china and cutlery and laying table for sixty-two.

Arthur Philipson put out handwritten place card. The wives warmed up sixty-eight bowls of soup—tins purchased by Janice and Julia—plated sixty-eight generous portions of fish and chips and prepared sixty-eight bowls of warm rice pudding and cold peach slices. All served by the lodge stewards. Costs were met by Billy's cheque and Janice's credit card. The six wives of Chandlery thoroughly enjoyed themselves preparing the improvised meal in a strange kitchen and eating their own six portions at the kitchen table. Billy's credit card bore the cost, sale or return, of forty bottles of wine. Having been told by Andy Thomas to help themselves to the Stourminster coffee, the hasty organisation had overlooked provision of milk. Brother Paul Miller saved that part of the day by dashing to a recently established open all hours shop and returning with a small crate of milk precariously balanced on the front seat of his sports car.

At the February meeting of Chandlery Lodge, two sets of minutes of previous meetings were read.

CHAPTER SIXTY

WHAT THE PAPERS SAID; WHAT A LITTLE WORLD SAID;
AND THE CONSEQUENCES WERE . . .
28–31 JANUARY AND BEYOND INTO 1988

The *Avonbridge Gazette* publishes late on a Thursday when it is delivered to homes who subscribe and is available in newsagents who remain open late. Astute pressman Gil Williams had ordered a print run of one and a half as many copies as usual, he should have doubled the order. Banner headlines announced: 'FREEMASONS EXPOSED!'

Photographs showed both group and individual portraits. Certain sections of the sufferers' anatomy, decency had dictated, were blacked out or, more sensationally, highlighted by stars. Names were named, occupations detailed, addresses—omitting house names or numbers— were cited. Mrs Scarlett Jones was quoted and photographically depicted posed in her Sunday best—ironically she was featured on page three. Dave and Molly Morris were shown standing outside their bed and breakfast—the free publicity did not result in the increase in customers they had hoped for, but did ensure their fifteen minutes of fame.

Never before had the gazette been so avidly read and re-read. It was eagerly seized upon, discussed and re-discussed in almost every Avonbridge home. It was not so well received in the Fisher, Jeffries and Hughes homes. Frank Fallowfield read it with disdain and decided it was best ignored.

Ray and Doris Hughes closed their furniture store after thirty minutes on Friday morning as it was obvious no sales would be made to the rude, curious persons walking around with the gazette blatantly held open. Doris managed to restrain her husband from hitting one impudent idiot who asked Ray to autograph his picture in the paper. They affixed a closed until further notice sign to the door, gave the employees a week's wages and told them to await further instructions next week, before taking flight in their car. Mr and Mrs Hughes booked themselves into the Royal Hotel, Torquay for four nights, 'until the dust settles,' they assured one another. They would not remain for the duration of their booking.

Judith and George Jeffries sat in their neat, dream home horrified.

The dream had become a nightmare; they could no longer remain in such
a terrible place as Avonbridge. Judith telephoned her sister in Sussex and
it was agreed, explanations to follow, that she and George would stay
with them for at least Saturday and Sunday nights. On Friday afternoon,
George Jeffries—overcoat collar upturned and trilby around his ears—
entered the offices of Corey and Pritchard Estate Agents and arranged
for their home to be offered for sale. Spare keys were left with the
manager, Robert Oldman, to facilitate viewings as the Jeffrieses would be
'unavoidably absent for an indeterminate time.' Rob Oldman managed to
keep his face straight whilst speaking with 'one of the strippers.'

Predictably, Maurice Fisher felt faint when confronted with his copy
of the gazette. Caitlin Fisher told him, as she always did, to pull himself
together. As he always did, Maurice tried to comply. Caitlin Fisher
vented her verbal wrath on the walls and windows of their cosy Grimley
Street home of twenty-four years. She returned to her Monday lunchtime
rant and Maurice, having little to say and less to suggest, sat mute whilst
his irate wife telephoned the police station to make a formal complaint.

'It's against person or persons unknown they say, Maurice, but I've
told them that rich Whitehouse-Martin and his buddy Baker are at the
bottom of this. You wait and see. I want to see them answer for their
violation of your person, Maurice.'

'Caitlin—you can't go around accusing people like that,' protested
Maurice.

'Can't I then?' stormed his raging wife. 'We'll see about that.'

To poor Maurice's dismay and distress, his headstrong wife next
telephoned Higgins & Wright, Solicitors, and insisted a writ be issued
against J. J. Whitehouse-Martin and B. Baker for assault on her husband
and others. Even the most eager for business lawyers need more than
a simple instruction before they can dash off unsubstantiated writs—
Maurice was relieved that Roger Wright counselled caution and, for the
time being at least, restrained his wife from actions he was sure they
would both regret.

The gossip and speculation of Friday and Saturday had not faded away
when the *News of the World* went on sale early Sunday morning. Local
newsagents, forewarned of the content, had doubled, trebled, and in one
case quadrupled, their usual allocations of the lurid scandal-sheet. Almost
every copy was sold. The same story as in the *Avonbridge Gazette* was
repeated, but in greater detail—some correct, some purely conjectural: all

eagerly accepted as gospel truth. The photographs were larger and bore more lurid captions. The bylines were: 'David Horseman and Gil Williams. Photography by Derek Peters.' (Young Peters was regarded with parental disfavour at home)

In addition to what had been published in the gazette, the national Sunday rag had photos of the Chandlery yard (courtesy of Derek Peters's gate climbing skills) and the victims' cars being driven from that same yard. The Morris's dog, Rags, had a small feature and photo which pleased his owners, but still failed to effect any increase in B&B bookings. An interview with Mr Douglas Fawner—secretary of the Masonic hall, Avonbridge, was interspersed with commentary.

> Mr Fawner stated that, 'The cleaner [Mrs Jones] found three naked men bound, blood-stained and gagged. It was an off-duty nurse who called me, but he didn't know what was upstairs.'
>
> The male nurse who found Mrs Jones in a disturbed state outside the Masonic hall was Greg Davies. He was assisted at the scene by colleague Philip Carlton. It was Carlton who telephoned the police to report suspicion of something untoward having taken place in the Avonbridge Masonic hall. Neither nurse was prepared to comment other than to confirm that they assisted Mrs Jones whom they subsequently entrusted to two detectives who returned her to her home.
>
> Douglas Fawner further said, 'They were alive. I went in and helped them. I took their gags off [but] I couldn't undo the knots [of their bonds].' Mr Fawner has since told us that the matter is 'none of [our] business' and refuses to speak further.

On Monday, a Masonic acquaintance cheekily asked Douglas Fawner, 'What're you doing talking to a *News of the World* reporter?'

'I haven't,' was the terse reply.

'You're quoted in the paper. Looks to me as though you gave them an interview.'

The Fawner home did not subscribe to, or purchase, the *News of the World*. After fruitlessly asking at two newsagents, Fawner eventually located a copy of Sunday's edition at a neighbour's house and was able to read his interview. In vain he protested his ignorance of ever having granted an interview. Even his wife, Marion, began to wonder how the interview had been reported and it was she who exasperatedly asked Douglas, 'Have you ever heard of this Jill Williams who you're supposed to have talked to?'

'I've never heard of Jill Williams,' answered Douglas. Then, in a sudden and uncharacteristic flash of insight, he said, 'Wait a minute . . . There was a man called Williams, said he was press, called at the hall. Are you sure it's Jill Williams?'

'Yes, of course. Look,' replied Marion handing over the mangled tabloid.

'It's spelled with a *G*, Marion. Not Jillian—Gilbert. It's him . . . he went away and then came back for something—a glove I think. He must have heard me talking to Rex Raymond on the telephone and written down what I said.'

Fawner held his head in his hands and contemplated betrayal and other negatives.

Time would prove him right. Within three months, the Masonic hall committee had suggested, as tactfully as possible but with undeniable intention, that it was time another brother 'had a go' at being hall secretary. The younger, enthusiastic John Robertson took charge of the hall administration at the April A.G.M.

Escaping the fallout from exposure in the *Avonbridge Gazette* by temporarily removing to Torquay or Sussex was easy; but the circulation of the *News of the World* was not confined to a small area of the United Kingdom. Ray and Doris Hughes, taking an almost relaxed breakfast in their Torquay seafront hotel, were at first irritated and then annoyed by the furtive looks and scarcely suppressed laughter in the dining room. With typical forthrightness, they confronted a nearby diner only to have the sadly familiar photograph of a naked Ray with other shameful images thrust at them. To cries of 'It *is* him' the Hugheses left the dining room. Shortly afterwards, they left the hotel. From a public telephone kiosk they telephoned their employees and the premier Midlands property agents. Whilst the humbled Hugheses toured Southern Ireland—where publication of the *News of the World* was still officially banned—their Avonbridge High Street premises was sold to a hopeful purveyor of fancy goods and their fine home was also easily disposed of. The Hugheses only re-entered Avonbridge to sign documents confirming disposal of their properties. Raymond Hughes's curt letter of resignation from Chandlery Lodge gave no forwarding address. The envelope was postmarked Cumbria.

Hiding away in a small Sussex village with one's sister/sister-in-law pleading intolerable problems with the lodge and the Avonbridge community as an excuse for leaving home made life for the pompous Jeffries briefly tolerable. Circulation of Sunday newspapers percolates into even the more remote parts of Sussex where they are read just as avidly, though more furtively, as elsewhere. Gossip and fingers of scorn move swiftly in small communities. Lodging with the deaconess of the local Methodist chapel with a false reason for arrival could not be tolerated. Judith's 'holy' sister asked, with little milk of human kindness, that her disgraceful relations remove themselves forthwith. The chastened Jeffries motored north into Norfolk where they sought refuge in a remote farmhouse pleased to have bed and breakfast lodgers asking, and paying, for an indefinite stay. During their second week in the flatlands of East Anglia, the Jeffries discovered a small cottage with a large garden offered for sale at a price they could afford. It had no near neighbours and the estate agent had either not read the *News of the World* or was someone with whom one should not play poker. George Jeffries returned to Avonbridge to sign off the sale of his property, superintend the removal firm's work—to their constant resentment—and deliver the minute books and other records of Chandlery Lodge to the Masonic hall. Carefully timing his visit to his place of shame, he gained access with the cleaner who had replaced Mrs Jones—thereby avoiding contact or communication with any Mason. His letter of resignation was left with the Lodge records. In common with Worshipful Brother Hughes, Jeffries gave no forwarding address. Neither he nor Ray Hughes ever attempted to join another Masonic Lodge.

The *News of the World* edition on that fateful Sunday was eagerly advised to the Fishers. Needless to say, they were not readers of the 'shameful Sundays', but there were many past recipients of Caitlin's verbal vilifications keen to acquaint her and 'poor little Maurice' with the fact that he was national news. The effect on the Fishers' already stressed systems resulted in diverse, but equally disastrous, nervous failings. 'Poor little Maurice' finally retreated into his innermost shell, curled up both physically and mentally and became wholly uncommunicative. Caitlin veered even further into accusatory hysteria, continually demanding justice from both the police and the judiciary. Her lawyers continued to ask for evidence before taking any action; she was frequently warned of the consequences of slander and libel and as often ignored the warnings. The police were more attentive—but still failed to appreciate Caitlin's conviction as to the perpetrators' identities. Superintendent Raymond tried hard to quell the spate of accusation stemming from Mrs Fisher and constantly assured her that her first formal complaint meant the incidents would be 'thoroughly investigated'. He did indicate that the initial request of the wronged men for no further enquiries to be made had delayed and, possibly, impaired the investigation. Caitlin Fisher neither understood nor wished to understand official prevarications. After a third interview, which was only allowed to maintain the peace within the police station, Raymond gave Mrs Fisher an official warning to keep the peace or be detained for her own good. The only good achieved for some time was to keep her away from the station.

CHAPTER SIXTY-ONE
INVESTIGATION AND FRUSTRATION
FRIDAY 29 JANUARY TO WEDNESDAY 3 FEBRUARY 1988

Detective Sergeant Paula James and Detective Constable Harry Carter-Knight were charged with resumption of the four-day-old cold case against 'person or persons unknown' for assault on Mr Maurice Fisher and others. They were both pleased to be given an opportunity to attempt to find a solution of the suspended case—Harry was happy that he might be able to probe the mysteries of the Masonic hall that had so intrigued him; Paula was glad to be in charge of something—albeit small. Apart from their own observations on the morning of Monday 25 January, all they had of any relevance were statements taken by Paula from Mrs Jones and by Harry from Dave and Molly Morris.

'It's not a lot to go on, sir,' said Paula to Superintendent Raymond. 'In light of what you told us the other day . . .' she stopped, looking nervously at her superior.

'You mean about me being a Freemason, Sergeant?' said Raymond.

'Well . . . yes, sir. If you don't mind . . . If you can offer us any suggestions as to what we should or shouldn't ask, or where we ought to go and when, we'd be grateful.'

'Relax, Paula. Ask whatever you like, if it's out of order then any Freemason worth his salt will tell you—I hope politely. Only visit the Masonic hall with permission. Almost all Masonic meetings are held in the evening from either five or six o'clock onward so avoid those times.'

'Thank you, sir,' chorused Paula and Harry, turning to leave. The superintendent held up his hand to detain them. He looked hard at each of them before continuing, 'This is off the record and don't dare tell anyone—and I mean anyone—you heard this from me . . . but, having thought about this and in fairness to both of you, I should tell you I am almost certain—and it grieves me to say so—that whoever did this to those four old brothers is almost certainly a Freemason. Either that or he has been . . . OK?'

'Yes, sir. Thank you, sir,' said two very surprised detectives.

After re-reading her statement and reviewing the difficulty of comprehension likely to be involved, the detectives decided another session with Mrs Jones would be of little use. The simple soul was not the most observant of beings, and when previously pressed on the matter there was nothing untoward she could remember until she had 'gorn up them stairs'. The two male nurses were traced and, not having seen the injured Masons at the time—they had, of course, seen the newspaper pictures—could add nothing to what the two detectives already knew.

Douglas Fawner seemed more intent upon excusing himself for tampering with the crime scene than in providing information. Having several times accepted his apologies and assured him he was not to have known and was not in any trouble, Paula and Harry eventually pieced together his small involvement. He had no knowledge of why or when the four injured parties had come to the Masonic hall. He had heard them complaining that it had been a long night—a fact appreciated from the sorry state of their lower bodies, despite the rudimentary receptacles of relief. He confirmed the detectives' suspicion that the chairs to which the four had been bound had not been in their usual positions. Pressed to do so he did, with reluctance, show them the temple room as it was usually arranged. The Wells Builders property cleaners had divested the premises of plastic sheeting, but despite an array of air-fresheners, an unpleasant aroma remained. Fawner divulged that Mr Baker had undertaken to have the temple re-decorated in the summer when no meetings were scheduled. Harry remained fascinated and some of his questions to Fawner bore little relevance to the investigation, that being so, Carter-Knight knew he dare not object to Fawner's evasive answers. Paula was amused by this diversion. Neither she nor Harry felt any wiser or further forward after interviewing Douglas Fawner, conversely, the interviewee's usual self-deception boosting his confidence, Fawner he felt he had acquitted himself well.

The Jeffrieses and the Hugheses had effectively disappeared, as they had committed no wrong there was no reason to instigate a nationwide search and whatever they may have added to the police's knowledge remained unknown. The detectives' appointment with Mr and Mrs Fisher proved little more informative despite the inordinate amount of time involved. Maurice Fisher remained comatose and unable to answer questions. Having confirmed this and offered their sympathies, Paula and Harry expected to leave with empty notebooks. In this they were disappointed and delayed as, to their frustration, Mrs Caitlin Fisher made several long, angry accusations against 'that Whitehouse-Martin and Baker lot'. Eventually, deep breath drawn, Paula used a short pause in

Caitlin's complaints to ask why she should suspect them. Glaring angrily at her, the furious Fisher wife expostulated, 'It's their idea of revenge for that disgraceful business at his ladies' night, of course.'

Tentatively, Paula sought clarification of a possible motive for the denuding, 'I'm sorry, Mrs Fisher, we don't know about that.'

Her enquiry unleashed another torrent of words.

'Disgraceful, it was. The lodge ladies' night, and my Maurice only trying to do the proper thing, just as it's always been done. That Mrs Whitehouse-Martin . . . from that Flower Patch shop with her stuck-up ways . . . she thrust herself at my Maurice and exposed herself. Then she started screaming. Poor Maurice was knocked over by her and her pals and she bled all over him. Anyone'll tell you what happened. There was fighting and shouting, and my poor Maurice lying on the floor with her blood all over him. He couldn't get up. They threw wine at me. You ask anyone who was there. Awful it was—her all exposed, screaming her head off and him staggering about holding his head and only me trying to help poor Maurice. We had to go to the hospital, we did and they weren't much help—told me to keep Maurice quiet and sent us home. They weren't as casual with the Whitehouse-Martin lot, I tell you.'

After more of the same the two ear-weary investigators extracted themselves from the Fisher home. Neither was sure what to conclude from the endless diatribe of denunciation and 'pity poor Maurice' which had assaulted their ears for what seemed far longer than the time actually expired.

'If we can find out more on this incident at The Swan, it might be a motive,' mused Paula.

'When is all this supposed to have happened?' queried Harry. 'If I remember rightly, Mrs Whitehouse-Martin was killed in an R.T.A. some time back.'

'You're right, Harry. There was a big funeral. It was about three years ago—just after I got posted here. But what has three old men sitting starkers got to do with the lodge ladies' night and all that she was raving about?'

They concluded it warranted further enquiry—but of a tactful nature. The following day they had a far more civilised and helpful session with Frank Fallowfield. They ascertained the time at which Fallowfield and Hughes arrived at the hall and why they had come. The old baker hadn't seen the note sent to Ray Hughes, but remembered what Hughes had told him—curiosity having decided him to accompany Hughes. Their later enquiries found no one who was aware of an urgent meeting with the caterer, the caterer himself was confused and affronted to realise his name had been used to lure the strippers—as everyone was calling them in casual conversation—to their strange fate . . . if fate it was. Frank Fallowfield also gave a sketchy, but ultimately unhelpful description of the perpetrator of the violations.

'Tall, well-built and walked with a bit of a limp. Not always, the limp that is, but most of the time. Dressed all in black, I'm pretty sure he used a cloak and tabard from the Knights of Malta degree.' Subsequent enquiries of Fawner confirmed a set of Malta clothing was missing. The only other hitherto unknown fact Fallowfield revealed was, 'His voice was very odd. Squeaky . . . but it sounded familiar. Couldn't place it at the time, but sitting around after he'd gone—couldn't do much else, of course—I remembered what it had reminded me of—don't think I'm losing me marbles, please—it was Mr Punch. The Punch and Judy shows we used to see at the seaside.'

Questioned about Caitlin Fisher's rambling accusations, Fallowfield chuckled, 'Got a nasty tongue on her, has that one,' he said. 'Tends to blow hot and cold—more hot than cold, if you know what I mean. Always felt sorry for old Maurice getting himself saddled with her.'

Interrupting him, Paula ventured to ask about Mr Whitehouse-Martin's ladies' night.

'Wasn't there meself,' replied Fallowfield 'No lady to take, ye see. Seemed a bit pointless if I'd have nothing to do except eat the meal and watch 'em dance—don't dance meself . . . oh, sorry, I'm digressing. What I gathered from talk afterwards, was that old Maurice somehow managed to make a mess of presenting the usual jewel to Mrs Whitehouse-Martin—nice lady she was, God rest her soul. Most seem to think he either trod on her dress or slipped and grabbed at the top. Whichever it was, the poor woman was suddenly . . . er, how can I put this . . . oh, yes, she was, as they say these days, topless. And . . . she . . . er—didn't like it.'

Paula tried to save the old man further embarrassment by questioning him on another aspect of Mrs Fisher's rant.

'Mrs Fisher told us there was fighting and Mr Whitehouse-Martin got hit in the head . . . At least that's what she seemed to be saying.'

Fallowfield seemed grateful for the change of emphasis, 'It's only what I heard, of course,' he said, 'but it seems there was quite a ruckus—though what started that I don't know. None o' my business. Young Whitehouse-Martin seems to have got something in his eye, certainly. Saw him a few days later with a patch on it right eye, if I remember aright . . . Look—if it's going to help your enquiry, though I can't see how or why to be honest, I do know quite a lot of 'em finished up at the hospital that night. Someone there'll know what damages they had if you ask.'

It was not easy to trace and then manage to interview the staff who had been on duty in October nearly four years ago. By the time Paula and Harry were able to question them, they had as clear a picture of the events of Friday 19 October 1984 as they needed. They also felt it was, whilst an interesting insight, not relevant to their current enquiry.

After seeing Frank Fallowfield, Paula and Harry conferred as to whom they could next interview. The Jeffrieses and Hugheses had disappeared without trace. Maurice Fisher remained mute and they had no great desire to renew face-to-face acquaintance with Mrs Fisher. Rather reluctantly, and realising they needed to proceed carefully, they decided that as Mr Whitehouse-Martin and Mr Billy Baker had been mentioned, they should see them—if only to eliminate slander from the enquiry. Paula's call to JJ's secretary elicited the information that he was somewhere in the Caribbean on a cruise. Paula realised this frustrated her intentions, but before she could politely end the call, she was given, unbidden, the additional information that Mr Whitehouse-Martin had left on the 16 January. Paula was unable to tell Harry before his appointment with Mr Baker.

Billy was surprised to be interviewed. He expressed his surprise and clearly stated that, much as he regretted the deplorable business at the Masonic hall, he could see no way in which he could be of any assistance. Harry had to negotiate the difficult problem of telling him he had been mentioned in Mrs Fisher's accusations. To the surprise and relief of the young detective, Billy burst out laughing.

'She's always making those sort of daft, unsubstantiated statements is Mrs Catty Fisher,' said Billy. 'How's she reckon I'm involved, I'd like to know?'

He looked, not unkindly, at Harry who, having caught his mood, was smiling.

'Well?' asked Billy. 'She must have offered some sort of argument as to how I was involved.'

'Not really, Mr Baker. She just seemed to think the whole thing was the fault of Mr Whitehouse-Martin and yourself,' said Harry. 'I'm sorry to mention it, but we had to follow it up.'

'It gets dafter and dafter,' replied Billy. 'Quite how and why does she imagine JJ and I would set about three, sorry, four old men?' he challenged.

'Well, sir,' said Harry—regretting having sought this difficult interview, 'as to how, we weren't told, but Mrs Fisher kept saying it was your "revenge" on her husband for something that happened at Mr Whitehouse-Martin's ladies' night.'

Billy was staring at him wide-eyed and in not as friendly a manner as had been the case up till then.

'That was over three years ago, young man. Maurice Fisher somehow managed to stick a jewel pin into poor Jenny—Mrs Whitehouse-Martin's—breast and then pull her dress off. If we'd wanted to take revenge we'd have knocked six bells out of the silly sod then and there. We didn't. There was some fighting and some accidents, and quite a few of us ended up at the hospital that night. It was all Fisher's fault in my view, but we've tried to put it behind us. Poor Jenny's dead and JJ— Mr Whitehouse-Martin—seems to have adjusted to life without her. He nearly lost an eye that night, you know.' Billy paused. He looked at the young police detective and pulled himself together.

'Sorry to go, on. That damn woman and her acid tongue always wind me up—even at third hand. I can see how she might think stripping old Maurice of his dignity—what little he's got—could be some sort of schoolboy revenge. But, and I'm sure you've considered this, why involve the others? And, if you manage to justify that, then you—and Mrs Fisher if she keeps persisting—need to explain how Mr Whitehouse-Martin and I could be in two places at the same time. JJ's cruising the Caribbean and my wife and I were with friends in Moreton-in-Marsh in the Cotswolds until nearly ten o'clock on Sunday night. As far as I can gather from talking to old Floury Fallowfield, the attacks—if that's what they should be called—took place much earlier that night.'

Billy stopped and gave the young detective the searching look that any recalcitrant employees had learned to fear—but Harry was not frightened. He felt inclined to express his thanks and leave, but thought he should confirm a few facts before leaving. He appreciated Billy's honesty as to a potential, if delayed, motive, 'Just for the record, Mr Baker, when did you first hear of the events of Sunday the twenty-fourth?'

'Monday afternoon. Alan Simmonds, the dentist, telephoned me. We had to re-arrange the Masonic installation because we'd been told the Masonic hall was being investigated by yourselves.'

'Thank you, sir,' said Harry—duly embarrassed. Adding by way of apology, 'We did release it later that day.'

'Agreed but . . . well, you'd seen the state it was in . . .'

Harry nodded, 'It couldn't have been fit for purpose that evening.'

'It took the best part of two days for one of our contractors to clear and clean it. And, if you've been in there since,' again he looked enquiringly at Harry who, again, nodded, 'you'll know a certain unpleasant aroma remains as a reminder of the twenty-fourth and twenty-fifth. It'll be re-decorated in the summer.'

'Yes, we had been told that, sir. Just one more thing, Mr Baker—just for the record and with no offence intended—is there any way we could corroborate when you left the Cotswolds on Sunday 24 January?'

'Well you could ask my wife, of course,' said Billy, 'but, I suppose, you'd expect her to support me. For a more independent confirmation, you could enquire of the friends with whom we spent the evening. I'll give you their details.'

Billy wrote the name, address and telephone number of their friends in Moreton-in-Marsh on an office memo pad, tore off the page and passed it to Harry. Harry thanked him for his time and information and again apologised that it had been necessary to bring Mrs Fisher's allegations to his notice.

'You've got your job to do, Constable,' said Billy—rising and proffering his hand.

They shook hands and Harry left. There were things about this job he was beginning to dislike.

Over the next few days, Paula and Harry re-read their notes and re-traced some of their steps—avoiding Mrs Fisher. All to no avail. Mr John Hipkins had been very clear that Janice and Billy Baker had left their home in Moreton-in-Marsh at 9.50 p.m. on Sunday 24 January. Peninsular and Orient Cruise Lines had confirmed that passenger Mr J. J. Whitehouse-Martin was travelling in the Caribbean on one of their cruise liners that had left Southampton on 16 January. The two detectives concluded there was little else they could do. The initial refusal of any investigation had left the usual preliminary routine work incomplete or not even begun. The daggers in the Masonic temple had been fingerprinted and showed only the prints of the victims. A uniform sergeant, whose wife regularly performed in local amateur dramatics had advanced her theory that the blood used on the victims could be what was known in theatrical circles as Kensington Gore—fake blood easily obtained from theatre suppliers; her theory had been confirmed, but chances of tracing the supplier or purchaser were so remote as to make any time spent pointless. The contractors who efficiently cleared and cleaned the Masonic temple had burned the plastic sheeting that covered the floor—rightly citing sanitation as their motive.

On Wednesday 3 February, the disappointed detectives reported their findings, or more accurately lack of findings, to Superintendent Raymond. He expressed neither surprise nor satisfaction.

'File your reports then, please, and we'll close this wild goose-chase. I'll have to do the brave thing and inform Mrs Fisher we've failed to find any justification for her allegations. Once more, I'll suggest she refrain from further accusations. Nothing more we can do. Thank you both for trying.'

CHAPTER SIXTY-TWO
An Apology and the Illumination of a Young Man
Monday 8 February 1988

The investigation was officially closed. On Monday 8 February, Inspector Gorman was surprised and slightly irritated to receive a telephone call from Mr JJ Whitehouse-Martin. Whitehouse-Martin enquired who had asked to interview him whilst he was away and for what reason. Not wishing to upset a prominent citizen, Gorman explained the matter had been settled but that he would send one of the investigating team to explain to Mr Whitehouse-Martin. Putting the telephone down with a sigh, Steve Gorman summoned Harry Carter-Knight.

'Harry—as you were part of the frustrated investigation into those four old fellows left in the nuddy at the Avonbridge Masons' place, can you go and see Mr JJ Whitehouse-Martin to assure him it's all over and apologise for any . . . well, you know the form. He's expecting you at eleven o'clock in his office at Avonbridge Hall.'

Harry Carter-Knight didn't really 'know the form' as his superior had so neatly phrased it, but he understood what was required of him. Nevertheless, he was nervous, JJ Whitehouse-Martin's reputation as the local money-man and business tyro was well-known and Harry had often heard him spoken of with some awe. And he had been vilified by that acid-tongued Mrs Fisher.

Several trucks were parked on the gravel in front of Avonbridge Hall. Harry parked as tidily as circumstances permitted, straightened his tie and checked his shoes before making his way through the open front door. Sounds of great activity could be heard. As Harry wondered whether it would be proper to shout a greeting, a tall, fair-haired, bespectacled and smiling man emerged from further down the hallway and introduced himself.

'JJ Whitehouse-Martin. Hello. Apologies for all the noise—we're having the place converted for a new project. Please come this way, Officer.'

Wondering why he had been apprehensive, Harry followed Mr Whitehouse-Martin into a spacious, well-appointed office. His host couldn't have been kinder or more charming, he thoroughly understood Harry's embarrassment and, brushing aside his apologies, offered his own for having caused Harry any inconvenience.

'Your boss told me it was all over on the phone, so I don't really understand why he's sent you along as well. Still . . . you're here, so you might as well have a coffee with me and fill me in on what I haven't learned since I got back about this peculiar business.'

JJ picked up the phone and asked for coffee for two—with biscuits, please.'

Indicating the chairs with an occasional table between them in the bay window he suggested they sat there.

'Excuse these—holiday photos.'

Teasingly, he thrust a large number of photographs that had been spread out on the table towards Harry, 'Case closed or not, you might want to glance at them—they're all date lined. My alibi for the time of the crimes, I suppose.'

'Thank you, sir, there's really no need,' said Harry—although he could clearly see the top two photographs were dated 25/01/88 and showed a Nassau road sign.

'We did, as a matter of routine, check with the cruise line to confirm you were sailing with them.'

For the next half hour they sat in two comfortable armchairs whilst Harry recounted not only the details of the discovery and the enquiry, but also his own short history, hopes and aspirations. Under JJ's gentle questioning, he admitted he liked dealing with and finding out about people—other than the Mrs Fishers of this world: JJ laughed. Increasingly, Harry confessed, he disliked the dull routine of endlessly trailing around asking the same questions—particularly as, in many cases, he knew those questioned knew little and cared less.

'I know its all part of the job,' continued Harry, 'and some of it might get left behind if I persevere, but its not what I hoped detective work would be.'

Harry suddenly realised he had digressed from official business to personal concerns, 'Oh, I'm awfully sorry, sir. Moaning about myself when I only came to apologise.'

'Don't worry about it, Constable. Thank you for helping me understand what's been going on. I did get a quick outline from my friend Mr Baker, but it's been interesting to hear your side. Not exactly a routine sort of case, I imagine?'

'No, indeed, sir.'

'It seemed to me,' continued JJ, 'from the way you spoke about it, that you were somewhat fascinated by the interior of the Masonic hall, young man.'

'Well . . . er, yes, I was. But we were told not to ask too many questions about the place and to stick to finding out what had happened there. One of my colleagues seemed to think it was all terribly secret.'

Harry paused, wondering whether he had said too much. He was swiftly re-assured, 'Nothing secret about it at all,' said JJ. 'The manner of recognition between Masons is, supposedly, safeguarded but, like most things meant to be kept quiet, there's always someone who can't be discreet. I've actually met an unprincipled salesman who, having unsuccessfully tried to impress me, actually boasted that knowing the Masons' grip had helped him to sell things. So, no, it's not a secret. You can easily find books in which the full ceremonies are written down, but that won't give you the full picture. I know a chap who read it all before he came in and, as he should have realised, spoiled his own enjoyment and appreciation. Freemasonry can be very worthwhile and very rewarding, not in a pecuniary way—this might sound a bit pompous, but it's not meant to be—but rewarding in the sense of life enhancing.'

'I see. Thank you, sir, most interesting.' Harry still hesitated.

'What is it you'd like to know, Detective—not as a detective, but as a man?' said JJ.

'Well, what do you do?' asked Harry.

'Big question to answer, young man—what's your first name?'

'Harry.'

'Well, Harry, here's the broad UK outline. All over this country there are lodges meeting regularly—some only four times a year and some as many as eleven times. At most meetings ceremonies are conducted—simply put, they're little morality plays. There's always a charity collection. We support many charities—not just our own: we don't brag about it, but some of us think it should be better known. We try to make sure any of our Masonic brethren in need are looked after—their families as well. And we do enjoy the social camaraderie at meals after the meetings—they're still referred to as festive boards although there are times when the festivity either gets out of hand or, even worse, never makes an appearance. Does that answer your question, Harry?'

'Yes, it does. But——'

'It leads to other questions?'

'Well, yes. All the display cases and boards looked impressive, but I was told to ignore them. And I wondered why.'

'Why they were there or why you were told to ignore them?'

'Both, really.'

'The displays and boards are Masonic history. The jewels commemorate all sorts of events and people. The boards simply state the names of whoever was top man in that lodge or chapter or other order in each year. Telling you to ignore them is a dictate of ignorance, I fear.'

'Thank you, sir. There's one other question I'd like to ask.'

There was a long pause. JJ decided to curtail the young man's embarrassment.

'You want to know how you become a Freemason?' queried JJ.

'Well—yes,' replied Harry.

'The strict protocol is that *you* ask someone whom you know to be a Freemason if you can become one. But that's not widely understood, I fear. I recently heard a sad but true story of two life-long friends—one a Freemason of some years standing, as his friend well knew—who met each other every Wednesday night for a drink, a chat and a game or two of cribbage. Someone asked them both, out of each other's hearing, why the outsider was not coming in. The outsider said he was waiting for his friend to ask him. The Mason said he was waiting for his friend to ask him. Silly situation and, so far, no one's knocked their heads together. If I've known someone long enough and sufficiently well to recommend them as a Freemason, then I see no reason why I shouldn't suggest they join and, if they don't object, conduct the necessary examination to confirm, well as I may know them, they are a suitable candidate.'

'I see,' said Harry. 'Thank you again, sir. I hope I get to know some Freemasons well enough to either ask or be asked.'

Before he left they talked more about Harry's ambitions. The more he heard, the more JJ became convinced this personable young man would be an ideal trainee for management of the conference centre. Eventually, he asked bluntly if Harry intended to remain a career policeman. There was a long pause before Harry answered.

'I honestly don't know, sir. As you know, I'm rather disenchanted with some of it. On the other hand, I haven't been at it long enough to really be certain whether it's for me or not. And if it's not, then I'm going to have to look for something else with prospects and a good pension.'

'Good answer, Harry,' replied JJ. 'Any time you feel you'd like to talk about your future again, here's my card. In my opinion, you're far too personable to be a copper. We do have vacancies for promising people from time to time, so if you continue having doubts, don't hesitate to get in touch.'

Harry was amazed. He'd come here to offer a grovelling apology and was almost being offered a job. He stammered his thanks and pocketed the business card—a very simple card, just J. J. Whitehouse-Martin followed by his address and telephone number in black print on white card. Over the next few months, Harry's thoughts would constantly return to his first meeting with JJ.

CHAPTER SIXTY-THREE
Avonbridge Masonic Hall
Worshipful Brother Billy Baker, 1989/1990

As he had promised, JJ was very much in attendance for the installation of his oldest friend Billy Baker as worshipful master of Chandlery Lodge. As Billy had done for him five years previously, JJ insisted on driving the master elect to the Masonic hall and having them both driven away at the end of a successful evening.

Hugh Kington, being a competent Mason, installed his successor and both he and Billy were warmly commended by the deputy provincial grand master, Chris Vernon, both in the temple and later at the festive board. JJ proposed the toast to the new master and then accompanied Worshipful Brother Sid Wear's singing of the Master's Song. It was a night to remember in the beautifully re-decorated hall.

The only unusual and unexpected intrusion into the usual proceedings was the discussion between JJ and the deputy provincial grand master. The P.G.M., Mike Copper, was keen to appoint JJ as a provincial warden, which would oblige JJ to attend a considerable number of installations plus other ceremonies during the year. JJ explained he was now a tax exile living in Guernsey and the duties of the office—necessarily carried out within the province—would mean he exceeded the quota of days in UK allowed by taxation law beyond which he would become liable for penal income tax. Great honour though it would be, the cost to JJ in UK taxation would make acceptance a very expensive exercise. A further problem was that JJ had been refused pilot training due to the defect in his right eye, which would prevent him swiftly transporting himself from the Channel Isles to his native county. JJ expressed his thanks, but regretted he must disappoint the P.G.M. His appointment as provincial treasurer the following June was to be his position for the next six years.

As planned by himself and JJ, Billy had a good year as master. He initiated two promising young men; performed two second degree and one third degree ceremonies—and saw another third done by past masters as tradition decreed. His late September ladies' weekend in Bruges was a resounding success. Whilst in the delightful Belgian town, Paul Miller,

Billy's senior warden, had a discussion with Brother John Robinson and the 1990 ladies' weekend was booked in Waterford, Ireland.

JJ desperately wanted to support his friend and brother in Bruges, but having no wife to escort at the ladies' weekend worried him. A solution became obvious during his mother and Claude's summer visit to his Guernsey estate. They, too, were anxious not to disappoint Billy and Janice, but the Sunday return journey with several stops on the way created a problem for Claude who was needed for Sabbath services. The obvious compromise solved two problems: Claude would miss the Bruges ladies' festival to attend to his clerical duties and JJ would escort his mother for the weekend—the cost of separate rooms was no problem for JJ. Although she missed Claude, Sylvia took a mother's pride in being escorted by her still handsome son: as a surprise present, JJ presented Claude and Sylvia with a long mid-week holiday in Bruges later in the year. One of many long remembered highlights of the festival was Janice's sparkling, witty response to the ladies' toast. In his short vote of thanks, Billy made particular mention of his friend and mentor JJ— gently reminding the assembled brethren that the concept of treating the ladies to a long weekend far away from home had been that of his proposer into Freemasonry. He made no apology for stealing the idea.

In the eight years following the Bruges weekend, the Chandlery Lodge brethren travelled by JBR coaches to resorts far from Avonbridge to treat their ladies. Many other Midlands lodges first envied and then emulated the idea—JBR Travel became an even greater success in the business empire spawned by Whitehouse-Martin money and inspiration. During 1990, Worshipful Brother Paul Miller instituted a summer Sunday luncheon for lodge families—another innovation giving domestic celebration for those unable to be away from work and home for two or three days.

The events of 25 January 1988 receded into distant memory and were less and less mentioned. The absence of the victims of January 1988 was neither mentioned nor a problem—indeed the more honest brethren of the lodge grudgingly admitted the absence of Jeffries and Hughes was more of a benefit than loss to the lodge.

CHAPTER SIXTY-FOUR
RETURN OF THE EXILE
1990 TO 1994

As January 1990 gave way to February, Billy and Janice become more and more concerned for JJ. Billy had never known his friend to fail at anything. Being refused pilot training had depressed JJ, but the extent of his sadness only became apparent after their return to the grange following Billy's installation of Paul Miller. Over the second brandy, JJ admitted to his friends that living in Guernsey was not all he had hoped for and, combined with being dependent on others for transportation, it even made the prospect of returning to the status of UK resident and taxpayer seem appealing. Much as they wanted him to return, the Bakers knew the decision must be JJ's alone so they plied him with more Remy Martin and let him talk himself into it. Once he seemed almost certain, the Bakers dared to tempt him by mentioning the imminent availability of a delightful, elevated house with swimming pool, gymnasium and grounds running down to the River Severn. It proved a determining factor.

The forthcoming sale was, as yet, known to very few—Janice and Billy being two of the few due to the fact that Janice had maintained the business records and tax return of the recently deceased owner, whose two cars had been supplied and serviced by B & J Cars. In the Bakers' opinion it would suit JJ ideally. The following day, Billy drove JJ through the lanes to the hamlet of Hawley Holt where, there being no one in residence, JJ walked freely around and fell in love with Herlways. The executors of the deceased were only too pleased to have a willing buyer even before engaging an estate agent, a mutually acceptable price was agreed and JJ bought the small estate and house which would become his base and principal address for the rest of his days. He arranged to leave Guernsey; his Channel Island estate would remain a holiday home for he, his family and friends.

JJ returned to the United Kingdom in the May of 1990—it having been prudent to remain a tax exile until the tax year ended on 5 April. Over the next seven months, he re-organised and re-arranged Herlways to suit his own tastes and was fortunate to engage Mr and Mrs Brice,

Eddie and Betty, he as gardener, general handyman and occasional chauffeur; she as housekeeper. They were well-paid and accommodated in the two-bedroomed cottage that served as a lodge to Herlways. There were two house warming parties; the first in late May and the second in early December when the same guests were able to appreciate the changes good taste and a deep purse had wrought. The second warming was closely followed by Chandlery Lodge Christmas party and JJ accepted the Baker family's insistent invitation to again spend the festive season at the grange, where he remained to see in 1991.

Whilst he thoroughly enjoyed his prolonged stay at the grange, the innocent queries of his godchildren, William and Jennifer Janice, as to Uncle JJ's new year's resolutions made him pause and begin to wonder how he was to occupy himself. Enforced idleness had led to his disillusionment with life on Guernsey, but having relinquished the day-to-day direction of his many businesses, he felt it unfair to those who had succeeded him to re-assume his former duties. The conference centre was complete and beginning to attract the sort of business he had instinctively known it would. He was not altogether surprised to learn that the successful applicant for under-manager with responsibility for security had been a former police detective named Harry Carter-Knight. When JJ made a chairman's visit to the old hall, he met Harry in his old office. It was now Harry's office. What could have been awkward was not, since neither wished it, indeed their mutual delight surprised staff who witnessed the initial confrontation. During the next three years, the chairman's visits to the Avonbridge conference centre were more frequent than strictly necessary. JJ and Mr Billy Baker seemed to be inordinately fond of the coffee served in the under-manager's office, and the sounds of laughter accompanying consumption of their morning beverage led some cynical employees to wonder whether there might be more than coffee in their cups. When the manager's position became vacant due to the first incumbent's problems with his distant family, the board's appointment of Harry as general manager surprised no one. His elevation to the board of directors followed, as did his initiation into Chandlery Lodge, sponsored by Worshipful Brothers Whitehouse-Martin and Baker.

The core business of the centre was conferences and annual general meetings of national and international companies. However, wedding receptions were also a profitable part of the conference centre's business, and none were more welcome than the nuptials of Detective Inspector Paula James and Edwin Harries—the groom being, at that time, master-elect of Chandlery Lodge. It was at their reception that Harry met his future wife, Ayisha Patel. Their reception a year later was an equally welcome event.

JJ tried to alleviate his boredom with life by joining or re-joining other orders of Freemasonry. Although they were interesting—some more than others—none totally absorbed him He accepted a few offices in other orders as they were offered, but found himself unable to summon the enthusiasm he saw in others. In Chandlery Lodge he declined the proffered posts of both secretary and director of ceremonies, was briefly tempted to become treasurer, but declined and became a lodge auditor, in which capacity he saved successive treasurers the problem—to them—of preparing lodge annual accounts. Attendance at his mother lodge became less regular and his imaginative excuses began to sound 'thin'—even to himself.

JJ's mood was not improved in March 1992 when he learned of the death of James Whiteman. He travelled north—staying with Terri and Gerald Armitage for the nights before and after the funeral. He was surprised to be asked at the wake if he could spare a little time to call at the offices of Millican and Knowles, solicitors to the deceased, but duly arranged to call the following morning; he was acutely embarrassed to discover himself the sole beneficiary of the late James Whiteman.

'It is not a large estate, Mr Whitehouse-Martin. There is no duty payable and costs, including, of course, our quite moderate fees, will not be excessive, so the proceeds will amount to a respectable sum,' pontificated the aging senior partner—wholly unaware of JJ's financial standing. The old lawyer was shocked to be asked to arrange immediate sale of the late Mr Whiteman's cottage, its contents and the car. JJ visited the property where, as a sentimental reminder of his friend, he removed a framed photograph of James in his prime, he also took the camera he had given James for Christmas 1987.

It had been JJ's intention to instruct Mr Knowles—Millican had passed on some years ago—to donate the entire proceeds of the sale to Masonic charities, but fearing he might precipitate Knowles into emulating Millican, JJ asked him to forward to him a cheque for the proceeds—less his fees. On receipt of Millican and Knowles's cheque, JJ rounded the amount up to the next nearest thousand and despatched cheques, each for half of the revised sum, to the Royal Masonic Benevolent Fund and the recently established Masonic Samaritan Fund. He requested the donations be recorded in memory of the late brother James Whiteman. The charities chosen were apposite: one caring for the welfare of impoverished Masons and their dependants and the other covering the costs of medical necessities for needy brethren, their families and dependants.

In 1994 Sylvia died. Although his mother had not suffered and her passing was peaceful, JJ felt an era had ended. She had influenced his life in an unobtrusive way and had never, as she could have, expressed any dissent as to the inequality of his father's disposition of his considerable wealth. Claude, now a hale and hearty, but bereaved, seventy-six, travelled from Hereford to Herlways in order to tell JJ in person as he felt the 'telephone can be so impersonal and distant', for which JJ was profoundly grateful. Sylvia had left precise written instructions as to the manner and content of her funeral and, in conformity with her wishes, Claude conducted the service. JJ, similarly obedient to his mother's wishes, delivered a moving eulogy in which, amongst his recollections, he said how delighted he had been to escort Sylvia to the first foreign ladies' festival of his lodge. He, Billy, Janice and Auntie Charlotte travelled together to Herefordshire in the JBR minibus. JJ had only twice visited the delightful Herefordshire cottage that Sylvia and Claude had moved to five years earlier following Claude's retirement, and where JJ had expected Claude to remain for the rest of his days. To his surprise, Claude told him at the wake that he intended to sell the cottage and travel with the Church Missionary Society to minister to the needs of those in deprived lands. In the opinion of JJ and many others, it was not a wise project for a man in his seventies, but Claude was set on the venture and, four months later, departed for the Dark Continent—as Africa had been known in his youth. Within a year opinions were vindicated. Claude was buried in the graveyard of a small Nigerian community to which, JJ was informed with African vigour, he had brought much comfort and support.

CHAPTER SIXTY-FIVE
Fresh Fields and Pastures New
1994 to 1997

Attending the conference centre as a shareholder for the September 1994 A.G.M. of a prominent public company, JJ discovered, in casual conversation (the progenitor of many solutions', a new passion to allay his boredom and provide peace and solitude; it would ultimately lead him to a brief renewal of happiness. The finance director of the visiting company had journeyed to Avonbridge in his own narrow boat on which he was both travelling and sleeping. JJ expressed an interest and was invited to inspect and imbibe. The following week, JJ hired a single-berth narrow boat and his enjoyable short trip confirmed his intention to acquire his own. Tardebigge Lock near Redditch were pleased to receive his instruction, and within a week a suitable boat was found which would be converted to JJ's specific requirements. Wells Builders began work on their first ever commission for a riverside wharf. Since JJ was not known for doing things by halves, Herlways' river bank became capable of accommodating three narrow boats—thus allowing future visits by some of JJ's acquaintances from his waterway wanderings. In April 1995, he assumed ownership of his own narrow boat which he named *Jenny*. The wharf was complete and he sailed leisurely and contentedly from Redditch to Herlways. Throughout the summer of 1995, JJ happily explored the inland waterways of Great Britain and, firstly as a matter of expediency and then because he found he enjoyed it, he taught himself how to cook on the small stove/galley of his splendid boat.

In late June of 1996, JJ embarked on a trip that became a turning point in his life. Travelling northward in the canal system, he turned west with the spontaneous intent to traverse the celebrated Llangollen Aqueduct from the Trevor Basin toward the Dee Valley town of Llangollen. Finding the riverside town delightful, he attempted to book a berth for the weekend and part of the following week. The refusal of his request accompanied by a look of absolute amazement awakened JJ to the popularity of the Annual International Musical Eisteddfod advertised around the town. Intrigued and now determined to prevail, JJ eventually found a berth at Trevor Basin available due to a late cancellation. Hiring a car in which to journey from Trevor to Llangollen for the second week of July proved a similar challenge, involving a taxi trip to Wrexham. The week's tickets for daily attendance, car parking and three evening concerts, made a further dent in his credit card, but the friendly ladies in the Eisteddfod office found him a single seat for the week, singles being more difficult to sell. He was seated in the centre block four rows back and five seats along the row. On an impulse, he joined the Friends of the Eisteddfod and was charmed to meet the delightful Welsh lady and Friends' chairperson, Dilys Davies.

Over the years, JJ had neglected his music. The week in Llangollen revived not only his love of music, but the spark of life extinguished by the death of Jenny. He experienced no guilt realising he had scarcely thought of his lost love during the week of the Eisteddfod. He enjoyed the competitions, the variety of music and dance and, particularly, the happy camaraderie of those around him. The only drawback to JJ's mind was the nightly uphill, wordless walk to the town cricket pitch utilised which was—apart from the square—the only car parking for patrons. The mass trek resembled what he imagined a refugees' mass migration would look like.

In the tented auditorium, JJ found himself forming a firm friendship with the married couple seated in front of him, Norris and Rose Tremain from Cheltenham. He suppressed a forbidden fondness—obviously unstated—for Rose. Standing five feet and four inches in height with natural strawberry blonde tresses descending to her shoulders, Rose's sole resemblance to Jenny was her mammarial magnificence. Norris appeared older than Rose, whilst he was certainly taller, he was also less noticeable than his wife and seemed less entranced than most with the events on stage—tending to wander away for long periods during the day. JJ enjoyed long discussions with Rose on music and the competitions.

Before the last night, JJ discovered and took advantage of the facility to reserve the same seat for the following year's Eisteddfod: everyone seated around him had done likewise. At the end of the week there was no awkwardness as the group to which serendipity seemed to have joined JJ embraced, exchanged addresses and parted with kisses and handshakes. JJ boated back to Herlways happily listening to the CDs of the various choirs he had bought on the tented site. Writ large across the second week of July 1997 in his diary was the single word, 'Llangollen'.

The family Baker were amazed at JJ's new enthusiasm. Though they tried hard to match his pleasure listening to the choir recordings, they had to confess themselves less enchanted than JJ. But they were happy for him, as Billy said, 'At long last old JJ's more like his old self.'

For the 1997 Eisteddfod, JJ had booked a berth on the canal bank within walking distance of the international show ground—thus avoiding both car hire and the refugees' rush. Despite not having seen him for almost a year, Dilys Davies gave him a warm welcome, as did others in the friends' tent. Before the first morning's competitions, JJ greeted those seated around what he already thought of as his seat, but they were all puzzled and a little concerned to see Norris and Rose's seats unoccupied—the Tremains were usually the first to arrive. The mysterious emptiness persisted until the break at the end of the second competition, when, as usual, almost everyone stood up and many left the main arena—some to relieve themselves; some to refresh themselves; some to view the hopeful tents of exhibitors and purveyors of all manner of goods and foodstuffs on site. JJ and others simply stood in their places relieving posterior pain.

As the interval drew to an end and the compère urged everyone to settle, JJ heard Alison further along his row saying, 'Oh—hello, Rose.'

Alison's voice had the falling inflection of surprise and enquiry. Rose was accompanied not by Norris, but by a severe-looking lady who seemed to find smiling difficult. Everyone around greeted Rose with a hug and a kiss and were subjected to a frown of censure from the newcomer whom Rose introduced as her friend and neighbour, Marion, who had driven them there.

Marion displayed neither friendliness nor neighbourliness.

Conversation ceased as the next choir took the stage to sing their competitive hearts out for the judges and the large audience. Despite the excellence of the singing, the small circle of friends were impatient for the next break when they hoped to learn how and why the miserable Marion was occupying Norris's seat. The next break was lunchtime—a longer interval. Rose, obviously aware her Eisteddfod friends should be informed—and preferably all at the same time—stood and, as the general hubbub of conversation accompanying the exodus to the refreshment tents retreated, she gestured them to gather around her as best they could within the closely packed seats. Marion remained seated. Rose, obviously emotional, spoke in short, staccato sentences.

'Norris died suddenly last New Year's Eve. It was a cerebral aneurism. Very quick. The doctors say he didn't suffer. Sorry I didn't write to any of you. It's been a difficult time. Marion's never been to Llangollen before, but when I said how much I'd miss it, she insisted on driving me. So, there it is. Now, please, can we all just have lunch and carry on enjoying the music—Norris would have wanted that.'

Having delivered her explanation, Rose wanted to sit down and unwrap her sandwich lunch. Obviously, though, she had to accept sympathetic and shocked hugs as everyone uttered their varying versions of apology at differing volumes. Eventually, those lunching outside the main tent departed to eat and discuss the unexpected news, those who only had packed lunches either stayed munching quietly in the main arena with some embarrassment, or took their food to eat on one of the many public seats outside. JJ, Alison and two others belatedly joined the queue for cooked lunch in the refreshment tent where they sat together and, feeling there was little to say, said little. All of her Eisteddfod friends duly took their seats for the afternoon as some show of support for Rose. There was a little general conversation with Rose during the first post-luncheon session, but halfway through the afternoon she and the mysterious Marion left with Rose's assurances that she would see them all later. Their seats remained unoccupied for the evening concert.

The following morning was devoted to dance. As had been his intention, JJ walked into the town, ate a big breakfast at the excellent café opposite the car park and strolled back to the high street intending to buy souvenirs and presents. He was surprised to see, standing alone on the opposite side of the street, a distressed Rose waiting for a break in the traffic. Watching her cross the road and walk towards the information centre it was obvious she had been—indeed still was—crying. She failed to see JJ until he caught her up and gently took her arm.

'Oh, JJ, I'm sorry—did I ignore you? I didn't see you. I . . .' She bowed her head and mopped her eyes. Without hesitation, JJ put his arm around her shoulder and led her to sit on a fortunately empty bench—JJ's arm still holding her heaving shoulders. After a while Rose took a deep breath and sat upright.

'Oh, I'm so sorry, JJ, I'm being a silly . . . This is awful.'

JJ began to remove his arm and apologise.

'Oh, don't be daft. It's not you at all. Really . . . in fact it's rather nice, thank you.'

The arm was replaced and Rose snuggled closer to JJ. As her sobbing ceased, JJ swivelled and looked into her reddened eyes—deep blue eyes in a round face with a little snub nose—framed by her luxuriant blonde hair.

'Something is obviously wrong, Rose,' said JJ softly. 'Do you want to talk about it here, or look for somewhere more private?'

Even as he said it, JJ realised that finding somewhere private in Llangollen during Eisteddfod was likely to be difficult. Rose knew this and, despite her distress, she smiled as she replied, 'Such as where?'

An entrepreneur and innovator isn't easily beaten. JJ recalled a maxim from a John Buchan novel he had enjoyed in early life, 'The best hiding place is under the light'. Adapting the maxim to the occasion, he helped Rose to her feet, escorted her across the high street and into the lounge bar of the Royal Hotel where, as JJ had suspected might be the case at ten o'clock in the morning, they were the only occupants. Briefly excusing himself from Rose, JJ found a young Welsh waitress who, easily persuaded by the £5 note pressed into her hand, agreed to bring a large pot of strong coffee and two big cups to the lounge bar. JJ returned to the lounge bar, assured Rose coffee was on its way and re-positioned a leather club chair to face Rose's similar seat.

'Do you want to tell me about it . . . or do I have to force it out of you?' he said gently.

'I need to talk to somebody, JJ, I don't know what to do. So . . . if you don't mind?'

JJ spotted the newly enriched Welsh waitress bearing a large silver tray, waved her over to the adjacent table and assured her he would dispense the coffee. Clutching the coins pressed into her hot little hand, the bemused but happy waitress left and, as instructed in a whisper, closed the door behind her.

'I don't mind in the slightest, Rose. Please talk,' said JJ in belated response.

As the—actually very good—coffee was consumed, JJ learned that Marion had been very disappointed with the music—it was not what she had expected—and after a bit of a row Marion had packed her bags and driven away to Cheltenham. They had not been close friends and Rose regretted accepting the missing Marion's offer to be a chauffeuse. Her principal problem was how to get back home to Cheltenham, there was no direct bus service and, as far as her B&B host knew, she would need to travel by several different buses or coaches at considerable cost. Should she be stranded in Llangollen beyond Sunday when her booking expired, he had further counselled her, she would have to pay premium rates for every other night under his roof, he had a business to run after all. Having paid for Marion's accommodation and been offered no refund, Rose was disinclined to pour more money into the coffers of her less-than-sympathetic host.

JJ assured her she could certainly be taken to Cheltenham, his guarantee.

'The first thing to resolve, young lady, is when.'

He gazed again into her deep blue eyes. Rose desperately returned his look and, suddenly, it all poured out, 'I need to get home as soon as possible, JJ. Not for me, but for my son.'

'You've got a son, Rose?' asked JJ—realising as he spoke it was a fatuous remark.

'He's fourteen—mature and sensible for his age. He wanted to come with me this year in place of his father, but I couldn't get a single room anywhere and the double we'd always had was reserved, and then Marion suggested, well insisted, that she bring me. Ant—that's my son—was to stay with her brother Harold. But now she's gone I can't imagine what she'll be telling him, and what Ant will be thinking and doing.'

Rose's outpouring ceased and she looked despairingly at JJ. He moved to sit beside her, he needed to clarify something.

'Forgive me, Rose,' he said, 'but quite how is miserable Marion likely to upset your son by saying she didn't like the music? Surely, by any criterion, she's in the wrong for abandoning you without transport?'

A long pause followed.

'You're right, of course, JJ,' said Rose. 'It wasn't about the music, although she did seem to have been expecting orchestras rather than singing. It was . . .' Rose glanced around the empty lounge to re-assure herself they were alone. 'Can I be frank with you, please, JJ?'

'I wish you would, Rose. Whatever this is needs to be sorted sooner rather than later, and I will help you, but I would like to understand, please.'

'Right. Don't be shocked, but that damned woman—excuse my language—actually accused me of being a lesbian whore before she stormed off in her silly little car. She's a maiden lady and I should have thought of that and been more careful. It was hot yesterday and, at her suggestion, we went back to the B&B to cool off and change. Without thinking, I just stripped off in the bedroom before going to the bathroom for a shower. She freaked. Nudity's never concerned me, but it surely concerned her. She screamed. Thank goodness there was nobody else upstairs at the time or heavens knows what they'd have thought was going on. Anyway, thoughtless me said there was nothing wrong with being naked, it *was* a bedroom, and then, more stupidly, I asked if she was going to shower. That was it. She started shrieking her hysterical accusations and shoving her things into her case before she stormed out. By the time I'd put something on and chased after her she'd driven off—much faster than she managed coming here. I was a bit upset—still am, of course, as you've noticed. I tried ringing home, but, of course, Ant's with Harold so there was no answer and they must have been out as well because there was no answer from there either. Then I ran out of coins—the miserable proprietor only lets guests use a pay-phone and he was out as well. I tried to persuade the local taxi firm to take me back—probably the biggest fare they've ever had—but they said it couldn't be done as it's Eisteddfod week Heavens knows what she's telling my fourteen-year-old son. So, you see, I do need to get home. I've telephoned this morning, but all Harold said was that Marion was home and was very upset before he put the phone down on me. I'm stranded here and . . . Oh, what can I do, JJ?'

JJ had been thinking as Rose talked.

'Right, Rose. There's a car hire firm in Wrexham I used last year and, hopefully, I can use it again. That'll get us—yes, I'll drive you, no argument please—back to Cheltenham. You say your son wanted to come to the Eisteddfod?' Rose nodded— this pleasant man she had sat in front of had become a dynamic man of action.

'Right,' continued JJ, 'I suggest, subject to his agreement, that we bring him back here today—either in your car or the hire—we can talk about that later. He can stay with me on my boat, or he can use your room at the digs and you can—no impropriety intended, it's a big boat with separate sleeping sections—stay with me. Again, we can sort that out on the way. What you need to do now is get whatever you need for the day from your lodgings whilst I get on to the Wrexham firm. If necessary, I'll have to buy them out if they start being awkward. OK?'

'Yes, yes, of course JJ. I don't need anything from the digs. But we'll need to sort out the costs of this——'

'Don't worry your lovely head about that, Rose' said JJ 'I need to find a telephone. Will you be alright here whilst I see what I can fix?'

Rose nodded. She sat back feeling amazed and grateful. Ten minutes later, JJ returned, apologising for being so long and assuring her that Wrexham were sending a suitable car down for them followed by a spare to return their driver. They would meet, the irony not lost on Rose, outside the local taxi firm's offices.

'Should be about an hour or, if we're lucky less,' continued JJ. 'I need to pop up to my boat and leave a note for my neighbours to keep an eye out in case I don't get back when they think I should. If you really don't have to get anything from your digs and don't mind walking, why don't you come with me? Better than sitting around.'

'Yes, JJ, I'd love to. You're being so kind. But, please, JJ, I'm not rich, but I'm not badly off and I like to pay my way. So, what's this car hire going to cost?'

'Nothing, dear Rose. I am rich. I don't flaunt it, or try to appear better than anyone else, but I own or part own a lot of property and several businesses, as well as my own rather opulent narrow boat—but that's of little consequence, here and now. If I can't help a damsel in distress—and a very attractive one at that—it's a sad state of affairs.'

'Oh, gosh. You're a fairy prince, JJ. I don't know what to say.'

'Well you can stop calling me a fairy for starters,' replied JJ.

For the first time since returning to Llangollen in 1997, Rose laughed. JJ joined in.

Together they walked up the steep pathway leading to the starting point for the commercial canal trips. At the top of the path they turned right and, after walking a further half mile on the tow path, Rose saw a wider section of canal where several narrow boats were moored. JJ led her to the largest and most conservatively decorated vessel, 'Welcome aboard, Madame,' he said, helping her to step from the muddy tow path onto the boat. As he unlocked the door into the cabin, JJ eased off his shoes.

'Don't like to seem fastidious, Rose, but I prefer to leave muddy shoes out here.'

Rose placed her walking shoes next to JJ's whilst he silently admired her delicate feet—but knowing this was not the time for flattery, he refrained from comment.

'Thank you,' he said, 'come on in and welcome. I'll just do a little note for next door and we can be off.'

Rose was astounded at the tidy, pristine interior. JJ proudly pointed out the lounge and diner, the kitchen (or galley), the shower room, and the stove.

'I don't want to appear forward or anything, JJ, but . . . where's the bedrooms?'

'The big double—that I tend to use, but I would willingly surrender to your son, or you—is in the bow, that's the front. The seats fold down to occupy the whole space. Similarly, the seats here in the centre area convert into either a single or a rather uncomfortable double. There's a curtain separating the front so, should you decide to stay here, you would be entirely private. And I promise to keep my eyes tight shut until you say otherwise should you decide to take a shower.'

JJ hesitated, 'Look, Rose, perhaps I shouldn't have offered you a berth. After all we hardly know one another and, well, with you recently widowed it's not quite . . . proper. The last thing I'd wish to do is—as they say in the best books—besmirch your reputation . . .'

JJ suddenly realised that Rose was laughing.

'*My* reputation, such as it is, has had more than its fair share of besmirching, JJ. Depending on which publications you read in the seventies, or your taste in films of that era, it's possible you'd be more likely to recognise me without my clothes on. But don't, as too many have done, misinterpret that.

JJ looked open-mouthed at this beautiful woman whom he had thought he had come to know a little. He definitely wanted to know more. Rose smiled enigmatically, 'Perhaps we could pass the time on the drive learning more about each other.'

'In light of what you've just said, there's no 'perhaps" involved, Rose,' said a perplexed and openly curious JJ.

The day was proving more interesting than the dancing had promised to be. JJ could hardly wait for the arrival of the hire car.

CHAPTER SIXTY-SIX

Rose—from Valley to University

1955 to 1975

Rose Antonia Rhondda Jenkinson was born on 1 March 1955 at Abercynon, South Wales, in the Welsh mining valleys. She was the only child of Idris and Mary Jenkinson. Her father was a former Welsh miner who had been invalided out of the mines due to lung congestion. Her mother had come to the valleys as Mary Abbott, the English district nurse, in order to be near her Welsh grandmother—marrying Idris ensured her continued proximity. With Mary's careful nursing, Idris recovered sufficiently to hold down an ill-paid job in the mine office until the pit, as did so many in the 1960s, closed. After which the Jenkinsons were reliant on Mary's earnings. To supplement her nurse's pay, Mary bought a second-hand Underwood iron-framed typewriter, taught herself shorthand and typing, and took in casual work. Such was the quality of her typing that she found herself with more work than she could manage, at which stage the twelve-year-old Rose was enlisted and a second cheap typewriter acquired. Since she felt it was a skill that might prove of use to her in later life, Mary taught her daughter shorthand and typing. She would never know how useful it would prove to be.

Idris gasped his last rasping breath in 1968 whilst straining for a high note during his favourite hymn. The chapel service was discontinued and Rose's father taken by strong men weeping to the nearby undertaker's. Despite their poverty, the Jenkinson's was a happy home. Although considered a star pupil, when Rose was sixteen she and Mary reached the inevitable conclusion that she must leave school in order to earn more money and supplement her mother's earnings. Before that decision could be implemented, Mary's mother, Grace, who had done the Pools for many years with no success, became a big winner, her half-share of the jackpot amounting to £42,462. The old lady had no idea what to do with her suddenly acquired wealth—lavish celebrations and holidays were things other people did and she had no wish to share their experiences. There were a few luxuries with which she spoiled herself, but her principal pleasure was the ability to help her daughter and beloved grand-daughter. With her mother's money, Mary bought a modest detached house suitable for her mother, herself and Rose; for the first time in their lives, they were not paying rent. Mary also bought a small car and learned to drive. To the delight of her teachers, Rose remained at school, became a prefect and was awarded examination grades which easily qualified her for Bristol University where she intended to study biology and anthropology. She was the first in her family to gain university entrance.

Mary and her mother shed proud tears in Bristol before Rose waved them off on their return journey to the other side of the Bristol Channel, an easy trip due to the seven-year-old Severn Bridge.

Rose's first year at Bristol was as happy and educationally stimulating as she had hoped it would be. She was popular amongst her fellow students, enjoyed hockey and student life, wrote home regularly and visited her mother at half terms and holidays. She shared a three-bedroom house with four fellow students—two girls and two boys. Rose shared a bedroom with Martha; Dorothy and Graham—already 'an item'— shared a smaller double; and Dean, by virtue of having negotiated the rental, was allowed the single room next to the bathroom. They rubbed along well together. Martha cooked on condition she did no washing up, most of which was left to Rose. When Martha fell into her first love and left, Rose found herself both cook and bottle washer; there were frequent arguments, and the only thing on which all four agreed was they would *not* be sharing digs for a second year. During the last week, having no further lectures to attend, Rose and Dean decided to finish the last wine from the communal store. As the wine went down, so did their defences. Giggling, they agreed they were probably the only two virgins in their year, a state of isolation they ought not to allow to continue. The consequent clumsy fumble and tumble on the badly sprung settee was neither satisfactory nor terribly enjoyable, the encore on Dean's single bed was not a great deal better, but they parted friends and never sought a repeat performance.

Two months into Rose's second year at college her grandmother died. Rose cried both at the funeral and in the dingy solicitor's office where Mr Emrys Williams informed her the old lady had left her £10,000. Acting on impulse, Rose bought a small flat in Bristol and invited two fellow students to share the second bedroom at less rent than they had paid elsewhere. Her world seemed idyllic, until her mother wrote to say she had met and become engaged to a lovely man. Before meeting Carl

Mortimer, Rose had reservations. Having met him, she questioned her mother's sanity and feared for her safety. The flashy financial adviser had obviously beguiled her mother, who had a fervent infatuation with him and all he said and did. Rose's veiled warnings were brushed aside. The furious argument in which Mary accused Rose of jealousy ended with Rose storming out and returning to Bristol, where she remained, resolutely refusing to attend the registry office wedding.

Her flatmates returned to their respective homes for the autumn vacation and Rose, in her first flush of infatuation, eagerly welcomed her boyfriend Gareth to stay. For two days and nights they wore only smiles—wandering around the flat unable to avoid groping and caressing one another if they had been apart for more than a moment. On the third day, Gareth had to return to Clevedon for his mother's birthday, promising to return that evening. Rose waved him off and left to buy some food.

When she returned, a police car was parked outside the flats and a sombre-faced policewoman waited at her door. Having established her identity, the officer informed Rose that her mother had been pronounced dead following a road traffic accident the previous night. Gareth was annoyed to find an empty flat on his return, from which he had to return to Clevedon later that night. He and Rose never spoke again.

Rose's return to South Wales was the most traumatic of her young life. Her mother was not the only victim of the accident; Mr Carl Mortimer, the driver of the vehicle, died in hospital a few hours after being admitted, blood tests proving him to have been in a drunken state at the wheel. Worse news followed. Mortimer had invested Mary's monies in high-risk funds that were now worthless and had also fraudulently double-mortgaged her little house and frittered away the proceeds. Rose was heir to nothing save shame and debts.

Emrys Williams, the solicitor, arranged a short-term bank loan against his personal assurance that the sale of Miss Jenkinson's Bristol flat would take place soon and cover the loan. There was enough over to pay for her mother's modest funeral. Through Mr Williams, Rose entered a legal disclaimer of responsibility for Mortimer's burial. She could not so easily rid herself of the remaining debts her stepfather had manipulated as being due by her mother. There was little relief in the life assurance policy that Mary had maintained—the proceeds of that were swiftly swallowed by the estate in bankruptcy of her mother. Old Emrys Williams patted Rose's hand; insisted that, in the circumstances, he was not asking her for any fees for his firm's services in the sad matter; and failed to brighten Rose's outlook by asking her to confirm the arrangement with the creditors whereby a percentage of Rose's future earnings would be taken until the balance of sums still due was cleared. Rose had no alternative but to sign the deed, drop out of university and seek work. She was no better off than before her grandmother had scooped half the football Pools jackpot, reflected Rose. She had to start over again—and from a less than promising point.

CHAPTER SIXTY-SEVEN
ROSE—FROM POVERTY TO PROSPERITY
1975 TO 1997

Rose Jenkinson, aged twenty, with debts the depths of which she hardly dared contemplate was, though she may have disputed it, fortunate. She did not have to look very hard for employment; the Bristol solicitors who old Emrys Williams had engaged to assist with the sale of Rose's flat had a vacancy for a junior secretary and typist. Recommended by Mr Williams, and bearing a flattering letter of commendation from him, Rose was interviewed and almost immediately offered a job with Hodges and Youngjohn. With all the associations of the last few months, she had no wish to remain in Abercynon and rented a very small, cheap flat in Clifton. With difficulty, and no social life or entertainment save a portable radio, she managed to make financial ends meet during the next year despite the 10 per cent deduction from her earnings taken by the ever-voracious creditors. She was lonely and loveless, yet remained cheerful and popular at work. From her Christmas bonus—kindly paid in cash by an understanding chief clerk—she purchased a music centre and several recordings that gave her some restful enjoyment in the evenings.

Rose was a conscientious worker and, by dint of application and study—for which she had ample time—she became a valued employee. She was scarcely aware of the advent of her twenty-first birthday, but her employers had taken note of her date of birth from her job application and Rose was amazed and emotionally moved by the surprise party they threw her. The party prevented her early return to her little flat and led to her being a little inebriated at her place of work. She was aware of the photographer—a client of the practice—who took a great number of pictures, particularly of Rose, and who promised her a souvenir album as his birthday present to her. She had not expected him to deliver the present in person to her little flat a few days later, even less had she expected him to make an offer that would, unbeknownst to her, effect the next major change in her life.

'If you'll excuse my saying so, Miss Jenkinson,' said Donald Bayliss, photographer, standing awkwardly inside Rose's front door, 'you are a very attractive young lady and, what is not always so with pretty women, you are very photogenic. Would you be offended if I asked whether you would agree to my taking a series of posed shots of you? You would be paid, of course.'

Rose had been on the point of refusing until the offer of payment was mentioned. In her ongoing penury the chance of any further income was not to be refused. Mr Bayliss's offer of an initial £25 with the possibility of more should she agree to him submitting her likenesses to various accepting publications, was a far better present than the very nice, bound album he had already presented to her.

'What should I wear, Mr Bayliss?' asked Rose.

'A smile is the most important thing, Rose. And its Don, please,' replied Bayliss.

There was an awkward silence whilst Rose wondered whether to press the point. Realising he may have been too bold too soon, Bayliss told Rose to bring her nicest dress and her bathing costume—preferably a bikini. 'If that's all right?' he added.

The lure of the money was still strong, so it was agreed that Rose should be at Bayliss's studio at 6.30 p.m. on the following Saturday.

When Rose confided her tryst with the photographer to Mrs Winters during the following morning's coffee break, that lady was of the opinion that Bayliss only wanted to get into her knickers and that she should stay away, if she knew what was good for her.

Somewhat deflated, Rose spent the next two days debating with herself as to whether she should or should not keep her appointment with Don Bayliss. She had no intention of entertaining carnal relations with him, but he had been kind and charming and the £25 would be very welcome. Rose's only bathing costume was a rather old one piece in which she had gone swimming during her first year at college: certainly not a glamorous garment in which to be photographed. She felt the expense of acquiring a bikini might be justified until she discovered, on a tentative Saturday morning shopping expedition, the price of two skimpy bits of brightly coloured material. Walking away from the stores feeling miserable, she found herself passing the end of the street in which, so his card stated, Don Bayliss had his Elite Photography Studios. Rose decided to call in and offer her apologies for the coming evening—it was the polite thing to do. In fact, so far as her future was concerned, it was the right thing to do, although Rose did not know that.

As Rose approached the doorway, a tall girl in a trouser suit and cap came hurriedly out—not so hurriedly that she could not stop to hold the door for Rose. As Rose passed her, she said, 'You're bloody late, luv. He's not very happy with you.'

The door closed behind a puzzled Rose. Deciding that the brief encounter had been a case of mistaken identity, she began the ascent of the long, straight staircase. As she neared the top she heard the street door bang and footsteps hastening up behind her. Another girl in a trouser suit—no cap, but a luxuriant head of long, flowing, jet-black hair was literally running up the stairs. Rose flattened herself against the wall to allow her to pass.

'Thanks dear—I'm late,' she said as she passed Rose and rushed to the right-hand door. Rose's second thoughts gave way to third ones—obviously Mr Bayliss was busy, perhaps she could telephone him.

'You coming, love?' she heard the dark haired girl say. She was holding open the door, clearly marked 'Studio' and looking impatiently at Rose. Pushing herself away from the wall, Rose muttered an apology, mounted the few remaining stairs and was able to catch the self-closing door the other woman had left swinging towards her and enter Don Bayliss's workplace.

The studio was vast. Separate small areas were decorated with background scenery and fronted by large white umbrellas and tall stands supporting lamps. On one of the small sets a naked girl posed for the camera. To her right, Rose could hear the nice photographer she had come to see mouthing obscenities at the dark-haired woman who was responding in similarly colourful language. The gist of the conversation, if it could warrant such a polite description, seemed to be that the woman was late and alone. Both of which situations appeared to pose Bayliss problems.

'Look, Don,' said the dark-haired woman in an almost threatening tone, 'I've spent 'alf the soddin' morning lookin' everywhere for 'er. You know it's not the first time bloody Flavia's gone walk about. I can't find 'er and that's that.'

'And where the —— am I going to find a busty blonde at a moment's notice, Tanya? Answer me that if you can,' yelled back Bayliss.

'Well I just passed one on the stairs,' said Tanya. She turned around. Rose was standing inside the door looking open-mouthed at them. 'Sorry, dear—come on in. Don't mind old, Don.'

She turned back to face Bayliss. 'See, Don, she's younger and better stacked than Flavia, so quit beefin'.'

Only now did the distracted Don Bayliss become aware of Rose. He began to stammer an apology, Rose did likewise, but the insistence of Tanya that Rose could be a replacement for the disappeared Flavia intruded on their mutual excuses. After the misunderstandings had been cleared up, Tanya persisted in her firmly stated opinion that Rose could be June.

'If she's not done it before, I'll 'elp 'er. So long as she's paid proper.'

Rose, feeling she ought to make some representation for herself, said that she would be quite happy with the twenty-five pounds Mr Bayliss had offered. This prompted another outburst from Tanya from which it emerged that twenty-five pounds was, in Tanya's words, 'A bloody insult.' Her protest that from what she could see Rose was worth ten times that, made Rose pay more attention.

It was patiently, but hastily, explained to Rose that replacing Flavia involved, as she had already suspected, being photographed in the nude. The overall assignment was for a calendar, and amongst the requirements of the printers and publishers was the specific insistence on a blonde girl to represent June. The lure of the money overcame any modest scruples Rose may have had, her few days' sexual abandon with Gareth had cured her of any shyness or inhibitions about exposing herself. She agreed to, as Tanya succinctly stated, 'Save Don's bacon,' and, together with her unexpected promoter, Rose disrobed in the well-appointed changing cubicles. Tanya was obviously well-practised since she was utterly naked long before Rose began removing her brassiere.

'Oh, Gawd, love, you ought not to wear one o' them comin' to a shoot,' said Tanya and, without a word of apology or by-your-leave, began massaging Rose's shoulders.

'Gotta get rid of the strap marks on yer skin, Rose. The camera can see 'em even if you can't.'

She leaned around the cubicle curtain to enquire of Bayliss whether 'A bit o' tan' might be needed on Rose. Apparently it would. From the large bag she had been carrying, Tanya produced a can of spray and proceeded to apply it all over Rose—instructing her to rub it evenly on her front whilst Tanya attended to the back. She then inspected Rose and, speaking more tentatively than before, she indicated Rose's lower regions.

'You'll need to get rid of the pubes if you want any more of this work, Rose.'

Rose was confused. Tanya produced another tube from her bag and advised that Rose should use the contents as instructed to remove her pubic hair.

'No time to do that now, dear. Keep yer 'and on yer a'penny for today.'

Rose had shyly observed Tanya's body to be utterly devoid of hair—despite her exuberant head of dark locks. Before they emerged to still Bayliss's impatient demands, Tanya attended to Rose's facial make up—explaining as she did so that her fair hair and complexion were great, but for the camera her eyebrows and eyelashes needed darkening if they were to show up on the prints. 'Leave 'em as they are and you'll look as though you've empty sockets and no eyebrows.'

As advised, Rose, clad only in a flimsy dressing robe, watched the unclad Tanya adopt poses and facial expressions dictated by Bayliss whilst he took what seemed an inordinately large number of photographs of her as Miss May. Rose was a quick learner and her stint as Miss June earned compliments from both Bayliss and Tanya. If she were honest with herself, Rose was so concerned with adopting the correct poses and showing the camera the expressions demanded, she almost forgot she was completely naked. Before she started to get dressed a discussion, instigated by Tanya, took place which resulted in a request for Rose and Tanya donning tiaras and very short white skirts in which they represented highly unlikely Santa's little fairies for the December page of the calendar.

Having spent what suddenly seemed an exhausting three hours posing and preening, Rose dressed herself. Before she left, Bayliss's assistant handed her cheque, having been checked for correctness by Tanya. Rose was astounded; in three hectic hours she had earned more than Hodges and Youngjohn paid her for a month's work. As they descended the stairs, feeling she should do more than thank Tanya, Rose suggested she buy them both a high tea at the nearby posh café. To her surprise and delight, Tanya accepted. When they had seated themselves and ordered, Rose noticed that since they had left the studio Tanya's accent—Rose thought it could be Cockney but was later laughingly told it was merely London (pronounced 'Landan') had disappeared. Tanya now spoke in clear, cut-glass Queen's English.

'Matter of fact, Rose, I'm thinking you could help me again tomorrow—if you're not busy. Flavia was supposed to come with me on a little film shoot and it'll help me and the film lot if you could come along.'

'What do I have to do, Tanya?' asked a rather nervous Rose.

'Not a lot, love. It's not a hard porn film if that's what you're worried about. It's one of these "you can be better if you try" sort of soft porn dos masquerading as educational. We just stand or sit around in the altogether for an hour or so with a lot of others, most of the men are poofs, so there's no hanky panky. I'll look after you. We get paid in cash for this one, no questions asked and no lies told.'

Tanya paused to check whether Rose appeared interested. Rose had no plans for Sunday. Even more money just for standing or sitting around in the altogether seemed almost too good to be true. Another exorbitant sum had been mentioned. Rose nodded her agreement.

Tanya smiled and continued, 'It's an early start, of course, all films are, but if that's OK, I'll give them a ring.'

Again, a bemused Rose nodded in silent acquiescence. This can't be happening to me, she thought. But it obviously was.

Tanya summoned a passing waitress and, in her posh voice that seemed to command attention, enquired if there was a telephone she might use. Assuring Rose she would be back before she knew it, Tanya left to follow the waitress's directions.

'You're on for tomorrow, love,' she said a few minutes later as she sat back opposite Rose and began giving directions to the location.

'Oh, gosh, Tanya, I'm sorry,' Rose interrupted. 'I don't have a car—and I couldn't drive it if I had, I'm afraid.'

The lure of riches receded for Rose, temporarily. Tanya seemed to be a permanent problem solver; in Tanya's car—a shiny new model to Rose's surprise—Rose was driven to her little flat only for as long as it took to gather up her night things and a selection from her small wardrobe as dictated by Tanya. Tanya then drove, rather fast Rose thought, to Cheltenham where not only was the morrow's shoot to take place, but where Tanya lived. Rose was introduced to Tanya's man, Carson, before being shown to a small, single bedroom and advised that they needed to get an early night as they would be leaving for the set at 5.00 a.m. It was the earliest Rose had ever risen. In her halcyon college days, 5.00 a.m. had occasionally been bedtime; here she was being told that she would be leaving her bed before cock's crow. Rose denuded herself of pubic hair using Tanya's depilatory cream before showering away the remains of the fake tan in Tanya's luxurious bathroom.

During depilation, and with no hint of embarrassment in what Rose privately felt a bizarre situation, the question of Rose's working name was discussed. Apparently, it was almost unheard of for anyone to 'work in the nuddy' under their own name—to avoid possible future problems—Tanya did not elaborate, but time taught Rose her meaning. Tanya's real name, Rose learned, after swearing to tell no one, was Doris Johnson. A totally confused Rose had no idea what she might call herself should she, as Tanya was promising, 'earn a small fortune with knockers like yours.' Allowing herself to be guided by her insistent new mentor, Rose agreed to adopt an abbreviated version of her own second, and never before utilised, forename. Tanya rather liked the sound of Tanya and Tonia—particularly as they both had the same vital statistics—the only differences being their colouring and Tanya standing two inches taller than Rose. Little did either of them appreciate on that Saturday evening how propitious their similarities were to become.

During the shoot, which was as boring and chilly as Tanya had warned, they were promoted to non-speaking, but more prominent roles as the dark and fair guardians of the mysterious private rooms in which apparently terrible things occurred. For these roles they wore very revealing dresses—Rose felt more self-conscious in her dress than she had in the nude. Tanya had been quick to extort more money for their further involvement, for which the still bemused Rose/Tonia could only be grateful. She was content to leave negotiations to Tanya. The only thing that puzzled her, and for which she sought enlightenment as soon as they were alone, was the query posed to her about her agent. Before Rose had been able to reply, Tanya had answered, 'John Carr and Son— same as meself,' (the London accent was back).

Tanya's patient explanation during one of the many breaks informed Rose that, 'You need an agent to negotiate fees and arrange bookings—I hope you don't mind me putting you down as with us? We'll sort the contracts out when we get back to Cheltenham. And don't let 'em think you've got a brain unless you need to—broaden your Welsh accent when you speak to most snappers—it makes them feel superior.

They returned to Tanya and Carson's spacious Cheltenham apartment on Lansdowne Road where it was explained in strict confidence to Rose that Doris Johnson and Carson Worth were actually Mr and Mrs Worth, but for professional purposes this was better not known, or spoken of. They were the sole proprietors and directors of John Carr & Son Limited (a clever combination of their real names)— Artistes Representation. Their charges—known as commission—were 10 per cent of fees negotiated and received plus the fairly new Value Added tax. Clients' fees were all paid into their business bank—clients' account—and forwarded to the 'artiste', less commission and VAT, within fourteen days. In the circumstances, they were happy to ignore commission on the two engagements Rose/Tonia had already done and been paid for. A contract was produced from Carson's business case and Tanya complained, as it seemed she always did, about 'having to wrestle with the damn typewriter.' Rose offered to assist and Carson and Tanya expressed surprise and delight at her keyboard skill. So much so that

Carson tentatively suggested she might like to work in their office besides being a client and model. The salary mentioned was far in excess of her Hodges and Youngjohn's pay—Carson explained it reflected the fact of their principal office being in London where Rose would be based with them for four days of the week unless she and/or Tanya were not working elsewhere. For modelling work Rose would be working freelance and would need to register as a self-employed person and submit accounts and a tax return every year. Carson felt certain that, if Rose was prepared to change her life in so radical a manner, it would be financially beneficial. He could recommend their Cheltenham-based accountant to deal with her accounts and taxation. Carson was older and more patient than his wife and suggested Rose sleep on it, and then let them know at the end of the week. Rose slept little that Sunday night. Driving her back to Bristol early on Monday morning, Tanya urged her to 'make the break, Rose—you'll not regret it.'

The decision seemed obvious—it was a win/win situation. She would be earning a better wage typing for Tanya and Carson and, since they seemed insistent she live under their roof, she would avoid paying rent on her Clifton flat; she would have no regrets about leaving there. It was the step into the almost unknown that seemed so final and frightening. During Monday at Hodges and Youngjohn, Rose remained distracted and undecided. A Tuesday telephone call for her. 'Private calls are frowned upon, Miss Jenkinson,' proved the persuasive push. Carson apologised for intruding upon her at work, but following the filming on Sunday her doorkeepers double act with Tanya had been admired and Carson had received an unexpected and dramatic offer he would love to accept—acceptance being dependent upon Rose's agreement. A reputable film company were anxious to engage the 'dark and fair ladies' for a feature film. The gross fees Rose would receive, less agent's commission, of course, could clear her dear mother's outstanding debts with something left over. In addition, an unprecedented double of the topless Tanya and Tonia on page three of a national paper was being mooted with a further staggering sum involved. Casting aside her doubts, Rose told Carson to accept the film and push for the page three feature. She would hand in her notice at Hodges and Youngjohn and begin anew.

Over the next three years almost every girlie magazine featured Tanya and Tonia in artistic, provocative, but never lewd poses reprising their much vaunted and popular 'twosome act'. As a double act, Tanya and Tonia featured in several 'skin flicks', two small feature films and one major horror film. In between, Rose re-organised and made more efficient the London and Cheltenham offices of John Carr & Son, earning her increased fees for her freelance secretarial services. For the first eighteen months of her new life, she lived with her agents and protectors, but in June 1978 she acceded to the repeated proposals of her besotted accountant, Norris Tremain, and became a married woman. The new Mrs Tremain resided in his Charlton Kings house whenever she was in Cheltenham, although the never-ending flow of work meant she was never in the Cheltenham suburb for long. Norris seemed content to be, at thirty-seven years of age, a married man whether his wife was at home or not, the status was more important to him than what many considered the obligations of a husband.

After a year of near inactivity in the marital bed, Rose chose, always with discretion, to seek sexual solace elsewhere. She had emulated her mother by buying and learning to drive a car in which she and Tanya— they alternated driving stints whenever they worked together—travelled all over England. Overseas engagements, arranged by Carson, had travel and accommodation provided. Free of debt, Rose ceased to worry about money and almost lost track of her earnings, Norris looked after all that. Her income tax and other statutory obligations were kept up to date and she was appraised of her personal financial position whether she asked or not. Rose Tremain, née Jenkinson, k/a Tonia, was becoming a wealthy woman.

Tanya was five years older than Rose. Ever open and honest, she had never made any secret of the fact that the career of a topless model was short—the flesh did not retain firm freshness forever and, according to Tanya, she, and probably Rose, would be finished by the age of thirty. True to her word, and not even risking the experience of finding herself unwanted, Tanya retired in 1979 at only twenty-nine and devoted herself to the ongoing success of John Carr & Son. Rose ceased to work in the John Carr offices, but modelling and even some acting continued to be offered and accepted. In the spring of 1982 she travelled to the South of France to appear in a French film directed by the fabled Jules Gaston. By her second weekend—no work on Saturday and Sunday by Gaston's decree—she had succumbed to his Gallic charms and the weekends were spent at a secluded villa outside Cannes. Rose's few days with Gareth were a pale adventure by contrast. She and Jules knew the *affaire* was simply a matter of sex, and no ongoing entanglement was implied or intended. Rose returned from Nice airport by Club Class flight, courtesy of Jules. Overnighting in London, she found herself, for the first time since puberty, missing a period. Instinctively, she knew she was pregnant.

On her return to Charlton Kings the following night she deliberately seduced Norris.

On the 20 February 1983, Rose gave birth to a healthy baby boy of nine pounds and five ounces. Norris was delighted. The boy was christened Anthony Norris Tremain and became, forever, acronymically and affectionately known as ANT. If Norris ever noticed that his son seemed to have inherited few, if any, of his physical characteristics, he never commented. Norris entered him for Stow School where he, himself, had been educated. Rose had, of course, given up work in 1982, but she continued to receive offers for television advertisements—having been considered successful in that medium before her pregnancy. The fees were welcome, but the residuals—repeat fees for ads the promoters considered were still selling their products—brought her an easy income and paid for the nanny necessary to care for young Ant whilst Rose shot yet more short promotional epics. Doris (she had dropped the Tanya tag) and Carson were happy to be both agents and godparents.

Norris tentatively suggested Rose return to office work as he was having difficulty finding secretaries willing to apply themselves to the vagaries of the programmable typewriters and computers now available. Rose was not keen on working for her husband whom, she had to admit (but only to herself) was a dull stick compared to the outgoing and extrovert characters with whom she had mingled in her frantic few years as a model and actress. Equally dull, she found, was the work of a chartered accountant's office: although many of Norris's clients hailed from the world she had almost left behind, any contact she had with them was either by telephone or letter and served to irritate her as second hand and almost voyeuristic. She did find the challenge of computerisation stimulating and met it with relish and, more so than others with whom she spoke, success. Despite this, Rose was restless and strangely unfulfilled in her new life.

A chance meeting in 1989 with Martha, her college first year room mate, whilst shopping in fashionable Cavendish House, provided the catalyst for Rose's resumption of education. She and Martha repaired to the coffee shop where they remained throughout a light lunch, discovering what each was prepared to disclose of their activities in the fifteen years since they last met. Martha had abandoned her first lover, studied hard, graduated with a first class degree; become a teacher, lecturer, wife and mother, and was now in her first year as a tutor with the eleven-year-old Open University. Rose had been aware of Harold Wilson's initiative in making higher education available to the masses, but had not taken sufficient notice of what was now so easily available. Talking with Martha, she realised that she could now, with accumulated earnings and financial freedom, achieve the degree she had once so keenly sought and had had to abandon due to her poor mother's foolish infatuation. Within a month, she had applied for and been accepted as an Open University pupil. The demands of parenthood and her studies took precedence, in Rose's order of priorities, over any advertising, modelling or office work. She had sufficient savings on which to live and purchase the books required for study, and Norris's practice, despite the lack of competent secretaries, brought in enough for them to live as well as they wished to, whilst providing for their growing son. Rose threw herself into her studies and, with diligence and some lack of sleep—the O.U. broadcasts were transmitted at odd, unsocial hours—she finally became a bachelor of arts in 1993. It was all she could do to remain dry eyed during the conferral of her degree in Walton Hall, Milton Keynes.

Her graduation would have been earlier but for the disruption of Norris's first heart attack in 1991. For three months Rose found herself, with the assistance of a sympathetic and competent staff whom she had found and engaged, effectively in charge of her husband's practice. She was relieved when Norris felt able to resume full-time work but, taking their doctor's advice, they sought more rest and relaxation than either of them had hitherto mutually enjoyed. Thus, in 1993, the Tremains first attended the Llangollen International Musical Eisteddfod. For their first two years of attendance, all three Tremains travelled to the Vale of Llangollen, staying in the best accommodation they could find for three at a small former farm in the village of Froncysyllte. At age twelve Ant began what were to be happy school days at Stow and, avoiding the shame of admitting to fellow pupils he vacationed with his parents, he ceased accompanying Rose and Norris to the Eisteddfod. Rose found a bed and breakfast in Llangollen from which they could, and did, walk daily to the competitions and concerts.

Having decided against the further period of intense study necessary to be a master of arts—a course had been urged upon her at two prestigious universities—Rose had little to occupy her still active mind. Eventually, she secured a part-time teaching post at the prestigious Cheltenham Ladies College. She enjoyed it and was popular with the staff—particularly the librarian Barbara Brownlow, whom she voluntarily assisted. As a consequence of which, when Barbara was due to retire, the authorities looked kindly on Rose's application to succeed her as college librarian. She was appointed to a post she loved in September 1996.

Norris and Rose continued to attend the Eisteddfod where they managed, due to someone dropping out, to secure excellent seats. They became permanent Eisteddfod guests at the F&B. Walking to and from the show ground saved daily car travel and car parking fees—Norris still counted small gains. Rose, and Ant until he ceased to attend, always enjoyed the singing and competitive aspect more than Norris, and since Rose insisted she would not be lonely with her Eisteddfod friends around her, Norris often absented himself during the day.

Nineteen ninety-seven was a year of contrasts for Rose. It began with her holding her husband's corpse in her arms on their front drive. The New Year party at a neighbour's house had been the usual eat-and-wait-for-next-year-to-start affair, but Norris had felt very unwell during the eating ('no reflection on your food at all, I do assure you') and with many apologies and early wishes for the coming year, they left at 11.30. He had felt strange in the car, but insisted there was no need to visit the hospital—such a call would not, medical opinion later stated, have affected the outcome. As he left the car, driven by Rose, Norris groaned loudly, leaned on the car holding his head and, as Rose ran around to his side, subsided into her arms. He was, she was told, dead before she lowered him to the ground. By the time an ambulance arrived, it was 1997. The irony of church bells and fireworks heralding his death would have amused Norris.

Ant returned from a party with friends to be told of his father's demise. Mother and son, principally mother, arranged what they felt to be a suitable funeral.

At such times, any help is much valued and the kindness of their near neighbours, Marion and Harold—unmarried brother and sister—was a great comfort. Prior to Norris's demise, they had had little contact and even less in common with their neighbours, but the Christian charity Marion and Harold felt they must extend to all in distress was, initially, very welcome for Rose. As the months passed, their continuing intrusion became slightly suffocating for Rose. Ant, with the resilience of the young, returned to Stow and avoided most of the stultifying care. Rose was glad of the excuse to leave the house for long days and most weekends to look after Norris's practice whilst continuing her school librarian's duties. A fellow accountant with an office nearby was, for agreed fees, administering the practice whilst a suitable buyer, whom he felt himself not to be due to the 'artistic' nature of the clientele, was found. At Marion's insistence, Rose had paid for her Eisteddfod tickets and confirmed the double room booking for Llangollen 1997. Marion

still regarded Rose as in her care and was adamant that, despite never
having been to an Eisteddfod, she would attend, and in order that Rose
should not have to endure 'the trauma of driving all that way', she would
transport her to Llangollen. Within the first few slow, tortuous miles
of the journey north, Rose began devoutly wishing she had not acceded
to Marion's dictate to drive. The journey took over an hour longer than
had been the norm and the trauma of being Marion's passenger was far
greater than would have been the obligation to drive herself. It was a
warning of worse to come.

CHAPTER SIXTY-EIGHT
Llangollen, Love and a Proposal
1997 to 1998

As they emerged from the café opposite the town car park, Rose had been hailed by an anxious looking, friendly Welsh woman—the wife of her B&B host. Wendy—that being her name—was eager to advise Rose that her son had telephoned an hour ago, but that she hadn't known where or how to find her.

'Did he leave a message?'

'Yes, yes, I was to tell you not to worry and that he's returned home.'

Rose had, with JJ's assistance and a small bribe, used the café telephone to speak to her son. The lad had been frustrated by the narrow attitude of Marion's brother, Harold, and had argued with him about saying his prayers. When Marion returned unexpectedly, Ant had remonstrated with her for abandoning his mother and Marion had answered, in tones of utter disgust, that his mother had exposed herself to Marion. Ant replied that his mother had once made a good living exposing herself. His rejoinder had sparked off further shocked protestations and accusations of wickedness and worse, resulting in Ant storming out of their house, returning home and locking himself in. Harold was, with boring regularity, coming to the door to tell Ant that it was not legal for him to be alone at his age, but, so far, despite pious threats, the authorities had not materialised. From what he heard, JJ adjudged Ant to be an intelligent and surprisingly mature fourteen-year-old.

Whilst no resolution as to who would sleep where had been reached, Rose told Ant that she and a good friend were coming to collect him and he should pack a case as he would be spending the rest of the week at the Eisteddfod. Ant was delighted. Rose was far calmer than when JJ had first encountered her that morning.

Rose and JJ discussed accommodation and agreed that it would be prudent and seemly in her son's eyes—despite his worldliness—were Ant to stay with JJ. Both Rose and JJ were honest and open with one another in admitting they would have wished it otherwise, and there was an unspoken understanding of future familiarity.

JJ and Rose journeyed from Llangollen to Cheltenham in some style and in far less time than it had taken Marion to drive the route two days previously. By the time JJ had treated Rose and her son to what was generally considered the best lunch available in Cheltenham, he and Ant had formed an unlikely, friendly bond. The lad was eager for the new experience of sleeping on a narrow boat, as he did for the remainder of the week. To allow her independence and the ability to return herself and her son home unaided at the end of the week, whilst JJ boated home at the leisurely pace of the waterways, Rose had driven her own car back to North Wales—following JJ in the hire car to Wrexham and then returning him to base.

The three of them enjoyed their week. With the frank perception of a bright teenager, Ant had told JJ that, 'You fancy my Mum, don't you?'

Not wishing to deceive the lad, JJ had confessed that he did, indeed, fancy Rose, but that Ant should not expect any sudden developments whilst the death of his father remained recent. JJ had no answer to Ant's statement that they hadn't seemed to have been very together for some time. But he took quiet comfort from the lad's view. By the end of the week, developments decreed there would be ongoing contact between all three for the foreseeable future. JJ had telephoned his partners in Whitehouse, Butler and Rock, chartered accountants who were agreeable to acquiring the practice of the late Norris Tremain. Establishing an arts wing to the Avonbridge firm was deemed to be at least a good, and at best a brilliant, strategy for further expansion. By 1999, Artistetax—the new style of the firm's arts wing—had established an office in Covent Garden, London and was expanding faster than even JJ could have imagined under the eager supervision of David Smith the London office manager. John Carr and Son were also growing apace and were sending all their new clients, and several of longer standing, to be represented by Artistetax for their business and taxation requirements.

JJ had, despite feeling it not quite right, sat up late every night in the narrow boat talking with young Ant and, as tactfully as he could, rationing the young man's intake of bottled beer. JJ learned that Norris had so constantly insisted that Ant become a chartered accountant and inherit his firm that Ant had developed a teenager's firm resolve not to so structure his future. Ant's ambition, JJ eventually elicited, was to be a professional sportsman—although quite which of the several sports at which he seemingly excelled would provide him with a living had as yet to be resolved. Ant was happy that he had found a grown up who did not mock his ambitions. Ant's unexpectedly high placing in the

British Amateur Golfers Championship at the age of sixteen sealed his destiny and, to his mother's delight, he eventually became a well-known international professional golfer with consistently high tournament finishes and earnings—the latter resulting in his becoming resident in Monaco and saving himself burdens of taxation. The savings were somewhat, though not wholly, offset by the high cost of living there.

When Ant returned to school in September 1997, Rose, by mutual agreement, spent most weekends with JJ. The initial excuse for seeing each other employed by both of them was to allow her to travel and stay on the narrow boat as she had wished to. Although they did cruise the Severn for an hour or so during weekends, the majority of their time together was spent in one another's arms and JJ's bed. They were both very happy with life and one another. At half term, Rose spent the week with JJ as Ant was on a rugby tour with the school. They visited London, ostensibly to see the potential new offices and to spend time with Doris and Carson, although they actually indulged in many of the touristy things neither had found time to enjoy previously.

In December 1997 Chandlery Lodge—who never held a lodge meeting in the last month of the year—held the usual supper and songs (i.e. carols, but they liked the traditional alliteration) evening at the lodge rooms for brethren, their wives and families. By unalliterated tradition, they always invited the widows of deceased lodge members. Brethren were expected to bring along any friends who might be interested in becoming Freemasons, and this resulted in two suitable gentlemen eventually being initiated in the following year. Norris had been a member of a Gloucestershire lodge, but had never been very active in the fraternity and, although she tried to understand JJ's position and enthusiasm, Rose was apprehensive of attending. Her fears were calmed by the warm welcome she received from several of the lodge wives and the near rapturous reception almost everyone gave to JJ. When she was able to quietly ask, she learned that during the year JJ had received grand rank (accorded the honour of being made an officer of United Grand Lodge).

During the early years of her former career—and since in less intensity—Rose had become used to the penetrating looks of many men as they tried to recall where they had seen her before, and the ensuing sly glances of some as they recollected when and how they had viewed her curvaceous charms. As time passed, the incidences of recognition had become less frequent, but on a December night at the Avonbridge Masonic hall it was obvious to Rose that some local brethren had been (might still be?) closet readers of certain glossy magazines. She and JJ giggled about the identities of those who had evidently recognised Rose as the former Tonia and their attempts to conceal from their wives their former cognisance of JJ's lady.

The only other peculiarity to what was a pleasant evening was the strangely changed to a friendly attitude of Mrs Caitlin Fisher towards JJ. JJ had been told she had attended the previous year and was, in Billy's words, 'remarkably well-behaved—for her'. Recalling Caitlin's former animosity, JJ was still apprehensive about meeting her but, to his surprise, Mrs Fisher seemed eager to talk with him, enquire how he was, and where he was now living. Although he would never have dreamed of inviting Mrs Fisher to his home, it would have appeared churlish not to divulge his address. Rose was curious as to who the pushy, thin woman had been, but JJ decided that reciting history was not appropriate to a pleasant night and gave the simple but true answer that she was the widow of his predecessor as master of the lodge.

JJ and Rose returned to Herlways where, before retiring, they discussed and finalised plans for spending Christmas and New Year together. At New Year, JJ proposed and was accepted. They agreed to delay their wedding for a year to avoid any ill-feeling on the part of those who might feel Rose's remarriage too soon. JJ had agreed to being appointed an assistant provincial grand master the following June and he would need to bed in to the demands of the new responsibilities with which he was to be honoured. His cup of happiness was full to overflowing. That the symbolic cup should lose any of its contents seemed inconceivable.

CHAPTER SIXTY-NINE
Mrs Caitlin Fisher—Woman and Wife
1934 to 1997

Despite her Welsh forename, Caitlin Meredith was born and raised in Cheshire where her father had established and successfully run his own light engineering firm. Her mother, wanting to preserve the memory of her Welsh grandmother, bestowed upon her second daughter and fourth child an unusual forename for an otherwise very English girl. She was a healthy and active girl and woman, and used her height to good effect on the netball courts of the North West. To her dismay, her breasts never developed to any appreciable size, and the family were quietly of the opinion that in the plain-faced, mousy-haired Caitlin, they had a lifetime maiden Meredith in their midst. It was, therefore, a considerable surprise when Caitlin brought home from the school at which, after teacher training college, she had secured a post, a diminutive man who quite obviously adored her. Bruce Meredith was only too pleased to acquiesce to this tiny science teacher's request for his daughter's hand, despite the six years difference in their ages.

Maurice's adoration of his wife was reciprocated, and the unlikely pair settled happily into married life. The drive in their lives definitely came from Caitlin, who was always keen to push 'dear Maurice' forward, despite his shy reluctance to progress. The incidence of push was debatable in their private life, but their sons were born in 1958 and 1960. With Caitlin's encouragement, Maurice acceded to her father's tentative suggestion he become a Freemason and, in 1969, Maurice Barton Fisher was initiated into a lodge in what, he learned, was the oldest Masonic province in England. Before he became eligible for any Masonic office in his mother lodge, Caitlin discovered a vacancy at a Midlands school for a head of science, for which she insisted Maurice apply. His academic knowledge gained him selection by a small margin—he was, after all, a small man—and the Fisher's found a useful bonus in that there was also a vacancy for a gymnastics and English teacher at the same school. They moved to Avonbridge and bought a small semi-detached house in Grimley Street where they were happy in their introspective way.

After a year in the Midlands, Caitlin, in telephonic consultation with her mother, decided that Maurice should pursue his Masonic life in the Midlands. After some weeks of simulated discreet enquiry, she discovered an acquaintance admitting to membership of a local lodge and willing to extend a Masonic invitation to her Maurice. Events took a predictable course and Brother Maurice B. Fisher became a joining member of Chandlery Lodge in 1972. His progress was unremarkable, but his timorous attempts were tolerated, and he slowly moved up the lodge hierarchy to be installed, to Caitlin's delight, as master in 1983. Maurice's ladies' night at The Swan was a more enjoyable evening than many had anticipated. Neither of the Fisher's sons were present. The elder had been rebellious and, disobeying his mother's commands to remain at home, joined friends on a drinking spree that ended in tragedy—the Fisher's first born was killed in a road traffic accident. The younger son was equally resentful of his mother's domineering attitude and attempts to control his young life, and at the age of twenty he married a Canadian woman five years his senior and sailed away to her native land. Caitlin and Maurice never heard from him again. They were, as they had been when they met and married, content with each other and cared little that no others seemed content to befriend them.

Caitlin wore her ladies' night jewel with pride, and her 1983 lady's speech, on which she laboured mightily for months, was accounted a success; better regarded for it's unexpected flashes of near-wit than might otherwise have been the case. Despite the controversy about trying to move the 1984 ladies festival overseas—something that Maurice, as Caitlin had said he should, had opposed as strongly as his habitually ineffective utterances allowed—Caitlin was still looking forward to the 1984 ladies' night. She would have another night at the top table and her Maurice would perform an important duty. She diligently rehearsed him using her treasured jewel. The actual fracas, that Caitlin insisted was entirely the fault of the Whitehouse-Martins and their friends the Bakers, would set in motion (rather slow motion) radical changes to what remained of the Fishers' lives.

Once the Stourminster Hospital staff had found the blood on Maurice's face, neck and hands was not his own, and he had no external injuries, the Fishers had been discharged. They had to find and pay for a taxi to The Swan where they retrieved their own car. Maurice, now more timorous than ever, was prescribed a nerve tonic and remained at home for three weeks. The appearance on television of a woman with a slightly low neckline (nothing beyond slightly was permitted at the

time) caused him to flinch and, if the appearance persisted, leave the
room. He resumed work in November, although he did not attend that
month's meeting of Chandlery Lodge. Life began to return to what, for
the Fishers, was normal, and Caitlin and Maurice enjoyed Christmas
1984 in their own rather childlike manner.

Encouraged by Caitlin, Maurice resumed his Masonic attendance at
Chandlery Lodge in 1985 and, with no responsibilities save the status of
a past master, actually enjoyed himself again. He was careful, as his wife
told him, to avoid more than fleeting contact with Worshipful Brother JJ
Whitehouse-Martin, and he generally returned home content. The Fishers
were not in attendance at any more ladies' nights as even the thought of
it caused Maurice to shudder and Caitlin to shake with anger. In 1987,
Maurice was appointed the Lodge representative to the provincial library
and museum committee, a far from onerous responsibility involving
no more than his attendance at a meeting of the provincial library and
museum committee once a year and making a report of that meeting to
the lodge. Maurice was cognisant of the relative unimportance of the
post, but Caitlin felt it an honour rightly bestowed on her precious little
man. Similarly, she exaggerated out of all proportion his membership of
the lodge committee—little realising that any past master automatically
acquired the right to attend such meetings. In the same manner, Caitlin
regarded the January 1988 summons for Maurice to attend an emergency
meeting concerning catering.

After he was returned to her care in late January 1988, Caitlin's
moods swung between concern for 'dear Maurice' and rage against
the perpetrators of the outrage against her man. Maurice declined
into a cataleptic trance that persisted for several months; he made no
utterance and seemed to understand little of what was said to him, or was
happening around him. He moved about the house almost as though he
were haunting his home. Caitlin's rage at those whom she perceived to
have caused this dire state, whilst deliberately ignoring the at least as sad
state of Jenny Whitehouse-Martin, preserved her physical health if not
her mental state. Her frustrated attempts to obtain satisfaction through
the law only increased her anger, and for months she was scarcely civil to
anyone. She had to do as the superintendent of police told her, but the
lack of any justice for Maurice continued to irk her.

Both by themselves and with their sons when they were young,
the Fishers had always thoroughly enjoyed Christmas. They embraced
the entire package amongst themselves whilst exhibiting an almost
Scrooge-like attitude to the rest of the world. Despite Maurice's ongoing

withdrawal into a world of his own, and his inability to work, Caitlin was determined, as they always had done, to have a tree for Christmas 1988. The usual five feet high and no more order was placed and delivered. The sight of the tree in their lounge began Maurice's return toward a more normal state of existence. As Caitlin wrestled the tree into the multi-coloured bucket they always used for the purpose, she heard his voice for the first time since October.

'Tree.'

Caitlin straightened up so sharply she snapped a branch of the 'new' tree.

Maurice repeated the monosyllabically accurate description of the seasonal greenery and found himself wrapped in an emotional embrace. As they combined to decorate the tree, his returning vocabulary expanded to name some of the well-loved baubles. The fervency with which Mrs Caitlin Fisher prayed and sang (slightly off-key) the usual carols surprised the congregation and clergy of St Michael's Methodist Church. As they emerged into a crisp Christmas day morning, anyone within earshot, whether they knew said Maurice or not, was made aware, 'Maurice is beginning to get better.'

The several doctors to whom Caitlin presented Maurice for opinion beyond the second such pronouncement all felt it unlikely he would recover his full reasoning and mobility, but there would be a 'gradual improvement providing Mr Fisher avoids stress of any kind.' Privately, the medical men felt life with Caitlin was unlikely to alleviate Maurice's condition. He became able to talk with Caitlin, but visitors were not welcome—even the persistent lodge almoner. The 1990 letter advising of Maurice's selection as a past provincial junior grand deacon made Maurice smile and Caitlin almost burst with pride. No amount of persuasion, including offers of transport to the provincial grand lodge meeting, could induce Maurice to venture beyond his home—even to receive his honour. Caitlin despatched a cheque for the honour fee with a very long letter explaining why Maurice would not be present in person; she fondly imagined it would be read in full to the accompaniment of murmurs of sympathy—nobody was unkind enough to tell her that it only warranted the single word 'apology' added into the records. In more hope than expectation, Caitlin purchased the appropriate dark blue apron, collar and jewel for Maurice to wear 'when he can return to his lodge duties.' It remained unworn.

Although her love for her little man continued unabated, Caitlin welcomed her weekly excursions to the supermarket. She had ceased work

when their sons were born; Maurice had been retired with a disability
pension and Caitlin received a carer's allowance so their financial state
was not a problem; they lived quietly, but as contently as Maurice's mental
state allowed. On a fine Friday morning in June 1992, Maurice expressed
a wish to sit outside in the sunshine whilst Caitlin was away shopping.
She had reservations but, not wishing to introduce stress by refusing his
simple request, she settled Maurice in a garden chair on the lawn with
a book and a drink before she cautioned (as in ordered) him to remain
where he was until she returned. She then locked the house and the side
gate before driving their little car—now her little car—to Freshbury's.
Due to the delay, she was later than usual and the car park was very full,
Caitlin had to park further from the store than normal—which annoyed
her since she was anxious to return home as soon as possible in case
Maurice . . . she was not sure in case of what, but she was concerned and
not as collected as she might have been. The greater number shopping at
the same time as herself also created delay—serving only to increase her
anxiety . . .

CHAPTER SEVENTY
Mrs Caitlin Fisher—Bitter Widow
1992 to 1997

Trevor Fenniman had been born with a small brain—an unusual but not serious condition if proper care were taken with him. He was physically fine and as he grew the lack of activity and stimulus for the lad worried his parents. He was, to all intents and purposes, a normal, very polite young man until conversation involved problems with which Trevor was unacquainted. Boys of his age were being employed and contributing to their upkeep and Trevor desperately wanted to emulate them by becoming a wage earner and helping his mother. He was strong and willing to learn as far as he was able. The job of gathering used supermarket trolleys from the Freshbury's car park was, the store manager considered, well within his capabilities and Trevor became a more contented young man. He derived simple pleasure from keeping the car park tidy and ensuring customers could always find a clean trolley near to the store entrance.

As time went on, Trevor nurtured an ambition to push larger and larger numbers of trolleys at once—in pursuit of which he became able to gather together and return to the store entrance at least twenty trolleys, a long train that few could or would manage. The inherent problem in this exercise was, as other store employees tried vainly to explain to Trevor, those unavoidable occasions when he could not see that the front of his train of trolleys was likely to cause difficulties for others. Trevor's solution to this problem was illogically simple, he would move his trains faster.

When Mrs Caitlin Fisher, already irritated and annoyed to have been kept so long away from her dear Maurice, emerged from the store, she discovered to her distress the weather had deteriorated and rain was falling. She hastened to her car, threw the groceries into the boot and, unusually for her, pushed the trolley behind the nearest car. Worrying about dear Maurice, she reversed her little car from its parking place, thrust it into forward gear and accelerated towards the exit. She was momentarily distracted by a wandering shopper and when her eyes refocused ahead, she saw an apparently self-propelling line of trolleys emerging from her left. Stabbing at the brake, her heel caught in the car mat and she depressed the accelerator causing the car to swerve, bounce off the rear of a parked Land Rover and collide at twenty-five miles per hour with the leading trolley. From there the car slid head on into a parked car that shunted onto two other innocent vehicles. In her haste, Caitlin had failed to fasten her safety belt and the collision propelled her into the windscreen—in transit her unsmiling mouth made tasteless contact with the steering wheel. Caitlin lost consciousness—thus failing to observe the confusion she and Trevor had created.

Trevor, too, was not fully aware. Having been suddenly and unexpectedly stopped in his tracks he had been winded and thrown on top of his trolley train from where he fell gracelessly to the ground, gathering multiple facial cuts, a dislocated shoulder and two broken ribs. He lost consciousness. Recovering and trying to rise, he gazed at Chrissie, a senior store lady who was bathing his face and telling him to lie still and be calm. Beyond Chrissie was a ruined train of trolleys impaled against parked cars and surrounded by agitated, very vocal shoppers. As Trevor closed his eyes, he heard the sound of an approaching ambulance siren.

Norman Wattinson, Freshbury's store manager, heard sounds of commotion from outside before Brenda, senior sales lady, screamed, 'Come and see what's happened in the car park, Mr Wattinson.' He came; he saw; he felt conquered. His trainee store manager was ineffectually directing traffic; Jean, the store first aider, stood transfixed holding the accident book. All around them shoppers and would-be shoppers milled, gazed in empty fascination, and did little.

'Go and help the injured, Jean,' Norman ordered her as he snatched the useless accident book from her before dashing back into the store past the open-mouthed security man to summon the police and an ambulance. Unbeknownst to Norman, a quick-thinking customer with a car-phone had already summoned emergency services and Norman was amazed and impressed as he re-emerged from the store three minutes later to hear the siren heralding an approaching ambulance. The subsequent intervention of authority closed the car park for two hours whilst attempts were made to resolve who or what was to blame, record the same and to discover the usual batch of blind witnesses. Friday's takings were deeply depressed, earning Norman an undeserved reprimand from head office.

The presence of two ambulances allowed Trevor to be first away—closely followed in the second ambulance by a confused and concussed lady—the contents of whose handbag identified her as Mrs Caitlin Fisher; she seemed more concerned about 'her Maurice' than her own injuries, although the car from which she had been extracted was a Skoda. Convinced she was confused, paramedic Geoff assured her of his mysterious certainty it could be repaired and would soon be running smoothly. The patient's impatient reply protested it was her husband she was worried about.

Unaware of any details, Geoff tried to comfort Caitlin, 'He's probably in the other ambulance, dear. Relax.' Simultaneous with the last word was an injection of anaesthetic and, wondering how and why Maurice had managed to be in an ambulance, a slightly comforted Caitlin drifted into a disturbed sleep. By the time she was discharged from hospital, Maurice was dead.

Ever obedient to his much-loved wife, Maurice had sat happily in the sunshine awaiting her return. After a while it grew colder and started to rain. Maurice sat on—consumed by the knowledge that Caitlin had been adamant he remain where he was until she returned. He was cold and wet. Maurice shivered and sat on.

The house adjoining the Fishers was that of Maureen and Michael Daley. They were both self-employed—working principally from home, he as a designer, she a skilled seamstress and milliner. They had moved in ten years previously, and although the same number of years younger than the Fishers, they were good neighbours who did what they could when asked, but were careful not to interfere. Every Friday they visited Maureen's parents, stayed for lunch and returned home in the late afternoon. On Maurice's final Friday, they had been pleased before leaving for their ritual visit to see him sat in the sun on the lawn; obviously he was improving from whatever it was—Mrs Fisher had not been at all specific. When they returned home at 4.30 p.m. they were alarmed to see Maurice still sitting outside in the rain. The Fisher's side gate was locked. Clad in his old black duffle coat with the hood up against the lashing rain, Michael climbed the fence between their properties and called out Maurice's name. Maurice's eyes flickered open, he stared in horror at what his confused mind interpreted as another attack from the creature who had denuded and left him exposed and, already in the grip of hypothermia, the diminutive former science teacher clutched his chest, groaned and slumped forward.

The ambulance man said it appeared to have been a massive heart attack, but the hospital doctor would confirm his diagnosis. He did. As the ambulance carrying the dead Maurice drove out of Grimley Street, it passed a similar vehicle containing his returning wife. Michael and Maureen Daley had to tackle the task of informing the widow Fisher of

her new and unsought status and then coping with the ensuing bout of
hysteria and incomprehensible railing against the wicked Whitehouse-
Martin and all his ilk.

Maurice Fisher's funeral at Avonbridge crematorium was poorly
attended. The Daleys felt obliged to support Mrs Fisher. One of her
sisters appeared, having travelled from the North West, but the Daleys
detected little sisterly affection and the sister departed swiftly after the
short service. Five stern men in morning suits white shirts and black ties
sat together and, afterwards, one after the other offered their sympathies
to Caitlin.

Maureen Daley's subsequent enquiry elicited the reply, 'They were
from Maurice's Masonic lodge—there should have been more of them.
At least that JJ had the sense not to appear.'

The Daleys, understanding little of the reply, nodded politely.
There was no wake and no refreshments. Four days later, the undertaker
delivered a china urn containing Maurice's ashes to 54 Grimley Street,
Avonbridge.

Caitlin found life without her little Maurice lonely and boring.
She tired herself out cleaning and re-cleaning the house. Television
transmitted little that she found interesting. She was pleasantly surprised
at the ongoing concern of the nice people next door and, indeed, it was a
tentative suggestion of Maureen Daley in 1993 that eventually stirred her
from home more than once a week.

'Would you like to come with me to my Towns Women's Guild
meeting tomorrow, Mrs Fisher? We've got a lady talking about exercise
and health who's supposed to be very good and quite amusing.'

Having nothing to relieve the monotony of life alone, Caitlin agreed
to accompany Maureen. The speaker was, as promised, interesting and
a little amusing—even to Caitlin. More relevant, as Mrs Daley had
hoped, the simple act of going to something new and different effected
some stimulus for Caitlin. Seven weeks later she joined the TWG. It
was something different—not anything she might have envisaged herself
doing, but it made a considerable difference to her life. After living
next door to one another for ten years during which they abided by
formality, she now addressed the Daleys by their first names and they
called her Caitlin. Michael mowed her small lawns—'No trouble at all
whilst I've got the mower out.' After a further year, inspired by a talk and
demonstration at TWG, Caitlin was bold enough to invite Maureen and
Michael to afternoon tea—her own scones and Victoria sponge.

Although she now brooded less, she still harboured a deep-seated desire to be revenged upon Whitehouse-Martin. She had no idea how she might accomplish that intent until she joined the Guild outing to a local amateur dramatic society's performance of *The Crucible* by Arthur Miller. It was not what she had expected. The title had attracted her since she thought it concerned chemistry—Maurice's pre-school preparations in the garden shed had utilised crucibles. So far as Caitlin understood the plot, it involved a lot of young women, motivated only by malice, having several of their pious elders condemned by bearing false and unsubstantiated witness against them. It was, as Maureen said, a thought-provoking play. It certainly provoked Caitlin's thoughts.

Almoner Terry Cox was surprised—actually amazed was the word he used later—when Mrs Caitlin Fisher accepted Chandlery Lodge's usual invitation to their December 1996 Christmas supper and song evening for lodge brethren, their wives and families, and the widows of deceased brethren. For four years she had firmly, abruptly, and almost rudely declined the invitation and Worshipful Brother Terry had almost decided not to bother her any more. His wife, Margaret, persuaded him to try one more time before giving up. Caitlin attended, was as pleasant as any in the lodge remembered her being, and drove herself home afterwards with her usual gift token (one for every widow) and the bottle of wine she had won in the raffle. She seemed, to general mystification, disappointed that JJ was not present. She promised to come again next year if she could and even expressed interest in the summer social. As it happened, she did not attend the summer social since she had already enrolled and paid for a four-day holiday in Llandudno with the TWG in the same week. She did, as promised, attend the 1997 Christmas gathering.

CHAPTER SEVENTY-ONE
Alecto—the Unceasing Spirit of Retribution
Tuesday 24 January 1998

The sight of a top of the range Jaguar car in Grimley Street was almost unprecedented. Curtains flapped as curious eyes observed JJ's car parked outside number 54. Many neighbours were aware that Mrs Fisher had a visitor in a posh car at 5.45 p.m. It was as Caitlin had intended.

Directory enquiries had supplied her with the telephone number for a Mr J. J. Whitehouse-Martin of Herlways. She had made two hastily disconnected calls before JJ himself answered the telephone—it was not essential that no other should be aware of her call, but she felt it would help, Caitlin had read a good many Agatha Christie and Ngaio Marsh thrillers in the last two years.

'Oh, Mr Whitehouse-Martin,' she said to JJ. 'It's Caitlin Fisher. We spoke a few weeks back at the lodge supper. I hope you don't mind me calling you, but after talking to you I got to thinking about what I ought to do with Maurice's lodge things—his aprons and jewels and so forth.'

'Well, Mrs Fisher, they are saleable—particularly, I think his provincial regalia that, if I remember correctly, he never had the chance to wear. If you like, I can put you in touch with someone.'

'Oh. Well, yes . . . but . . . I wonder if I could ask you to collect them from me, please. I'm still not sure about strangers and as you followed Maurice—is followed the right word?'

'It'll suffice.'

'Oh, good. Well, as I know you, would you be so good as to call on me and collect the case and everything?'

There was a short pause. JJ felt Caitlin was being unduly cautious— but, again, he didn't like to seem churlish. Caitlin was almost holding her breath.

'If that's what you would like, then that's what we'll do,' said JJ. 'Would it be convenient if I called after work today—say five thirty plus?'

'That would be lovely,' replied a delighted Caitlin. She gave JJ her address and directions (superfluous but politely acknowledged) and promised a cup of tea should he so wish. JJ felt it unlikely.

The date did not 'register' as of any relevance with JJ; Caitlin was overjoyed: ten years was a not uncommon celebratory anniversary and it would serve very well. She felt she had been very patient. She knew it was unlikely that either Maureen or Michael would be away from their home that evening. Everything else she had meticulously planned to the last detail. The day could not pass quickly enough, but she knew she should not anticipate too soon; one hour would be more than enough for the final details and she set herself to a crossword puzzle book until 4.30 p.m. Allowing for a little lunch she completed four puzzles—three without having to cheat by looking at the answers in the back of the book. Now, it was time.

Caitlin put the puzzle book away, looked around the lounge to be sure it was still clean and tidy and went upstairs. From the back of what had been his wardrobe, she extracted the parcel with the big apron and collar and Maurice's Masonic case. Opening both for the first time since before his death, she removed the aprons, collar, past master's jewel, gloves and ritual book and placed them neatly on the bed. She placed the case on the floor before rehearsing the hoped for moves and re-aligning the case. Everything was in place. Caitlin experienced a surge of adrenaline within herself. Time to change. Caitlin Fisher stripped herself and, avoiding any sight of her naked body in the mirror, quickly donned older, pre-prepared underwear. Her warm tights were replaced by stockings and her old, doctored suspender belt. The dress destined for the charity shop had been retained as it suited her newly planned purposes: it had been worked on diligently and, barring any unforeseen hitches, would pass inspection and easily convert as intended. By five thirty a grimly determined Caitlin Fisher was seated in her lounge where she could see arrivals without appearing nosey.

'Keep calm, Caitlin,' she said aloud to herself.

At 5.35 p.m. two fresh-faced, dark-suited young men with permanently fixed smiles approached Caitlin's front door. Their expressed intent to talk about God was swiftly rebuffed and they departed to the next rebuttals. By the time Caitlin opened her front door to JJ, the modern missionaries were far away along Grimley Street.

'Oh, Mr Whitehouse-Martin. Come in, please. I'm a bit disorganised since we spoke, I'm afraid,' said Caitlin—hoping her prepared script did not sound too rehearsed. 'Maurice's things are still upstairs—I laid them out for you to see but, I'm sorry, I suppose I ought to have brought them down here. I didn't think—it's a bit distressing seeing them again. Would you mind looking at them upstairs, or shall I gather them up and bring them down?'

This was a crucial moment, if he said 'downstairs', Plan B would apply. To Caitlin's relief it was all too easy.

'No need to move them around, I can go up and get them, if it's all right with you,' said JJ with a smile.

'I'll show you the way, Mr Whitehouse-Martin, don't want you getting lost, do we?' simpered Caitlin and, without waiting for any objections, she led the way up the stairs, along the short landing and into the rear bedroom.

'Here they are,' said Caitlin, indicating the aprons with her left hand, as she positioned herself at the head of the bed.

'Ah, yes. Should be no problem finding a buyer before next June,' said JJ. 'Can I take the case as well?'

'Oh, please do—it's of no use to me,' replied a now taut and expectant Caitlin. This was almost too good to be true, she thought. As JJ bent to take the case from the floor, Caitlin swung the heavy urn dealing JJ a crashing blow to the side of his head; his glasses broke and he collapsed, unconscious, onto the bed—strewn in Maurice's ashes.

Quickly, Caitlin gathered the Masonic things—she had to ease one apron from beneath JJ's inert body—slung them untidily into Maurice's wardrobe and locked the door, she could tidy that up later. Next she wrested JJ's jacket from his shoulders, shook the ashes from the jacket onto his shirt and waistcoat and placed the jacket, inside out, on the floor. Undoing his belt she pulled down his trousers and underpants. Caitlin gasped—Maurice had been nothing like this—but he was a small man and . . . enough of that. Concentrate Now she tore her ready-to-tear dress to reveal her shoulders. The bra could stay where it was—no need to overdo it, and anyway she was still sensitive about her breasts. She had grown her nails and now she scratched JJ's face and right hand until they bled before taking his right hand and, not without difficulty, inflicting similar injuries to her right shoulder, right hip and upper right leg. She tore her panties through on the right and broke the almost severed suspender. JJ was still unconscious. Time for witnesses. Caitlin screamed as loudly as she could; having left the landing window open she hoped the sound would carry. Holding her torn dress and panties to her in such a way that her injuries remained visible, she ran, still screaming, downstairs, out of the front door and across the front garden to Maureen and Michael's front door on which she leaned sobbing and banging. With commendable haste, Michael opened the door and Caitlin, as she had intended, collapsed into his hall.

The ambulance and police car arrived at the same time. Maureen accompanied Caitlin to the hospital where her scratches were dressed— they were not very deep, and a sedative administered. A policewoman trained in assault and rape cases attended her and took a preliminary statement before telephoning the station. Caitlin slept. The nurses were mystified by her satisfied smile, but attributed it to relief or indigestion.

A confused JJ, with a massive headache and broken glasses, was examined even before he began to recover.

'Open and shut case of sexual assault, dirty b——' was the older police patrol officer's sweeping, cynical opinion.

JJ was, none too gently, assisted to don his pants and trousers. The belt was withheld. Shards of porcelain and scattered ashes were gathered as evidence. Once he felt able to walk, JJ was supported from the bedroom, down the stairs and into the back of the police car. Still confused, he imagined the police car was taking him to hospital. His queries were answered with insults about his cleanliness and morals. It wasn't until he was frogmarched into Stourminster Police Station and charged that it fully dawned on him what had happened. His throbbing brain recalled his right to one telephone call. Being still denied his jacket with his diary and his solicitor's telephone number, he called Billy— he knew his number—and asked his old friend to get young Morton down here as soon as possible. In the presence of Walter Morton, JJ was formally charged with assault and attempted rape against Mrs Caitlin Fisher. He was detained overnight pending a bail hearing.

CHAPTER SEVENTY-TWO
WORCESTER MAGISTRATES' COURT
THURSDAY 26 FEBRUARY 1999

A plea of not guilty and a counter-suit of malicious falsification of evidence and assault on his person was all JJ and the best legal brains he and Rixon Reed could find to offer in his defence. He had no witnesses. He could not recollect telling anyone of his intention to visit Mrs Fisher—indeed his initial recollection had been very little due to concussion and he was still confused on some matters. His entire defence was his good character. In simple terms, the case comprised his word against that of Mrs Fisher.

JJ felt utterly alone. He knew it was wrong to feel so, Billy and Jan were in the public gallery of the court and he had both a solicitor and barrister defending him. But there was no Rose. She had cried for him when he had been bailed and returned to Herlways dirty and dishevelled from his night in the cells. She had been horrified at the actions of Caitlin Fisher and had told him, as had Walter Morton and Billy, that he could not possibly be guilty of rape—particularly of such an unattractive old woman. But journalists—some journalists—are adept at slanting a story, particularly when it reflects badly on someone successful, and far too many still believe that whatever is printed in a newspaper—any newspaper—must be true.

JJ's arrest, indictment and subsequent bailing on his own recognisance at a very high sum was a matter of public record and, therefore, available for reporting. And comment. And several informed (by whom it could not, of course, be revealed) reporters felt the presence in his life of a woman who had 'shamelessly exposed herself for a living' must have been the catalyst driving a respectable and successful businessman to an act of wanton sexual assault. Once the facts and resentful opinions had been read, some citizens of Avonbridge and district felt moved to commit their opinions of JJ and of Rose to paper. Unsigned and anonymous vilifications on paper were delivered by Royal Mail to Herlways and the offices of Wells Holdings. To begin with, Rose treated such missives with the contempt they deserved but, as the written invective continued and became joined by telephoned vilifications, shouts in the street, and even a painted insult on her car, her strong nerve began to weaken. She became morose and convinced herself that her presence in JJ's life was deleterious. She tried to explain this to JJ, who refused to countenance such silly notions. In despair, Rose left Herlways early one Monday morning to return to her own little Cheltenham house and her beloved job . . . leaving JJ his engagement ring and a tear-stained note expressing her hopes that he would forgive and forget her. For JJ there was nothing to forgive, but he never forgot Rose. She never returned to Herlways or Avonbridge.

Even a relatively inexperienced barrister could have made Mrs Fisher's case credible. Her barrister was experienced. With some difficulty he managed to confine his client's evidence to the events of 24 January 1998, despite her repeated attempts to make mention of her late husband. The only mention of 'dear Maurice' was the use of his urned ashes as Mrs Fisher's weapon of defence.

'Would a bereaved and besieged widow smash her late husband's remains unless she were desperate and fighting for her honour, your honour?'

Costs and damages were awarded against Jonathan Justin Whitehouse-Martin. A suspended sentence of three years was imposed and he was bound over to keep the peace. Mrs Fisher wore a black dress and what Billy and Jan described as an evil smile. The Bakers walked beside their friend, fending off the persistent press, to their car. Pointing his car towards Avonbridge, Billy felt he was driving a broken man, Rose had left him and he was now a convicted sex criminal. Little did he know how soon more heavy straws were to be added to the camel's back.

CHAPTER SEVENTY-THREE
REMONSTRANCE, REBUTTAL, RESOLUTION AND RESIGNATION(S)
MONDAY 9 MARCH 1999

Chandlery Lodge No. 5591

Your attendance is requested at an emergency meeting of the lodge committee at the Avonbridge Masonic hall on Monday 9 March 1999 at 6.30 p.m.

Agenda: to consider the lodge re-action to the sentencing of Worshipful Brother JJ Whitehouse-Martin P.A.G.D.C.

The urgently prepared summons was hand delivered to suitably qualified brethren of the lodge by a reluctant lodge secretary and others at the insistence of the master and three other past masters. Delivery to Herlways was effected by a less than honest brother who deliberately waited until the narrow boat moored at the wharf below the house cast off before pushing the envelope through the front door. Such a sad attempt at deception met its just reward, since both JJ and Billy now had mobile phones. The narrow boat returned to Herlways wharf within the day.

Worshipful Master Owen Miles presided over a stormy and not very fraternal meeting. It was obvious that an attempt had been made to keep JJ away. His entry into the room accompanied by Billy triggered an awkward silence before Alan Simmonds and Paul Miller rushed forward to shake his hand and, rather too volubly, extend their sympathies at what they felt to be a miscarriage of justice. Since the Magistrates' Court judgement was the catalyst that had caused the meeting to be called, this did not make for the most comfortable beginning to the evening.

'It just got progressively worse,' Billy later related to Jan.

Worshipful Master Miles opened the meeting, and reading from the summons, stated the only matter on the agenda. As he finished speaking, JJ asked, politely, if he might be allowed to address the assembled brethren. He was refused.

'I think, Worshipful Brother Whitehouse-Martin, that those who asked for the meeting should be allowed to speak first,' said the red-faced master. He then asked Worshipful Brother Frank Manners—a recent joining member and church warden—to state why he and others felt the meeting to be necessary. The meeting was subjected to a sermon on the sins of man against weak women—specifically a widow of a past master of the lodge. The words 'living with a wanton woman' were uttered, drawing from JJ a terse request to define wanton.

'I don't need to,' replied the ill-mannered Manners.

'You do if you're using the adjective inaccurately,' answered JJ.

The master gavelled for order. The conclusion of the ill-mannered spiel was a proposal that JJ be told to resign.

Before the master could fully regain control of the evening, Brother Laurence Holman, a regular worshipper at the same church as Brother Manners and an obvious devotee of the impolite brother, loudly seconded the proposal. Again JJ asked if he might speak, but was shouted down by the piously angry brethren. The stentorian tones of Worshipful Brother Frank Fallowfield, now the senior past master of the lodge, stilled their insistent voices. He suggested the master only allow one person at a time to speak and, since he had twice asked permission to address the meeting, JJ be allowed to state his point of view. With obvious reluctance, the master called upon Worshipful Brother Whitehouse-Martin to say a few words.

Sensing the insensitive atmosphere, JJ abandoned his original intention of explaining his innocence—which he had done continually since his arrest and arraignment. Maintaining his dignity, he spoke firmly and calmly.

'Worshipful Master, Brethren. It is a matter of public record that I have consistently protested my innocence of the charge for which I was recently convicted. I have no proof that I was framed—that being the planned intent of my accuser. My intended appointment as an assistant provincial grand master was withdrawn as the other rulers of the province, whilst expressing regret, felt it might reflect badly upon Freemasonry. That I have to respect and it is no concern of this lodge to pass comment upon the decisions taken by our rulers. You should know that their decision was transmitted to me personally, with sympathetic understanding and no pre-judgement. I had hoped to receive a similarly Masonic reception and hearing here in my mother lodge. I am surprised that Brothers Manners and Holman, feeling as they do, have felt themselves able to sit in lodge with me on the few occasions I have attended in the last ye——'

'It's been difficult,' interrupted Manners rudely.

'Had I been aware of creating disharmony, even towards so

inharmonious a member, I would have withdrawn and expected him to do likewise,' replied JJ. 'Now that I am aware of Brother Manners and Brother Holman's narrow, intolerant views, I have no difficulty in stating myself unable to sit in lodge with them. Unless, as I feel unlikely, they intend to apologise and withdraw their proposal—and memberships—I shall be writing to Brother Secretary to tender my resignation.'

JJ looked hard at Manners who, as expected, almost shouted that he was not guilty of sin and there was no reason for him or Brother Holman to resign.

'My proposal remains as made and seconded,' he concluded smugly.

JJ rose from his seat.

'I feel there is no point in my remaining. Please excuse me, Worshipful Master.'

As JJ left the room, further uproar broke out with accusation and counter accusation creating an unruly cacophony. At length, the master restored order. Despite Worshipful Brother Fallowfield stating that it had been rendered obsolete, the proposal of Brother Manners was put to the vote by show of hands. Twelve were in favour and eleven against. The Master pompously instructed the secretary to write to Worshipful Brother Whitehouse-Martin asking that he tender his resignation from Chandlery Lodge. The secretary, Worshipful Brother Edwin Harris, answered that as JJ had already expressed his intention of resigning it would be a pointless waste of time and paper writing to ask for that resignation.

'I shall, however,' he continued, 'acquaint Brother Whitehouse-Martin with the sad outcome of this vote. I shall forward his anticipated letter of resignation to yourself, Worshipful Master, together with my own and, I imagine, several others. In respectful emulation of Worshipful Brother Whitehouse-Martin I now ask you to excuse me from what remains of this meeting.'

Worshipful Brother Harris's dignified action was, in turn, followed by the departure of ten others—including Frank Fallowfield. At the suggestion of Worshipful Brother Peter Hordern, they walked to his print shop where there was an ample supply of writing paper and envelopes. Edwin Harris drove home with his own and ten other letters of resignation from Chandlery Lodge. Three days later he delivered to Worshipful Master Miles a parcel containing twelve letters of resignation. To Owen Miles plaintive query as to who would read them at the next lodge meeting, Edwin gave the curt reply that it was not his problem, but that of the worshipful master.

Whatever arguments Billy and Alan Simmonds advanced, JJ remained obdurate. He resigned from every other Masonic lodge, chapter or preceptory of which he was a member. Of the other eleven resignees from Chandlery Lodge, five were already members of other lodges. To the muted delight of their brethren, Stour Lodge admitted six joining members in April and May of 1999. They included the promising young Brother Harry Alan Carter-Knight.

CHAPTER SEVENTY-SEVEN
AVONBRIDGE AND WORCESTER
BOXING DAY 1999 AND BEYOND . . .

Michael Daley was a quiet, thoughtful man who always regarded himself as fair and honourable. He was a good designer and, as he would be the first to admit, could have been more successful professionally and financially had he promoted himself more forcefully. He and Maureen moved to Avonbridge in 1988 when he was awarded the profitable contract for the internal design and conversion of the hall into a conference centre following his much-admired designs for the latest Wells Estate. The contract fees for his work allied to both their recent annual accounts secured them a mortgage on 52 Grimley Street—the first home they had actually owned. The sudden, unexpected death of Michael's widowed father in 1990 enabled the Daleys to pay off their mortgage. Since they liked their little house, and despite their increased prosperity, they saw no compelling reason to move. They bought a new car each and effected improvements to the home they had only envisaged in dreams. They were a contented couple.

For the first ten years of their residence in Grimley Street they were on more friendly terms with other nearby residents than with their immediate and attached neighbours. They continued to address the somewhat aloof Fishers as Mr and Mrs until after Maurice's death. That had been a shock, but they, Maureen particularly, had brought some comfort and interest into Mrs Fisher's—Caitlin's—life. Michael would never forget the traumatic time when, responding to cries of distress and beating at their front door, he had tried to catch Caitlin who was gasping about rape and said, 'I think I've killed him.' As any good citizen would, Michael had summoned his wife to aid their bleeding, dishevelled neighbour and called 999 to summon the police and an ambulance. Having made a statement of what he knew to the police patrol officer, Michael observed a bandaged and handcuffed man being escorted from next door, but it was only as he was turned to sit in the police car that Michael recognised the man as Mr Whitehouse-Martin—effectively his employer. He was shocked but, as Maureen later stated, you never can tell about people.

The Daleys had nervously given evidence at the trial, Michael had been selfishly relieved that his work for the accused's companies was never mentioned by either side's barrister. Driving Caitlin home after JJ had been sentenced, they were both shocked at her violent reaction to the suspended sentence as being far too lenient and her ongoing condemnations of JJ. They tried to dismiss it as nervous re-action to the trauma of re-living her ordeal, but her comments that JJ had had it coming for a long time and that he and his cronies were all against Maurice, failed to fit the image of the man for whom Michael had been working.

Michael and Maureen had both enjoyed a particularly good working year in 1999 with several new clients and customers and profitable contracts. Although they were not known for their hospitality, both had been raised in homes where it had been customary to entertain and it seemed natural to them that on Boxing Day 1999 they should invite a few friends and neighbours to join them for drinks and light refreshments. Maureen's culinary skills allied to selective purchases from the local delicatessen and the advice of the nearby wine shop ensured their guests were well-pleased with the Daley's Boxing Day party. They felt obliged to invite Caitlin as she could have been offended had she seen so many arriving at their door whilst she remained alone. For the early part of the evening she had been affable and seasonally polite, and Maureen and Michael were pleased she seemed happy. As the evening wore on so did the effect on Caitlin of unaccustomed consumption of wine. As numbers began to thin, Maureen realised Caitlin had sat herself in a corner with a glass and bottle and was freely replenishing one from the other. She called Michael's attention to the possibly problematic state of their neighbour. Both he and a recent and valued customer looked towards the imbibing old woman.

'Are you alright, Caitlin?' enquired Maureen rather loudly.

'Yesh, thank you, M'reen. Lovely party.'

They realised, with amused tolerance, Caitlin had imbibed too freely but, after all, it was still Christmas. Maureen, watched by the few others still present, decided she should relieve Caitlin of the bottle, but Caitlin seemed to feel possession entitled retention and clung tightly to her wine.

'Glad you're enjoying yourself,' said Michael—feeling he should support his wife.

'Maurish loved Chrishmash, you know,' trilled Caitlin. Her beaming countenance suddenly became ugly as she continued, 'He can't any more, though, becaush of that Whitehoush-Mar'in man. Wicked he ish. They were all againsht Maurish, you know—but 'ticularly him.'

Maureen and her distinguished customer, realising the state of Caitlin, tried to help her to stand. She wobbled on her feet but clung grimly to the bottle she now waved about to emphasise her shtatemensh.

'I got 'im, though, din' I?' Caitlin continued. 'I got 'im in the end.'

Michael stiffened. Maureen gripped Caitlin's arm more tightly.

'What do you mean, Caitlin?' asked Michael. Somehow he dreaded the reply.

'You know I got 'im, Michael . . . you were there. Even if he di'nt get put away for it, I still got 'im.'

'How did you do that?' asked the well-dressed lady helping Maureen to hold Caitlin.

'Got 'im 'reshted, din't I? They believed me . . . all of 'em . . . 'shif he'd want shexsh wi' an old woman like me. But I made 'um 'lieve me, di'nt I, Michael?'

The room had gone very quiet—the remaining guests and their hosts all looking at Caitlin with a mixture of horror and distaste. Urged on by a penetrating look from Maureen's customer, Michael asked the question that several present now wanted answered, 'Do you mean you trapped Mr Whitehouse-Martin, knocked him out and made it look as though he tried to rape you?' said Michael as calmly as he could.

'Corsh I did, Mikul. But they carn' prove it, ye shee? . . . They all b'lieved me. I got 'im . . . and 'e got 'is jusht deshertsh, din't he? They should've put 'im in jail, tho' . . . shu'nt they Michael?'

Suddenly, Caitlin seemed to realise there were more people present than just Michael and Maureen. She looked around with a half smile.

'Can you take this side of her, please, Michael?' enquired the distinguished lady. Stepping in front of Caitlin, Detective Inspector Paula Harries (née James) continued, 'Mrs Caitlin Fisher, I'm arresting you on suspicion of perjury and perverting the course of justice.' She then gave Caitlin the customary caution. She apologised to her hosts and asked for permission to use their telephone A car was summoned and two burly policemen escorted/supported Caitlin Fisher to Stourminster police station where, at 11.00 p.m. on 26 December, she was formally charged and detained in the only available cell remaining. Paula had, with further apologies, asked everyone at the Daleys if they would make statements of what they had heard.

On the 9 January 2000, Worshipful Brothers Billy Baker and Alan Simmonds attended a lodge at Rainbow Hill, Worcester, as guests of an old friend from their rugby days. They enjcyed the ceremony and were intrigued, as is often so when visiting lodges, by the subtle differences in ritual. At the festive board, Billy sat next to a Worshipful Brother Roy Packenham who, it emerged in conversation, assisted in the provincial library and museum. At this time, Billy was still not aware that Caitlin had been arrested and Brother Roy's enquiry about his friend JJ, brought from Billy his usual response that he was as well as he could be for a man who'd been framed, asked to leave his lodge and left Masonry completely.

'Sorry—I didn't know he'd resigned,' replied Roy. 'If you don't mind me asking, what's happened about all his regalia?'

'As far as I know, he's still got it,' answered Billy.

'Well, if he wants to get rid of it, we can help,' said Roy.

'Thanks . . . I'll tell him.'

'If you'd remind him—only if he wants to of course. He knows we deal with regalia, of course. He was going to let me have a set of provincial deacon's stuff he was collecting from some widow some time back. But I never heard any more.'

Billy thought for a moment before asking, 'When was this, Roy?'

'Oh, ages ago. I'd forgotten until now.'

'You couldn't be more specific, could you, Roy? It's important.'

'Is it? I dunno. Ages ago it was. Wait a mo' . . . it was in January because we did all the happy new year bit. . . . It wasn't last year so . . . yes, it must have been two years ago. Yes, because we'd just seen off our friends from Canada who'd been with us for Christmas when he rang. . . . Why's it important, Billy?'

Trying to contain his exasperation, Billy explained that JJ had been unable to prove that he had been invited to call on the woman who had framed him. Roy had not followed JJ's case, but now realised that he had, unintentionally, been in possession of what could have been significant evidence. He assured Billy that he would be prepared, if asked, to repeat on oath what he had told him and gave Billy his address and telephone number. The following morning, Billy telephoned Rixon Reed to tell Gerry Quinn, JJ's solicitor following the retirement and death of his Uncle Charles, that he had discovered fresh evidence. It was only then that Billy learned of the arrest of Mrs Fisher. Gerry Quinn took details of Roy Packenham and assured Billy that he was pressing for a judicial review of JJ's case in light of the arrest and that the further evidence was 'all grist to the mill.' That night, JJ and Billy both had too much to drink and Billy, with Jan's blessing—she had expected it—stayed the night at Herlways.

CHAPTER SEVENTY-FIVE
Worcester Magistrates' Court
Thursday 13 July 2000

The Worcester courtroom was less well attended for the trial of Mrs Caitlin Fisher than it had been for that of Mr J. J. Whitehouse-Martin—sadly the disgrace of a successful person attracts more attention than the disgraceful conduct of a deranged widow towards that same successful person. The judge had several times to ask Mrs Fisher to confine herself to the facts of the case and not to tax the court's patience with tirades on her deluded view of her late husband's persecution. On this occasion it was Mrs Fisher who had no witnesses appearing on her behalf. Testifying against her were a recently commended detective inspector, several upright citizens of Avonbridge, and a retired engineer from Worcester who had never even seen Mrs Fisher until he appeared in the witness box. The evidence of the latter was not, strictly, relevant to the prosecution of Caitlin Fisher, but was introduced in order to establish a formerly disputed fact relating to JJ's version of what happened on 24 January 1998.

Mrs Caitlin Fisher was found guilty of perjury under oath and attempting to pervert the course of justice. The final nail in her coffin had been the discovery during a search of her house, authorised by a court order, of her diaries in which a clear entry in her own handwriting on 24 January 1998 stated: 'Whitehouse-Martin; 5.30 p.m.' followed by several exclamation marks; she had always maintained JJ had called unbidden and unannounced. Caitlin was condemned to three years confinement but, in consideration of her age, the sentence was suspended. The judge imposed a heavy fine on the still complaining widow and also awarded costs and damages against her. Her long-suffering counsel pleaded Mrs Fisher's poverty and a court scrutineer was appointed to establish her means and ability to pay.

The case was over within the morning despite the delays to procedure by the accused. In the afternoon, a court sitting under the same judge dismissed the former indictment and sentence of Mr J. J. Whitehouse-Martin who was awarded a judicial pardon.

Reimbursement of his costs and damages plus compensation was generously waived by JJ. Such conduct was unprecedented in the good judge's experience and he felt, whether it was correct to or no, obliged to thank Mr Whitehouse-Martin.

CHAPTER SEVENTY-SIX
HERLWAYS
AUGUST 2000 TO EARLY FEBRUARY 2001

His exoneration by the court felt like a Pyrrhic victory to JJ; he had given up most of his business involvements whilst waiting for his original trial since staff—particularly female staff—tended to treat him with extreme care and most of his lady employees and customers avoided any one-to-one contact with him. The pariah feeling persisted in social circles. Masonic constitutions permit a brother who has resigned to attend any lodge once as unattached, and JJ had twice succumbed to repeated pressure and accepted invitations. But he had not felt universally welcome or socially comfortable, indeed on his second and last attendance at a lodge, despite having paid for a meal, he apologised and left after the ceremony and bought a Chinese takeaway meal which he had eaten alone at home. Billy and Jan continued to visit him, as did their children. Terry Cox, the former almoner of Chandlery Lodge, telephoned at least once a month.

Whilst awaiting his trial and feeling that the world, apart from a select few, had already judged him, JJ had passed his time keeping fit in his home gymnasium and swimming pool; playing and listening to music, and voraciously reading almost everything in book form he could lay his hands on. His attempts to contact and be reconciled with Rose grew less and less frequent, and after he had wrongly been found guilty he abandoned hope of ever seeing or hearing from her again. To Billy's great relief, JJ had refrained from descending into an alcoholic haze of amnesia. Until his court pardon, his well-stocked cellar had remained almost intact. On the evening and night of his being pronounced judicially innocent, he and Billy vainly attempted to redress the situation.

In the sober light of day, and as they struggled to emulate the light, Billy asked JJ whether he had, as yet, decided what to do to re-invigorate his life. However they looked at every aspect of his former life, neither of them honestly felt JJ could step back into any of his former activities without, at least initially, creating awkwardness and embarrassment. JJ was adamant he had no intention of returning to Freemasonry, even joining a lodge in another province—an option that could easily be available to him. Although his original flair had improved their fortunes, none of his business interests had been badly affected by his absence, and JJ felt muscling his way back in—possibly by replacing or moving someone sideways—would not be fair or useful. So far as his thinking had proceeded, and he had had little time to ponder, he intended to spend more time travelling the inland waterways and, possibly, writing. Billy had to be content with his friend's intentions—at least JJ would be doing something other than exercising and reading.

Three days later, JJ cast off the narrow boat *Jenny* and puttered gently northward. He re-explored the potteries before, by some almost morbid intent to confront his ghosts, travelling to and mooring at the Trevor Basin for the night. The following morning, driven by he knew not what, he passed over the Llangollen Aqueduct and moored himself for the night in the Llangollen basin. The Eisteddfod was over; the tented extension to the international pavilion had been collapsed and removed; the town was strangely quiet compared to the bustle of Eisteddfod week. For want of something to do, he took a trip on the steam railway that was rather disappointing since the majority of passengers were schoolchildren on an odd form of history lesson, and once he arrived at the end of the present railway's tracks he found little to do save return to whence he had come. Back in the town, he bought a few books from a pleasant little bookshop in an alleyway; purchased a few postcards of the town; sat in a café to write and address them and bought stamps at the post office. At the last moment, he withdrew the card addressed to Rose as being, perhaps, bitter and thoughtless. After wandering up and down the high street, JJ enjoyed a solitary dinner at a pleasant restaurant beside the River Dee— the proprietor was pleased of his custom, but as JJ was his only customer it was obviously not a profitable night and he seemed impatient for JJ to depart. His lack of patience turned to shame when confronted with the generous gratuity bestowed upon him by this English customer. JJ walked alone to his narrow-boat and slept fitfully. He was uncertain what he had hoped to find, although it was certain he had not found it. The following morning he embarked on the return journey to Herlways.

Travelling on a narrow boat at a maximum speed of four miles per hour allows plenty of time for thought. By the time JJ tied up at his own moorings, he had made some decisions in detail, decisions from which he did not veer. He resumed his morning exercises and swim after which the rest of his days were spent either on the telephone or at his desk and computer. The cellar remained as it had been following his and Billy's last celebratory encroachment on its contents. The house was clean and tidy due to the ministrations of Mrs Brice, the housekeeper. She and her husband, Eddy, remained in the small lodge and Eddy's pride in the gardens was considerably greater than that of his employer and paymaster.

From Christmases past, the Brice's had become used to a flurry of deliveries, so they were not surprised by the arrival and departure of several large lorries one weekend in early December 2000. Betty Brice was surprised the following Monday morning to find cardboard boxes and packing cases stacked in the large Herlways lounge; no explanation was offered. She was also surprised and disappointed that JJ did not erect a Christmas tree, or make any concession to the festive season by way of decorations. Both Brices received a Christmas bonus as had always been so and, for the first time ever, JJ asked Eddy if he would be so good as to post for him an enormous quantity of Christmas cards. JJ had been a good employer and it concerned the Brices that he seemed to intend spending Christmas alone. As casually as she could, Betty asked JJ if he would be going out on Christmas day. He would not. Suddenly emboldened, she blurted out an invitation for him to have his Christmas dinner with her and Eddy.

"Onest, Eddy, I thought 'e were goin' ter cry.'

'Well . . . is 'e comin'?'

'Yes, 'e is. 'E said 'e'd be 'onoured hand delighted.'

And on Christmas morning, JJ walked down his own drive to the Brice's little lodge carrying two parcels and several bottles. Once initial embarrassments had been smoothed by the consumption of gin and tonic or 'small' sherries ('Oooh, not that much, sir . . .') the three strange companions enjoyed a delicious dinner, more wine than the Brices were used to—or had ever had—and, a novelty to Betty and Eddy, a glass each of Green Chartreuse. Before he walked—quite steadily—home, JJ helped a rather unsteady Betty load the dishwasher whilst Eddy snored tunelessly in the small snug. The Brices remembered Christmas 2000 with great happiness for the rest of their lives.

The year two thousand and one received little welcome at Herlways. JJ sat up and watched television until midnight, switched off the set and walked steadily upstairs where he drew back the curtains and watched the almost three hundred and sixty degree firework display exploding in the sky. He noticed, with pleasure, a couple of rockets nearby that had almost certainly been launched by Eddy Brice. Not even an hour of the new year had elapsed before JJ Whitehouse-Martin was asleep in his bed.

In early February, a Mr Gerry Quinn knocked at the front door of the Herlways Lodge and politely requested Mr and Mrs Brice to be so good as to come up to the main house in about half an hour for a few moments as a small favour to him and Mr Whitehouse-Martin.

Thirty minutes later, the two bemused Brices stood at the front door of Herlways debating whether they should just walk in as Betty did to clean, or ring the bell. Their problem was solved by JJ opening the door and bidding them welcome with thanks for coming. They followed him into the dining room where Mr Quinn again greeted them and added his thanks for their presence. By this time, both Betty and Eddy were utterly confused as to why they should be summoned and fussed over. They both felt rather disappointed when they were sat down to watch JJ sign his name on a large piece of paper and then asked if they would sign and write their own names and address as witnesses. They had no idea what the purpose of the exercise had been, but were gratified and further confused when, as he showed them out of the front door, JJ pressed an envelope into Eddy's hand and said, very quietly, 'This is my thank you for what you just did. Never tell anyone about this, spend it on yourselves and don't put it in the bank.' When opened, the envelope contained two bundles of £250 labelled 'Betty' and 'Eddy'.

CHAPTER SEVENTY-SEVEN
I Did It My Way
Late February and March 2001

After Betty and Eddy Brice had witnessed JJ's signature, the matter was never mentioned again. In the following two weeks, Betty noticed the cardboard boxes in the lounge were steadily be ng unpacked and disposed of. JJ constantly apologised for any mess, although there was little. The cardboard was flattened and neatly stacked near the log store and JJ asked Eddy to burn it whenever he had a moment. No explanation was offered and the unpacking was always done in the even ng and at night. The Brices did notice the garden lights on the river path were often burning late at night, as were the lights in the narrow boat. Eddy was sure JJ had been out in the narrow boat at night—something that was not permitted on the river—but Betty told him he must have drunk too much and imagined it.

On Friday 16 February, JJ asked Eddy to accompany him to the post office in order to assist with the thirty same-s zed parcels he was posting. On their return, JJ handed Eddy a similar parcel as he dropped him off at the lodge. It was addressed to Mr and Mrs Brice. In answer to Eddy's understandable, 'What's this, sir?' JJ told him it was a little present and the note inside would explain. Eddy waited until he and Betty had had their tea before, together, they opened the parcel—it was a hard-backed book by someone called P. C. Wren entitled *Beau Geste*. The Brices were not great readers. Betty thought it might be something about the police. They referred to the typed note.

'This is a good yarn,' the note began—Betty now thought it must be about knitting—'I enjoyed it and I hope you will too, if you've not already read it. You may find it illuminating.'

Betty and Eddy disagreed as to which of them should attempt to read it first and in the end, predictably, neither of them ever read the book. Thirty other recipients either had or did.

On Friday 23 February, Betty found the lounge furniture all placed against the walls. The last of the boxes and packing cases were gone and two lines of new, upright chairs were arranged facing the window—before which stood JJ's two favourite armchairs with their backs to the window. Two side tables and a small desk set around the armchairs completed the arrangement. JJ apologised to Betty and asked her if Eddy would be so good as to burn all—he stressed all—the packing that was now outside. He offered no explanation and, in answer to the query Betty simply could not contain, replied that it was necessary and that he was just getting things in order to save trouble later. Both Betty and Eddy's weekly pay-packets contained a £50 bonus with a little note explaining that it was to 'help celebrate my birthday'. The Brices began wondering whether their employer was quite right in the head.

As dusk descended on Sunday 25 February 2001, Jonathan Justin Whitehouse-Martin walked purposefully down his unlit garden path to the river moorings, boarded his narrow boat and started the engine. He eased the boat upstream, executed the difficult turnabout and drifted back towards Herlways. Instead of turning to his own mooring, he steered to the opposite bank where he tied up and jumped ashore on the grassy river bank. Carefully, he secured the two mooring ropes he had gone ashore with to two stakes driven into the ground before returning to his boat and casting off trailing the two ropes. The current was not strong, for which he was thankful, and he returned to the Herlways mooring where, again, he jumped ashore with two further mooring ropes which he tied to the usual bollards. Pulling on the ropes secured to the opposite bank he manoeuvred the narrow boat to the centre of the river, lowered the anchor and carefully tightened the two sets of rope until he was firmly secured. There would not be—or should not be—any river traffic at night but, just in case, JJ lit both port and starboard mooring lights before raising the anchor. The *Jenny* floated serenely in the centre of the river.

JJ went below and, with infinite care, prepared his favourite meal—sausage and herb mash with onion gravy. The ingredients were all ready in the small refrigerator, as was a bottle of his favourite Chablis. He opened the wine, poured himself a large glass and sat down to enjoy a hearty meal he thoroughly enjoyed. Not wanting it to go to waste, he finished the wine, cast the bottle into the river and washed up. He then removed from the bow bedroom several stored cans and scattered their contents around the boat—both inside and out—and on the ropes securing the boat. In the galley he poured the contents of a smallish brown bottle into a glass and, taking the glass with him, climbed to the top of the cabin where he lay down and secured himself with the ropes placed ready, swiftly swallowed the contents of the glass and pulled the small chain that led to the cabin below. The chain ignited a spark.

'What's that glow, Betty?' asked Eddy Brice glancing through their window.

They both stared through the window before hastening outside and towards the house and the distant yet increasingly bright glow in the sky. Once he had gained a vantage point from which he could identify the cause, Eddy turned and ran towards his house, yelling to Betty that Mr JJ's boat was on fire and he was calling the fire brigade. Betty, now seeing more clearly than had her husband, wondered what the fire brigade could do for a boat surrounded by water. As she watched, the two strange spouts of fire from the rear of the boat disappeared and the blazing boat veered sideways before starting to drift downstream. It gathered pace and disappeared around the bend in the river. All that Betty could see was the glow in the sky as it grew more distant and began to fade. Herlways was all in darkness. With a feeling of deep dread in her heart, Betty rang the front door bell. There was no answer.

CHAPTER SEVENTY-EIGHT
Something to Your Advantage
Friday 4 May 2001

As Executors of the estate of the late Mr Jonathan Justin Whitehouse-Martin, we are charged to invite you to attend Herlways—his former home—on Friday 4 May 2001 at 3.00 p.m. where you will hear something to your advantage. Refreshments will be provided later in the dining room.

This letter is as instructed and dictated before his death by the deceased.

Yours Sincerely,

Gerald Quinn. Walter Morton

The thirty recipients of the letter 'dictated before his death' were all curious as to what would be revealed. Most hoped that they might learn why there had not been, and seemed unlikely to be a, memorial service for their late friend. A few perceptive individuals, having read the copy of *Beau Geste* sent to them before JJ's death, were reasonably certain why there had been no service of remembrance. Twenty-nine beneficiaries sat down to hear Gerry Quinn carry out his late client's wishes. Mrs Rose Tremain had telephoned Rixon Reed and begun explaining to Gerry why she felt unable to come to Herlways, the good solicitor had interrupted her to say the late JJ had advised him she may not wish to attend and he would be writing to her immediately after the meeting, 'with an enclosure.'

When the twenty-nine were all seated in the upright chairs facing Messrs Quinn and Morton, Walter Morton rose and thanked them for attending. He explained that this gathering of selected persons was as instructed by the late Mr J. J. Whitehouse-Martin who had very specifically instructed his executors not to sanction or, if possible permit, any memorial service in his memory. Mr Quinn would read to them the actual words of the deceased outlining his testamentary wishes and whilst this was not the actual legal will, it contained precisely the same gifts and legacies as the formal document. The legal will would be available for inspection by anyone so wishing after they had all heard the late JJ's wishes in his own words. The meeting had been delayed as the unusual nature of the late JJ's death had created difficulties with the Coroner's Court.

He then introduced Gerry Quinn who initially stood to ask if anyone would object to him sitting down whilst he read as the document was 'somewhat lengthy—though I am sure it will be of great interest, and I tend to feel it probably has literary merit.'

No one objected. Gerry Quinn sat down and began to read.

'This is the last will and testament of I, Jonathan Justin Whitehouse-Martin of Herlways in the county of Worcestershire where, I hope, you are all now gathered. With all respect due to my executors, I have not used the dry legal language deemed necessary for the proper will—of which a copy is available for the inspection of those so inclined. The following reflects my true and last gifts to those who have been dear to me.

'One. To my dear and almost lifelong friend Billy Baker I leave my thanks for his companionship, his unfailing cheerfulness and his support in my times of emotional need. I also bequeath to him my motor vehicles, which he has faithfully maintained or had maintained, and one fifth of my holding of shares in Wells Holdings Limited.

'Two. To my almost equally dear friend, colleague, inspiration, and finance director Mrs Janice Baker I leave my profound thanks for her sagacity, advice and—in the nicest sense—love. I also bequeath to her my late wife's, Jenny's, jewellery and one fifth of my holding of shares in Wells Holdings Limited.

'Three. To my dear friend Mrs Zoe Connolly, I leave my thanks for her kindness and help in my early education and her zealous industry in aiding Janice to establish and make successful what was my first speculative business venture. I also bequeath to her one tenth of my holding of shares in Wells Holdings Limited.'

Over the next half hour, Gerry Quinn, with frequent recourse to the glass of well-diluted whisky—another of JJ's instructions—read JJ's expressions of gratitude and material legacies. His further shares in Wells Holdings were divided amongst his fellow directors and, in most cases, founders of the various disparate parts of the empire. These included his two godchildren, William and Jennifer Janice Baker, who were now both active in the company. William, now managing director of Wells Holdings, inherited the Guernsey estate where he had enjoyed recent holidays and stated his wish to spend his honeymoon. JJ stated that whilst he ought not to display favouritism, he was especially fond of the young lady who had, to her early embarrassment, been known as JJ Junior, and had succeeded her clever mother as finance director of Wells Holdings and had recently married a fine man. Since the couple had not, to JJ's knowledge, yet acquired a home, he bequeathed them Herlways with the fond hope that they would retain, and continue to retain, the services of Betty and Eddy Brice. After disposing of his Wells Holdings Shares, JJ then bequeathed, with more expressions of personal gratitude and affection, some of his holdings in the stock market followed by cash gifts to friends and supporters in Freemasonry and other organisations in which he had, at one time or another, been active.

The final dispositions were:

'Twenty-nine. Mrs Rose Tremain to whom I leave the diamond ring with which we became betrothed; my deepest regrets and understanding that "events and persons beyond our control" caused her to withdraw from the engagement; the sum of at least £500,000; my Birmingham properties; plus the residue of my estate after the settlement of duties and costs.

Thirty. Lastly (but by no means least) to Mr Harry Alan Carter-Knight my thanks for his friendship despite the disparity in our ages; my apologies for an ongoing deception (this puzzled everyone—and only Harry was, eventually, aware of the meaning); plus £10,000 and my Masonic cases and regalia in the hope he will be able to wear all or most in the fullness of time.'

When Gerry Quinn closed the last page and took his final, large sip of whisky and water, he was rewarded with a round of applause. Walter Morton rose to inform everyone that, as promised, there were refreshments in buffet form in the dining room. Whilst everyone ate he would endeavour to distribute any bequests of a portable nature as JJ had wished and instructed. The distribution of share certificates, cheques and larger tangible assets would follow as soon as probate was complete but, at this time, neither he nor his fellow executor were willing to speculate as to how long that might be. Billy received the keys and registration documents of JJ's cars. Janice took home Jenny's jewellery. Her daughter, Jennifer Janice, who had wept more than anyone at the announcement of her legacy, arranged an appointment with Mr Quinn to effect early, undated advance completion of some necessary paperwork. Harry, possibly the most embarrassed person present—although Zoe ran him a close second—walked away with JJ's two Masonic cases.

CHAPTER SEVENTY-NINE
HARRY CARTER-KNIGHT'S HOME
SUNDAY 6 MAY 2001

Saturday was always a busy day for Harry Carter-Knight being, as ever, a favourite day for weddings. There were two at the conference centre on 5 May and, by the time Harry arrived home, he was in no mood to explore JJ Whitehouse-Martin's masonic cases. On his return from church on 6 May, encouraged by his wife Ayisha, who was openly curious, Harry decided to 'see what I'm supposed to become entitled to wear.' Hefting the larger case onto the bed—like many men, he kept Masonic regalia in his wardrobe—Harry snapped the locks and raised the lid. Secured in the body of the case by interlocking elasticated ties were aprons and collars; clipped into the pockets in the lid were a selection of Masonic jewels. Immediately below the ties and on top of the regalia was an envelope marked confidential and addressed simply 'To Harry'. Beneath his name was typed, 'Please open and read sitting down and alone.'

Harry and his wife looked at the envelope before Aysisha said, a little huffily, 'I suppose I'd better leave you to it then?'

'I suppose you should,' replied a slightly concerned Harry. Adding 'Shan't be long . . . I hope.'

Ayisha left thinking, not for the first time, what an odd lot these Masons were.

Harry sat on the bedside chair with the unopened envelope in his hand. This was even more mysterious than the manner of JJ's death and the gathering to hear his will. Mystery or not, Harry knew he would only discover what was in the envelope if he opened it. Not having a paper knife in the bedroom, he used his pen to slit the top of the envelope. Inside were typed pieces of paper—the top one headed with JJ's Herlways address. Discarding the envelope, and now anxious to resolve the mystery, Harry sat back to read a letter from a dead man.

> Dear Brother Harry,
>   I apologise for the unconventional manner of this missive but, having read it, I trust you will understand my caution. There

would, in my opinion, be no practical purpose in publicising what I am about to reveal to you although, at your discretion, you may wish to show this to just one other person in strictest confidence.

I hope you either read or re-read *Beau Geste* and can understand the Viking funeral I executed upon myself. The law is very clear that suicide is a crime, although it seems to me it corroborates Dickens's assertion that 'the law is an ass' since the only successful prosecution for the crime could be against an unsuccessful person. Besides yourself, there were thirty recipients of the book, and I like to feel that at least some of my friends made the connection. I was very specific with my legal advisers that there should be no memorial service: whilst there would be those who would sincerely wish to attend, I could not bear the thought of those who would attend for hypocritical reasons, or simply for a free meal afterwards. This letter is the only proof of my actions on 25 January 1988, and is confidentially entrusted to your care. Unless my judgement is badly skewed, my confidence is well disposed.

From the excellent work you have done at the conference centre and on security matters throughout the Wells Group, I know you dislike loose ends and unsolved mysteries. You and I first met when you were despatched to assure me an investigation had been abandoned. The case was in no way the crime of the century—or even the year—but I always felt it unfair to yourself and Paula that you were forced to leave an investigation incomplete and a mystery—if mystery it was—unsolved. At our first meeting the photos I was so anxious to display to you had become obsolete, but I clearly recall the searching look you gave me when I cheerily referred to the holiday photographs—which by no chance whatsoever were on the table where we took coffee—as 'my alibi'. After all, the case was closed.

I always felt that had Mrs Fisher been less hysterically strident and more reasoned in her accusations of me as the perpetrator of her 'dear Maurice' being 'exposed', your superiors may have taken her more seriously. If DNA testing had then been available, a thorough investigation would, surely, have discovered me. As it was, poor, silly Caitlin brooded for ten years before taking the law into her own deceptive hands. Fortunately, her own inability to hold her loosened-by-alcohol-tongue and her desire to gloat secured my pardon. By then it was, for society and for the mean-minded Masons of Chandlery Lodge, too late as the damage to my reputation had been done. The unforgiving are rarely willing to admit their errors. My second great love left me, for which I bear her no ill will, and—rightly or wrongly—I felt myself without credibility in Freemasonry and left.

I consider I had a good life, but I could see little purpose in prolonging it. The date of my demise was precisely sixteen years after the tragic death of my dear Jenny.

Illogically, as I now realise, I blamed her descent into dementia and death on the three old misguided Masons who ruined her ladies night and unwittingly caused her to re-live a trauma from her past that destroyed her powers of reason.

You will, by now, have realised that the denuding of Brothers Jeffries, Hughes and Fisher was my doing. My big regret at the time was that dear old Floury Fallowfield somehow learned of the bogus meeting I had called and decided to attend; he had to be treated similarly to the others for my protection and the success of the scheme. There have been times when I was sorely tempted to confess and apologise to him, but I was taught to be cautious and discretion prevailed.

How it was done was very simple, and I now tell you merely to clear an unsolved case. Had you, at our first meeting, still been on the case and examined my holiday photos with a critical and suspicious eye, you would have noted that I did not appear in any picture. The snaps were taken in the West Indies at the time of the outrage in Avonbridge, as the date and time stated on each picture proved. The cruise company confirmed Mr J. J. Whitehouse-Martin was a passenger on their voyage to the Caribbean as it was the name in which the holiday was booked and the name on the passport presented at the commencement of the trip.

But I was *not* on the cruise. The passenger was my late friend and lookalike Brother James Whiteman from Lichfield. He only came to Avonbridge once and never visited Chandlery Lodge, although I attended his Staffordshire lodge several times. We had business dealings and I was able to be of help to James when his wife was dying and, later, when he, too, contracted a terminal disease so, as the saying goes, he owed me.

The only person who was aware I had not left the UK was not, as you may be thinking, Billy Baker, but another who shall remain anonymous but assisted me in the matter of transport and lock-picking. Since suspicion may have fallen on Billy, I made sure that he and Jan were in London for the weekend and persuaded them to make a visit to his old friend in the Cotswolds on their return journey; fortunately it was a lengthy visit. Whilst James enjoyed what was his last holiday, I lived at his house apart from the few days I spent dossing—the only description for the self-inflicted misery I endured—at the rear of the empty former DIY shop premises on Avon Street. Other details that I made sure were untraceable to me were the purchases, in October and November of 1987, of fake blood as used in theatres, the mask, and the swazzle (used by Punch and Judy men to produce the 'squeaky' voice). Those I bought in London, posing as a keen member of an amateur theatrical company. I disposed of them in several rubbish bins around Lichfield along with the gloves I wore the entire time I was in the temple.

I have often regretted my revenge. The intention was to subject those I felt most at fault to a similar embarrassment and shame as my poor Jenny had endured.

You may feel, and it would be understandable, that Caitlin Fisher's plot against me was justified; it has occurred to me ever since she wrought her revenge.

Whatever opinion may be held by any, I am no longer around to hear it voiced and it troubles me no longer.

I hope this has cleared a long unsolved mystery for you. Should you so choose to show it to her, Paula Harries will, I trust, be the only one besides yourself to read this. I wish you well in what, I feel sure, will be an enjoyable and successful life—both in and out of Freemasonry.

Yours Sincerely, Fraternally and (very definitely) finally,

JJ.

AFTERWARD
2001 TO 2024

Chandlery Lodge never recovered after the resignation of JJ and the subsequent departure (the diehards termed it defection) to other lodges of twelve more brethren. It struggled on with an ageing membership failing to attract any initiates to replace those who died or gave up. In 2012, the few remaining brethren endeavoured to mount a celebration of the lodge's seventy-five years existence; few from other lodges and fewer from the province attended. The members were reluctantly persuaded that their lodge had become little more than an old men's dining club: the lodge warrant was surrendered in 2013 and it ceased to exist.

In 2005, an offer to absorb the ZoNice Hair and Beauty salons into a nationwide consortium was happily accepted by Zoe and Janice. Forty years of hard work and deserved profit left them well able to contemplate retirement. Zoe and Gareth moved permanently to Spain where their children and grandchildren enjoyed free holidays for years to come.

Janice and Billy retained their directorships of Wells Holdings whilst they gradually transferred their shareholdings to their son and daughter without incurring tax penalties. Their involvement after 2002 was confined to attending board meetings to which they travelled from their permanent Aberdovey home.

William Baker was a successful managing director of Wells Holdings— guiding the different divisions through the troughs of national recession. He married and had two happy, healthy children. William was initiated into Stour Lodge at the age of thirty, became their worshipful master eight years later, accepted a past rank appointment in Provincial Grand Lodge and took little further interest in Freemasonry. After their honeymoon and three years holidaying in Guernsey, the estate was sold. William and his wife were keen walkers and spent all their leisure time tramping the hills and ancient pathways of Britain.

Jennifer Janice Baker qualified as a chartered accountant at twenty-one, and after serving three years with Price Waterhouse Cooper—as the former Price Waterhouse had become—left to manage the Avonbridge practice of Whitehouse, Butler, Rock & Co. in tandem with her new responsibilities as financial director of Wells Holdings. Having inheriting Herlways, she debated with her husband, Sam Anstruther, who was Terri and Gerald's son, whether she should or should not retain the property. They decided they should live there and effected alterations to make Herlways their own. Entry from the house and grounds to the riverside was permanently closed, and for a time the wharf became deserted. Later, an opportunity to purchase the adjoining house and grounds and the wayside inn beyond was eagerly embraced; the wharf was renovated and extended and an ultimately very profitable hotel and marina established. Their son became a chartered accountant and succeeded to his mother's posts.

Harry Alan Carter-Knight was embarrassed by his legacy of JJ's Masonic regalia. His wife, Ayisha, was not keen on the further nights out entailed in his Masonic activities since he—too frequently in her opinion—also worked evenings at the conference centre. Harry never attained sufficient Masonic stature to wear his inherited senior regalia and it was, eventually, donated to the provincial museum to be sold for their funds. In 2003 Ayisha inherited her parents' open all hours corner shop on the outskirts of Wolverhampton, the Carter-Knights left Avonbridge and Harry became a profitable, if not ecstatic, shopkeeper. Ayisha was unable to conceive and, in 2006, the Carter-Knights adopted a daughter whom they named Sophia Ranee. She was a bright, impulsive child who did well at school, was accepted for entry to Oxford University and departed on the almost mandatory gap year of travel. In 2024 she and a friend bought tickets and attended an open golf tournament in Italy where she met a mature, good-looking and charming golfer.

She accepted a trip in his private jet to Monaco.

Rose Tremain remained a school librarian in Cheltenham. She sold the Charlton Kings house and bought a delightful little house close to the college from where she walked to work every day of term time. The income from the Birmingham properties and her invested half a million pounds were far more than she needed for the life to which she was committed. Her holidays—school librarians have school holidays—were spent in her son's, Ant's, apartment in Monaco where her wealth enabled her to shop. Ant was rarely in residence, his success as a world-ranked golfer on the international circuit taking him all over the globe in his own private plane. Rose never married again. She kept a photograph of JJ next to her bed in Cheltenham from where Ant removed and packed it away after her death at the early age of fifty-five in 2010.

Her sole heir was the already rich Anthony Norris Tremain—the well-known international golf professional who now became one of the world's wealthiest men.

He was also noted as a ladies' man, frequently photographed with glamorous models and actresses on his arm. It was not the only part of his anatomy they lovingly clung to. In 2024, Ant met a forward young lady at a tournament in Italy to whom he offered a lift to Monte Carlo via Nice airport. The young lady had nowhere to stay in Monaco and accepted Ant's kind offer to stay at his apartment; they shared bed and breakfast.

Ant never expected to hear from Sophia Ranee again. When he did it was to learn of her pregnancy—a state she attributed to him and was prepared to prove should he not agree. He agreed. They were quietly married in a Wolverhampton Registry Office and returned to Monte Carlo where Sophia was delivered of a healthy son weighing nine pounds and two ounces. A son who would, in time, inherit immense wealth, join Freemasonry and, ultimately, find himself disillusioned.

AFTERWORD

The first successful criminal prosecution using DNA evidence occurred in January of 1988 and was a murder trial. Despite the sameness of the date, it is highly unlikely such an infant criminal science would have been available to a provincial force for a case, or cases, of assault—indeed it did not become widely available for some years. Nonetheless, it did dictate the timing of this book's first chapter. JJ's assertion, in his letter from beyond, of possible detection should DNA have become involved indicated the general ignorance that has grown since the use of DNA became widely used by police forces and reflects the portrayal of its use in crime novels, films and television programmes.

It is frequently, and correctly, stated by the United Grand Lodge that Freemasonry is *not* a religion. It has regrettable similarities to the major religions of the world inasmuch as what is a good, viable core of merit and a code—or guide—for one's conduct through life has become elaborated and often almost submerged by dicta. There are, regrettably, Freemasons who regard their hobby (for such it is) with more respect and dedication than their religion and hold the ritual—much of it cast in the almost arcane language of the eighteenth and nineteenth centuries—to be Holy Writ. They are, due to their own misunderstandings and the failure of their predecessors to properly advise them, losers. Freemasonry is not secret; it never should be, or have been, and only became so in Britain due to Hitler's persecution of the Fraternity that he equated with Jewry allied to deep-seated (and equally secret) fears that Britain might lose the Second World War. For the losers in Freemasonry, the only secret is the sad fact that they still firmly believe it *is* secret. The dedication of those eager to boost their own ego is largely due to the fact that one may, in too many lodges, however inept, proceed in the basic form of Freemasonry—The Craft—by doing little more than serving one's time and doing as one is told. The ritual terms it, 'rising to eminence by merit.' Any serious debate on the matter must include consideration of what is, or is not, meritorious.

There is much to be gained by becoming a Freemason: it can complement and supplement one's life. It can also compliment one's ego and dominate, even destroy, one's life and livelihood—that has happened. Like any hobby, Freemasonry needs to be kept in proper perspective. There are ridiculous things in its practice and ridiculous brethren perpetuating them on no better comprehension than the fallible reasoning 'we've always done that'.

Unless a brother strays from the path of rectitude (is convicted of serious illegality) then, certainly at provincial, district and metropolitan level, he can become a provincial, district or metropolitan grand officer and wear a dark blue apron—although too often vaunting ambition has been mistaken for zeal in the cause. Those considered worthy become grand officers and have a bigger dark blue apron.

There is no better antidote to antediluvian attitudes than a sense of humour. Recognition of the ludicrous. Yet should one dare to criticise, or find one's brethren a source of amusement, then elevation to dark blue may be tempered. This may be exemplified by the authors of a dozen and more comic operas famous and much admired in their time and beyond: Gilbert and Sullivan. They were both Freemasons. They were, arguably, equally talented and responsible for their joint success. Sir Arthur Sullivan, who wrote the music, became an officer of grand lodge (grand organist). W. S. Gilbert, an outspoken humorist, wrote the satirical and, some felt, critical plots and lyrics, but did not become an officer of grand lodge.

As fewer and fewer young men find themselves able to devote the hours and financial outlay necessary for a time-consuming and costly hobby, the situation satirised in Gilbert's *The Gondoliers,* enhanced by Sullivan's music, tends to arise:

> So to the top of every tree
> Promoted everybody.
> . . . .
> In short, whoever you may be,
> To this conclusion you'll agree,
> When every one is somebodee,
> Then no one's anybody!
>   (Lyrics written in 1889.)